The general's ▨▨▨▨▨▨▨▨▨▨▨▨ thick, cloying p▨▨▨▨▨▨▨▨▨▨▨ tread carefully. "I do not know him, General. To say I saved Sage's life would be to say I was acquainted with him. I am not. He is an enemy combatant."

"You defended him against one of DawnStar Corp's chief sec officers."

"I did so because having the Terran Army and DawnStar at each other's throat can only be beneficial to us, General. United, they provide a much more serious threat level." That was only part of the truth. Zhoh had also respected the way Sage had fearlessly marched in to face Velasko Kos despite the odds being against him. A warrior recognized the bravery of another warrior, even if that warrior was the enemy. General Rangha was not conversant with that concept.

"That division is what I want you to concentrate on, Captain. Since this Sergeant Sage is so interested in combatting the cartels, make certain you aid him."

"Sir?" Zhoh looked at his commanding officer in surprise.

Rangha snapped his primary in annoyance. "The Terrans use some of the same spies we do. Make certain that information about the different cartels out in the jungle makes its way into the hands of the Terran Army. Keep them busy chasing those people because the profits those black-market enterprises make find their way into the money purses of several key members of the *Quass*, from what I am told. They will not be happy with Master Sergeant Sage's success."

Reluctantly, Zhoh admitted to himself that it was a good plan.

By Mel Odom

The Makaum War

MASTER SERGEANT: BOOK ONE
GUERILLA: BOOK TWO

GUERILLA

THE MAKAUM WAR: BOOK TWO

MEL odom

HARPER Voyager
An Imprint of HarperCollins*Publishers*

This is a work of fiction. Names, characters, places, and incidents are products of the author's imagination or are used fictitiously and are not to be construed as real. Any resemblance to actual events, locales, organizations, or persons, living or dead, is entirely coincidental.

HARPER Voyager

An Imprint of HarperCollins*Publishers*
195 Broadway
New York, New York 10007

Copyright © 2015 by Mel Odom
Cover art by Gregory Bridges
ISBN 978-0-06-228444-0
www.harpervoyagerbooks.com

First Harper Voyager mass market printing: September 2015

Harper Voyager and) is a trademark of HCP LLC.

Printed in the U.S.A.

10 9 8 7 6 5 4 3 2 1

For Michael Kent, PhD, who opened doors for me at academia and watched my back during the zombie invasion at the gun range!

GUERILLA

ONE

Covered in perspiration from the thick humidity caused by the surrounding jungle vegetation and Makaum's normal tropical heat index, Master Sergeant Frank Sage crept down into the valley toward his mission objective. Truth be told, not all of the perspiration was from the mugginess. The grim awareness that he could be discovered by Phrenorian security measures at any minute and end up DOA the second after kept his nerves wound tight.

If he ended up KIA on this op, Sage figured Colonel Halladay would have the answer they were looking for concerning the secret base the Sting-Tails had built despite treaty limitations between the Terran Alliance and the Phrenorian Empire. The Phrenorians were supposed to be restricted to an ambassadorial detail and some trade explorations. Charlie Company was there to help police the planet.

Of course, no Terran expected the Phrenorians to honor those treaties except when it was convenient. Evidently, convenience was no longer a factor on Makaum. The Sting-Tails had changed the rules of engagement without notifying anyone. Colonel Halladay hadn't wanted to proceed until the reports from the local scouting band had been confirmed.

That was Sage's mission. He'd said yes instantly because he was on Makaum under protest. He'd wanted a reassignment to the front lines of the Phrenorian War.

Now the Sting-Tails had a base, one that had been missed up until a few days ago.

An ovoid ebony Phrenorian drone zipped through the night sky, almost invisible against the deep velvet even though the unmanned aerial vehicle was nearly two meters across and a meter deep. The spy device's profile momentarily blurred the crisp whiteness of the stars and one of Makaum's five moons as it stopped to hover just above treetop level. Stationary now, it looked like a black hole in the starlit night.

Ahead of Sage, Jahup leaned into the inky shadow of a *wock* tree. The tree's fragrant blossoms thickened the humid air with the sour sweetness of decay. The pale, alabaster flowers only opened at night and were large enough to encompass both of Sage's fists together. Flurries of *neerts*, mothlike creatures that ranged from a fingertip in length to ten times that in adults, fed on the nectar. They also glowed in the dark, which presented a potential hazard for Sage and his partner because they could be skylined against a mass of the *neerts*.

Jahup hadn't spoken in the last hour since they'd entered the red perimeter zone Sage had designated. The young Makaum scout took orders well. Lean and wiry, he moved as silently as a falling leaf despite the verdant undergrowth beneath the towering trees that insisted on making Sage's progress difficult.

The tree trunk, almost three meters in diameter, provided adequate shelter for Sage as well as Jahup, and the Terran sergeant settled in against the rough bark adjacent to the young Makaum scout. That way they each had a field of view that overlapped. They weren't safe, but they were as safe as they could be under the circumstances.

Though he'd only known Jahup for less than two Terran months, Sage had no qualms about putting his life in the young man's hands. Jahup had proven himself as a warrior during the battle against DawnStar. Having grown up on Makaum, Jahup was as much a part of the tropical planet as any nocturnal creature in the jungle around them.

Jahup glanced at Sage, and the sergeant knew the young man was assessing him. Both of them knew Jahup was putting himself at risk more than Sage. Jahup could have done the recon much easier alone than with Sage because his jungle skillset was sharper. But the young scout wasn't knowledgeable about Phrenorian battle weapons. Sage was there for the military looksee.

Frowning slightly, Jahup looked away from Sage. The sergeant knew his companion wasn't happy with the Terran's abilities in the jungle. Compared to Jahup, Sage moved like a wildebeest in a china closet. The dissatisfaction showed in the narrowing of Jahup's dark hazel eyes and his tight-lipped mouth. He'd tied his long dark hair back. Oil created from a mixture of crushed *aldu* ants and *polst* berries and smeared over his exposed flesh broke up his light green skin color. It also served to scare away bloodsucking insects.

The carnivorous ants were nearly as long as a man's hand. A swarm of them could strip an adult down to bare bones in a matter of minutes. Luckily the *aldu* lived in hills and rotted trees far from civilized areas. The ants would eat mammals—a rarity because the Makaum people were the planet's only mammals, descendants of a generation starship that had crashlanded on the planet hundreds of years ago—but preferred to prey on the world's insect, reptile, and fish species, and lived apart from Makaum City and outlying villages.

Collecting the ants to make the camouflage oil was dangerous. Sage respected Jahup and his hunting companions for the danger they had faced in doing so.

The Makaum scout wore clothing made of spider silk, thin and wispy, and dyed green so dark it was almost black. The coloration was intentionally broken in an irregular pattern with slightly lighter patches of green. The survivors of the generation ship crash had quickly learned to stay alive on the hostile planet. Sage didn't think the camo ability of the Army's combat suits could offer a better disguise than the spider silk.

Sage wore the same clothing and oil, but he felt naked and vulnerable without his combat suit and weapons. His skin was darker than Jahup's, a gift from his South-American mother, as was the crow's-wing black hair. He got his height and broad shoulders from his father, a career military man whose family had Norwegian roots.

Breathing shallowly, Sage counted the passing seconds, estimating the drone's speed at somewhere near twenty klicks per hour. He glanced briefly at the device as it continued tangent to their hiding spot. Something had alerted it. The slight throbbing noise made by the baffled engine created sound waves that registered as a slight pressure against Sage's eardrums rather than a truly audible event. Someone unfamiliar with it wouldn't have known what it was.

The noise reminded Sage of an owl's swooping passage

on Terra. He'd been born and raised there, and his soldier father had trained him to hunt in the wilderness and survive on the land at an early age. Abruptly, the drone halted and changed direction, flitting toward Sage and Jahup's position. Moving slower now, the drone's engine noise beat more harshly against Sage's eardrums. He opened his mouth and swallowed hard to equalize pressure.

His right hand drifted up to the hilt of the long knife, or short sword—he had heard the weapon described as both—sheathed over his right shoulder. The Makaum warriors called the weapon an *etess*, and blacksmiths beat them out on anvils in the sprawl's marketplace.

Blade work wasn't something the Terran Army focused on in combat, but the skill wasn't overlooked because Phrenorians gloried in hand to pincer combat when the chance arose. Sage had an affinity for long knives, but he didn't want to have to use it. For a second, he mentally cursed the Phrenorians and the drone, then stopped because that was wasted effort. If the drone had picked them up on its sensors, cursing was no defense.

Unfortunately, the long knife was the only weapon Sage had carried along on the excursion. Nothing else, including tech, had been possible to bring. The security system around the Phrenorian base would detect a Roley gauss rifle or a Birkeland coilgun because the near-AI was programmed to seek out tech. Even the Smith and Wesson .500 Magnum pistol Sage habitually carried as a backup to the energy-based weaponry would be detectable because of the offworld metallurgy.

Wearing an AKTIVsuit anywhere near the Phrenorian base was out of the question. During his twenty years as a Terran Army soldier, Sage hadn't often walked into a hot zone without the armor, enhanced senses, and stepped-up speed and strength afforded by the Armored-Kinetic-

Tactical-Intelligence-Vestment suit. He missed the 360-degree HUD most, but he felt confident in his own and Jahup's abilities to spot danger while they were in the jungle. Sage just didn't like giving up that edge. The young Makaum scout had managed to get into the area, discover the Phrenorian base, and get out again without getting caught.

So far, they hadn't been caught tonight.

Maybe. As a sergeant, Sage had been trained to consider all the ways an engagement could turn, good and bad. The possibility remained that the Phrenorians had noticed Jahup and his hunting band and had intentionally let them go, knowing they were going to report the base to the Terran military forces at Fort York.

The base could be a suck, just a plant to make the Terran Military waste time, energy, and resources while the Phrenorians hid assets elsewhere. Or it could be used as a political chit if Terran forces attacked it. Even though the base wasn't supposed to exist, any aggression on Charlie Company's part wouldn't sit well with the Makaum people.

Colonel Halladay hadn't wanted to take the chance that the Phrenorians had a base here and go unknowing. Sage hadn't wanted to let the opportunity slip by either. Besides that, even a fake base would possibly be ruled a treaty breach. So he was here, underequipped with a native scout half his age for reinforcement and no exfiltration waiting on him. And he had to hope nothing went sideways.

Colonel Halladay had told Sage up front that the reconnoiter mission would be off the books, unsanctioned and unsupported. Live or die, Sage and Jahup were on their own.

The drone drew closer, hovering only twenty meters

away. Sage discovered he was holding his breath and made himself breathe. Getting anaerobic wasn't going to help. Oxygen was necessary no matter how the next few minutes played out. He already had a map of his exit strategy worked out in his mind. Jahup knew it too.

Having an exit strategy didn't mean it was going to work, though. All it would take was one signal from the drone and the surrounding jungle would fill with Phrenorian warriors. There would be no escape because Sage and Jahup would never reach the extraction point before the enemy net closed around them.

A sudden hum trilled through Sage's body. Long experience told him it was the reverb caused by an energy weapon discharge. If he'd been in an AKTIVsuit, the onboard near-AI would have informed him of the occurrence. But he'd experienced attacks outside the suit as well.

The energy release from the Phrenorian weapon caused painful twinges to echo in the bionic lung Sage had received less than two weeks ago. Made of organicsim polymers coded with his DNA, the lung didn't show up on the drone's sensors. The organ operated just like Sage's original bio equipment had before it had been ruined by a laser blast while in conflict with DawnStar Corp and Velesko Kos only days ago.

Sage held himself steady, though he expected the drone's unseen energy beam to tear through the tree where he had taken cover. Instead, the gauss blast knifed into the tree canopy twenty meters above him.

A sudden shriek filled the air and Sage recognized what the noise came from before he saw the multi-legged body tumbling limply toward the ground. At nine or ten meters across, the *kifrik* was small compared to most of the giant spiders Sage had seen. The long legs fought to grab the branches and trees, but they lacked the strength to hold on.

The *kifrik* slammed into the ground and lay sprawled. Covered in stiff, coarse hair, the creature's reddish black body almost disappeared in the darkness. Normally a *kifrik* tended to stay with its web and subsist on other insects and lizards caught in the sticky strands, but sometimes one would get curious and creep across the canopies almost soundlessly to investigate things that caught its attention.

Sage didn't know if the *kifrik* had been stalking Jahup and him, or if something else had caught its attention. The creature's presence reminded Sage that no one was safe out in the Green Hell, the Terran soldiers' nickname for Makaum.

The drone sailed over the *kifrik*, hovered for a moment to scan the dead creature, then sped away to drop back into its security route.

Releasing a tense breath, Sage mentally flagged the drone and the two others he'd noticed on his descent from the ridgeline. They'd also skirted four fixed-point sec-sweepers that scanned for ground approaches by climbing through the trees. The jungle provided security because of its density, but the same proliferation of trees and branches created inroads for enemies clever enough and skillful enough to use them.

With three of Makaum's moons now in the sky, some of the darkness faded. Sage pulled the spyglass from the spider silk backpack he wore and wished he had a Kozuki Digital Peeper or the AKTIVsuit's vid capabilities instead. The spyglass was a native instrument and would be undetectable because it was low-tech.

Sage made a mental note to beef up the security around Fort York regarding low-tech approaches. The anti-Terran faction of the Makaum had gotten more demonstrative since the Army had started hitting the drug cartels so hot and heavy out in the jungle. Many of the locals had enjoyed the wretched excess provided by the corp-sponsored cartels and bio-pirates. But others had been working with the cartels and were angry over losing the illegal revenue.

Slowly, Sage scanned the Phrenorian base, barely able to suss the structure out from the jungle. Camo tech covered the polycarbonate shell and blended the building into the background, but the lines were too straight and stood out to a trained eye.

The Sting-Tails had been clever about construction. They'd shoehorned the base into the hillside at the bottom of the valley. A swift-running river over fifty meters across meandered through the valley, coming down off the mountain to the north in a series of plunging waterfalls that looked silver in the moonlight.

Sage guessed that the Phrenorians were using generators located under the surface of the river for a power source because that was what he would have done if he'd designed the fortification. He raked the treetops above the rounded blister of the base's roof and spotted solar collection shields reaching up forty meters to break the canopy. Somewhere out in space in low planetary orbit, a group of Phrenorian satellites gathered solar radiation and channeled it to the base in beam transmissions.

The Terran Army and the corps used satellites for solar collection to power Fort York as well. The energy exchange was virtually untraceable.

Moving the spyglass slowly, Sage searched the surrounding grounds. He kept both eyes open, the same way he would while looking through a sniper scope. One eye focused through the spyglass to take in the magnification, the other to watch over the surrounding landscape for movement. He switched effortlessly back and forth between eyes.

For fifteen minutes, Sage held his position. No tracks existed through the jungle, so the Phrenorians didn't come by crawlers. They also didn't come by jumpcopter or another kind of aircraft. With the satellite recon the Terran Army maintained on the area, anything aerial would have been spotted.

Personnel in the clandestine operation were probably permanent. Nobody in, nobody out would make spotting people coming and going difficult.

Even if the Phrenorians in the base were living off the land, which they could do on Makaum, there still had to be information and critical supplies going into and out of the area.

Moonslight gleamed on the water and Sage suddenly realized how the Phrenorians could move through the area relatively unseen. He shifted the spyglass and tracked the flow downriver, watching as the tributary widened a little before disappearing around a bend in the valley.

At the same time, Jahup dropped a hand onto Sage's shoulder, drawing his attention immediately.

Sage slipped back out of sight and glanced at the young scout.

Slowly, because quick movements drew attention in the dark, Jahup pointed upriver toward the cliffs where the waterfalls spilled down onto a tumble of broken rock.

Tiny figures stood skylined against the night for a moment, dark shadows blocking out the starlight. Then they made their way over the rise and down into the valley, occasionally masked by the silver spray of the falls.

Cautiously, Sage traded places with Jahup and brought up the spyglass to his eye again. He peered at the figures and only made out glimpses of the small group walking through the trees, but he identified the Phrenorians easily.

On average, the Sting-Tails stood taller than humans.

The chitinous exoskeletons, four "lesser" arms, and segmented tails gave them more than a passing resemblance to Terran scorpions. The primary arms that came out from the shoulders ended in huge pincers big enough and strong enough to crush a man's head. Generally their exoskeletal coloration ran the gamut of blue and purple, the preferred colors of the Phrenorian elite, but there were greens and dark reds mixed in. They wore little armor because their chitin was as tough as any AKTIVsuit, and oftentimes only a little less dense than shielding on the Army's heavy combat powersuits. Only bare latticework featuring yellow and red plates protected their abdomens and provided a tactical platform for weaponry and supplies.

All of the Phrenorians carried weapons, rifles and sidearms, and they looked alert. Several anti-grav "mules," floating flat cargo carriers, transported heavy loads strapped aboard them.

Sage wondered if the polymer crates carried supplies or equipment. Either way, it was a lot of material.

A door on the blister irised open as the new arrivals approached. A dozen Phrenorian warriors stepped out, fanning into position on either side of the opening. Another Phrenorian, this one colored deep blue and purple, stepped out as the supply train came to a halt.

Evidently a conversation took place, then a PAD glowed briefly, revealing the alien features of the Phrenorian officer. The Sting-Tails' heads narrowed as they went from shoulders to forehead. Three pairs of oily black eyes gleamed above the Phrenorian's slash of a mouth. *Chelicerae*, tiny arms that resembled the Sting-Tails' lesser arms, surrounded the razor-slit mouth. Another pair of eyes, not seen at the moment, was set into the back of the warrior's head.

One of the newly arrived Phrenorians stepped forward

and pressed a lesser hand against the PAD. In that brief instant of pale light, Sage recognized the warrior.

Zhoh GhiCemid was, according to Terran military intel, a high-ranking warrior in the Phrenorian Empire. Information experts had tracked GhiCemid at the scenes of several major battles in the Khustal System. The Pagor System had fallen and the Sting-Tails were making a major push into new territory. The Loki System that contained Makaum was only a short distance out of the way for them.

No one knew what Zhoh GhiCemid was doing on Makaum, but everyone knew the stakes had been raised.

Silently, Sage watched Zhoh GhiCemid and his warriors disappear into the blister. When the door irised closed again, he leaned back, collapsed the spyglass quietly, and considered his options. After a minute he glanced at Jahup.

The young scout signed quickly in the code they'd worked out before leaving Fort York. *We go.*

Sage shook his head and signed back. *We stay. See more. Then go.*

Jahup frowned and let out a short breath filled with irritation. *Dawn soon.*

We go before dawn.

Reluctantly, Jahup nodded.

Sage didn't want to chance another recon. Getting caught might accelerate the Phrenorians' plans. The Terran Military needed to know everything he could discover now. He lifted a waterskin from his hip and drank deeply to stay hydrated, signaling for Jahup to do the same. Then he settled in to wait.

TWO

J-Keydor Node
Stronghold RuSasara
Makaum
4917 Akej (Phrenorian Prime)

Captain Zhoh GhiCemid of the Phrenorian Empire's Brown Spyrl struggled to keep his fury under control as the sec door closed behind him and he stepped into a well-lit, broad hallway. He knew he was failing to keep his emotions to himself when the lieutenant to his left took a half step away and the sergeant on his right dropped a lesser hand to the pistol holstered at his hip. Zhoh's anger radiated in waves of edgy pheromones, signaling a warning to those around him. He smelled the cold stink of himself and concentrated on being calm.

"Are you well, sir?" Lieutenant Sibed DenSkel asked. The question was designed to allow Zhoh to take no offense.

"I am fine, Lieutenant," Zhoh replied. He wanted to tell Sibed that getting called from his bed in the middle of the night like a youngling was not how an honored warrior was to be treated. But he knew the lieutenant was only following orders. "Have your sergeant stand down before I take his actions as an affront to me."

"Yes sir." In a strident voice and with a fearful and angry pheromone release of his own, the young lieutenant ordered the sergeant to remove his hand from his weapon.

Reluctantly, the sergeant did so. He kept his emotions and his scent under control.

"Excuse Sergeant Orek. General Rangha insists that we remain vigilant, and the general can be very exacting."

Zhoh said nothing. Any response he made to acknowledge the explanation would have been seen as a sign of weakness. He was getting tired of seeming fragile to warriors he should have been commanding. His patience was wearing thin on this planet. The Empire was not being as forceful as they should have been in pursuing their goals on Makaum. Either the planet was worth conquering or it wasn't. If it wasn't, the warriors here would be better served stationed somewhere else. And if the Phrenorian Empire wanted the world, General Rangha should have been pursuing that more aggressively.

The hallway held doors to several rooms. Some of the rooms were open. Most of them were quarters for warriors who watched silently as the small party strode by.

For more than two Empire Standard months, Zhoh had served on Makaum, watching and learning, and waiting to seize an opportunity that would put his military career back on solid footing. He had learned what the Terran Army was doing, what the (ta)Klar were doing, and what the Makaum factions were doing. He had thought he'd known what the Empire's warriors here were doing, which was very little.

However, that wasn't so. He hadn't known anything about this base until tonight.

Two hundred meters into the installation, they approached a lift against the wall.

Zhoh's *chelicerae* tightened in displeasure, and he knew the subtle fragrance of his pheromones changed as well. The lift was an open invitation to invaders, a way to trap all who served below. Doubtless there would be other escape routes, but the chokehold was too attainable.

"Things are not as they seem, Captain." Sibed waved his left primary hand toward the featureless wall beside him.

Glancing at the wall, Zhoh noticed the faint outline of half a footprint at the juncture where the wall met the floor. He smudged the footprint with the claw on his big toe. "Your secrets would be better kept if you maintained cleanliness, Lieutenant."

"Of course, Captain." Sibed's embarrassed pheromones mixed with resentment and anger. "I will make note of this." He placed his top right lesser hand against the wall. Pale infrared lights cycled under the wall's surface.

Zhoh glanced around the hallway. "You have other points of egress from the hallway."

"Yes sir." Sibed watched Zhoh with the eyes in the back of his head.

Certain that the lieutenant would not tell him where all of the entrances were, Zhoh remained silent. If he had designed the fortification, he would have put a few of the doors in some of the rooms as well. Doing so was expensive and redundant, but it would help with security. There would be other surprises hiding behind the walls too, and many of them would be lethal. The waiting lift so readily in sight probably didn't do anything. It was bait in a very lethal trap.

A section of the wall slid to the side to reveal a lift large enough for six Phrenorians. Other wall sections probably held fighting points where warriors could trap invaders or kill them at will. The setup impressed Zhoh. It meant that whoever had designed it had recognized the chances of one day being found out. Or maybe, when the installation had served whatever purpose it was there for, it would be turned into a kill box against enemies.

Those enemies could get in, but they couldn't get out.

Sibed gestured for Zhoh to precede him.

"You go first, Lieutenant." Zhoh still wasn't certain why he'd been brought to the command post, and he was certain that was what this place was. General Rangha could have been merely throwing his weight around, or he could have summoned Zhoh there to kill him. Either was possible given Zhoh's current predicament.

With the ill-fated brood his treacherous wife had given birth to, and the blame she had placed on him for the genetic defects that had required the immediate deaths of those spawn, the titles and office Zhoh had been given by the Phrenorian Empire primes had been negated. He was just a warrior once more, and only bravery and success would lift him back to a place of honorable standing in the Empire. He should have been at the front of the war, leading warriors into battle and claiming the flesh of those he defeated, eating those enemies and joying in victory, not shepherding researchers working only to create poison to sell to the humans and other lesser species.

As he stepped into the lift, Zhoh slid a lesser hand closer to his Kimer particle beam pistol and another to his *patimong*. In close quarters the honor blade would prove instantly more lethal. If things went badly, he would bury the length of orange-red *daravgane* resin in the sergeant's thorax. The *patimong* would have no problem slicing through the sergeant's chitin. The blades were designed to do exactly that.

The other accompanying warriors started to board the lift too, but Sibed waved them back. It was an obvious attempt to put Zhoh at ease, or to show that Sibed did not fear Zhoh, but that didn't insure that weapons would not come out.

Or that the lift would not explode somewhere deep in the bowels under the base. It was a trap that Zhoh had used before. He had entered the lift because sometimes chances had to be taken in order for enemies to reveal themselves.

Sibed waved a lesser hand with a key cube over the control panel. Lights glowed briefly, then the lift dropped at a rapid rate and stopped to shift sideways for a time, shifted still again, then dropped some more before shifting twice more. The path to wherever they were going was not straightforward. Zhoh's equilibrium rocked slightly, but he maintained his balance.

The lift did not blow up. That thought had crossed Zhoh's mind, that Rangha might have called him to his death. His wife's father wanted him dead. He dropped that thought from his mind, knowing that he shouldn't even have considered that.

At least, he shouldn't have had to allow distractions along those lines. Yet here he was, on this blighted planet with no real chance of war glory ahead of him.

Zhoh also knew the installation was larger than he'd imagined earlier. A lot of resources had gone into the construction.

Angrily, he wondered if it was all a waste. The commanding officer in charge of the Phrenorian army on Makaum wasn't known for his abilities in the field. General Rangha wasn't even a blooded warrior.

Finally the lift doors opened onto another hallway that was narrower than the one above. A dozen warriors stood on guard along the way. They wore particle beam rifles and pistols and *patimongs*, and dressed in *raintai,* the ceremonial armor of warriors who guarded the Phrenorian primes.

The distinctive armor was constructed from a spyrl's blood-kin warriors fallen in a victorious battle, symbolic of the glory their forebears had won. The armor pieces were all deep purple and blue, thick layers of chitin processed with *sul'kala* oil made from the apodemes that attached a Phrenorian's muscles to his exoskeleton and made him stronger.

Zhoh struggled to keep his anger and contempt under control. As a general recognized by the primes, Rangha could choose to have his private guards wear the armor, but doing so could be to honor the warriors that had pledged to lay down their lives before their general's. Or such a show could be considered boastful.

Zhoh considered the present choice as boastful. General Rangha had achieved his rank through privilege from the Empire based on his bloodline. Sometime in the distant past, one of Rangha's ancestors had been a hero to the Phrenorians, a warrior who had made a name for himself in battle against harsh odds. His descendants had been partitioned out of dangerous service to continue breeding strong warriors.

That way of thinking was changing these days. Defeating the Terrans was proving to be more difficult than the Empire had at first believed. Warriors died quickly in battle against the Terrans. Although the humans were more fragile with their soft bodies and thin bones, they did not quit or turn away from a fight. Zhoh would never respect the Terrans because there remained so much weakness in them, but he would acknowledge their ferocity and dedication to battle.

If the war against the Terrans was to be won quickly, Phrenoria needed to bring out their best warriors now. Zhoh had championed that line of rationale for the last six years, until the time Sxia, his wife, had delivered their malformed brood only months ago.

That old anger settled in over the new and Zhoh got control of himself as he walked at the lieutenant's side. Their footsteps echoed in the hallway. One day Sxia would pay for her betrayal, and her father would bleed for the political favors he had pulled in to salvage his daughter's future and bury her genetic defects. She would never again have a brood. That had been taken from her, and blame for that had also been placed at Zhoh's feet.

Zhoh would have no other wife, and there would be no children to carry on his name so that he would be forever remembered. His present hadn't been the only thing that had been taken from him. His future had been stripped away as well.

None of the guards looked directly at Zhoh, but they all took notice of him. Some tightened their grips on their weapons, but not enough to be offensive about it. He was a renowned warrior, one who had killed hundreds of his opponents, and no few in personal combat. They were wise to be wary of him. Zhoh took a shadow of satisfaction at that.

Sibed stopped in front of an inset door. Massive hinges on the side gave an indication of how thick the entrance was and how much it weighed.

Zhoh's respect for the general dropped even further. A true warrior wouldn't hide away in a hole in the ground.

As if guessing his thoughts, the lieutenant said, "General Rangha isn't all that is protected within this vault."

Zhoh chose not to answer.

With a hiss that revealed the airlock within, the huge door recessed a meter, then swung to the side, revealing the massive room on the other side. Where Zhoh had only expected the general's living quarters, the vault had to be at least a klick square and half that deep, lit now by bright lights. Several war machines, ranging from heavy powersuits to tracked assault vehicles ten meters tall to aerial manned and unmanned vehicles, gleamed in the brilliant incandescence. Machine oil stink overlay everything.

An assault force lay ready and waiting before Zhoh. All thoughts of his anger drifted away from him as he gazed on the collection of armament.

"I can smell your surprise from up here, Captain Zhoh," a mocking voice stated.

Using his rear eyes, Zhoh glanced up the wall behind him and spotted General Rangha leaning on a balcony overlooking the floor and the immense room. The general supported himself on his primary hands. The great claws fastened on the waist-high railing.

Rangha's age showed in the dulling luster of his chitin. His days of *lannig*, the moulting process that promoted growth all Phrenorians went through till their final years, were behind him. He had seen his final rebirth. There was no stronger body awaiting him these days.

Although his hair didn't turn gray as a Terran's did, the thin black braids festooned with awards his ancestors had won in service to the Empire were dull and flat. His exoskeleton wasn't as broad and as formidable as Zhoh had expected, and he knew the old general hadn't been challenged physically in a long time. There were no scars on his chitin. Pain and struggle made a warrior larger and stronger. Rangha had not experienced much of either. Like his guards, he too wore ceremonial armor.

"Greetings, General." Zhoh turned and performed a small bow. "May your next *lannig* be ruthless and painful and grow you ever stronger so that you may serve the Empire."

The traditional greeting was proper, but Zhoh hoped it shamed the general all the same, drawing attention to the fact that such a thing would never again happen for him.

"And may yours test you," Rangha called down, "to the limits of your endurance."

That was a thinly veiled curse, or perhaps a threat. Zhoh was not certain which it was. Of course, it was also a traditional response among Phrenorians. *Lannig* was a painful process.

Zhoh bowed again and snapped a primary hand at the guards in their ceremonial armor. "Had I known the occasion merited formal dress, I would have come properly attired."

"Stronghold RuSasara, as this place is known, stands on tradition, Captain. You were not so informed because your manner of dress is not a reflection of this place."

You are not—and will not be—any part of this place. The general's words couldn't have been any clearer. Zhoh kept calm through willpower, barely able to withstand the continued rebuke around him.

"You must have many questions, Captain."

Stubbornly, Zhoh refrained from stating the obvious. He might have questions, but the general would tell him only what he wished him to know.

Rangha snapped one of his primary hands and the loud, flat clap of chitin striking chitin echoed across the cavernous space. "Come up, Captain, and let us talk."

THREE

In shadowy darkness, Noojin waited irritably and anxiously atop a narrow two-story house across the street from the Terran fort, wishing that Jahup and the big sergeant would return soon from their "secret" mission. Jahup had been excited about going, about spending time with the sergeant, and he'd told Noojin more than he'd been supposed to. Like a fool, he'd sworn her to secrecy.

That was wasted effort. She was part of his hunting band. They had placed their lives in each other's hands for years. There was no closer-knit relationship, not even in families.

She was still angry with Jahup and the sergeant for not allowing her to go along. She was as good as Jahup in the jungle, and much better than the sergeant. If anything, the big-footed offworlder would probably get Jahup killed clomping around the jungle as he did.

She made herself stop thinking about Jahup getting hurt. That wasn't going to happen, and it was a waste to dwell on it. She wouldn't let it happen. Grandmother Leghef had told her several times that the power of the mind could control the future. It only took a strong mind.

The Terran fort stood brightly lit in the night, a sharp contrast to the Makaum dwellings and public buildings around it that bore the colors of the jungle and seemed to melt into it. Until the offworlders arrived, people had risen with the sun and gone to bed shortly after sunset. There had been little to do at night and several of the nocturnal predators were more dangerous than those that hunted by day.

Powerful lights lit the fort, illuminating the grounds and paths between the Quonset huts where the soldiers slept and day-to-day business was carried on. Other sec lights monitored the hangars that contained the fierce engines of destruction that Jahup was so interested in.

In the heart of Makaum, the Terran Army had erected an alien fortress that warred with the environment. At the other end of the city, the Phrenorians, the (ta)Klar, and the corps all did the same. It was as if a sea of technology and *otherness* strove to form a barrier around the Makaum people. The effect was suffocating and Noojin found she didn't like being in the sprawl. She preferred being out in the jungle hunting.

Some looked on those offworlder efforts to grow their own world on Makaum as a step toward security that the Makaum people had never had. Migrating jungle creatures had threatened the city at times, but the people had always rebuilt. Those attacks were natural things. The offworlders were not.

Noojin felt that the city was being imprisoned. Roads into and out of Makaum now had checkpoints managed by the Terran Army. The offworlder word *checkpoint* sounded harsh and explosive, and as offensive as it was. Before, people who lived in the city had been free to come and go as they pleased. Now "identification" had to be presented to travel the roads close to the fort, and no one was allowed at the embassies except those who were invited.

The restrictions were intolerable.

An *eanga*, glowing a soft violet, flitted through the air near Noojin's head and distracted her angry thoughts. Only a few centimeters in length, the small winged lizard was probably curious to find her seated there. She lifted a hand and called it to her with her mind.

Come.

For a moment, the *eanga* hesitated. Its small, vaporous thoughts brushed up against hers. Although those thoughts weren't completely decipherable, just as hers weren't to it, Noojin knew the little creature was searching her intentions for any predatory overtures. There were things, creatures as well as plants, that could lure victims into traps from which there was little chance of escape.

She thought only happy thoughts at the *eanga*, then slowly reached into her kit for the journeycake she'd stuffed there in anticipation of the long night of waiting for Jahup's return. She held a crumb between her thumb and forefinger.

Cautiously, the *eanga* flitted in and darted its tongue out to test the crumb. Satisfied there was food and nothing threatening, the lizard rested on Noojin's hand. The tiny claws were sharp and dug in to hold, but they didn't cut into flesh. Folding its wings, the *eanga* perched there. Slowly, she brought it in closer to her body and offered it her warmth. So many of the lizards were attracted to the Makaum simply because of the heat their bodies radiated. Absentmindedly, Noojin stroked the tiny creature as it fed.

Her eyes raked the empty training grounds that she and Jahup used to watch. She'd never had any real interest in the offworlders, but Jahup did. Noojin suspected that interest had something to do with his father dying so young. There was an incomplete part of her friend that she sensed but could not understand. For some reason unknown to her, Jahup had illusions of finding that missing part among the offworlders. Or, rather, among the soldiers because they could be so fierce.

Jahup enjoyed watched the offworlders as they trained in hand-to-hand combat and with their weapons. He liked the offworlder rifles and pistols. Noojin didn't. She preferred the bows and the spears their band used while hunting. Everything they needed to take meat could be gotten with those weapons, and those things that couldn't be safely taken with them—like the *kifriks* and the greater *khrelavs* and others—needed to be left alone.

Over the last few months, Noojin had tried to correct Jahup's thinking, but it was as if the older he got, the more stupid he became. Males, Noojin had discovered, had a tendency for stupidity. Especially if they were allowed to gather and share fermented drinks. She had hoped Jahup would never turn out like those men did.

They were both seventeen, recognized as adults in their community. They served in an adult capacity by taking meat from the jungle. When they were younger they had thought alike. Now Jahup insisted on being something Noojin didn't entirely understand.

That was frustrating. And scary. She also wanted to stop thinking about it.

Wrapping her arms around her legs as she sat on the tree bough that helped provide support for the house's roof, Noojin wished again that the offworlders had never found their planet. Before the Terrans and the Sting-Tails and the (ta)Klar and the corps had arrived, the Makaum had lived good lives.

Most of her people would not agree with her. They enjoyed the technology and wealth brought by the off-worlders. Many of Noojin's friends occupied their free time with games and music and clothing they had never before seen. In fact, they enjoyed free time that they had never before had because of the wealth the offworlder corps spread around.

Those friends never paid attention to the great holes left out in the jungle where offworlder miners dug out the bones of the planet. Sometimes, if the large digging crawl-ers excavated too close to the city, small earthquakes shook the homes and buildings and caused minor damage.

The greedy Makaum never saw the waste wrought by the offworlders either. Offworlder soldiers and bash-hounds killed creatures out in the jungle to keep them from their camps and compounds, and sometimes simply for pleasure. Thousands of pounds of meat Noojin's people could have used were eaten by carrion feeders or simply spoiled in the heat.

Some of the migratory herds of edible lizards had re-treated deeper into the jungle as a result, their numbers diminished. Getting them now required hunting bands to forage deeper into more treacherous lands, and to carry meat greater distances to return to the city. It was always a race to get back, to escape the carnivores that hunted them, and to keep the meat from spoiling.

Some of the bands had quit the hunt and found other jobs within the city. The hunting bands talked among themselves and warned the *Quass*, the Makaum govern-ing body, that soon the people would become dependent on food provided by the offworlders. They would no longer be autonomous. They would no longer be free.

From within the house Noojin sat on, someone played one of the consoles brought by the offworlder traders. The music was eerie and unnatural, nothing like the wood-winds and stringed instruments used by musicians in the city. The sound was uniform, not unique like the songs the musicians played. Blue light emanated from a window below and faded into the night.

Noojin sensed Telilu before the girl made herself known, though she had climbed the tree soundlessly.

"Hey," she called softly from behind Noojin.

"I already knew you were there, Twig."

"Don't call me that."

"If I had been a *kifrik*, I would have already snared you in my web and wrapped you for my dinner." The state-ment was harsh, but the young had to learn early the dan-gers held by the jungle.

"I'm getting better."

"You are." Noojin turned the girl and ran her free hand through Telilu's green-tinted hair. She was eight years old, slightly built, and her hair felt as fine as spider silk. Like Noojin, she wore shorts and a pullover top with a small kit and knife belted at her hip. She was Jahup's younger sister.

"Oooh." Telilu crouched down and sat beside Noojin. Her eyes rounded as they lit on the *eanga* still feeding on the crumb. "Can I hold him?"

"Her. And yes you can. But you have to be careful so you don't scare her." Gently, still thinking safe thoughts, Noojin transferred the tiny lizard over to the smaller girl. "What are you doing up so late?"

"I couldn't sleep." Telilu traced the tiny folded wings with her forefinger with rapt attention.

"Your grandmother will be worried about you if she finds you missing from your room." Both of Jahup's parents were dead, and brother and sister had been raised by their grandmother.

"Quass Leghef," Telilu said in a mocking tone that told Noojin she and her grandmother had had another disagreement, "is too worried about Jahup to be worried about me." She was silent for a moment, then spoke more softly. "I'm worried about him too."

"Why?"

"Because Grandmother's head is filled with bad things."

Sometimes Quass Leghef could see parts of what was to come. Noojin had never wanted that kind of ability. It would be horrible. "What kind of bad things?"

Telilu shook her head. "I don't know. She makes sure I can't get into her thoughts, but I know they're there. She can't hide *everything* from me."

"No, I suppose she can't." Noojin threw an arm around Telilu.

"You're worried about Jahup too."

Noojin didn't even try to hide her fears, just made sure that the younger girl couldn't peer too closely into her mind. "I am."

"Why?"

"Because Jahup is out in the jungle."

"At night?"

"Yes."

Telilu shook her head. "That's dumb. The jungle is even more dangerous at night. Is he hunting?"

Noojin supposed that was the truth. "Yes."

"That's even dumber. We have more than enough meat." Telilu shifted the journeycake morsel and made the *eanga* creep across her hand to get the food again.

"Meat goes quickly. You've seen how much Old Vorves eats."

Telilu smiled and her eyes shone. "Denas eats more."

"Maybe. And they aren't the only ones with healthy appetites." Noojin brushed hair from the younger girl's face.

On the other side of the tall fence, two soldiers walked steadily along a well-packed training field. They carried their rifles across their chests and talked quietly among themselves. One of them laughed and the other joined in.

Noojin didn't know what they were talking about but she suspected whatever it was, it wasn't very different from what other young men their age talked about. The Terran men, and the women, tended to be similar to the Makaum people. They had diverse rites and traditions, and other interests, but in many ways they were alike.

That was one of the arguments Jahup's grandmother constantly put forth during disagreements over the off-worlders. Quass Leghef believed that ultimately the Makaum had more in common with the Terrans than with the Phrenorians or the (ta)Klar. Both of the other off-worlder races were too alien, too far removed from what the Makaum knew.

Noojin had a different view of the Terrans. She had been kidnapped by Velesko Kos and she had known what the man intended for her. The man had planned to take her and use her. She had been ready to kill Kos or die before she let that happen. Nightmares of the violation that had nearly happened still lingered in her mind in the small hours before dawn. Quass Leghef told her those memories would fade in time, but Noojin was not so certain.

As Telilu sang a little song to the *eanga,* a small pack of shadows stole down the tree- and bush-lined alley between the fence line and the nearest house on the other side of the street. The soldiers at the fort kept defoliant sprayed on their training grounds, so that area was clear of plant growth. The line of demarcation was clear, though, because the Makaum didn't like the offworlder sprays. The threat remained that the chems would get loose in the jungle and hurt the environment.

When the Terrans first came, there had been a lot of new sicknesses. Even after they'd administered their vaccines and cleared up the outbreaks, the Makaum people had mostly chosen to stay away from the offworlders.

Then the Phrenorians had come, but those kept mainly to themselves except for trade negotiations and diplomacy issues. Many Makaum people appreciated that aspect of those offworlders. Privacy was a valued commodity.

Feeling tense, Noojin watched as the soldiers kept walking and the shadows clustered in the alley. Her senses went on high alert and she felt the same excitement thrilling through her veins as she did when the hunting band rousted a large predator from the jungle by mistake.

Moonslight sparked silvery fire from metal in the hands of the shadow and Noojin knew she was staring at an ambush. Whoever was in that alley intended to kill the Terran soldiers. Even from this distance, she could sense that. Their thoughts were loose and fiery, not totally guarded.

Knowing she had no time to waste if she was going to save the soldiers, Noojin caught up her nearby bow and slid an arrow free of her quiver hanging from a branch. As she stood, she put arrow to string, drew back till the stiff insect wing fletching glided along her cheek to her ear, and released.

The arrow skated through the leaves and stayed on course, sliding over the top of the mesh fence, and then struck the nearest of the soldiers in the side of his head. Noojin trusted the polycarbonate shell to deflect the arrow before it did any damage. Splintered on impact, the arrow dropped to the ground, but it had smashed into the soldier hard enough to stagger him.

Military training took over and he went down, presenting a smaller target profile as he searched for his attacker. Judging from the way the other soldier moved, the first had warned him.

Noojin knew about the armor's onboard near-AI, and she knew the software—whatever that was because it sounded like magic to her—would track the arrow's flight back to her. She grabbed her quiver and pulled it over her shoulder, then reached down for Telilu, catching the young girl under the arms and scaring the *eanga* away in a frantic flutter of wings.

"Time to go," Noojin whispered into the startled girl's ear. She tossed the bow ahead of her into the brush behind the dwelling. "Fall softly." She took two steps and vaulted into space on the other side of the house. Behind her, gauss blasts tore the trees above the house to shreds and someone inside the dwelling screamed in terror.

FOUR

J-Keydor Node
Stronghold RuSasara
Makaum
5023 Akej (Phrenorian Prime)

ieutenant Sibed led Zhoh up a narrow stairway that let
out into General Rangha's offices. The younger officer
did not speak and Zhoh asked no questions. The footsteps echoed in the cavernous weapons vault behind them.

Built into the wall behind the balcony, the general's
personal office overlooked the immense room and the
weapons standing in neatly ordered ranks. Massive and
orderly to match, the office had been designed to intimidate and provide an illustrious history of the man behind
the large *daravgane* desk.

The orange-red resin piece of furniture was calculated
to impress visitors even further. *Daravgane* was prized on
Phrenoria, and was found in no other place. The resin was
drawn from the sacred primordial predators on the home
planet. The great beasts swam in the Phrenorian seas and

were regarded to be distant ancestors of the Phrenorians. Draining the *daravgane* was the most dangerous thing a warrior could do, and usually he did so only to create heirloom weapons when sanctioned by a prime after he'd made a name for himself on the battlefield.

To have drained enough *daravgane* to create the desk of one piece was astonishing as well as bordering on self-aggrandizing. Zhoh had never seen nor heard of anything like it. The desk was carved into a block of translucent solidity, then inlaid with darker pieces of *daravgane* so deep a red they stood out against the orange.

The images carved into the desk celebrated the achievements of a warrior armed with a *patimong* and using an *arhwat*, one of the original chitin bucklers, not one of the electromagnetically enhanced units carried by present-day warriors.

Rangha stood behind the desk, ramrod straight and as imposing as he could. He was still half a head shorter than Zhoh and not nearly so wide, and the captain took pleasure in that distinction. "The warrior in that image is Faylas HatVeru, my ancestor, at the Battle of Arquacha."

Zhoh bit back a scathing retort. With the family name of HatVeru, the general's claim to distinction came from matriarchal lineage. He did not even have a true pedigree of entitlement to his position or pride.

"I have heard of Faylas HatVeru," Zhoh said. "He was a very brave warrior. Skilled and deadly in melee against his enemies."

The Battle of Arquacha was legendary. Hundreds of songs and stories had been sung and told of the warriors and the combat. The land had become a sea of blood.

"I am all that is left of the HatVeru family." Rangha's voice carried a threatening timbre, and Zhoh knew the man recognized the unspoken disrespect that he held back. "Faylas HatVeru was a great commander and fierce warrior. The Empire wanted that preserved."

So neither you nor your family before you has fought in a true battle in over four hundred years. Not only that, but your bloodline has thinned. That happened when a family tried to stay within the prime lineages. That was why Sxia's father had pursued Zhoh's father to set up the mating match, wishful of fresh blood to carry on his brood. Instead of a legacy, Sxia had borne damaged goods that had to be exterminated.

Zhoh kept the thought to himself because if the words were spoken, they could not be taken back. The insult he would give so lightly was punishable by death, tantamount to suicide. He would not die that way. He would live and he would glorify himself in the war, and he would return to avenge his name.

"As you know, Captain, bloodline is everything in the Phrenorian Empire. Those warriors who cannot deliver children to claim more prizes for the Empire are quickly forgotten."

Zhoh stood there and accepted the affront. As a lesser warrior, he was a target for rebuke and admonishment. Also, his failure to produce healthy offspring was a matter of public record. No lesser warrior could bring the subject up, but the general had free rein.

Rangha snapped a primary at one of the chairs before the desk. "Sit."

After adjusting his weapons, Zhoh sat and curled his tail around the chair leg so the appendage would be out of the way. He breathed in through his carapace and distanced himself from the room, turning off his emotions as he'd been taught by his father and by his first instructors when he'd entered officer training at Ath'ormy Academy.

The general did not sit and chose to remain standing.

His primary hands hung at his sides while his lesser hands crossed his narrow, thin chest.

"The presence of this stronghold has surprised you."

"The fact that we have not used the war machines that reside in that hangar surprises me." Zhoh knew his statement bordered on insubordination, but it was also the truth and all within the room knew that.

Walking to the balcony, Rangha peered out at the aerial units sitting idle on the ring of decks that clung to the walls. "You look out there and you see a way to take Makaum, do you?"

"With those weapons? Yes, I do. Those are more than the Terran soldiers have." Zhoh didn't hesitate about answering.

"You have been on this planet for two months, Captain. Yet you did not know about this place." Rangha turned back to him. "Do you think it is possible there are Terran bases like this one that you do not know about?"

"The Terrans do not have this kind of equipment at their disposal." Zhoh believed that. The spies they had in place among the humans were thorough. "The Terran Army does not have a space station circling the planet. They believe their precious Fort York is enough to hold Makaum. They use the space they have leased from DawnStar's space station. We know everything General Whitford has brought onto Makaum."

"We do," Rangha agreed. "However, General Whitford could send for reinforcements from the Khustal System. Those units could be Gatestreamed into orbit around Makaum within days." The general snapped a primary in the direction of the hangar. "Can you guarantee the Phrenorian Empire War Council that you can take this planet before the arrival of those reinforcements? And hold it once those arrivals took up arms against you?"

Everything in Zhoh screamed to respond in the positive, that he *could* do such a thing. But the truth was that he *might* be able to deliver on those terms.

"Can you guarantee that?" Rangha demanded.

Zhoh forced himself to answer. "No."

"Neither can I, and having to do so is almost an insult to my revered ancestor." The general's response was cold and brittle. He took a breath and it hissed out of him when he released it. "A premature use of the weapons we have here would alienate the Makaum people, perhaps even unite them against us. Our standing here is improved as long as they are at odds."

The Makaum people were no threat in Zhoh's mind. If not for the (ta)Klar and the Terrans, taking the planet would require no time at all, and within weeks a new supply route could ferry natural resources to the Khustal System. Those supplies were increasingly necessary, though the humans did not yet know that.

Instead of thinking about any of that, though, Zhoh focused on the one word that Rangha had inadvertently given him. *Premature.* A *premature* use of the weapons . . .

So there was a plan in place for them. Even as he recognized that, Zhoh also knew that was a question he could not ask. If the general had wanted him to know those plans, he would have offered that information.

Anger coiled inside Zhoh as he sat there in that office and knew that he was being kept from that knowledge on purpose. The lack of information—the lack of *trust*—was the general's way of dismissing him as an inferior.

And it was the way of the Phrenorian Empire.

Zhoh's anger was tinged with fear at being so far from the good graces he had always enjoyed, and he hated himself for it. He had never dreamed of being ostracized from the Empire. He had always been a loyal warrior. He had even married Sxia because his father and her father had agreed on the future of their families. Sxia was above Zhoh in station, but Blaold Oldawe had no sons to carry on the family name. The union should have brought them strength. It had before the primes, but the birth of their younglings had changed all of that.

Looking back on things now, with the knowledge that Sxia had been the only child Blaold Oldawe and his wife had had, Zhoh should have known the family was hiding something. According to stories, Blaold Oldawe and his wife had lost the rest of their brood in a tragic accident at a young age.

Cover-ups and lies spun out of that family. Zhoh knew that now, but he had never before encountered them on such a level. Blaold Oldawe had needed an heir. Blaold would be free to adopt a young male from another family to look after his holdings. Sxia would live an easy life, and Blaold would have a champion who owed him everything until the day he died.

Zhoh warred against the shame and outrage that threatened to spill over him, maintaining a level emotional state only by promising himself there would be an accounting. One day he would kill Sxia and break her open, then eat his fill of her and excrete her into the nearest dung heap. Then he would go after her father with the taste of his daughter on his breath.

"Why have you brought me here, General?" Zhoh was surprised at how calm his voice was.

For a moment, Rangha's *chelicerae* twitched in surprise before coiling back into place around his mouth. "You have a part to play in this as well, Captain."

The statement could have been mistaken for a peace offering. Zhoh recognized it as yet another insult, telling him that out of this grand plan the Empire had, a crumb still remained for him. He was so ashamed of the way he looked forward to it.

"Of course, sir. I follow the will of the Empire."

"So far the Terrans have been distracted by the drug cartels set up by the corps. This new sergeant—" Rangha hesitated.

"Sage, sir. Master Sergeant Sage."

"Exactly." Rangha's primary snapped irritably. "I was told you saved this man's life."

The general's accusation came out layered with thick, cloying pheromones that warned Zhoh to tread carefully. "I do not know him, General. To say I saved Sage's life would be to say I was acquainted with him. I am not. He is an enemy combatant."

"You defended him against one of DawnStar Corp's chief sec officers."

"I did so because having the Terran Army and Dawn-Star at each other's throat can only be beneficial to us, General. United, they provide a much more serious threat level." That was only part of the truth. Zhoh had also respected the way Sage had fearlessly marched in to face Velesko Kos despite the odds being against him. A warrior recognized the bravery of another warrior, even if that warrior was the enemy. General Rangha was not conversant with that concept.

"That division is what I want you to concentrate on, Captain. Since this Sergeant Sage is so interested in combating the cartels, make certain you aid him."

"Sir?" Zhoh looked at his commanding officer in surprise.

Rangha snapped his primary in annoyance. "The Terrans use some of the same spies we do. Make certain that information about the different cartels out in the jungle makes its way into the hands of the Terran Army. Keep them busy chasing those people, because the profits those black-market enterprises make find their way into the money purses of several key members of the *Quass,* from what I am told. They will not be happy with Master Sergeant Sage's success."

Reluctantly, Zhoh admitted to himself that it was a good plan. One of the major benefits of the Makaum civil unrest lay in how it kept the people separated. Polarized as they were by their wants, they could not change treaties or make decisions with any real speed. At this point, confusion was a potent weapon.

But there was another potential problem.

"The plan is good, General." Zhoh was not going to give Rangha credit for coming up with it. Doubtless the strategy had been drawn up by the War Council leader assigned to the Makaum action. "However, the (ta)Klar will not hesitate to take advantage of the situation to champion their own interests."

"Do not concern yourself with the (ta)Klar at this moment, Captain. As always, those creatures play their little political games behind the scenes, and this time they continue to be too far behind. They will take far too long to stop us. We gain momentum every day." Rangha pulled open a desk drawer and took an ivory object from within with one of his lesser hands. He set it on the desk.

Zhoh recognized the alabaster grin of a human skull at once. Taking such prizes in combat went against the rules of engagement between the Terran Alliance and Phrenorian Empire. Rangha would only get chastised by the primes and the War Council if it was discovered he had the artifact. Rank had its privileges.

"I killed this human in combat on Akalo," Rangha said. "For four days and three nights, I stalked him until he had no place left to run. Then I confronted him." He dropped a primary hand onto the skull with a resounding *crack*. But the skull remained whole.

Zhoh barely held back a sneer. Akalo was an outlaw world on the fringes of the Pagor System that had fallen nine years ago. The planetoid wasn't part of the war and had existed only for spacefaring crews to pursue their vices. It was only a place the war had gone through, a blip on the path to victory. One day it had been there, and the next it was gone.

"I killed him and I ate him and I claimed his head." Rangha's pheromones broadcast the sickening stench of pride. "I promise you, Captain, we will claim many skulls here."

"Yes sir."

Rangha's *chelicerae* twitched expectantly, as if the general had wanted a more robust response.

Zhoh wasn't going to give it. He sat and waited till he was dismissed, and he was glad to be going.

FIVE

"Did you see who it was?" Sergeant Pearson's voice sounded surprisingly calm and he stood his ground.

Still in a kneeling position, still panicked that he might be injured, Corporal Trevor Anders sighted along his Roley EMR 6 out of habit. Locked into the AKTIVsuit, with the onboard near-AI doing the calculations for him, he didn't have to aim. The suit more or less did the aiming. He just had to make the decision to pull the trigger, and that had happened without him truly thinking about it.

"No!" Anders yelled. He swept the Roley over the rooftop across the nearby intersection where the suit told him the missile had come from. He still didn't see whoever had fired the projectile that had hit him. He sucked in air and listened to his heart slamming in triple time. It was the first time outside of boot that he'd been shot, and the experience ripped away any ideas of how calm he would be in combat. The veterans had told him the Army was 99 percent boredom and 1 percent frenzy during firefights.

"Calm down, Corporal," Sergeant Pearson said. "You're on comm. There's no need to shout."

Anders cursed. He'd forgotten about the comm. He'd been—maybe still was—reacting to being shot. Thankfully he was still alive. He wasn't even injured. The projectile had hit him right in the head. *Right in the head!* He was never going to take that helmet off when he was on patrol again. *Never.* He was lucky he was with Pearson tonight. Pearson was a stickler for rules and regs. *Otherwise . . .* Anders didn't want to think about that.

The main sec channel officer buzzed them over the helmet comms. Like Pearson, her voice was calm but held a hint of edginess. "What's going on out there, Lima Three? I've got reports of gunfire."

Anders let Pearson take the call as he searched the area.

"Roger that, Control. We popped off a few rounds after someone took a shot at us."

"Do you need sec units, Lima Three?"

"Not yet. We're confirming the situation. Looks like a lone attacker who just wanted to score pride points. Took a shot at us with an arrow. We're uninjured."

"Affirmative, Lima Three. I'm standing by."

"Appreciate it."

"Do you see who did it?" Anders asked. He made an effort to hold it together. He'd been on the ground on Makaum only a few weeks. He'd been on the space station with Master Sergeant Sage when the sergeant lit up the bashhounds in the Azure Mist Tavern. Anders had thought all the soldiers in the place were going to get killed by cyber-enhanced bashhounds that night. No love was lost between the Army and the secmen.

Since then Anders had been on patrol a few times out

in the Green Hell, but nothing had ever happened. Except getting confronted by some of the local wildlife. This was a direct attack by another intelligent being. This had been personal.

"No, but you lit up that rooftop pretty good."

Switching to infrared and increasing the magnification on his HUD, Anders looked at the white meat of the shattered tree branches. A half dozen of them were bigger around than he was. The depleted uranium balls had smashed through everything he'd fired at. Flames danced along some of the limbs.

"Probably got whoever shot me too." Anders heard the pride in his own voice. He was from Lincoln, Nebraska, and nothing had ever happened there. That was why he'd joined the Terran Army. He'd wanted to see the stars and fight the enemy.

Now he'd probably racked up his first kill, an attacker he hadn't even seen. Part of him felt sick at the realization, but the rest of what he felt was fierce pride.

"Yeah, but maybe you better hold off on the celebration."

Anders swallowed bile. "Why?"

Pearson kicked the broken pieces of an arrow that lay on the ground. "Because whoever shot you with this knew it wouldn't hurt you."

Anders stared at the arrow. "That doesn't make any—" Before he could finish speaking, Pearson grabbed him and pulled him back toward the barracks. Unable to stop himself, Anders sailed through the air as a section of the fence's wire mesh turned into molten metal and blew up, spraying composite links out like shrapnel. They rattled against his armor. A follow-up flash bomb specifically tailored to take out the HUD visuals burst like an exploding nova.

The electric-white flash rendered Anders blind right before he struck the ground.

Visual systems are temporarily off-line. Stressors are evident in your nervous system. Do you require medication to remain combat ready? The near-AI's voice was feminine, as sexy as Anders could select. Only it didn't sound sexy now.

Anders struggled to get control of himself as Pearson kept him pinned down. The corporal spoke calmly. "Control, Lima Three requires backup immediately."

Pearson's words were lost in the loud explosion and sudden flood of agonizing heat that followed. Anders screamed as the suit tried to fight off the incendiary attack. On his faceshield, systems started failing, then he felt the flames eating into his body.

0358 Hours Zulu Time

Noojin struggled to roll over and force herself to drag her knees under her as she fought to suck in oxygen. The impact had driven the air from her lungs. Her first thought was for Telilu, hoping the girl was all right. The second was that the rounds from the soldier's rifle had come within millimeters of them—he had almost killed them. And the third was that two stories was a long way to fall without preparation.

She pushed herself up to her knees and looked around as the echoes of gunfire rang in her ears. She tried to pull in air again, and this time she succeeded.

"Telilu! *Telilu!*" Her voice came out in harsh barks.

Images of the little girl's body ripped to pieces by the gunfire threaded through Noojin's mind, layering one horrible nightmare onto the next. Other images of the child impaled on a tree branch followed. Noojin didn't accept any of them. She would never be able to

explain what had happed to Jahup or Quass Leghef if
Telilu was hurt.

Or worse.

Banishing that thought from her head, Noojin forced
herself to her feet. *It will* not *be worse! I won't allow it!*
"Telilu!"

"I'm up here."

Following the sound of the girl's voice, Noojin looked
up into the trees and spotted Telilu clinging to a branch
three meters from the ground. Her face was scrunched up
fearfully and tears shone on her cheeks, but Noojin saw
no blood.

"Are you all right?" The ringing in Noojin's ears persisted as she reached up for the girl.

"I'm okay. But why did the soldiers shoot at us?" Shaking and uncertain, Telilu climbed down the branches and
dropped into Noojin's waiting arms. She clung tightly, her
arms wrapped around Noojin and her small body quak-
ing all over.

"I shot at them first."

"Why would you do that?" Telilu's voice took on a
sharp note of accusation.

"I wanted to warn them. Someone was about to attack
them." Noojin paused long enough to gather her bow
and quiver. Some of the arrows had spilled out, but some
remained. She didn't want to be reduced to her knife if
things turned out badly. She wanted to keep Telilu safe.

"Who would—"

The deafening thunder of a close-proximity explosion
blew away Telilu's question and a sun seemed to dawn on
the other side of the house. Hot wind blew through the
space between the structures.

Noojin hunkered down and protected the younger girl
as much as she could. Two more explosions followed,

each one louder than the last, and long bursts of automatic fire chopped into the rolling detonations.

Creeping between the houses with Telilu held tightly against her, Noojin stopped at the corner and peered back at the alley where the attack had been launched. Before she could focus through the harsh light spreading in a pool across the ground at the foot of the fence, a man ran into her, knocking her down and coming down on top of her in a tangle of limbs.

Noojin released Telilu as the girl cried out. Placing herself in front of Telilu, Noojin drew her hunting knife and crouched warily as the man sprang to his feet.

Even in the scant moonslight, she recognized his blunt features and the burn scarring that mottled his left cheek and turned his ear into a twisted stub.

"Mosbur." Noojin held her knife down and ready.

The man had been a hunter, one of the best trappers she had known. After the ships had come, he had become a guide for the drug cartels and bio-pirates. Last year he had been brought in wounded, nearly dead. No one had ever learned how he'd been injured, and Mosbur had never told, but everyone suspected it was related to criminal activity.

Mosbur searched the ground for the pistol he'd dropped during the collision with her, but the blazing light given off by the explosions had night-blinded him. His outstretched hands raked over the grassy jungle floor and exposed roots of the trees. He cursed her luck and his, and Noojin had no doubts about what he intended to do with the pistol when he found it.

Another man ran through the alley and nearly plowed into Mosbur.

"Let's go!" the new arrival shouted. "The Terrans will be on us!"

"This girl has seen me!" Mosbur protested.

The second man turned and clawed for the pistol belted at his waist.

Before he could get the weapon clear, Noojin grabbed Telilu and fled back between the houses, hoping that she didn't encounter any more of the ambushers, hoping that the man's vision wasn't good enough to allow him to shoot her.

A laser beam snipped a lock of her hair and the stink of it burning filled her nose. She tightened her hold on Telilu so much that the girl instinctively fought back despite her fear. Noojin tried to think calming thoughts at her, but she was screaming inside her own head and knew that she was failing.

Ahead of her, twisting flames coiled against the fort's fence line and the building nearest it was a mass of fiery debris. A shadow came toward her and she spotted the rifle in the gloved hands, picking out the armored soldier carrying the weapon in the next instant.

"No! Don't shoot!" Noojin dropped to her knees and covered Telilu with her body, expecting bullets to rip through her at any minute. She remembered to call out again in Terran the second time.

Another shot from the laser pistol in the hands of Mosbur or his companion struck the armored soldier and burned a bright spot on his thigh near Noojin's head.

Autofire ripped out in a steady roll.

Then the soldier stood before her, towering above her, and said, "Don't worry. I've got you."

Noojin almost felt safe, but she didn't trust the Terrans any more than she now trusted Mosbur and his friends. Her world was never going to be the same. She held onto Telilu and stayed down while the Terran troops set up a defensive perimeter in the area.

SIX

Restlessness clouded Sage's mind as he watched the base on the other side of the swiftly moving river. Almost an hour had passed since Zhoh GhiCemid had disappeared within the structure. Sage wanted to know more because he knew Colonel Halladay would be as frustrated as he currently felt.

But they were running out of time on the scouting op. Dawn would come in a little less than an hour. They would be hard-pressed to clear the danger zone without being seen by the drones and the sec systems in that amount of time.

Jahup touched Sage's shoulder lightly.

Sage turned to face the younger man.

We go? the young scout signed.

Sage hesitated only a moment before signing his reply.

Yes. We go. He hated pulling out with so little information. What they had discovered had only confirmed they
had a big problem on their hands, and that knowledge led
to more questions. Just as he was about to move away
from the tree, Jahup put a hand on his shoulder again.

Wait.

Following Jahup's pointing finger, Sage slid back to the
tree and glanced back at the Phrenorian base as the door
irised open again. The sec drones pulled in closer to the
river and viewed Zhoh's departure from the base.

This time Sage noticed the three by three-square formation of warriors around Zhoh that told him the Phrenorian warrior didn't exactly have the run of the place. In
fact, the Sting-Tails escorting the captain treated him
more like a prisoner than a commanding officer.

That was interesting.

The guards walked Zhoh to the riverbank and stood
there waiting. After a couple moments, a small underwater sled surfaced. The craft hardly caused a ripple in
the river due to its streamlined design, and the camo
skin closely blended it to the darkness of the water. Only
the lack of refraction from the moonlight gave the vehicle slight dimension. It looked vaguely elliptical and
rode the current effortlessly.

Sage identified the sled as a Phrenorian *Tonbel*-class
submersible that was equivalent to the Terran Navy's Sea
Shadow. The Sea Shadow served as armed transport craft
that ferried men and materials in shallow water for assault
and support. Like tank crews, the Sea Shadow only carried
four personnel on board: a commander, pilot, gunner, and
loader. The cargo space was small, but the armament packed
a serious punch. It wasn't designed for sustained firefights,
but the presence of the boat indicated that the Phrenorians
had more muscle at their fingertips than otherwise believed.

A hatch swung open upward and a faint hint of light issued forth. Sage guessed the light source was infrared or something in a band that Phrenorians could see that humans couldn't because the area remained dark to him.

One of the guards nodded to Zhoh and he boarded the vessel without a word. The door closed and the submersible slipped back into the river and vanished.

The guards stood there a moment longer, then returned to the base and disappeared within.

Tensely, feeling exasperated, Sage hunkered down against the tree and kept watch. The Phrenorian base was there, just as Jahup had said it was, but no one knew what purpose it was supposed to serve. The structure was a ticking bomb waiting to go off.

Minutes passed and Sage put his emotions to one side to concentrate on the exfil from the area. He had some information, not everything he wanted, but enough to initiate a more informed investigation into the matter. He just needed to return with it.

The sec drones settled into a patrol pattern that was different from the previous one. Guards walked the area too, but they had to work hard not to be seen as well, so they didn't venture far.

Sage signed to Jahup, nodding to the nearest sec drone. *When that one disappears behind the tree line, we go.*

Yes. Impatience tightened Jahup's eyes and turned his mouth into a hard line.

Slowly.

Jahup shot Sage a disgusted look and signed back. *I'm more worried about you than any mistake I might make.*

If the situation had been any less tense, Sage might have grinned at that. But it was the truth.

The sec drone cut back behind the tree line thirty meters away and Jahup led the way into the jungle. The young scout's eyes were better than Sage's, more used to the environment and operating at night without HUD assistance.

The young man's ease with the jungle made Sage realize that he needed to incorporate some training with his soldiers in the brush without the AKTIVsuits. The Phrenorians depended a lot on technology, but they hadn't gotten away from their roots as independent fighters. Still, Makaum wasn't a home twenty for them either, and they tended to rely on their tech onplanet. Learning to operate, if necessary, without full military gear on assignment behind enemy lines might give the Terrans an edge at some point.

Sage stored that in the back of his mind and concentrated on moving through the jungle without making a sound or drawing attention from the drones or the local predators.

Submersible *Ituri*
Yeraf River
West of Makaum
5071 Akej (Phrenorian Prime)

Aboard the submersible, Zhoh kept his anger under control. The boat's commander wisely elected not to stick his passenger in the cargo section and instead let him ride up front in the control section. That affront, if it had come, would have resulted in someone's death.

Outwardly, Zhoh appeared calm. His position as a captain in the Brown Spyrl would allow nothing less. But since the birth of his defective offspring, only disrespect had come his way. If it were not for his family's standing with the Phrenorian primes—if not for *his* standing—he would have already been dead.

Lieutenant Yuburack had already attempted to kill him.

Zhoh rubbed his primary hands together as he remembered killing Yuburack. The chitin claws grated against each other. The lieutenant had been the first being Zhoh had dispatched since being called up on review and his assignment to Makaum. He thought about that for a time, remembered the taste of Yuburack as he'd eaten his conquered foe. There was no greater satisfaction than excreting a vanquished opponent onto a dunghill. There was not enough combat on Makaum. Yet.

The Terran sergeant was a worthy foe. Sage had proven himself in battle against the DawnStar drug traffickers. The man's bravery in standing up against Velesko Kos had been impressive. Soon, Zhoh knew, his and Sage's paths would cross, and that would be the end of the sergeant. Zhoh trusted that.

However, Zhoh set his sights on a greater game. Perhaps General Rangha believed himself untouchable in his present position, too well dug in to be unseated by an ambitious underofficer because of his family's history. Zhoh didn't acknowledge that. Nor would he acknowledge that. A warrior made his own history, and *lannig* changed everything.

The submersible's command section held the four crewmen. The pilot and copilot, the navigator, and the comm officer occupied large chairs in the nose of the craft. Computer projections hung in the air before them and revealed the river's depth, width, and speed in various colors. They cruised at a depth of five meters below the surface and stayed ten meters above the river bottom.

Rangha's base of operations was well thought out. Zhoh conceded that. But it also left the general cut off from the main strength of the warriors. Rangha had not been visible at the legitimate Phrenorian enterprises the Makaum

Quass had allowed. Zhoh believed a leader should always be front and center, leading his warriors into battle and spending time with them every day.

This was something Zhoh realized he shared with the Terran sergeant.

Despite his current situation, balanced precariously on a sword's edge between command and contempt, Zhoh remained in front of his warriors. They knew who he was and what he stood for. In spite of his wife's father's efforts to undermine his command—and to have his life taken— Zhoh had gained support when he'd stood up against the DawnStar bashhounds.

Zhoh enjoyed that memory, and he started planning how to build on that. He opened a comm link to the submersible commander. "Commander."

"Yes, Captain Zhoh?"

"How long will our voyage last?"

"We'll stay with the river for another three hours, Captain. Then we'll deliver you to a group of warriors who have overseen harvesting efforts in the jungle not far from the sprawl."

"What will you do after you see to my delivery?"

"I can't tell you that, sir. General's orders."

Zhoh ignored the affront because he knew it didn't come from the man. He turned his thoughts to Rangha. Before he could form a plan of action, Zhoh needed more information about the general. He opened a private comm link to Mato Orayva, his second-in-command, and sent a ping.

Mato wasn't just a junior officer and eager for advancement through the ranks, he was also part of Zhoh's family spyrl. He was young and hungry, wishing to earn glory and advancement through bravery and battle. Getting sent to Makaum hadn't set well with him either. Like

Zhoh, Mato believed he was destined for greater things. Zhoh knew that, properly counseled, Mato would reach his desired position.

Another warrior's need to excel was a weapon in the hands of the right superior officer. Zhoh knew how to be that officer, and Rangha had made the situation easier by spilling his dislike of Zhoh over onto his second-in-command.

Before the comm connection was made, a warning light flared to life on the navigation screens.

"Attention," the boat commander called out. He stood in the middle of the control center and swayed easily on his feet. "Captain Zhoh, you will want to make certain you're buckled in. We have attracted the attention of a *jasulild.*"

Zhoh recognized the creature from the studies he oversaw at his assigned project. The *jasulild* was equivalent to a Phrenorian *muyec*, except that the Makaum creature was not so dangerous. On Phrenoria, warriors braved the depths of the seas to dive into the fanged mouth of a *muyec* and eat their way free of the creature. Zhoh had done it the first time before he was old enough to be trained as a warrior.

"Is this a problem?" Zhoh asked.

"We're not going to allow it to become one." The commander's voice turned steely. "Pilot, course correct eight degrees to starboard and accelerate."

"Yes." The pilot made the adjustments.

The swift acceleration pushed Zhoh back into his seat. As he watched, the *jasulild* filled the navigation screen. The creature was round and huge, far larger than anything Zhoh had seen on Makaum. Purple-blue scales, the coveted hues for a Phrenorian warrior, covered the *jasulild.* Its mouth opened wide enough to engulf the submersible and only blackness appeared on the other side of the rows of sharp teeth. Zhoh had a new respect for the Makaum fishermen who brought *jasulild* meat back to the sprawl for vendors to sell.

With a flick of its tail, the *jasulild* course corrected as well, easily approaching the submersible in a smooth, effortlessly glide.

"Captain Zhoh," Lieutenant Mato said over the private comm link.

"Give me a moment. It appears we are under attack." With danger so imminent, Zhoh felt excitement thrill through him.

"Sir?"

Zhoh sat forward in his seat and thought about his chances of surviving in the river if the submersible was destroyed. Even though Phrenorians had come from the seas, they were no longer at their best in that element. His primary lesser hand curled around the hilt of the *patimong* while two lesser hands on his left side prepared to release the seat restraints. His segmented tail coiled restlessly around the seat's legs.

"Commander, there are three other creatures nearby," the navigator called out. "We have their attention now too."

If the commander was worried, he didn't show it. He remained standing. "Copilot, make a note. We need to find out why these things are massing here."

"They're spawning," Zhoh said.

The commander looked at him. "How do you know this?"

"I can't tell you that."

The Phrenorian Command kept units separate, compartmentalizing all war efforts so they couldn't be easily compromised. Zhoh's current assignment was with the biological weaponization effort. His teams learned the flora and fauna of Makaum so they could use the information against the Terrans and the local inhabitants. They were currently stockpiling a strain of Makaum virus that looked surprisingly lethal. They'd also started inoculating Phrenorian warriors against it so the virus wouldn't affect them when it was released.

"If you want to clear the river of them, you'll need to seed the riverbed with *byryj*."

"What is that?"

"A type of aquatic kelp. It renders *jasulild* eggs sterile, as well as other freshwater species. *Jasulild* and others of their kind can sense *byryj* and stay away from it during their spawning cycle."

"You can get this for me?"

"I can."

The commander nodded. "I would appreciate that."

"Of course." The task was small and easily done, and Zhoh knew the favor could pay off in the future. On the viewscreens, the *jasulild* grew hugely as it came closer, and the thing opened its mouth still wider.

"Weapons officer," the commander said.

"Yes."

"Clear the way."

"Yes sir."

The submersible was equipped with lasers, solid projectile weapons on the conn for above surface encounters, and torpedoes. It was also equipped with sonic cannons. The weapons officer fired those and generated a wave blast that ripped the lead *jasulild* to crimson jelly and flotsam that churned in the river. Another two blasts destroyed the other three creatures that swam toward the submersible and the way was clear again. The boat slid through the blood-stained water.

"Mato," Zhoh said, turning his attention back to the comm.

"Yes, Captain."

"I want to start digging more deeply into General Rangha's operations here."

Mato was silent for a moment and Zhoh knew it was because getting caught committing such betrayal might result in getting served to carrion feeders, and would definitely lead to getting assigned to somewhere even worse than Makaum. However, not obeying orders from a superior officer would be career suicide, even if that superior officer was committing treason. If Mato went to the general or one of the general's adjutants with Zhoh's intentions, Mato would forever carry the stigma of being untrustworthy.

It was a no-win situation for the lieutenant.

Although he considered it a weakness, Zhoh acted to soften the situation for the other warrior. "I swear to you on our ancestors that you will be rewarded for your efforts, Mato. I will take over command of the Phrenorian military on Makaum, and you will remain my second-in-command. Grow as I grow. *Lannig* changes everything."

"*Lannig* changes everything," Mato answered, but he did not sound so certain of that. "I will do as you say."

The response was automatic, and Zhoh heard some of Mato's anxiety, knowing that only touched the surface of the emotions that ran through the younger man.

"Tread carefully," Zhoh admonished. "Until we remove the general from this command, he will have the support of the warriors we want to win over."

"Of course."

"Good hunting. I will be there within a few more hours." Zhoh broke the connection and stared at the navigation chart of the river bottom as the submersible shot over underwater terrain.

The Phrenorian War was heating up on other worlds, and it was pushing toward the Loki System. If the War Council of the primes was correct, and Zhoh felt that it was, Makaum would soon be part of the campaign. The Phrenorians needed a world that would guarantee resources to the fleets and armies. They would need Makaum to establish a toehold in this solar system.

He intended to be the warrior who delivered Makaum to the Phrenorian Empire. And if he had to stand on General Rangha's corpse to do it, so much the better.

SEVEN

Just as the sun thrust pointed fingers through the fog that clung to the treetops, Jahup reached the spot where he and Sage had left the two-wheeled crawlers that had brought them to the site. A thin nanobot-operated camo sheet covered the crawlers and perfectly emulated the surrounding jungle with only a minimal tech footprint. Drones had to be within a few meters to detect the signal. Centimeters from the camo sheet, an onlooker wouldn't have noticed anything out of the ordinary. Even the wind was accounted for as the circuitry made adjustments.

Ten meters from the site, Jahup went to ground behind a stand of trees atop a small hill. Jahup reached for Sage's arm to pull him down, but Sage knelt beside his companion.

Wait, Jahup signed. *Make certain not discovered.*

Sage nodded and didn't bother to explain that he had planned to do the same thing. He counted down ten minutes and the sun eased higher, burning off more of the white fog caused by the humidity. The diurnal insects and lizards took up their routines, hunting food and some of them stalking each other.

If any Phrenorians had been waiting, the creatures wouldn't have been present and that void would have given them away. Sage noted that the repellant Jahup had made still worked because they weren't bothered.

When the time had elapsed and he was satisfied no one was watching the site, Sage tapped Jahup on the shoulder and nodded toward the hidden site. Sage led the way, walking down into the lower part of the jungle and stepping behind the camo sheet.

A slither above drew Sage's attention to the upper branches of the tree. With a rush of scales, the *omoro* descended and lunged toward Jahup.

The creature was four meters long from the tip of its ridged snout to the thick, stubby tail. The scales were thick and ridged, uneven in most places, and looked like a pile of rocks strewn along its length. The head was a craggy mass with a bone ridge that flared out a half meter from between its eyes to the back of its skull. Two more ridges almost as large jutted out along the jaws, framing a meter-long maw filled with rows of serrated teeth. When Makaum built a predator, it didn't hold back. The *omoro* looked like a spear as it streaked toward its intended prey. Ten powerful legs propelled it forward in a hypnotic choreography of synchronized thrusts.

By the time Jahup realized the danger he was in and tried to move aside, he was already a half step too late. Fear widened the young scout's eyes.

Sage drew the *etess* from over his shoulder and the hide-covered hilt felt solid and secure in his hand. The sharp blade ripped free of the sheath and he hoped it would be enough to handle the *omoro*. Sage slammed into the giant lizard and felt the breath go out of him. He stumbled and tried to regain his footing, but the *omoro* grabbed his thigh with one of the heavy-clawed feet, yanking him to the side.

Jahup's dive had almost taken him clear of the attack, but the *omoro's* back quarters swung around and caught him in the chest with its stubby tail. Jahup flew backward and crashed against a nearby tree, striking his head hard. His arms relaxed at his side.

Sage didn't know if the young man was alive or dead. The *omoro* twisted and squirmed like a boneless thing, managing to turn in all directions seemingly at once. Knotted in a ball, man and creature struck the ground.

Sage landed on the bottom, but knew he couldn't stay there and live. The *omoro* ripped at him with its great claws, digging shallow furrows across his chest, stomach, and thighs as Sage kicked away and rolled to his feet. He was conscious of the absence of the AKTIVsuit, too aware of the armor he didn't have.

He brought the *etess* up in both hands and stepped into a fighting stance. The *omoro* looked like a spring coming uncoiled as it flipped and flopped on the jungle floor. One of its feet caught in the camo netting and trapped it for a moment.

Hoping to take advantage of the *omoro's* bad luck, Sage quickly stepped forward and swung the *etess* at the lizard's head. The blade *clanged* home, but didn't bite into the creature's flesh as Sage had hoped. Only a few small pieces of scale tore away. Sage set himself again and thrust at the *omoro's* nearest eye, thinking that the organ had to be vulnerable.

The blade pierced the eye and dark purple blood wept down the *omoro's* cheek. Screaming in rage, a deep coughing bellow that echoed in the jungle, the lizard opened its mouth so wide it looked like Sage could have stepped in. He pulled on the *etess*, but the weapon didn't come free. Just as he was about to yank on the blade again, the *omoro* jerked once more and tore the *etess* from Sage's hands.

Unarmed, Sage stepped back, hoping that the monster was in its death throes. With only a little warning, the *omoro* launched itself at him once more. Sage threw himself to the side and got to his feet only a split-second before the *omoro* twisted around and came for him.

As he ducked aside, Sage thought of trying for his weapons on the RDC, but he knew he'd never reach them. Spotting a tree limb as thick as his arm and a meter in length in the undergrowth, he snatched it up. When the *omoro* came at him, Sage swung the limb as hard as he could, catching the lizard in its open mouth. Teeth shattered and broke, flashing yellow-white in the dulled gleam of sunlight streaming through the deep emerald leaves.

The *omoro* roared in rage again and started to come around. Knowing he needed a weapon and that he couldn't continue dodging the creature's quick strikes, Sage focused on the *etess* and ran for it, pitting his speed and strength against that of the monster he faced. His hand closed on the hilt just as the *omoro* swung around at him.

Instead of backing away from the creature's attack, which would have been the instinctive response, Sage moved forward. He slapped the clawed leg aside with the sword and vaulted on top of the lizard's thick body. His boots held against the *omoro's* uneven hide and allowed him to step up onto the thing.

Reacting at once, the *omoro* tucked and rolled. When it reached its back, the lizard opened it jaws and curled up toward its intended prey.

Sage tried to ignore the rows of serrated teeth framing the pink gullet, but he couldn't. They could close on him, and whatever part of him was left inside the *omoro* would be gone, cut or torn away. Purple blood leaked into the *omoro's* mouth from the ruined eye.

He knew there had to be a brain somewhere in that massive head, but he had no idea how big it was. He also trusted that the creature's palate was softer than its craggy hide. Lining himself behind the blade in a heartbeat, ignoring the whipping claws for the moment, Sage shoved the *etess* forward.

The blade bit into the pink flesh, slowed only for a moment, then rammed on in. The mighty jaws continued closing and Sage yanked his arm back, loath to release his only weapon. Even as fast as he was, he wouldn't have been able to get clear of potential injury if the *omoro* hadn't choked on the blade and the buckets of blood draining into its throat.

Squalling in renewed fury and pain, the *omoro* twisted to the side in an effort to get its feet under it. Sage leaped off of the creature, managed to avoid the flailing legs and tail, and scanned his new battlefield to prepare for his foe's next attack.

The *omoro* hacked and coughed blood as it righted itself. It looked around with its one good eye and spotted Sage. It growled as it came forward, much slower than it had moved earlier, and blood poured from its mouth. Two steps later, the *omoro* shivered all over, froze in place with purple froth dripping from its snout and front legs, and collapsed.

"Is it dead?" Jahup called from behind Sage.

Sage watched the creature for a moment, saw that it wasn't moving, and let out a breath. "It had better be."

Jahup walked up beside Sage and stood uncertainly,

swaying. He held his *etess* in one hand. "I thought it had me."

"I thought it had me too."

"It should have."

"Thanks for the vote of confidence."

"I've never seen a single man win a fight with an *omoro*."

Sage regarded Jahup with a small grin and a lifted eyebrow. "Maybe I'm not so green in this jungle as you think."

Jahup looked back solemnly. "If you kill another in the same way, then I'll believe it."

Sage frowned and felt a little angry and nonplussed, then he spotted the smile Jahup could scarcely hide and knew the scout was baiting him.

"Nope," Sage said as he turned back to the camo sheet and the waiting equipment, "the next one's yours."

0519 Hours Zulu Time

Under the protective netting, the sunlight was dimmer and the heat was blunted. Two Rapid Deployment Crawlers sat under the trees. Both two-wheeled vehicles had fat all-terrain tires, and both were stripped down to only essential equipment, a magnetic-powered engine, a powerful driveshaft that turned both wheels, a seat, and enough suspension to survive drops from twenty meters—if the rider didn't lose control on impact. Or wasn't already dead from enemy fire. The matte gray and green paint allowed the crawlers to present a low profile while on the move.

Reaching his crawler, Sage stripped out of the Makaum clothing and pulled a black hardsuit with Terran Army markings from the equipment saddlebags. He pulled the

AKTIVsuit on, then tabbed the sec code into the hidden wrist controller and felt the armor activate, locking into place and hardening up. Medical subroutines came online, comparing Sage's current condition to what was programmed in the memory. The suit ran on an electromagnetic feed broadcasted from Terran Army satellites in orbit around Makaum.

The saddlebag yielded a pair of boots and gloves. He pulled on both and felt them lock into the combat suit. Taking out the helmet, he pulled it onto his head, securing it as well. Flexible, ablative scales slid out of the helmet and snaked down around his neck. A reinforced column covered his spinal cord.

For the moment, the faceshield remained blank. All systems were off-line. Neat letters from the suit's near-AI scrolled across the inside of the faceshield.

State your name and rank.

"Sage, Frank Nolan. Master Sergeant Terran Army Charlie Company." Voice recognition confirmed his identity and the helmet came to life. The 360-degree view opened on the faceshield and a map overlay of his current location ghosted into view over that, spreading out ten klicks from him in all directions. The top-down view came from the satellite feeds.

Welcome, Master Sergeant Sage. Your biometrics scan reveals that you are approaching physical exhaustion. Do you require stims?

"Negative. I'm fine." Sage didn't care for the chem cocktails the hardsuit could pump into him. He preferred true clarity of mind.

He took his weapons out of the armored case strapped under the saddlebag on the right side. He fit the Smith and Wesson .500 Magnum revolver into the shoulder holster under his left arm. The silver reticle that matched up with the weapon instantly dawned on his faceshield, paired by the smartlink in the grip and in the biometric link grain in his palm.

The Birkeland coilgun triggered a red reticle as Sage slid it into the holster on his right hip. He slung the Roley gauss rifle across his back and made certain the violet reticle for the weapon was present.

The near-AI juiced a message across Sage's faceshield. *One member of your present team is not prepared.*

Sage turned slightly. A few meters away, Jahup struggled with his helmet, unable to get the piece locked into place. "Need help?"

"No." Jahup sounded irritated. He jerked on the helmet again but still didn't succeed in pulling it into place.

Sage ignored the young man's answer and walked over to him. He took Jahup's helmet in both of his hands, twisted, and leaned it forward a little, fitting it more precisely into the hardsuit's collar. The armored plating extended from the helmet and locked into the hardsuit with a series of rapid *clinks*.

Through the transparent faceshield, Jahup looked equal parts annoyed and appreciative. "Thank you."

"No prob." Sage dropped an armored fist onto Jahup's helmet to test the connection. "You have to hold the helmet just right to get it on. Takes time to learn it." Sage felt guilty because the scout's training had been abbreviated. Still, having the hardsuit was better than not having it while out in hostile territory. "You keep using it, suiting up will become something you don't even think about when you do it."

"Okay." Jahup pulled out his own weapons.

Sage pulled up the note app and made a reminder for himself to make certain Jahup saw the company armorer to ensure the AKTIVsuit was up to spec. Jahup had only recently been issued armor, a hand-me-down that had survived when the soldier inside hadn't. After the scout had agreed to work with the Terran Army following the events of the action against DawnStar, Sage had wanted Jahup properly outfitted. A lot of potential enemies existed within the corps, and Jahup had been identified as one of the soldiers even though he'd only been at the site to save Noojin.

Jahup hadn't mentioned his part in the attack on the illegal drug factory to anyone, but word about his presence had gotten around through DawnStar's people who had been at the site. Sage still wasn't certain where that was going to leave Jahup in the eyes of his own people. Some of them lauded him as a hero. Others seemed to think he had betrayed them by taking a position with the Terran Army.

Noojin, the young girl who worked with Jahup's hunting band, didn't like her partner crossing lines. She liked to keep her distance from the Terran Army. Jahup still hunted meat with his band, since those efforts also served as scouting expeditions. Sage figured those trips were a lot more interesting these days than they had been.

Jahup climbed aboard his RDC and switched on the magnetic drive. The crawler shivered to life and rocked forward until Jahup restrained it.

Back on his own vehicle, Sage brought up the shared comm link. "You lead. I'll follow."

Jahup nodded without turning around, picking up Sage on the 360-degree view afforded by the helmet. Twisting the throttle, Jahup hunkered down over the crawler and rocketed through the jungle's underbrush.

Sage accelerated, following closely behind as they sped

through the jungle. Keeping the RDC on track was mind-numbing as the hardsuit's AI and past experience kept track of Jahup's route and the terrain without any real effort on Sage's part. Idle, without true focus, his head filled with questions concerning the Phrenorian base and what the Sting-Tails had hiding there.

EIGHT

They're afraid of us, Sergeant."

Sergeant Kjersti Kiwanuka knew the assessment made by the corporal standing next to her was accurate. Kiwanuka didn't need the hardsuit's vision multiplier capabilities and body language interpreter software package to recognize the fear that gripped the Makaum onlookers and made them restless while causing them to stand packed together. She'd been in plenty of places where she'd seen it before—from both sides of that line that kept the two groups separate.

The Makaum people stood well back of the yellow warning laser array that marked the blast hole created during the ambush. The sizzling yellow lines were almost too bright to stare at with the naked eye, and the warning hum that accompanied them intensified when any non-military person approached.

The lasers wouldn't do any real harm if physically encountered, but they did interfere with the central nervous system and render most intelligent creatures nauseous. Unfortunately, most of the life-forms on Makaum didn't have high-functioning central nervous systems and went through the lasers with impunity. As a result more soldiers had to be assigned to the barriers to keep out wandering reptiles and the larger insects.

And the increase in armed guards worried the locals even more.

"I know they're afraid," Kiwanuka said. "We're afraid too."

Army sec drones zipped by overhead, scanning rooftops and trees. One sniper, properly armed, could take down a soldier in a hardsuit. Ten could take down just as many. The snipers might not get away, but escape might not be one of the goals of the next attack.

And Kiwanuka was certain there would be another attack. Whoever had hit them last night had drawn blood. That was sure to incite continued violence.

Corporal Pita Brandvold shook her head. "After I heard the Phrenorians had negotiated treaty rights with Makaum, I came here hoping I could do some good for these people." She took a breath that was audible over the comm link. "I'd heard they were peaceful, just kind of blown away by all the attention. I can't imagine what having alien worlds drop down among them has done to them. But I want to help."

"I know." Kiwanuka hadn't been on Makaum by choice. She'd been assigned there after losing an arm and assaulting an officer during a battle in the Kimos system. She'd had the arm replaced with a bionic one, not flesh and blood, because the cyberlimb would be a better weapon than an organic one, and because the demand on her circulatory system would be diminished.

Since she'd lost her arm just before she'd attacked the officer and nearly killed him, the assault charges against her had been ameliorated, but her field service report was flagged as still "under review." The Army could sideline her at any moment. She'd intended to simply put in her time on Makaum, keep her nose clean, and get through the probationary period.

Still, a soldier didn't spend time at a post without becoming attached to the people she served with, or the people she was assigned to protect. That bond was something a lot of soldiers didn't talk about, but it was there. Part of it was pride, wanting to do the job right, but part of it was a sense of community, a sense of belonging—no matter how briefly—to a place.

But that sense of community faded quickly when one of the locals attacked the post and seriously injured—or killed—a soldier.

"I've just started gaining the trust of some of the kids in this sprawl," Brandvold said bitterly. "Do you know how hard that is?"

Kiwanuka didn't know firsthand, but she remembered how the children in Uganda had acted when medical people from outside the country had arrived to help during crises. Kiwanuka's mother had been from Norway and was working in a medical facility when she'd met her future husband, a diplomatic attaché. Even after years of service inside Uganda, even with children of her own who had been born in that country, most citizens still considered her mother an outsider.

Offworlder. Kiwanuka heard the word circulate in the crowd that watched with hostility and speculation and, yes, fear. There was always that division of *us* and *them* when two or more cultures shared space. People often tried to get past that, to pretend that it didn't exist and to say that it didn't matter, but the division was too sharp, too ingrained.

The soldiers regarded the Makaum people with the same reined-in hostility. Little trust existed at the moment. Everyone was an outsider.

Kiwanuka had been an outsider all of her life. Her father's people didn't consider her African enough, and her platinum blonde hair—which she'd gotten from her mother—set her apart from the children she had grown up with. And her mother's people, and most Europeans, considered her to be African, not white, because of the dusky hue of her skin. On top of that, she hadn't wanted to follow her mother into medicine or her father into diplomacy. She'd had no path either of her parents approved of or offered mentorship for.

Her only choice that had allowed her to be herself was the Terran Army. That was her family. And they'd just been hurt by the people they were supposed to be there protecting.

Some of those people, Kiwanuka reminded herself. *Only a handful.*

That was all that had shown on the sec cams. The handful of locals had slipped through the shadows and launched the attack from hiding. So far the vid forensics people hadn't been able to identify any of them.

She pulled up the med stats on Corporal Anders. He'd been most injured during the attack. The bomb had been a combination of acid and flammable substance, concocted to eat through an AKTIVsuit's armor and burn the soldier inside. The attackers hadn't developed that on Makaum. They didn't have the resources. The weapon had been offworld tech. Evidently when it came to murder and destruction, the anti-offworlder people didn't mind going to offworlders to upgrade their weapons. It was peacekeeping they couldn't deal with.

The med reports weren't accessible. Kiwanuka had no idea how the young corporal was doing. The surgeons would have him sedated now, but once he came out of that fog he would be traumatized and more frightened than he could ever remember.

Flexing her bionic hand that looked human but wasn't, Kiwanuka remembered her own recovery after her life had been saved. Her parents hadn't found out about her injuries till weeks after the attacks. One of her father's diplomat friends had told him, and he had told Kiwanuka's mother. Then her mother had called to discuss organic limb replacement, and she'd been shocked to hear about the cyberlimb. Kiwanuka and her mother didn't agree on much even now.

Kiwanuka took a deep breath and let it out as she surveyed the Makaum people. More were still arriving. Some in the back were getting louder, trying to whip the others into a frenzy.

Only a handful, she told herself again. *There are a lot of people here still worth saving. We are here to help them. They will recognize that again.*

Still, that number of anti-Terran dissidents was growing, though. She'd seen the reports filtering through to Colonel Halladay. Taking down the DawnStar cartel had been a major victory to the military mindset, and to many of the Makaum people, but other Makaum natives didn't like the Army's heavy-handedness in acting without permission.

Permission was a gray area. Everything in the fort was under military jurisdiction, and permission had been granted to shut down drug dealers inside the sprawl and keep the general peace. Exterminating outlaw drug labs in the jungle had slipped into the gray. Putting those labs out of business had turned into an undeclared war that persisted.

Some of the Makaum people, and the soldiers, blamed Master Sergeant Sage for the increased hostility. But Sage hadn't initiated the attacks. Colonel Halladay and Sergeant Terracina, now KIA on one of those drug lab hunts, had started the mission. Sage had just been more successful at it. DawnStar was involved with a PR nightmare, not only on Makaum, but in other systems as well. The Terran Alliance now had their operation in other systems under review. That was no doubt that improprieties would be found.

DawnStar was trying to put distance between themselves and Velesko Kos, painting him as a loose cannon within their ranks. The spin doctors would fix that eventually. DawnStar Corporation was too large, too well embedded in most systems to be easily chased away.

The current situation onplanet had turned nastier. The Quass, and the Makaum people, were more divided than ever. The Phrenorians and the (ta)Klar had taken advantage of that, stepping into more prominent roles and spreading the wealth to win over supporters.

The Phrenorian base, if that's what it was, would cause another major shift in alignment when it was announced, but Terran military intelligence circles weren't sure what shape that shift would take. Having the base turn out to be a false alarm would probably be best, but Kiwanuka didn't believe that would be the case.

"I was supposed to spend the morning giving inoculations against disease brought here by interplanetary corps," Brandvold said. "The Nys'ale brought in a variant of the *Isummy* virus, which could be lethal to local infants if not taken care of. I wasn't supposed to be preparing to shoot some of those people."

Corporal Brandvold was cross-listed on her MOS, serving as a med tech and as a rifleman. She'd joined the Terran Army to get the training she'd wanted for her eventual return to a medical career in civilian life.

"We're not there yet, Corporal. Don't borrow trouble." Kiwanuka nodded toward the fence. "Right now we're just here to secure the perimeter. As soon as reconstruction's complete, we'll go back to business as usual."

"We might, Sergeant, but I don't think those people will."

Kiwanuka didn't have anything to say to that, so she didn't try. Her comm popped for attention and she shifted over to a link where Colonel Halladay was waiting for her.

"Sergeant Kiwanuka." Halladay sounded calm, but his voice held a note of tension that Kiwanuka could hear because she knew him.

"Yes sir."

"I was told there were witnesses to the attack."

"Yes sir. Noojin and Quass Leghef's granddaughter."

"Jahup's sister and girlfriend?" Halladay's calmness slipped away.

"Yes sir."

"What were they doing there?"

"I didn't ask, sir. I secured the scene and made certain the two girls were out of harm's way." Kiwanuka didn't know if Noojin had been part of the attack or if she'd just gotten caught in the middle. Kiwanuka had spotted the broken arrow with transparent blue insect wing fletching in the confrontation area when she'd arrived. It didn't make sense that Noojin would have been part of the ambush while shepherding the young girl. Kiwanuka thought she knew what had happened, but she wanted to hear it for herself.

"Did they see who did this?"

"Private Welchel informed me the girls told him someone tried to kill them, sir. They'll have to be interviewed to find out what they know."

"Bring them in."

"Yes sir." Kiwanuka handed off control of the attack site to another sergeant, let Lieutenant Murad know she'd been called away, and went to get the girls.

Private Welchel had intercepted the girls and brought them into the fort through the hole in the fence. She'd immediately locked them down in an armored personnel carrier.

Crossing the parade grounds that showed fresh wounds from the tracks of the massive main battle tanks that had drawn a line in the sand with their presence, Kiwanuka headed for the APC. The tracked vehicle stood eight meters tall, seventeen meters long, and five meters wide. They were called Invincible Bubbles, and mostly they were. Capable of carrying a cargo of four powersuits, or twenty soldiers, or tons of equipment and materials, they were workhorses in ground campaigns but were difficult to use in Makaum's jungles.

Kiwanuka reached the APC and laid her palm on it, juicing her ID and authorizations through the alloyed skin. A lot of soldiers felt the physical contact was a joke. A Bubble's weps would cut down anyone not cleared by security for 1,000-meter access, so if anyone got that close, the crew already recognized them as friendlies.

But the touch logged the person into the Bubble's records, something flesh-and-blood soldiers sometimes forgot to do in the heat of a battle, or just because they were lax. Kiwanuka left her hand on the behemoth's armored shoulder and let the link flare to life.

"Something up, Sergeant Kiwanuka?" a man's voice asked over the comm.

"I need the two civilians and enough sec to manage a transfer on-post."

"Copy that."

Kiwanuka stepped back. A moment later, the door opened, a short stair extended, and two armored soldiers stepped out locked and loaded. After a short time spent confirming a physical visual recon, Noojin and Telilu followed.

Neither of the girls was bound, but both had small bandages on their arms and faces. Kiwanuka had been told the injuries were superficial and had been sustained from a leap off a house. Kiwanuka figured they were both lucky to be alive from a leap like that in the dark.

Noojin's weapons had been confiscated. She'd been carrying several knives, a short sword, and a bow and quiver of arrows.

Kiwanuka glanced at the arrows, saw that they had the same dark blue insect wing fletching as the one that she'd noted earlier at the confrontation site, and captured a digital image to her hardsuit's memory. She ordered the faceshield to go transparent, so Noojin could see her. They'd met after the DawnStar cartel business. They hadn't gotten to know each other well, but there was something about a woman talking to a woman that broke down barriers.

"You can't hold us like prisoners," Noojin stated in a hard tone. She held the small girl before her, hands on the thin shoulders, in a protective manner.

Or maybe those barriers wouldn't be broken. Kiwanuka tried not to let her frustration show.

The small girl still looked frightened and shrank back into Noojin's loose embrace. "Have you seen my grandmother?"

Kiwanuka answered the youngest child's question first. In the sergeant's eyes, both of the girls were still kids.

"Quass Leghef is busy at the moment, I'm afraid. But she knows you're here and that you're in good hands. She trusts us to take care of you." Kiwanuka wanted to emphasize that.

"We're *prisoners.*" Noojin took an aggressive step toward Kiwanuka.

One of the soldiers standing guard took a step forward to block her way.

"As you were, Private," Kiwanuka said.

After a brief hesitation, the soldier nodded and stepped back into formation.

Kiwanuka turned her gaze to Noojin, who met her attention full measure.

"You're not prisoners," Kiwanuka replied. "You're being projected."

"In this?" Noojin snorted derisively as she pointed at the Bubble. "Do you really think it's better than your fort? The people who did this have big enough weapons to destroy this crawler."

Maybe that was true, maybe not. The answer didn't matter to Kiwanuka at the moment. She also thought Colonel Halladay was going to have his hands full talking to the girl.

"We have somewhere to go," Kiwanuka announced. She adjusted her faceplate and darkened the material, then turned and started walking toward the command post where Halladay was working.

In her 360 view, Kiwanuka saw Noojin standing her ground stubbornly. The hard set of her jaw told Kiwanuka that she was going to resist. One of the soldiers put a hand on her shoulder, but Noojin immediately shrugged and pushed the hand away.

The soldier took a step closer and put his hand in the middle of Noojin's back. This time she had no choice but to take stumbling steps or be shoved along. She called the soldier all of the obscene names she'd learned in Terran English. The list was well fleshed out and even Kiwanuka heard some terms that were new to her.

Abruptly, several shouts arose from the assembled Makaum natives. More had joined the mob and tempers were flaring. In the helmet's view, Kiwanuka saw one man take a swing at another, then when the combatants were roughly shoved apart, another man close to the action took a swing at one of the men trying to keep the fighters apart. That only started two more fights, which in turn turned the whole gathering into a vicious kicking, hitting, and spitting scrum.

The mob teetered as they fought. Men went down under fists and feet and tripped others. Suddenly, the group staggered into the laser field and a dozen people had their senses shaken and stirred. A handful of them got sick, throwing up and going boneless, causing even more problems for the crowd.

Kiwanuka got her charges moving, but she watched the developing violence.

"Lieutenant," a soldier bellowed over the comm link. "Permission to use dispersal gas and microwave repellers."

Before Murad could reply—the lieutenant was still green but coming along, so he was slow to make a call—a shrill, melodic whistle cut through the air.

"Grandmother!" Telilu shouted. The girl started to run toward the soldiers and the mob.

Kiwanuka grabbed Telilu and wrapped one arm around her. "Wait, little one. It isn't safe."

Telilu looked at Kiwanuka in disdain. "It's Grandmother! Everyone is safe with Grandmother. She is Quass."

"Just a moment," Kiwanuka said.

"You can't stop us," Noojin shouted. She fought to get free of the soldier that held her but she didn't have the strength. "We're not prisoners."

Kiwanuka lifted her eyes to meet the girl's gaze. "Do you want to take her through that?"

Face twisted in rebellion, Noojin calmed herself and reached out for Telilu's hand. "It's okay, Twig. We'll stay here. The Quass will come for us."

Kiwanuka released the girl and was relieved when her two charges stood still and watched the crowd.

The effect of the whistle was instantaneous. Since Telilu had assumed her grandmother was there even though she hadn't seen her, Kiwanuka assumed that the whistled tune had something to do with the identification.

The mob quieted quickly, splitting out into groups and standing by meekly.

Through the chasm created between them, Quass Leghef strode like a general taking the battlefield. She wore a green and gray *kifrik* silk gown bright enough to stand out even in the early morning. A silk headdress covered her head and face, but the material was transparent enough to see the lean, brown features seasoned with a few wrinkles. Her hair was black but shot through with gray strands. She was small, barely five feet tall, and thin. She carried a wooden staff a foot taller than she was.

She stopped in the middle of the crowd and surveyed them with narrowed eyes and tight lips. "Look at yourselves," she said in a hard voice. "Fighting among yourselves like savages."

Many of the people hung their heads, and Kiwanuka

couldn't believe the change that had overtaken them so quickly.

"When the ship that carried our ancestors crashed on this planet and scattered hundreds of bodies of the dead throughout that inhospitable jungle filled with predatory things our people had never before seen, they knew they had to trust each other to survive. That's what they did. That's what *we* did. And that's what we must do in the days that follow this one if we are to survive."

Kiwanuka had to hand it to the old lady. She knew how to dish out guilt with the best of them.

"Now," Leghef continued, "go home. All of you. Get back to your families and your jobs. Make something of today. Don't let these events affect the good that you can do for the rest of the day."

There were a few grumbles, and maybe even a half-hearted attempt to argue with the Quass, but the mob went away, drifting in clumps to the other side of the street.

Then Quass Leghef turned to Kiwanuka. "Return my granddaughter and Noojin to me."

"I can't, ma'am," Kiwanuka responded. "I'm under orders to take them to Colonel Halladay."

Leghef walked over to Kiwanuka and peered up at her. This close, even though she was short, the little woman was intimidating. "What does the colonel want with them?"

"They saw the people who attacked our soldiers."

The Quass shifted her gaze to Telilu and Noojin, and it was obvious she was awaiting an answer.

Wrapping her arms around herself, Noojin shook her head and didn't quite meet the Quass's gaze.

"There was a man who tried to hurt Noojin," Telilu said excitedly. "But Noojin hurt him and we got away, and then the soldier protected us."

Leghef put a hand on her granddaughter's shoulder. "Did you know this man?"

Telilu shook her head. "It was dark and I couldn't see him." She took her grandmother's hand in one of hers. "May I go home now? I'm sleepy."

Leghef smiled. "Of course you may." She glanced up at Kiwanuka meaningfully. "You may take Noojin to see your colonel, Sergeant, but I will be taking my granddaughter home with me. She saw nothing and I would prefer to take care of her myself."

Kiwanuka knew Halladay wasn't going to be happy that a local politician had pulled rank on him. But she also knew from looking at Leghef's face that the older woman wasn't leaving without her granddaughter. Losing a friend on the Quass would not be something Halladay wanted either.

"Yes, ma'am." Kiwanuka stopped herself just short of thanking the Quass.

Noojin started forward. "Quass, what about . . ."

Leghef shook her head, cutting Noojin off. "No. You'll be staying here."

"I didn't *do* anything."

Leghef tapped the fletching of an arrow in the quiver one of the soldiers carried, then she pointed at the broken arrow that remained on the ground. "I think that you did, and I think that you owe Colonel Halladay an explanation about what you did." She paused. "You'll be safe with these people. I'll make sure of that."

"I only warned the soldiers about the trap," Noojin protested.

"Tell the colonel that."

"Quass . . ."

Leghef remained firm. "You're a hunter, Noojin. One of the most important lessons you learn as a hunter is to stand by your actions. If you only wound a creature out in the jungle, you have to follow it until you are able to put it out of its misery. And you should not have allowed my granddaughter to get caught up in this affair."

Chastised, Noojin stepped back and didn't speak again.

"No harm will come to this girl," Leghef said to Kiwanuka.

"No harm, Quass Leghef," Kiwanuka agreed. "I know how to stand by my actions."

A faint smile touched the Quass's thin lips, then it disappeared. "What of my grandson?"

"He's not here, ma'am." Kiwanuka was sure the Quass had been read into Sage and Jahup's op into the jungle, but she wasn't going to acknowledge that.

"When will he return?"

"I don't know. That time is flexible."

The Quass's shoulders rounded a little more, like a burden had been dropped onto them. "Please tell Colonel Halladay to keep me informed in all of these matters."

"Yes, ma'am."

Holding her granddaughter's hand, Leghef turned and walked away. Her honor guard formed a sec detail around her. The soldiers manning the breach in the fence stepped aside so she and her party could pass once more.

Kiwanuka's stomach unclenched and she drew in a deep breath. She had never talked to the Quass before, had never expected to because they moved at different levels in all the political jockeying that took place on Makaum, but she understood now why Leghef was Quass. The woman possessed a gravitas that Kiwanuka had seldom seen.

Waving to the soldiers with her, she headed back to the meeting with Halladay. The day was shaping up to be a busy one on all fronts, political as well as military, as the top brass figured out what to do about the attack. The Army couldn't just sit this one out. A statement had to be made.

She watched Noojin in the HUD, studying the young girl and wondering how much she knew. She'd fired the arrow to warn Corporal Anders. That meant Noojin had seen something. And if one of the men had tried to kill her and the Quass's granddaughter, Noojin had seen even more.

Noojin's jaw was set and her back was straight in obvious rebellion. Getting information out of her was going to be difficult. Kiwanuka was glad she wasn't the one who was going to have to attempt it.

NINE

atest sim disks! Movies old and new! Action-packed adventure tales! Erotica! Come see the beautiful men of Dardorn! Come see the beautiful women of Halinog as they perform the Forbidden Dance of Limber Shadows!"

"All-terrain bicycles! Personal ATV riders! Don't walk when you can ride!"

"Come enjoy the zesty taste of Mongolian beef! Enjoy the fusion of spices that will provide a unique culinary experience!"

Ignoring the hawkers lining the bazaar located near the center of the sprawl, Sytver Morlortai strode across the hard-packed earthen road that cut through one of the offworlder hubs that had popped up on the backwater planet. Merchants from dozens of different worlds had Gatestreamed to Makaum to sell their wares. Many of those merchants were there to entice newbies with their flashy tech and manufactured goods. Others were there to sell to the Terran soldiers, offering products not sanctioned by the Terran Army.

And a few of those hawkers would be spies who would learn what they could and sell information about the Phrenorians to the Terrans, or the Terrans to the Phrenorians. Maybe there would even be some information about the (ta)Klar, but information on those people was hard to get. That was one of the reasons Morlortai had come to Makaum.

"Insect repellant!" The last was offered by a young woman at a brightly colored pushcart featuring a gigantic wasp that was actually small by Makaum standards. "Guaranteed to work!" She held up a wristband to display the merchandise. "White noise generators that will turn away the fiercest bloodsuckers! Don't risk disease when a small payment will protect you!"

Morlortai continued past her. She attempted to intercept him, but he held up a hand and warned her away. She was good-looking enough to attract the attention of someone who thought talking to her might lead to a romantic liaison.

Scowling, the young woman acted like she'd had no interest in him and approached an older Makaum woman who seemed tentative about visiting the market.

Morlortai continued walking and scanned the other people in the area. He knew urban areas, even ones this primitive, and he knew how hunters approached prey. So far, he was neither. He'd come to the bazaar to investigate a potential business proposition.

Most of the offworlder buildings were prefab domes of colored plascrete dozens of different hues that had been dumped into place by corp-owned aerial transport vehicles. The domes were wired for solar power beamed down from corp-owned satellites. Nobody went into business on Makaum without the corps getting a cut of the action.

That was about as genteel as thieves could be.

Of course, the corps owned most of the bashhounds that enforced security in the sprawl too. Most of the sec troops represented corp interests while others hired out to various enterprises. When the *aldoede* hit the spinning *iangoero*, though, the bashhounds' loyalty would still be with the corps.

From what Morlortai saw, the corps had nailed down most of the sprawl. The rest was divided by the Terran Army and the Phrenorians. No one except the (ta)Klar knew how much they controlled.

A small part of Morlortai's eroding morality felt bad for the Makaum people. He'd seen backward worlds ground under the heel of the technologically superior. There wasn't much left after the corps took what they wanted. He walled that sympathy away. Until a people could protect themselves, they were all victims. The split in the population was undermining their ability to assert themselves, and they would realize that too late.

As a Fenipalan, Morlortai had seen his own world succumb to the Black Opal Corp. After Fenipal had been discovered near a newly built Gate, the Black Opal Corp had descended on the world and stripped it clean of minerals, reducing it to a wasted toxic husk before the Terran Alliance could step in. Once the Alliance troops arrived, all they could do was slap bandages on mortal wounds. Fenipal was a walking corpse, slowly dying because the planet had been sucked dry and poisoned by offworlder machinery.

Fenipal's economy had been based on technology five generations behind what the Black Opal Corp had brought. So many people loved tech that they embraced each iteration and forgot all the old ways of doing things.

Seeing Makaum people nearby showing off "technical" marvels to their peers made Morlortai remember his own early years.

No one on these backward planets knew the trade goods they held today rendered their futures moribund. Their children would never have the lives they did because the technology jump erased the need for educations that were then taken for granted.

Morlortai had been fortunate because he understood violence and he'd learned to focus on his own survival. He'd joined an offworlder enforcement group and become a bashhound. He'd worked to support the Black Opal efforts to preserve their investments, and he'd helped loot his planet. His own survival had been all that had mattered to him, so he had learned to defend himself and kill anyone who threatened him.

He turned out to be very good at it.

When the Black Opal Corp had pulled out ahead of Terran Alliance interference, remaining on Fenipal hadn't been an option. Morlortai had spaced with the bashhound team that had trained him and found his own pathway through life. He hadn't had a home since, but worlds remained open to him. There was always someone willing to hire an assassin.

As he gazed at his surroundings through his 360-degree HUD, Morlortai gave only fleeting interest to passersby as he walked toward the location where he'd agreed to meet his prospective clients. Most of his attention was invested in staying alive in hostile territory.

Soon-to-be hostile territory. Morlortai hadn't done anything criminal onplanet yet. Other than arrive under a false identity. His stolen background would take weeks to penetrate if someone started digging. Looking at the pack of thieves that pinged the facial recognition software juicing through his faceshield and wore other names than their own, operating under a false name was a slight infraction of the law on Makaum. In fact, he was pretty sure the local laws hadn't even considered such a thing. The planet's inhabitants lagged far behind the developing interstellar relationships evolving around them.

Morlortai's hardsuit looked scarred and ill used, but that was just a patina of disguise. Beneath the worn exterior, the physical enhancements, stimpaks, and built-in weps were cutting-edge.

Fenipalans were humanoid, two arms and two legs, and could be mistaken for Terrans at first glance. Anyone who didn't know the milk-white skin and pale gray hair might still think they were Terran. They were slightly shorter than Terran average, underweight when compared to Terran average, but physically more resilient, with denser bones and stronger muscles. Fenipal's gravity was 1.2 Terran standard and Fenipalans tended to have redundancy systems for major organs. Morlortai still possessed two hearts, but one of them was a bionic construction, courtesy of a bulky Losool who had moved much faster than the assassin had assumed. The Losool might have burst Morlortai's heart with a bullet, but had paid for that with his head.

Morlortai pulled up the map overlay of the sprawl and took the turn indicated to reach his destination. The alley was narrow and two stories tall, filled with roots that tore through the ground and branches that stood out from the sides of buildings constructed by the Makaum. The buildings had been evacuated once the offworlders had negotiated trade rights and dropped in around them. Morlortai ducked the branches and stepped over the exposed roots.

No one followed him.

At the other end of the alley, he didn't break stride, but he took in the area in a sweeping glance. His contact had chosen well. The three-story building had also been built by the Makaum and was festooned with growing vines, shrubs, and small trees. No Makaum lived there anymore. A group of Zukimther mercenaries had moved into it and used it as a headquarters while they "provided" protection to small merchants who couldn't afford bashhounds.

A few food carts dotted the open space in front of the building. Thieves, offworlder and Makaum—though Morlortai saw few of those, came here to trade with the Zukimther. The mercs provided a small black market for goods, not enough for them to ship offworld, but enough to keep them living well.

Morlortai figured the mercs were on Makaum because they were hiding out. The Zukimther fought for credits, usually only for whom they believed the winning side would be, but sometimes wars didn't go the way they were supposed to go. Out of funds, temporarily on the run from hostile opponents, they holed up on backwater worlds until they could resupply themselves and build up another war chest by sponging off criminal activity.

It wasn't much different from what Morlortai did, but Morlortai *always* had another contract working and three or four set up in case that one went sideways.

The Zukimther mercs stood almost three meters tall and were massive in armor designed to make them look even larger. Brown patches spotted their yellow skin where it was visible. Twin ridges of bone ran across their hairless heads, from just above their eyes to their shoulders, and provided a natural armor. More bone overlaid arteries in their four arms and both legs. Having those additional arms made them even more deadly, but they were strong, not quick. With the natural armor and the tactical gear they'd strapped on, they were hard to kill.

Morlortai knew how to kill them, though he bore scars

from his first encounter with a Zukimther merc. After nearly getting killed, he'd learned fast. He flexed his left wrist and brought the compact gauss cannon mounted under his arm online. The fingertips of his right hand grazed the *waraw* at his right hip. At the moment, the weapon resembled a black tube as thick as two of his fingers and no longer than his hand. It was something a trade courier might carry a datastick containing bills of lading in.

"Did your contact mention anything about Zukimther mercs?" a quiet voice asked over the private comm link Morlortai had assigned for the meeting.

"No." Morlortai pinged Turit's position, and even then he had a hard time spotting the Angenen on a small balcony of a building that held an angled view of the rendezvous site.

As an Angenen, Turit almost fit in on Makaum. His people were lizardlike, covered with gray and green scales. They tended to be long and thin, narrow shouldered and narrow hipped, but they were wiry and quick, so flexible as to be almost boneless. His face was elongated, framed around powerful jaws that jutted out twenty centimeters. Speech was hard for him, but the translator/enhancer he wore around his neck allowed him, once he had trained to use the device, to articulate well enough. His black reptilian eyes were close-set like a human's instead of on either side of his head.

Turit sat at an uneven table and wore the somber brown robe of a Banatia priest to cover his armor. He hoisted a small bottle of local beer and managed to take a sip, which was a feat with that mouth. The pack on the floor beside him contained an Imhat squad automatic weapon capable of spraying depleted uranium rounds that could tear through the armor the Zukimther mercs wore. Massive and strong, the mercs were still big targets.

"You know I hate those *anckals*," Turit said.

An *anckal* was a particularly disgusting carrion feeder

on Queormu. It looked small and cuddly till it started burrowing through the corpse of a fellow soldier, then its hair, slicked back by blood and body fluids, revealed the stringy, muscular body that was an engine built for eating dead things.

Morlortai had signed the team up for a campaign on Queormu and things had turned out badly. They'd ended up living in underground trenches with *anckals* for weeks. Turit had especially hated them because the creatures hid in corpses and tended to pop out unexpectedly. There wasn't much that bothered the Angenen, but the *anckals* did. He just despised the Zukimther mercs on general principle.

"We're not here to do business with them," Morlortai replied.

"You hope."

"If it turns out that way, then we turn down the job. There will be another. On a world like this, there always is."

"The payoff will be cheap."

"This job, or another, is only a cover. The one we're here for will pay out well."

"With a real good chance of getting dead. Phrenorians are hard to kill."

Mirthlessly, Morlortai grinned. "That's why they pay us so well. Imagine having to kill Phrenorians for what the Terran Army has to do it for."

Turit snorted derisively, something that took a lot of skill to do through a translator. The device hadn't been designed to deliver that particular reaction.

Morlortai started up the steps leading into the building and one of the mercs put a hand on his chest.

"This building's off limits, *cr'tontor*."

A *cr'tontor* was an intestinal parasite native to Zukimther. Whenever they infested a body, it was always a race to get them out before they produced larva that invaded every system in the host. They were also considered a delicacy because the pharmacological venom produced by the creatures was a natural painkiller. "Harvested" *cr'tontor* were filled with the venom, and when prepared carefully, could produce an experience that would wrap the eater in dreams for days.

If it was prepared incorrectly, the diner risked death or infestation. Despite the aphrodisiac qualities promised by those who sold *cr'tontor* as a repast, Morlortai had never been tempted to try it.

"I'm expected," Morlortai said. He resisted the impulse to place the gauss cannon in the center of the merc's chest and trigger it. The round would easily tear through the armor and blow out the merc's heart. Morlortai didn't care for the Zukimther mercs either. "I was told to meet someone here."

"Clear your faceshield."

"That's not part of the deal."

"It's part of my deal, *cr'tontor*."

Amused to a degree, Morlortai smiled. "Is that a term of endearment? I hear you people like eating parasites you've dug out of your own *eenas*."

The merc thrust his face down at Morlortai in an effort to be threatening. "They can also be fed to people we don't like."

"Try it and you'll find out if you've got any parasites in you right this moment."

The merc hesitated, trying to think of a comeback or if he could risk ignoring his orders and breaking Morlortai. That struggle made him grimace.

"Let him go, Nalaw," one of the other mercs said from a short distance away. He was bigger than the merc confronting Morlortai, and he wore his scars proudly. "We have our orders."

"He has not proven who he is."

The second merc looked at Morlortai.

Holding his left hand up, leaving the hidden gauss cannon aimed at the merc in front of him, Morlortai juiced a holo through the display in the palm of his hand. A bright red, three-dimensional geometric shape appeared in the air a couple centimeters above the display. It rotated slowly, then glowed silver as it was scanned for identification.

"We have confirmation," the second merc said. "He is allowed to pass."

With obvious reluctance, Nalaw stepped back slightly, barely giving Morlortai room to pass.

"I've got him," Turit whispered over the comm link. "If he twitches wrong, he'll be dead before he knows it."

Through the HUD, Morlortai magnified his view of Turit. The Angenen leaned back against the wall behind him and Morlortai knew the Imhat SAW was hidden in the folds of the voluminous robe. The cyber link between Turit and his weapon would guarantee the shot.

Ignoring Nalaw because the merc was dead meat if he made a mistake, Morlortai stepped past and continued into the building. As he entered, he spotted three Phrenorian warriors conducting business in one of the large rooms.

One of the Phrenorians sat at a table too small for him. Another stood at the door, and another at the window overlooking the front of the building.

There would be others. The Sting-Tails never traveled in small groups when in hostile territory.

The Phrenorians gave no indication they noted Morlortai, but the assassin knew that wasn't the case. He also knew that Turit was correct, that their real target would be hard to kill.

But Morlortai would find a way to get it done.

TEN

While following Jahup through the jungle, Sage got pinged for a private conference with Colonel Halladay over his helmet comm. Leaning over the handlebars of the RDC and fighting with brush that slapped him along the way, Sage felt tired from being up all night stalking through the jungle. He was looking forward to some serious rack time. Unfortunately, he knew he wasn't going to get that even before Halladay contacted him because he couldn't relax with the Phrenorian base waiting in the shadows.

"Top," Halladay said over the link after the comm officer connected them. "You answered, so I'm assuming you're still alive."

"I am, sir." Even it if hadn't been for the agreement that Sage would run silent on his return to the fort unless things turned dicey, the colonel's voice held serious overtones that indicated something had gone wrong. On top of the discovery of the Phrenorian base.

"You're running later than expected," Halladay continued.

"We got in closer than we'd hoped. Didn't get seen. Unfortunately, we confirmed what we'd been told, but I can't give you much more than that until I see you. What I do have for you, I'd rather let sit till we're in private."

"Understood." Some of the fatigue in Halladay's voice lifted and Sage knew he'd tweaked the man's interest. "We have a situation here. Last night, the base was attacked."

Twisting the throttle, Sage shot across the jungle, dodging trees, uneven terrain, and low-hanging branches to overtake Jahup. They had been traveling in single file. Waving the young scout over, Sage pulled to a stop behind a copse of trees on a hillock that gave them somewhat of a clear view around their position.

Jahup's tight body language and constant staring at Sage gave indication of his irritation. Though the younger man had been fascinated by the two-wheeled RDCs because there weren't any in Makaum, he wasn't happy with the noise the vehicles made. As a scout, stealth was one of the chief weapons in his arsenal. He didn't like losing it in spite of the speed the RDCs gave them.

Sage kept the Roley ready in his hands as he talked to Halladay. His gaze roved restlessly, and he used his peripheral vision to pick out movement in the dense shadows. So far none of the local predators showed undue interest in them.

"How bad was the attack, sir?"

"Two of our walking sentries took the brunt of it. I think the attack was more a statement of intent than a solid assault. Corporal Anders collected a mass of burns that's going to require some skin grafts. He's being taken care of now."

"But he'll pull through?" Sage remembered the earnest

young man he'd met in the DawnStar space station upon his arrival. Anders had been exactly the kind of inexperienced soldier Sage had been turning out while assigned to boot camp. He'd known most of them wouldn't make it back from wherever they confronted the Phrenorians.

"Anders will be fine, Top. The attack was violent, but limited in scope. The attackers breached the outer perimeter and hit one of the training buildings with rockets. The perimeter will be taken care of by this afternoon. It'll take a couple days to regrow the building."

"Do you think the attack was a kickback from the drug cartels?"

"We believe it was orchestrated by the anti-Terran Makaum faction."

"What makes you think it was the Makaum people?" Sage asked.

"Because Noojin saw them."

Sage gazed at Jahup, who knelt only a few meters away against a tree trunk and watched over the surrounding jungle. "Did she know them?"

"We think so. She's not saying. If it hadn't been for Quass Leghef, we wouldn't have been able to hold her here."

That surprised Sage. Quass Leghef was protective of her people's independence. She was also Jahup's grandmother, something that had surprised Sage when he'd learned that.

"The Quass," Halladay continued, "has told Noojin she's supposed to cooperate with us too. The girl is maintaining her silence."

"Why?"

"I think she wants to keep things private. The Quass's granddaughter was with Noojin when the attack happened. Anders nearly killed them both. Noojin fired an arrow into Anders's head, which the helmet deflected, to warn him about the ambush. Anders reacted to the attack. He's still green. A lot of them are. Thankfully Noojin cleared herself and the girl from the rooftop where they'd been."

Noojin was a skilled hunter. Sage had seen her operating with Jahup when they'd been out in the jungle. The girl was headstrong and independent. She didn't much care for him and only put up with him because she wanted to be with Jahup.

"I think Noojin is staying silent because she intends to take care of the situation herself," Halladay continued. "One of the ambushers tried to kill her and the Quass's granddaughter on his—or her—retreat after the attack. Needless to say, the Quass is highly motivated to assist us in finding out who did this."

"Maybe she is," Sage replied.

"Something on your mind, Top?" The irritation in Halladay's voice scratched through to the surface.

"Just thinking out loud, sir." Sage searched the jungle and listened to the quiet *tick-tick-tick* of the RDC's cooling magneto drives. "The Quass is supposed to be in control of her people. If she leans on us to take care of this problem, that's going to undermine her authority with the community."

Halladay cursed lightly. "That had crossed my mind too. You saying it like that makes me even more suspicious of her letting us keep Noojin. She knows we can't do anything to the girl, just hold her for a little while, as long as the Quass doesn't object. Letting us have her could just be lip service to the joint effort we should be having. The Quass seems like a sweet little old lady. I've never had any problems with her."

"You don't get to be Quass by being a pushover, sir."

"I suppose that's right. How far out are you?"

Sage pulled up a map on his faceshield and estimated the travel time. "About four hours if we push it." That would mean tearing through the jungle at faster speeds than they'd traveled at so far.

"I think I can keep Noojin here for that long. She was waiting around last night for Jahup to return. I can trade news of his impending arrival to keep her hanging."

"That will probably work, sir." Sage glanced at the chronometer reading on his faceshield. "There's no activity on the part of the Phrenorians?"

"No, but if the local anti-Terran movement gains traction, we're going to have a more difficult time doing our jobs."

"Copy that, sir. Jahup and I will be there as soon as we can."

"Be safe, Top. We need you back here."

Sage let that roll in his mind. For the last six years on the training fields, he'd felt useless and wasted. Now he was needed and that felt good. The comm link faded from his faceshield and he turned toward Jahup, knowing the other man still wasn't used to the 360-degree provided by the helmet, because he was looking at Sage.

Instead of the Roley rifle, the scout held a recurve bow with a nocked arrow in his hands. That weapon would have been more silent than the Roley, and something—or someone—killed with it wouldn't have sparked curiosity in a Phrenorian patrol. It was a good choice.

"Saddle up." Sage threw a leg over the RDC and switched the engine on. The crawler started with a low hum. "We need to travel fast."

Jahup nodded and mounted his crawler. He took the lead, zipping through the jungle.

Close behind, Sage settled into the ride, his mind already racing through the problems that awaited him at the fort. Everything was escalating. The Phrenorian fort was only part of it.

Interview Room D
Security Building
Fort York
0714 Hours Zulu Time

The door to the prison cell (Noojin refused to use the term "interview" room even though that was clearly written on it in her native tongue because that was really just a lie) remained closed. Two armored guards stood to either side of it inside the room as well as out.

This wasn't an "interview."

Noojin sat in one of the gel-cushioned chairs that conformed to her posture and movements. It was one of the most comfortable chairs she'd ever sat in. Only the chairs maintained by the corps were more comfortable. She'd sometimes accompanied Quass Leghef during those visits. Telilu had wanted to see the offworlder structures and the DawnStar space station once. The Quass had asked Noojin to accompany them because not even Jahup could control the young girl.

Noojin had been impressed by the amenities, but the view of Makaum from space had been unsettling. The planet had looked like an alien place from the space station observation blister. To her, Makaum the world had looked remote and uncaring.

It hadn't looked like home.

That was her biggest fear. On Makaum, she was defined. She was a scout, part of a hunting band that provided meat for the community. But if she was taken out of that, she wasn't sure who she was.

How could Jahup feel so certain around them? Noojin wanted to scream out her frustration, but she carefully kept it locked down.

There was a knock on the door, then the lock cycled with

harsh clicks that echoed in the nearly empty room. Noojin
knew the grinding and the emptiness were supposed to
intimidate her. They did, but she refused to reveal that.
She remained seated and didn't adjust her posture. She
wondered who would be sent to talk to her. Whether it
would be the female sergeant who worked with Sergeant
Sage. Despite her dislike of the Terran Army, Noojin did
like the white-haired sergeant because she knew her own
strengths and did not try to hide them.

Noojin was surprised when Colonel Halladay walked
into the room. He was the last person she had expected.
Then she thought maybe Quass had experienced a change
of heart and sent the colonel himself to apologize for "interviewing" Noojin.

"It's about time." Noojin stood, folded her arms, and
glared at the guards.

"Time for what?" Halladay studied her with interest. He
was a little shorter than Sergeant Sage, not as broadly built,
and had piercing green eyes. Despite the fatigue that clung
to him, his uniform was sharply creased, his tie carefully
knotted, and he stood straight. He held a PAD under his arm.

Noojin also noted that the colonel's hip holster was
empty. The only people with weapons in the room were
the guards. Her hopes sank a little at that. The only reason
the colonel would enter the room unarmed would be if he
was going to continue her arrest.

"To let me go home." Noojin had no choice but to continue with the bluff. "You have no right to hold me."

"I have every right."

"I alerted your guards to the danger they were in."

"You did."

"Then why do you insist on holding me?"

"Because I want you to go on protecting my troops,"
Halladay replied. "If I let you out of here before you tell

me who was in the group this morning, I'll be putting my soldiers in jeopardy. I'm not going to do that."

"I don't know who attacked your soldiers."

"I don't believe you."

Unable to stop herself, Noojin screamed and balled her hands into fists.

Both soldiers started to step forward but Halladay raised a hand to stop them. "As you were."

The soldiers stepped back.

Halladay pulled out a chair on the other side of the table and sat down. "It might surprise you to know that I have two teenage daughters, and that I can tell when they're lying to me. Or *omitting* something. You can throw all the temper tantrums you want to, but I promise you that you're not leaving this room until I'm satisfied."

Frustrated, feeling trapped in the small room, Noojin grabbed her chair and tried to rip it from the floor. But it didn't come up.

"The chairs are locked to the floor," Halladay said helpfully. "It keeps people from making their situations worse."

Stepping back from the chair, Noojin kicked it. When nothing happened, she kicked it again and again.

Halladay just sat on the other side of the table and didn't react.

Noojin quieted herself and sat down, afraid that if she kept on kicking the chair and seeing nothing happen, she was going to cry. She refused to cry in front of the offworlders. She also refused to answer Halladay's questions. She folded her arms and stared at him. Terran girls were not as tough as she was, and the colonel was going to get a quick lesson in that.

ELEVEN

Morlortai climbed the winding stairs inside the Makaum building, surprised at how large it was on the inside. Perhaps that was only the perspective of the place, or the fact that it was so empty. Or it might have been the mix of artificial light from bulbs and tubes along with the phosphorescent glow from lichen and moss growing at certain intervals along the walls and ceiling.

Judging from the signage on some of the walls and things he spotted in certain rooms, the structure must have once housed learning centers for the Makaum people.

He could almost imagine the Makaum children sitting in those classrooms and listening to whatever it was that was taught there. The images in Morlortai's mind dredged up some of his own, of the time before the Black Opal Corp ships had descended on Fenipal. He had sat in similar class-rooms, then only a few years later the Fenipalan economy had fallen and the world had struggled in its death throes while the Black Opal Corp bashhounds used them as slaves to loot their own planet.

"Are you good?" Turit asked over the comm link. The connection was scratchy, uncertain.

The calm voice refocused Morlortai, though his thoughts had never strayed from his own self-survival. He remained aware of his location and the dangers around him.

"I'm fine."

"Someone has a damper in the building. The farther you go, the harder it is to keep track of you."

"Don't worry. If I need you, you'll know by the explosions."

Turit laughed, but the sound was hollowed out by the comm damper and sounded far away.

On the third-floor landing, Morlortai turned and walked through a curtain of hanging vines that pulled away at his touch. The long, thin tendrils curled away from him and he had to stop himself from releasing blades into his hands.

"They won't attack you," someone said. "I was told those plants are part of the Makaum people's filing network in this treehouse. Supposedly the vines log your scent, the way you taste, your DNA—although that isn't the Makaum word for it—and record the time you pass through. Their word means something more like *essence*. What makes you *you*."

The speaker was a bashhound that stood in front of a closed door. His hardsuit, like Morlortai's, bore no identifying marks.

"Does it?" Morlortai asked.

The bashhound shrugged. "Above my pay grade."

"Then why hasn't it been destroyed?"

The bashhound laughed. "I think it's one of those stories people tell. There's no way those vines could do all of that. And no way they can get a DNA sample from anybody in a hardsuit. The only thing Makaum tries to do is eat you. Besides, you can cut those vines down or burn them back to the ceiling, they'll be back again—same length—by tomorrow."

Morlortai flicked a knife from his armor, grabbed a handful of the tendrils, and sliced them free as far up as he could reach. He examined the cut ends, searching for micro-circuitry as the vines curled up and twisted as if they were trying to escape his grasp. Micro-circuitry would explain how the plant would be able to do all the things the bashhound claimed.

All Morlortai saw was plant matter. He put the knife away, then wrapped the vines around his fist and tucked the bundled mass into a sealed thigh compartment built into his suit. He'd have Polsulim check it over when he got back to his ship. Even though he didn't plan on returning to this building after this morning, Morlortai liked to know things. If the vine grew here, chances were good it grew other places as well.

"You can look all you want," the bashhound said. "All the corps have looked too, but they didn't find anything."

The corps didn't have Polsulim, who happened to be one of the best reverse engineers of organic things Morlortai had ever heard of. And he could make a bomb out of nearly anything.

"Same side," the bashhound called out as Morlortai moved on.

It was an old merc saying, a hope that two professional warriors who met again would be fighting on the same side, not against each other.

"Same side," Morlortai said. He didn't mean it, though.

The bashhound meant nothing to him and the man would be easy to kill.

0726 Hours Zulu Time

Before entering the room at the end of the hall, Morlortai hit it with a quick burst of X-rays and infrared to reveal who was inside. There were three beings. Two of them were human, armored, which was to be expected, but the third being was a surprise.

Over the years, Morlortai had worked for a lot of species, and seen even more worlds, but he'd never fully trusted the (ta)Klar. As a rule, they were devious and underhanded, and they always got the better of a deal.

For a moment, Morlortai considered just walking away. He could find another job to do on Makaum. The world was practically bursting at the seams with people who wanted someone else dead.

On the other hand, no one was ever quite wired into a world and culture and place the way the (ta)Klar were. Whatever the (ta)Klar wanted, it was second to the job that Morlortai had come to do. And that job was big.

Morlortai palmed a small canister from his left thigh compartment and strode into the room.

The two humans were good, not like the man in the hall. Their assault rifles rose automatically, covering Morlortai without actually pointing at him. They stood on either side of the table and the (ta)Klar seated on the other side.

The fact that the (ta)Klar was so vulnerable was the only thing that kept Morlortai from flinging the canister in his hand and taking his chances with getting out of the building. Turit and his team waited outside to cover him.

The (ta)Klar were a small race and looked fragile, but they were hard to kill because they'd altered their own DNA over the centuries to give themselves limited regeneration abilities. A lethal wound didn't necessarily kill a (ta)Klar if he or she had a chance to heal, which sometimes took only minutes. They were resilient enough to be almost supernatural.

Morlortai had heard stories of (ta)Klar taking several gauss blasts to the face and still surviving. The female merc who told Morlortai the story had said the (ta)Klar had come back even better-looking than he had been.

The (ta)Klar seated at the table was a little more than a meter tall and maybe twenty centimeters broad at the shoulders. The bright blue skin seemed to contain an inner glow, but maybe the phosphorescent lichens or moss helped provide that effect. The head was small and perfect, ageless, but it was covered by thin, wispy white hair that was just long enough to lie down. The (ta)Klar possessed two large black eyes that allowed them to see underwater because they were an aquatic species, and gill slits that covered their necks and the sides of their chests. They were noseless and had small mouths for feeding and communication.

Like any (ta)Klar out of the water, this one wore a hydration suit and a glass helmet with a built-in translator. The backpack was a portable rebreather that cycled the water, allowing the (ta)Klar to travel on land for hours at a time.

"Come in, *Dran Morlortai*," the (ta)Klar said.

The voice streaming from the translator was female, but that didn't mean anything to a (ta)Klar. Along with all the size and the ability to breathe air—not planned as Morlortai had heard it—for their regen ability, they had also given up secondary sexual characteristics. Rumors held that all (ta)Klar were vatborn and had been for centuries.

"I am called Merih It'dra. Please sit with me." The small hairs on the being's face shifted gently as the water cycled through the helmet.

The *Dran* was an honorific among the (ta)Klar, but they threw the title around with anyone they did business with, so Morlortai didn't buy into the attempted ingratiation. The translation, according to the (ta)Klar, was "grand and august."

"I have some ground rules," Morlortai said. "I expected whoever I'd be meeting would waive the 'no bashhounds' rule we agreed on. That actually happens more than you would think."

Merih responded with spread hands. "As you can see, I offer no threat. If we had met one-on-one, I would have been at a disadvantage. This was not acceptable."

"Two on one is?"

"Two on one is more acceptable."

"I'll bet these aren't the only ones. There are others nearby."

Merih nodded, and the two bashhounds shifted uneasily, letting Morlortai know the (ta)Klar was telling the truth now.

"There are four other bashhounds in rooms around us," Merih answered.

"Sounds like you didn't need me. You could have just had these beings do whatever you want me to do."

"That was not acceptable. We want this assignment to end in results that are satisfactory."

"Why me?"

"You were recommended to us."

"By whom?"

Merih named a woman that Morlortai knew who arranged assignments. The name didn't mean anything to the bashhounds, and it wouldn't even if someone checked into it later because the woman used a different name for each contract she set up. The name Merih had just mentioned was already an artifact, a thing of the past that had turned to dust.

The broker had pushed the contract to Morlortai because he'd already let her know he was going to be on Makaum. She'd arranged the other contract as well. Once everything worked out, it was going to be a good payday.

"You said something about ground rules," Merih stated as she sat there with clasped hands and waited expectantly.

"I have only one." Morlortai waved the hand that held the canister. "This is a plasma grenade explosive enough to take out this entire floor, and it's wired to the beating of my hearts. If either of them stops, the grenade detonates. I'll already be dead or close to it, so you people won't live much longer." He looked at the three beings across from him. "Any questions?"

Merih shifted uncomfortably and inclined her head. "It will be as you say."

"Good. Have your sec team put their guns down."

"Please do as *Dran Morlortai* says."

The bashhounds slowly put their weapons on the floor and moved away, stepping slowly backward with their hands in the air. The hardsuits would have built-in weapons, but Morlortai wasn't going to the extreme of having them deactivate everything.

"Will you join me?" Merih waved again to the seat across from her.

Lowering his hands, Morlortai crossed to the chair and sat. He placed the plasma grenade on the table. "Let's talk about the job."

Merih held up a hand and juiced a holo built into her glove and the image of a Makaum male popped up.

The man was older, with gray hair and a stooped posture. He had extra weight on him and it centered in his gut. More images of the man cycled through the hologram projection, showing him in traditional Makaum dress as well as offworld styles.

"This is Wosesa Staumar, one of the local leaders of the Makaum," Merih said.

"A member of the Quass?"

Merih smiled, but the expression didn't look normal on her face, but it slid into place easily enough that Morlortai knew she had practiced it. "You have familiarized yourself with the Makaum?"

"Yes." Morlortai never took on a job where he didn't know how the terrain fell. Preparation was 90 percent of the job and 100 percent of the success.

"Good. But this man is not a member of the Quass. He represents business arrangements. Before the arrival of the corps, he operated the sprawl marketplace. Since that time, he has managed to insert himself in trade agreements between the corps and his people, most of whom do not like to deal with offworlders."

The Makaum were living in a fantasy. Once the corps found you, you were dealing with them. They changed the world a being lived in every day.

"He has also ingratiated himself with the Phrenorians," Merih said.

"Because he thinks the Phrenorians are going to take this planet?"

"Of course not." Merih shook her head, a very human gesture that told Morlortai she had spent a lot of time working among humans. "The (ta)Klar are going to take this planet, *Dran* Morlortai. That is why we are here."

Morlortai ignored the pompousness of the (ta)Klar. Anyone who worked with them had to learn to ignore that.

"Staumar has aligned himself with the Phrenorians because they bribe him."

"The Phrenorians don't usually go in for bribes. Generally they just kill whoever doesn't agree to do things their way and talk to the next person who takes over that position. It doesn't take long to find someone who will see things their way."

"Normally, that would be the case. However, things on Makaum are too well balanced between the Phrenorian Empire and the Terran Army."

"The Terrans have a fort onplanet and the Phrenorians don't."

Merih nodded. "Exactly. If that balance were to change, if the Phrenorians were to build a fort of their own, they would not be content to simply stand by."

"That would make things harder for you too."

"It would. So we've contracted you to change the balance."

"By killing Staumar."

"And making it look like the Terran Army did it, yes."

Morlortai sat quietly for a moment. "I heard about the attack on the fort this morning. Things are tense between the Terrans and the Makaum."

"We want to take advantage of that by moving quickly."

"How quickly?"

"We would prefer Staumar to expire—messily—tomorrow night. There will be a public festival then and his death while in attendance will have great impact."

"We had agreed on a five-day window." Morlortai acted upset, but the accelerated schedule, with the bonus of all the unrest, would put his next target in sight a little easier.

Moving up the time should be no problem, but a professional never accepted a change at the last minute without increasing the price, and he was a professional.

"We would compensate you for your shortened timetable."

"Triple the amount. Half now, half when the job is done."

Merih didn't hesitate. "Agreed."

When Merih immediately put through the cred amount on Morlortai's credstick, the assassin knew the (ta)Klar had managed to hide something from him. It didn't matter. He had thirty-eight hours to figure it out, and the team was already 50 percent ahead of what they had expected for the contract.

TWELVE

Even though he was tired, Sage picked up the target-lock warning ping on his faceshield immediately. By the time he recognized what it was and yelled, "Jahup! Take cover!" the unidentified person's outline showed up on his faceshield and the trajectory software kicked in, revealing a round streaking for Jahup.

Instead of abandoning the RDC like Sage had told him, Jahup accelerated, perhaps thinking he could outrun whoever was shooting at them, or perhaps he was hypnotized by everything taking place on the faceshield. The boy still didn't have enough time in on the combat simulator for the helmet and HUD to be second nature.

Already leaping from his RDC, Sage tucked himself for the impact against the ground. Right before he hit, he took over control of Jahup's RDC and shut it down. The two-wheeled crawler immediately fell onto its side, just as the software was programmed to do. Sage had had the motor pool install the override on Jahup's RDC just in case the scout panicked.

Sage hit the ground and his HUD display scrambled as it tried to make sense of the visuals juicing through its circuitry. The RDC had been doing a little better than 100 KPH at the time he'd left it. Bouncing off the ground, still controlled by his momentum, Sage skipped like a stone and struggled to regain control of his fall.

Two depleted uranium rounds sped in his direction. The HUD tracked both of them intermittently, and one of the rounds struck a nearby tree with a trunk thicker than Sage's leg. The projectile cored through the tree trunk, reducing at least a ten-centimeter square of it into kindling. As Sage hit the ground and rolled again, the tree fell, narrowly missing him.

Sage kept his arms crossed over his chest, one hand knotted in the Roley's sling, and his chin down. He kept his legs tucked and trusted the armor to do its job. That was what a soldier was supposed to do when he was in a situation he had no control over.

Control over his careening skid came back, though. Contact with the ground slowed him as it hammered him at the same time. He slammed into a tree on his left shoulder and felt something fracture at the impact in spite of the armor. Momentarily stunned, he struggled to roll to his stomach. Once he was there, it took two tries to get the Roley off his shoulder and into his hands.

Administering stims, the suit's near-AI informed him.

"No." Sage didn't want a stimpack coursing through his body. He liked to remain in control, and the stimpack shut down some of the critical thinking and problem processing a soldier needed to stay alive. Command believed a soldier who thought he was bulletproof could get out of a situation better than one who concentrated on survival alone. Stimpacks could trigger a berserker rage, allowing a soldier to take a lot of damage before going down.

Sage crawled on his knees and elbows, looking for Jahup and searching for whoever had shot at them. Double vision plagued him and he couldn't quite catch his breath.

Parameter override. Soldier is more damaged than acceptable. Administering stims.

Sage cursed as he felt the pinpricks at his jugulars. The chems ripped along his systems, powering through on the deluge of adrenaline already flooding his body. The pain went away and his double vision sorted itself out.

Deploying extra oxygen. The AKTIVsuit routinely scrubbed carbon dioxide buildup from the suit's contained air and could filter fresh oxygen into the interior atmosphere from outside air if necessary. When sealed off from outside resources, the suit's onboard air bladder provided a few hours of air in open space, underwater, and in hostile environments flooded with unbreathable atmosphere.

Gratefully, Sage sucked in a lungful, feeling the extra oxygen move through his body. That wasn't as bad as the stims. The oxygen cleared a soldier's head and allowed him to operate on a reduced breathing capacity if that was a problem. Oxygen was fuel.

"Find Private Jahup," Sage ordered. The military designation wasn't legitimate yet, but the boy had to be entered into the system.

Searching. Private Jahup located.

A blue-limned figure showed up on Sage's faceshield. Jahup lay in a heap 63.7 meters from the overturned RDC and wasn't moving.

"Confirm Private Jahup's condition." Sage settled in behind the Roley. The sniper targeting screen opened up on his faceplate, magnifying the image and painting the man on the ridge overlooking them just long enough to get the distance. The targeting recalibrated for five hundred meters and Sage raised the rifle. He selected depleted uranium munitions for the rifle because an electromagnetic burst wouldn't scramble a target's EM field at that distance. His finger settled over the trigger and he squeezed with the reticle over the man's head.

Cannot confirm Private Jahup's condition. Range is too distant.

Riding out the Roley's recoil, Sage fired again, this time aiming for the man's center mass. Fired only a second apart, the first round hit the man's helmet and evacuated everything inside, and the second round knocked the man down.

The faceshield picked up two other people on the ridge as they took cover behind trees and boulders. For a moment, the foliage and underbrush hid them, but Sage switched over to thermal imagery and the hostiles stood out as red and yellow silhouettes. He targeted one of them as the reds began to cool, letting him know their opponents had cutting-edge hardsuits with built-in cooling capabilities. They also had training, knowing that Sage would use thermal imaging to pick them out.

Squeezing the trigger twice more, Sage watched as one of the rounds cored through the tree the target hid behind, then slammed the person backward. The second round struck a boulder just a few millimeters from the tree and cracked the stone into chunks. The flattened ricochet punched into the target as well, just before the armored figure struck the ground.

Two more hardsuits joined the surviving one, but they were moving more cautiously now. The one who had dug in unleashed a barrage of fire that tore through the jungle around Sage. Two of the rounds skimmed off his armor.

Reaching into a thigh compartment, Sage removed a smoke grenade, set it off, and tossed it a couple meters ahead of him. The grenade hit and rolled in the underbrush, then exploded with a *whumpf!* Almost immediately, dense red smoke filled the area and started spreading out.

Sage pushed up and got moving. The pain from the repeated contact with the ground had been walled away. He'd feel it later, but he didn't at the moment. His right leg felt weak and he wondered if he'd torn something or sprained something, but the hardsuit compensated almost immediately and his gait smoothed. All he needed to do was move and the hardsuit's muscle memory would pull him up to full performance.

On the run, Sage pounded through the trees and leaped over a twelve-meter-wide creek. His boots sank nearly thirty centimeters into the soft bank on the other side, but the suit's musculature pulled them free without breaking stride. He ran opposite from where Jahup lay. The boy was alive or dead or wounded, and there wasn't anything Sage could do about any of those things except try to stay alive himself.

The hardsuit functioned perfectly, getting the strides right and managing the rough terrain without a hitch. Sage held the Roley at port arms before him, using it as a barrier as he ran through branches and circled back toward their attackers.

"Identify hostiles," Sage commanded.

Identification failed. Hardsuits are not registered or are masked.

Sage figured the people belonged to a small drug lab in the area. His team had taken down a few of the bigger ones, as well as the DawnStar operation Velesko Kos had been running, but that hadn't put everyone out of business. Makaum was too rich in pharmacological resources for criminals to ignore the profit potential.

They'd also kill not to get caught.

Jahup still hadn't moved. All things considered, it was better if he wasn't 100 percent to stay down.

Sage just hoped the boy wasn't dead. He dragged his thoughts from that and focused on the men ahead of him. Three of them remained viable.

The circular path Sage was taking had cut the distance between himself and the gunmen to 376 meters. They were also starting to anticipate his speed and were getting closer to him. When a round clipped his left shoulder, tweaking the injury he'd already suffered, he went with it, following the momentum to the ground. He rolled like he'd been badly wounded and came to a rest on his back. Underbrush covered him as he pointed the Roley at his targets.

He managed to get off three rapid rounds, watching as one of the shooters took a round in the chest that split the armor open. Unless the shooter had a really good onboard med system, a corpse hit the ground.

The second round missed, but the third round caught a shooter in the ribs. Off balance, the shooter spun and dropped. The third shooter looked at the two nearby and decided to escape.

On his feet now, Sage broke from the circular route he'd been following and ran straight for the ridge. The hardsuit's boots tore into the turf and threw divots behind him, but he managed six-meter strides. He crashed through brush, leaving broken branches and uprooted saplings in his wake.

As he started up the hill, Sage noticed the rough road that had been cut through the ridge in front of him. Someone had cleared a path almost four meters wide. Shorn stumps showed where trees had been cut down and potholes left empty spaces where big rocks had been removed to enable vehicles to pass. The thick canopy of interlaced branches blocked an aerial view of the primitive road.

The first shooter Sage reached was dead. The damage to the hardsuit and all the blood that had leaked out was proof of that. The second shooter was still moving a little farther up the inclined path. Sage raised the Roley and heard the roaring rush of a magnetic drive coming over the hill.

He shifted his aim just as a six-wheeled boxy mud-brown ATV shot over the hill. The ATV had an open top and roll bars to protect the driver and passengers. A cargo net secured the crates in the crawler's storage space at the rear. A mini-rail gun swiveled at the top of the roll bars and the near-AI warned Sage of a potential target lock.

At the top of the ridge, the ATV went airborne, the mini-gun lost the target lock it had acquired, and Sage's round ricocheted from the reinforced undercarriage. Twenty meters down the hill, the ATV landed on the shooter, who had managed to stand. The shooter went down under the spinning tires but caused the ATV to list to one side. Sage fired again and the round skimmed along the crawler's side, leaving a scar at least a centimeter deep.

The three wheels touching the ground grabbed traction and forced the ATV forward. The mini-gun swiveled again, either on autopilot or under control of the shooter behind the ATV's steering wheel.

Sage's faceshield tinted red in warning, letting him know the mini-gun had him in its sights. He squeezed off another round that chewed through the roll bar by the driver's head, leaving the bar shuddering and jerking, throwing off the mini-gun's target acquisition.

Depleted uranium rounds ripped through the trees along the path near Sage and chopped into the ground, throwing up fist-sized clods and leaving craters. The driver steered for Sage, turning the ATV into a weapon. Even if impact with the ATV didn't kill him, Sage knew the crawler would pin him up against the trees and the mini-gun would finish him off.

He turned to retreat into the jungle, aiming for a thick copse of trees, knowing they would block or at least slow down the ATV. Before he reached them, a round caught him in the back and threw him off-stride. Unable to re-cover his footing, Sage fell and listened to the crawler's magnetic drive coming closer. The HUD's view was dif-ficult from the angle he was lying in, but he saw trees going down before the ATV. He forced himself to get up, but the soft ground betrayed him in his haste and he fell again. The hardsuits were heavy. He should have remem-bered that.

Rounds cut through the trees over his head like a scythe cutting through wheat. The trees toppled and Sage's faceshield tinted full-on red again, letting him know the mini-gun had him locked once more.

Frantic, Sage rolled to the side and tried to bring the Roley up. The ATV was ten meters out and closing quickly as the mini-gun roared and flashed. Rounds ripped gouges in Sage's hardsuit, but none of them hit him squarely. The armor held—barely, and the near-AI let him know that.

Take a defensive position!

Just before Sage could drop the Roley's sights over the driver's helmet, the man jerked sideways and spilled out of the seat. On autopilot, the crawler continued coming and the mini-gun stayed locked on Sage. He leveled the Roley on the mini-gun and squeezed the trigger just as the ATV-mounted weapon exploded into flying scrap. Some of the rounds cooked off in midair, adding to the noise and smoke and confusion.

Rolling again, Sage managed to get out of the ATV's path. It rolled on another six meters into the jungle before jamming into a huge boulder.

"Sage." Jahup sounded excited over the comm link, but Sage didn't blame the younger man. His own blood pressure and heart rate were up because of the stimpack.

"I'm here."

"I thought he had you."

"Me too." Sage rolled to his feet and got up, feeling time snap back into place around him. He walked to where the crawler continued grinding away at the ground with all six wheels. He switched off the power. "That was good shooting."

"I was lucky. I don't know how the round didn't hit a tree. There are a lot of trees between you and me."

Sage glanced at the jungle and silently agreed. "Lucky's good. It was bad luck these guys saw us, so having a little of it come back our way kind of evened things out."

He walked to the back of the crawler and saw a number of protective black cases inside the crates. He'd been wrong about the shooters working on a drug lab. They'd been stealing plants, mushrooms, and other flora.

"Were they making drugs?" Jahup asked.

"No." Sage picked up one of the protective cases and scanned the information contained on it. "They were bio-pirates. Gathering up samples." He put the case back and stared around the jungle. "I don't know if this is all of them, so let's be careful looking."

1151 Hours Zulu Time

The biopirates had operated from a small camp set up in a tree hut constructed eight meters from the ground. The hut was five meters by five meters and two stories tall. Lab tools and a small kitchen occupied the lower floor and bedrolls were on the second floor.

There were no other biopirates.

The dead were a mixed bunch. Two of them were Tyxetis, who were mostly humanoid but had double-jointed limbs, and hooves instead of feet. Two of them were Terran. And the remaining one was a Worall, a being covered with light green fur and an opossum's narrow features.

Three of them were in the criminal database in Sage's files. Two of those were wanted for murder in addition to other crimes.

"They might have been stealing plants," Jahup said as he stood at the lab on the first floor of the hut, "but that wasn't all they were doing."

The hut was dark with shadows due to the mosquito netting that covered the windows. Evidently the transplas sheets hadn't kept all of the bugs out. Or maybe the netting was part of the hut's disguise.

"What do you mean?"

Jahup tapped a transplas container where yellow spores sprouted on a piece of rotting meat under a grow light. "The spores are *vesgar*. They're hallucinogenic. The offworlders who trade in this call it Snakedream. When the spore is properly prepared and ripe, you burst it and breathe it in. The spore dust moves slowly and comes up in a twisting stream." He took his hand back. "If it's not prepared correctly, it causes brain death."

"That doesn't sound like something someone not from this world would know," Sage pointed out.

"*Vesgar* occurs naturally in the jungle," Jahup replied. "*Honits*, small flying lizards, eat the *austa* plants that grow at the top of the canopies. The *honit* can't digest the seeds. If the *honit* dies before it can pass the seeds, which happens when a predator fails to kill them, the seeds turn into spores. But only in *honits*."

"Why?"

Jahup shrugged. "We don't know. My people learned to stay away from *vesgar*. We destroyed it where we found it. It is the offworlders who have turned it into *product*. They are the ones who embraced the evil the spores contain." Anger colored the young man's words.

Sage thought about the attack on the fort that had happened that morning. He wondered how Jahup would react to that. The boy was torn between two worlds as it was.

"The biopirates didn't learn about *vesgar* on their own," Sage said. "Someone had to tell them about it. Someone had to show them how to cultivate it and prepare it."

"I know." Jahup faced Sage. "But your people brought the temptation to my world. If your people had never arrived, we would not have the problems we're now facing."

"My people are here to help," Sage replied. "The Army isn't like all offworlders."

"Yet some of them have cooperated with the drug manufacturers and others who steal from us."

"That's right. Some of them have. But most of us haven't. We're here because we want your people to get a fair shake on the interplanetary scene. You've worked with us. You've seen that."

Jahup looked like he wanted to say something, but he didn't.

"Would you have shown an offworlder how to find *vesgar*?" Sage asked.

"Never."

"Why?"

"Because it is evil."

"Yeah, I heard you say that. But one of your people

showed somebody, Jahup. That's how people are. Not all of them have the same values. When people are given choices, they don't always do the right thing."

"No! *We* were not like that. Not until the arrival of your ships. Not until you brought your war to us."

"The war was going to find you," Sage said quietly. "It's been headed this way for a while. We didn't bring it. We're trying to stop it. We're trying to protect your world."

"Can you?" Jahup demanded.

Hearing the harsh, ragged fear in the boy's voice, Sage realized that the anger wasn't from the discovery of the *vesgar*. And it wasn't anger. It was fear about the Phrenorian base. Seeing that fortress out in the jungle, knowing what it was, had made the war more immediate to Jahup. His world was suddenly more fragile than he'd thought it could be.

"Can you stop the Phrenorians?" Jahup asked. "Because if you can't, if my people make the wrong choice by joining you, then they will be killed by the Phrenorians."

"If you work with the Phrenorians, they'll make slaves of you. I've seen it happen. They'll strip this world down to nothing, take everything they want, and leave you people to die. If you're not dead before they accomplish that." Sage met Jahup's gaze. "You and your people don't get the luxury of sitting this one out. If nothing else, that base we found should tell you that. The Phrenorians want Makaum, and they'll take it if they can. If we hadn't come—if the Army hadn't come—Makaum would have been lost to the corps and then to the Phrenorians. One of the problems we have facing us now is that your people are trying to stay out of things, not choose one side or the other. That's not going to save you."

For a moment longer, Jahup stared at Sage, searching

for something, but Sage had no clue what the boy was looking for. Sage knew the decisions were hard. He'd seen his mother and her family have to make similar decisions when war had ravaged their country in South America. At the time, Sage had been young, but the things he'd seen, all the death and carnage, had stuck with him.

In the end, his mother had lost her country, her home, and things had never been the same for her again despite her husband and son.

Sage put a hand on Jahup's shoulder. "All I can promise you, Jahup, is that I'm not going to quit on you. I'll be here. I'm not going to leave."

Jahup nodded. "Not everything is in your hands, though, Sergeant." He turned and walked away.

Sage watched the boy go, knowing there was nothing he could say.

THIRTEEN

Ahead of Sage, Jahup passed through one of the checkpoints to the fort. The gates slid smoothly to the sides as the RDCs approached, already alerted by Sage when he sent their identification on ahead. The boy stood up on the crawler and took note of the constructor bots repairing the damage to the training building. New steel gleamed in the afternoon sunlight on the patched portion of the fence that had been burned through.

Jahup slowed down and almost stopped.

Sage rode up beside him and opened the comm link between them. "Come on. We've got a lot to do."

"You knew about this?" Accusation rang in Jahup's voice.

"I knew." Sage wasn't going to lie to him.

"You didn't tell me?"

"No, I didn't. We were concentrating on getting back

alive. You didn't need to be distracted about this then. We couldn't do anything about this while we were out there."

"What happened?"

"We'll talk about that when we get inside."

Jahup sped up through the gate and raced toward the blocky motor-pool building, where crawlers, Bubbles, and other rolling stock sat outside in neat rows. Jumpcopters occupied the top two floors.

Sage noticed that the motor pool had more armed soldiers standing guard today than normal, but didn't know if that was in response to the attack or to the fact that Jahup was riding in. He sped up and followed the boy into the massive building.

"You're late, Top." Colonel Halladay stood in the doorway of the hallway leading from the motor pool dressed in a hardsuit. His helmet was adhered magnetically to his hip and he carried a Roley slung over his shoulder. The colonel didn't usually carry an assault rifle through the fort.

Sage leaned the RDC on its side and booted the kickstand into place. Jahup parked his crawler beside Sage's. He fidgeted, as if uncertain what to do, but Sage knew he was upset.

Sage took off his helmet, slung it at his hip, and saluted. Halladay returned the salute, and Sage was aware that the three of them held the attention of all the motor-pool personnel in the cavernous space.

"We ran into some trouble on the way, Colonel," Sage replied.

Halladay glanced at the new scars on the RDCs and frowned. "What trouble?"

"Biopirates, sir. We were on them before we knew it. They reacted and Jahup and I were forced to defend ourselves. There were casualties, and we shut down another operation."

"We'll talk about that later." Halladay waved a hand. "You two follow me." He led the way down into the underground hallway that connected all the buildings.

1422 Hours Zulu Time

"What happened to the fort?" Jahup demanded. He emulated Sage, standing in front of the colonel's desk at parade rest.

Sage throttled the urge to dress Jahup down. If Jahup had been a regular soldier, he would have.

A nerve twitched high up on Halladay's cheek and he hesitated just a moment before taking his seat. "You're a recent recruit, Private Jahup, and not fully trained in how chain of command works, so I'm going to ignore the tone you're presently taking with a superior officer. If, however, you were regular army and completely trained, you'd be in the brig in two minutes. Are we clear?"

Jahup's jaw flexed and he nodded.

Sage cleared his throat.

Glancing at him, Jahup realized his mistake and quickly returned his attention to the colonel. "Yes sir. We're clear."

"Good. Now the two of you have a seat and let's talk about what you found. Then we'll talk about the fort."

1447 Hours Zulu Time

Since Sage and Jahup hadn't learned much, actually, about the Phrenorian base other than it existed and Zhoh GhiCemid had been there for reasons unknown, though he didn't look like he was in control, what they knew to tell didn't take long, but it gave them a lot to think about.

Halladay had a steward bring in sandwiches and black coffee and they ate while they talked.

"You don't know how much of the base is underground?" Halladay asked.

"No sir." Sage set his coffee cup on the colonel's desk and knew he shouldn't have drunk it. With the residual effects of the stimpack still rattling around in his system, he felt restless. He needed some serious rack time, but he didn't think that was likely to happen anytime soon. Not until the ambush was dealt with.

The colonel leaned back in his chair and took a breath, then made notes on his PAD. "What would you put out there, Top?"

"If I was going to attempt to take this planet from an opposing military force?"

Halladay nodded. "I can't see any other reason for the Sting-Tails to build a stockpile out there."

"I'd put in everything I could. Rolling stock. Air support. Powersuits. Weps."

Jahup's hands knotted, but he didn't say anything. It might have been easier to have the discussion without the young man present, but Sage knew they would have had a fight on their hands. He was sure the colonel knew that too. Jahup had already seen the base—twice. He'd assured Sage and Halladay that he hadn't told anyone else.

"I would too," Halladay said. "We need to find out what they have in there."

"The Phrenorians are breaking treaty," Jahup said. "Tell the Quass what the Phrenorians have done."

Halladay turned to Jahup. "What have they done?"

"They have put a fortress out there and filled it with weapons."

"Did you see any weapons?" Halladay kept his voice quiet and calm.

Jahup hesitated. "No, but—"

"Then we can't tell the Quass the Phrenorians are stockpiling weapons."

"Why else would they have it there?"

"For research purposes. Just like their treaty says they can. They're identifying flora and fauna just like our science teams are, and like the corps are doing. All according to treaty."

"The Quass can demand to see what is out there," Jahup said. "That is also according to treaty."

"Okay, let's say the Quass throws its weight around, that *enough* Quass members agree to pull rank and demand a review from the Phrenorians to challenge them for a look inside that secret installation of theirs. And you know many members of the Quass are looking at the Phrenorians for support, not us, because the Phrenorians want *all* Terrans gone from Makaum."

Jahup's mouth and eyes tightened and his shoulders rounded. Getting the Quass to agree to risk offending the Phrenorians was next to impossible and Sage knew the boy was aware of that.

"But let's, for the moment, imagine how such a visit would go," Halladay continued. "The most passive way would be to allow a review team made up of Quass to visit the site. They bring the Quass members in, show them around, show them all the science experiments and observations they've been doing. Most of that isn't going to be anything those Quass members will know anything about."

Jahup's cheeks darkened with anger, but he kept himself in check. He knew the limitations of his people.

"So they see nothing out of the ordinary because the

Phrenorians have hidden their secrets really well. It's what I would do." Halladay's face remained grim. "But there's another way such a demand by the Quass could go. Feeling pressured, knowing they're about to be exposed, the Phrenorians could decide that then was as good a time to spring their attack as any and they'll kill those Quass members." He paused. "Then this sprawl becomes the battleground that the Terran Army is here to prevent."

Horror widened Jahup's eyes.

Sage knew the boy had been thinking about such a thing. The attack by DawnStar on Sage and Kiwanuka in the sprawl marketplace had nearly destroyed one of the Makaum people's oldest landmarks. That had been the first time the Makaum had had a taste of what was coming if war broke out, and it had split the Quass and the populace even more. Some of the people and the Quass had faulted the Terran Army for causing violence to erupt in the sprawl, and others had seen the Phrenorians as saviors because Zhoh GhiCemid had taken advantage of the moment and ridden to the rescue.

"Then the Phrenorians have won," Jahup said quietly.

"No," Halladay replied. "They haven't. Since we know about the base, now we can do something about it. If we can figure out more about the base, we can launch a preemptive strike."

"You mean just attack them?"

"Yes."

"If you do that, you'll be breaking the treaty."

"*Before* we do that, if we can, we have to win the Quass over to us."

"Do you think telling them about the base will convince them there is a threat?"

"If you hadn't seen it, would you believe it?"

Jahup didn't reply.

Halladay tapped his pad. "Why do you think that fortress is filled with weapons? Because Sage told you it was?"

"No, because putting weapons out there would be the smart thing to do. It's like when I lead a band hunting a *quekton*. I station hunters in front of and behind the *quekton* in case we don't bring it down quickly. You put spears and bows in the bush to protect your flank."

Halladay shook his head. "Sounds like a good assessment, but I don't know what a *quekton* is."

"It's one of the native lizards, sir," Sage said. "Dinosaur-sized. Mean, ugly, and smelly. Hard to kill." He'd only seen a few of them out in the jungle and he'd given them a wide berth.

"They're intelligent too," Jahup added. "Natural predators, and trying to take them out in the jungle is dangerous. We only hunt them when we're desperate for meat, when the hunting has been scarce. Which it has been more and more since offworlders have moved further away from the sprawl."

That had been the outlaw drug labs and biopirates. Some of the hunting bands had been attacked by offworlder criminals defending their turf.

"With these extra bows and spears in place, your odds of taking the *quekton* increase," Halladay stated.

"Yes," Jahup agreed.

"Do you think most of the Quass will think like you think?" Halladay asked. "That the Phrenorian base is filled with weapons?"

Jahup let out a disgusted breath. "No. Most of my people have never been hunters. They've lived in the sprawl and tended gardens and built homes. My grandmother tells me our people have gotten soft. Back in the Dark Times, after the Crash, our ancestors had to learn to survive. Mostly they hunted and stayed on the run. Not much technology survived with them, and they had to abandon the ship for many years because the jungle there was so hostile. By the time they were able to return, not much of the ship was usable, and the survivors didn't know how to use it anyway. The captain and crew had died."

"We have to find a way to prove that the Phrenorian threat exists," Halladay said, "and do it at a time we can take advantage of that. Do you understand?"

"I'm a hunter," Jahup replied. "Of course I understand. You build a trap and you have to wait for your prey."

"Good. In the meantime, you can't tell anyone about this. Only Sage, you, and your team will be given information about the base. We have to keep it quiet until we have leverage."

"I understand, but I don't like the idea of keeping this a secret from my grandmother."

"I don't either," Halladay admitted. "I'm going to draw a lot of heat from my general when I tell him, and if I tell him, he's going to have to tell the diplomats. If the diplomats get involved, nothing is going to get done and everyone will know only a little. So we've got to figure out what we're going to do and be quick about it."

"The first thing we do is step up security around the fort," Sage said. "Given the attack this morning, that will be easy enough and not put anyone on alert. The Phrenorians will expect us to be more agressive."

"We've also got to decide how we're going to handle the attack," Halladay said.

Sage knew that was true, and he knew that Halladay was concerned about affecting the tentative acceptance the Makaum showed to the military. "Doing nothing isn't the answer, sir."

"No. But first we've got to find out who the attackers were."

"I thought you had a witness."

"I do, but she's not talking."

Jahup leaned forward. "Who is the witness?"

"It would be better if you let us handle this," Halladay responded.

"It has to be one of my people. No Phrenorian would give you information, and no corp member would tell you unless there was a payoff involved, and no other off-worlder would want to get involved because he or she would be vulnerable to retribution."

The young man was smart, quick to pick up on things. That was one of the things Sage respected about him.

Halladay flicked a glance over to Sage, letting him know he could choose how to play the situation.

"You're right, Jahup, it is one of your people," Sage replied. Holding back the information wasn't possible. As soon as Jahup was out with the soldiers, or at least in the sprawl, he would know who the witness was. "Noojin was with Telilu and they saw the whole thing. Noojin alerted the soldiers who were in danger and probably saved their lives. But she's not telling us anything."

Jahup took a moment to assimilate that. "Let me talk to her."

Sage shook his head. "That's not going to happen. I'm going to talk to her first."

Coolly, Jahup sat back and folded his arms over his chest. "She won't tell you anything."

"She has to. I'll make her see that."

FOURTEEN

S he's tough," Halladay said as he stood beside Sage at the observation window that peered into Interview Room D. "I've got two daughters, both about Noojin's age, and despite being gone as much as I am, I still have a good relationship with them. I know girls." He sipped his coffee. "I spent a couple of hours with Noojin. Came at her from every angle I knew. She's not going to crack. I think we're wasting our time here. She's not going to give up what she knows. If she knows anything."

Sage peered at Noojin as she sat in the chair inside the small room. In her mind, he knew, she wasn't in that room. She was someplace else, maybe on a hunt or talking to Jahup. She had a predator's mindset, a sniper's cool calm. She would understand how to sit still and not think and just let time pass because time worked against the people who were holding her and she knew it. Quass

Leghef had given permission for the Army to keep her for now, but that wouldn't last.

"With all due respect, there's something you're forgetting, sir." Sage focused his mind, knowing he had to be sharp to talk to Noojin. He was freshly showered and wore a clean set of ACUs, not the hardsuit, which was getting repaired. He would have been better if he'd managed to get some sleep before interviewing the girl, but that wasn't going to happen.

"What do you think I'm forgetting?" Halladay asked.

"That she's not your daughter. That she's not just a kid. You have to approach this girl a different way. We have to raise the stakes and take off the kid gloves."

"I came down pretty hard on her. Threatened her with locking her up no matter what the Quass says."

"She figures she's going to be able to handle anything you throw at her. Especially with the Quass looking out for her. You have to move the threat off of her and let her know that she and the Quass can't control everything. She's not the only one in danger. She just hasn't seen that yet." Sage adjusted the meal box he had under one arm, palmed the security panel to release the locks, and opened the door.

Noojin flicked back to awareness as Sage entered the room. Her eyes took him in, then darted to the door behind him as if she was expecting someone else. She only looked disappointed for a moment when the door closed behind Sage, then she wiped that response from her face. She wasn't going to let him see weakness.

Without a word, Sage sat on the opposite side of the table from her and put the meal box in front of her. He took two disposable sporks out of his pocket and placed them, and napkins, on the table as well. He'd brought enough food for both of them. The sandwiches in Halladay's office earlier had taken the edge off his hunger, but hadn't filled him up.

Blazing with unspoken defiance, she pushed meal box away.

Patiently, Sage reached for the box and opened it. The meal consisted of Makaum food, roasted lizard meat and jellied insects that Jahup had sworn were Noojin's favorite. The spices in the meal filled the room. Sage removed two bottles of amber *corok* juice. The small melons were popular on Makaum and grew readily. He twisted the tops off the bottles and slid one over to Noojin.

"You should eat," he told her.

"I'm not hungry." Her tone dripped with rebellion.

"You're hungry, and you're thirsty. Colonel Halladay says you haven't eaten or drunk anything since you've been here."

"I am a prisoner, not a guest."

"Yeah, you are a prisoner." Sage looked over the breaded meat in the meal box. The pieces were finger length and about as thick, and the breading was golden-brown and flecked with red and purple spices. "Jahup said *slor* was your favorite meal because it was so dangerous to hunt."

Noojin sneered at him. "You don't hunt *slor*. You kill those that hunt you—if you can. We're just fortunate that they're edible and that killing them isn't wasteful." She shot him a look of disdain. "If you were to encounter a *slor* without your combat suit, with only the weapons we use to hunt, it would kill you."

"Maybe." Sage tore into the meat and discovered that it was surprisingly good. He chewed and swallowed. "This morning I killed an *omoro* with an *etess* before it got to Jahup. Probably saved his life. Maybe an *omoro* isn't as big as a *slor*, but it's faster and more lethal in some ways. And I managed that without the help of other hunters."

She blinked as emotions twisted within her. Sage had deliberately told her about the attack on Jahup to get her head out of her own situation.

"You're lying," she said.

"No. You can ask Jahup. After we're finished here." Sage took another bite and chewed.

"You're going to let me out?"

Sage swallowed. "After we've finished talking, sure. If you had answered the colonel's questions, you could have been out of here a long time ago."

She crossed her arms. Her pointed chin rose in open defiance. "The Quass is forcing you to release me."

"Nope." Sage wiped the grease from his hands on a napkin.

"She will."

"Not till after we've finished this talk."

"Do you think you can get me to answer you when the colonel couldn't?"

"I know I can." Sage didn't look at her, didn't give her any kind of direct confrontation. She would have become even more sullen over a challenge like that. He just spoke the words like it was already the truth. It was. She just didn't know it yet.

"Try all you want. I'm not saying anything. I can wait until Quass Leghef orders my release. Which will be soon."

Sage gave her a flat stare, the kind he used on a green soldier in boot who had just failed an inspection. "She won't do that. Not until we release you."

Noojin worked her jaw like she was going to say something, then she chose to remain silent.

"That attack this morning blurred a lot of lines between the Army and the Makaum people," Sage said. "The Quass knows those lines have to be straightened out again if we're to be effective. And she wants us to be effective. Otherwise the Phrenorians will take this planet."

"You keep making the Phrenorians out to be monsters. The only thing I've ever seen them do is save you when you confronted DawnStar the second night you were here, and they put out the fires that burned part of the market-place after your fight with the DawnStar Corp triggered that. Terrans are the monsters."

"Terrans didn't attack the fort last night and nearly kill two of my soldiers. So maybe we need to figure out who the monsters are."

She ignored him. "Where is Jahup?"

"In the med center."

Concern wiped away her rebellion and fear gleamed in her eyes. Her voice tightened. "Is he all right?"

"He's fine. He fractured a couple of ribs when he crashed the RDC after some biopirates tried to kill us. The doc is looking after him. In a few hours, he'll be fine." Sage was scheduled for a med visit as well, as soon as he finished the interview. The shoulder separation he'd suffered from the fall he'd taken from the RDC and the impacts from the gunshots were painful now that the stimpack had worn off.

"What happened?"

"I guess both of us want to know that." Sage reached into the meal box with one of the sporks and picked up a chunk of vegetable he didn't recognize. Like the meat, the vegetable was well seasoned. He popped it into his mouth and ignored Noojin glaring at him.

Her stomach rumbled and she looked embarrassed, just like a girl again, not a hunter or a young woman.

Sage finished swallowing and took a sip of the *corok* juice, finding it cool and sweet. "You saw who attacked the fort. I need to know who it was."

"What would you do to them if you could find them?"

"I don't know yet. Let the Makaum people know they can't do that kind of thing again. Turn them over to Quass Leghef for punishment. The Army doesn't care what happens to those people, they just want to send a message that something like this morning won't be allowed to happen again."

"Would you kill them?"

"Only if I have to."

Noojin reached out for a piece of meat and began to eat. She paused her chewing long enough to say, "The Quass won't be patient forever."

"After the attack on the fort, Quass Leghef has to make a statement to your people, and to mine too. She made a treaty with the Terran Army that we would be welcome here. That her people would accept soldiers being here. Last night, some of her people broke that treaty, and Quass Leghef and her peers are responsible for that."

"Some of the Quass members no longer want you here."

"Yeah, I know that. After this morning, there are a lot of soldiers who don't want to be here either." Sage had already heard some of the grumbling that was taking place.

The soldiers at Fort York, for the most part, were green and not used to getting shot at. Only the teams that Terracina and Sage had taken into the jungle had been tested under fire, and the attrition rate during the ambush that had killed Terracina had given pause to a lot of soldiers.

"I've been told the general is talking to military intelligence about the wisdom of keeping Fort York open for business since we apparently don't have the support of the people the way we did in the beginning. Military command is trying to decide how badly they want to help you people maintain your freedom. The Phrenorian War is spreading, getting bigger, and some of it is headed this way. This planet's resources make it a prime target for exploitation. The Phrenorians won't say *please* and *thank you* when they get here."

"Trying to scare me isn't going to work. You're just as bad as the Phrenorians. You weren't killing Phrenorians out in the jungle, you were killing Terrans and other off-worlders. And it wasn't a Phrenorian who captured me and tried to—" Noojin dropped her eyes and wouldn't meet his gaze. Her hands shook just for a second, but she quickly regained control over herself.

Sage kept his voice flat because they were going to deal with the truth. "No, it wasn't a Phrenorian. You're right about that, but it was the Army who got you out of that."

"It was you that nearly got us killed. Jahup had the band out there looking for drug labs as much as we were looking to take meat. He wanted you to notice him. He misplaces his trust in you." Noojin took a ragged breath. Part of the reaction was going without food for so long, but part of it was the residual trauma. "You were there to kill Velesko Kos. You only happened to find me while doing that."

"Jahup found me and told me they'd taken you. We came looking for you. Saving you became part of the mission. Jahup made certain of that. He saved you. We helped. We wouldn't have gotten into that drug lab if it hadn't been for him."

She looked away from him and made herself eat.

Sage let silence hang in the room for a time while she ate. She was back in that underground lab, a prisoner again, a victim. He knew he had to let her come back from that on her own, and he trusted that she would. She was tough.

Besides the meat and vegetables, the meal box contained flat bread that was chewy and had a nutty taste.

Sage took a piece and continued eating and watched as Noojin calmed herself.

"I want to tell you a story," Sage said.

She rolled her eyes at him, and Sage had to wonder if that was something she'd picked up from offworlder women or if the eye roll was a trait of all females.

Sage sipped the juice and wished he had coffee. He also wished he didn't have to dig inside himself so much to convince her, because he didn't like talking about his past, but he knew he had to be honest too.

"I grew up in a village not much different than yours. It was called Sombra de la Montàna, which means, more or less, 'Shadow of the Mountain.' It was called that because it was located in a mountainous area of Colombia, not far from Bogóta. It was a rough, inhospitable piece of country, but it was where my mother and several generations of her family had lived working crops and herding goats."

Noojin narrowed her eyes at him in disbelief, no doubt thinking he was lying to her.

Sage took his PAD from his thigh pocket and laid it on the table. He tapped the screen and the holo program popped up an image of a small village. Dusty roads wound through thatched huts clinging to the side of a long hill. Vegetation was sparse and the trees were twisted things that looked spindly and weak. Goats and chickens walked freely around the yards. The people dressed in simple white cotton clothing. The children were barely dressed at all, and their skin was dark from the sun, like Sage's own skin. With the blue sky overhead, the scene looked calm and restful, not at all like the hardscrabble life Sage had experienced there.

Despite her attitude, Noojin stared at the image and watched the people and animals walking around the village. Everyone had jobs. Goats had to be tended, gardens had to be worked, and laundry had to be done in the stream that flowed nearby.

Most of the vids released in the marketplace through offworlder vendors offered immersive experiences for tourist spots. People who used the vid equipment could walk on sandy beaches, play games of chance in elegant casinos, surf white waves near Hawaii and the pink waters of the Bay of Uskosh on Rodapol and the frigid, ten meter waves of the Enthormwar Sea on Belseris. Or they could ride horses or fly on *delusks* on Rydis or swim with *skelale* on Claseras.

The simsense vids allowed users to go to pleasure spots. No one wanted to go to places like Sombra de la Montàna.

"My father was assigned to a scout unit during Mexico's war with Colombia. The United States had joined Mexico against the terrorists that were launching attacks on the both of those countries from Colombia. Sombra de la Montána was a lot like Makaum in the early days. Not involved in the war, but it affected my mother's people.

"The Army established a FOB, a forward operating base, near Sombra de la Montána because the terrain lent itself to guerilla action. My father's unit performed surgical strikes against the Colombian leaders, going into the city, hitting targets, then fading into the jungle."

"So he was a soldier? Like you?" Noojin asked, interested in spite of herself.

"Yeah. He was special ops, a guerilla, trained to work behind enemy lines." Sage advanced the vid and showed some of the battle scenes from that war. Burning vehicles occupied streets filled with victims' corpses. "My father's unit was up against some really bad odds, but they held it together."

"Your mother and father met there?"

"They did. Some of the men in Sombra de la Montána traded goods with people in Bogóta. They would
bring back information about the Colombian soldiers.
One of those men was my mother's brother. My father
ate in her father's house and listened to the reports from
her brother. According to my father, he fell hard for my
mother. He wasn't a soft guy. He didn't believe in love
at first sight, and he was a soldier with a mission. But he
always said there was something about my mother that
he just couldn't pull back from." As Sage looked at the
vid images, he could remember sitting with his father
on their back porch, talking about his mother after she
had died. Both of them had been emotionally distraught.

"He married her."

Sage nodded. "I was born there the following year, and
the war went on for eleven years before the Colombian
army overran Sombra de la Montána. My mother refused
to leave even though my father begged her to take us out
of the village. Later, when the Colombians invaded, my
father and his unit evacuated as many of the people as
they could. They got my mother and me out, some of the
other villagers, but not many of them. My grandparents
and uncles and aunts and most of my cousins were killed
when the Colombians rolled into the village."

"You think that because you tell me this story, I'm
going to tell you what I know?" Noojin stared at him,
clearly unimpressed.

"No. That story was just to let you know we have more
in common than you might suspect. And it was to set up
the story I'm going to tell you now." Sage delved back
more deeply into the memories, and this one he didn't
like telling at all. In his whole life, he'd only told it to a
handful of people.

"Sad stories aren't going to break me. If I want those, all I have to do is walk through my sprawl."

Sage ignored her, but he had to clamp down on a small spark of anger before it got out of control. "Before the Colombians destroyed Sombra de la Montána, I had a friend who lived there. His name was Danilo Arango. When I was eleven, he was fifteen. We hunted and fished together. Danilo had a girlfriend named Soraya, who was his age."

The room's environmental controls kicked on with a slight thump. Noojin sat on the other side of the table and feigned disinterest, but Sage knew she was listening.

"Danilo loved Soraya," Sage went on. "I used to get mad at him and give him grief over it. He ignored me because he was happy being with her." He pushed the emotion away and concentrated on putting words together. "He was spending more time with her than he was me. Then one morning, Soraya was found dead outside of the village. Someone had raped her and killed her. No one had seen anything. No one knew how such a terrible thing could happen."

"Did anyone find out what happened to her?" Interest lighted Noojin's eyes.

"I went to Danilo and talked to him. He told me that two men from another village caught him and Soraya the night before. They stabbed him and thought they'd killed him, but he saw everything they did to Soraya. Later, when he got strength back, he stumbled back to the village."

"Didn't he tell anyone what happened?"

"Me. He told only me."

"His parents didn't notice that he was wounded?"

"Danilo was an orphan. With the war going on, there were lots of orphans in the village."

"You didn't tell anyone?"

Sage shook his head. "Danilo asked me not to." In his mind, he could see his friend at the back of the hut where they'd bandaged him up. "He swore me to secrecy. I was a kid, and I took things like that seriously. I guess I still do."

"Why didn't your friend want anyone to know? Was he ashamed?"

"Maybe he was ashamed, but mostly he wanted revenge on those two men that hurt Soraya. He was afraid no one would believe him. I don't know if anyone would have, and if they would have done anything about the murder of one girl. Times were very confusing then. That was only weeks before the Colombians attacked the village, so Soraya's death was a small thing compared to all the other fear people had." Sage pushed images of Danilo from his mind, but it was hard. He still remembered the wound in his friend's chest and the pain in his eyes. It was an old story and the hurt was almost thirty years gone, but it lingered. "After Danilo healed up, he disappeared. Three days after that, some of our hunters found Danilo dead, his throat cut, out in the jungle. He was dressed up in battle paint and carried a warrior's weapons. A bow, machete, and an old laser rifle that didn't hold a charge for long. Nobody but me knew why he was dressed that way."

"Did you tell anyone then?"

Sage nodded. "I had to. I couldn't keep that to myself. To my way of thinking, I'd let Danilo get himself killed. So his death was partly my fault. By the time I told my father, the Colombians were almost upon us. We had to get ready to leave."

"What about the men that killed Danilo and Soraya?"

"They got away. Nobody ever knew who they were. Danilo never told me their names. He might not even have known. He went after them and they killed him. Or someone did."

A flicker of anger ignited in Noojin's eyes. "You think to frighten me with that story? To make me think about being the only person who can name those men that attacked the fort? To consider that they might want to kill me?"

"Or maybe Telilu?"

Noojin drew back at that, and Sage knew he'd made her look beyond herself.

"You're sure you can take care of yourself," Sage said. "But can that little girl protect herself?"

"She doesn't know who they were."

"Maybe those people don't know that. Then she'll be even more vulnerable because she'll never see them coming."

That had never occurred to Noojin. Horror twisted into her face as she considered that.

Sage went on softly. "There's a young soldier in the hospital ward right now who has to undergo skin grafts and other surgery for simply doing his job. He's not much older than you and Jahup, and he's going through a lot of pain, and he's got physical therapy ahead of him before he's himself again. He's only been on Makaum a short time. He arrived when I did. He hasn't made any enemies."

"I tried to warn him."

"I know, and that's why you're going to give me the names now. Because you want to protect people."

She shook her head.

"And because if you don't tell me," Sage said, "Jahup is going to want to know who almost killed you, and who almost killed his little sister. He's not going to leave this alone."

"I won't tell him." Desperation gleamed in her eyes.

Sage kept his voice soft and insistent. "Jahup's going to keep asking, and keep asking, until one day you do tell him who those men were. And when you do, what do you think Jahup is going to do? Sit back quietly and let those men get away with it? Even if you don't tell him, he's going to start asking around, and he may get close enough to the people behind the attack to get himself hurt because he doesn't know who they are either. Because you didn't tell him."

Noojin wrapped her arms more tightly around herself, and from the slow panic easing into her features, Sage knew he'd gotten to her.

"Jahup won't let them get away with it," Sage said. "Once he knows those names, and he'll get them eventually, he'll go after those men. And he'll probably get himself killed because he's not going to be ready for them." He let the silence between them grow heavier. "You don't want him doing this alone, and don't think the two of you are good enough to do this on your own."

When Noojin looked at Sage again, tears sparkled in her eyes. "I don't want Jahup hurt."

"I know. Neither do I. That's why I'm here. Those guys nearly killed you, and they nearly killed his little sister. Jahup won't let that go. You know that."

Noojin wiped her tears on her sleeve. "I didn't see all of the men."

"That's fine. Give me the names of those that you know and I'll take it from there."

FIFTEEN

Noojin couldn't believe how weak she'd been. Crying in front of the Terran sergeant was embarrassing. She didn't cry in front of anyone. She wasn't some empty-headed female who couldn't control her emotions. She was a hunter. A *good* hunter. She wasn't this emotional person who couldn't control herself.

True to his word, Sage had freed her from the interview room, but she also believed that he knew she had nowhere to go. She couldn't be with Jahup, though that was what she wanted most of all, because Jahup would ask the questions the sergeant said he would ask.

And she didn't want to go home to the small house she shared with three friends. They were merely acquaintances, people to live with, not family. Her family, like Jahup's mother and father, were dead. She was like the orphan in Sage's story.

She walked to one of the small commissaries set up throughout the fort, drawn by the smell of coffee. Makaum didn't have coffee, though some of the off-worlders were now experimenting with planting some seeds. The Quass and the trade council had seen a market for coffee beans. Many of the Makaum people had developed a taste for it.

The commissary was about half full of soldiers. Men and women in hardsuits sat at tables and talked quietly among themselves. Most of them stopped talking when Noojin entered, and she realized coming there was a mistake. She just didn't have anywhere else to go.

They knew who she was. Her skin and her hair and her clothes immediately set her apart from them. None of them trusted her.

Noojin stopped and turned around, ready to head for the door, then she noticed Sergeant Kiwanuka standing behind her.

Like many of the others, Kiwanuka wore a hardsuit and carried weapons. Her helmet hung at her hip. She smiled at Noojin. "I'm having coffee. Care to join me?"

Noojin wanted that because she didn't want to be alone, but she didn't want to talk to anyone either. Still, she felt she had something in common with Kiwanuka. She also knew that Kiwanuka hadn't just happened to find her there.

"Sergeant Sage sent you, didn't he?"

Kiwanuka didn't try to lie or avoid the question. "Yes. He and I both thought you could use some company right about now."

"I told him everything I know."

"I believe you."

"Doesn't he believe me?"

"He does, but he also wants to make sure that you're okay. I'm here for you. You've been through a lot."

"I'm fine." Noojin made her words cold, trying to put that hard exterior back into place. If she needed anyone by her side right now, she needed Jahup, but that would be too complicated.

"I can see that. However, I'm going to have coffee, and I wouldn't mind some company. You can talk—or not—as you wish. What do you say?"

Noojin looked at the door. "If I leave, you're going to follow me?"

"Yes. The master sergeant wants you protected."

"From what?"

"From anyone who wants to hurt you."

"Doesn't he trust the soldiers here?"

Kiwanuka smiled. "You're not in any danger from the soldiers, Noojin, but there are outsiders on base. We've got things locked down tight, but there are still citizen employees at the fort. Sage wants to make sure you're out of harm's way in case the men from this morning have friends. Quass Leghef would expect nothing less." She paused. "I know you like coffee. Jahup says you've developed a taste for it."

"He's telling everyone what I eat and what I like to drink."

"Not everyone. Just the master sergeant. Sage told me."

"Where is Jahup? Why isn't he here?" Noojin felt betrayed by his absence.

"Master Sergeant Sage suggested Jahup give you some space for a while. He's still down in medical."

Concern filled Noojin and for a moment she forgot about her problems. "Has something gone wrong? Sage told me Jahup was hurt."

"It's nothing serious. The sergeant decided to have Jahup sedated so he could sleep while the nanobots repaired his ribs. Jahup had been up over thirty-eight hours. Sleep is a good thing right now."

"Do you know where Jahup and the sergeant went while they were gone?"

Kiwanuka shook her head, then took Noojin by the elbow and guided her to a small table in the corner.

"You wouldn't tell me if you knew."

"Not if I was told not to, no."

"Then how do I know you don't know where they went and what they were doing?"

"Because I'm telling you I don't know. If I knew and wasn't going to tell you, I'd tell you I wasn't going to answer your question. That's how you know."

A server came by and Kiwanuka ordered two coffees. Noojin sat in silence and Kiwanuka didn't speak either. The coffee arrived and she waited till it cooled a little before sipping.

"What is Sage going to do about those men that attacked the fort?" Noojin asked when she couldn't endure the silence anymore.

"He's going to make things right."

"How?"

"I don't know."

Noojin stared into her coffee and tried to find answers in the dark liquid, but none appeared. "I've betrayed my people by giving those names to Sage."

"No, you haven't. Those people betrayed you by breaking treaty. Evidently at least one of them would have killed you. Probably Jahup's sister as well." Kiwanuka held her gaze. "This has to be settled before someone else gets hurt."

"Do you think Sage is going to be able to do what he's doing without hurting someone?"

Kiwanuka hesitated for just a moment. "That depends on what those men do."

"If this goes badly, things between the Makaum and your people are going to be worse."

"The master sergeant is aware of that. That's why he's going to work through channels."

Med Center
Fort York
2034 Hours Zulu Time

Sage came out of the twilight sleep he'd been put into and felt a little more rested. Unfortunately, two hours of sleep only put a sharper edge on the fatigue that filled him.

"You feeling okay, Top?" The med tech beside Sage's bed wore all white and looked earnest.

Leaning forward, Sage sat up on the bed and felt a momentary wobble of dizziness that sorted itself out when he closed his eyes and reopened them. He tested his injured shoulder, moving it in a circle. The muscles felt a little stiff and sore, but none of the pain he'd been feeling before the doctor had programmed the nanobots to fix his rotator cuff was there now.

"Feels right," Sage answered.

"You'll have to do some physical therapy to get it back to peak."

"Yeah, I know. I've been here before. Am I good to go?"

"Gimme a thumbprint and you are." The orderly extended his PAD and took Sage's thumbprint. "I've sent the PT schedule to your PAD, Top, and scheduled you with one of our rehab people."

"Thanks." Sage already had ACU pants on. He slid out of bed and pulled on clean socks and his military boots, then slipped into a fresh olive-drab tee shirt and ACU blouse. He ran a hand through his short-cropped dark hair, but knew he wouldn't feel clean again until he'd showered and shaved. There was something about a hospital room that always seemed to leave a residue.

After checking the patient list, Sage went to see Private Trevor Anders in the ICU ward. Sage stepped through the clean zone and walked to Anders's bed.

The private lay quietly on the sterile white sheets. Cell-stim fluid packs covered Anders's legs up to mid-thigh. Other minor burns marred his upper body and the right side of his face, but all of those looked like they were healing well. Nanobot reconstruction worked quickly.

Sage was about to leave, but Anders must have sensed him standing there because the young man's eyes flickered open, took a moment to focus, then locked on the sergeant.

"Hey, Top," Anders said in a drowsy voice that indicated he was on a constant pain-management feed.

"Anders, how are you doing?" Sage stopped beside the private's bed.

"They tell me I'm doing good." Anders licked his dry lips and looked up at Sage blearily. "They also tell me you're going to get the guys who did this to me."

"I am. Want a drink?"

Anders smiled. "Yeah. Like you wouldn't believe. But it feels like I've already gone over my limit."

Sage picked up the water bulb next to the bed and held the straw so Anders could get to it. The man sipped a little and swallowed slowly, then pulled away.

"Thanks, Top."

"Sure." Sage put the water bulb aside. "Anything else you need?"

Anders shook his head and glanced away. "I can't believe I got taken by surprise like that. Stupid mistake. I was thinking there was no way anyone would try to attack the fort. I figured patrol was just a waste of time."

"Patrol is never a waste of time, soldier. We do it to stay safe and stay sharp, but no matter how thorough you are, surprises happen. You lived through this one, so that means you probably learned something. Focus on that."

"Yeah." Anders grimaced. "The thing that bothers me most is I nearly killed that girl and that kid. I was too quick on the trigger. The suit read the arrow shot as an attack, plotted the trajectory, and I came up firing instead of confirming the target. I should have held off till I knew what I was dealing with."

"You should have looked for cover. When you're attacked, you find or create a defensive position first thing. That's something you've learned. We'll work on it in training when you get back on your feet."

"Okay, Top."

"You just get back in fighting shape, soldier. That's your job right now."

"I will, Top."

Sage nodded to Anders and headed back out of the ICU. He stopped at the outer ward and checked on Jahup. The young man looked small on the hospital bed, and guilt crept in over Sage when he thought about how he'd risked Jahup's life taking him out to the Phrenorian base. He hadn't thought about it until now, but Jahup was only a couple years older than Danilo was when he'd been killed.

Captain Karl Gilbride, one of the senior medical people on post, saw Sage and walked over to join him.

"Can I have a word, Top?" Gilbride was almost as tall

as Sage. His brown hair was neatly clipped, a little long by Army regs. His face was square and handsome, and he had a rep as a lady's man.

"Of course, sir." Sage stopped and faced the man. When they'd first met, they hadn't gotten along well. Gilbride was used to doing things the way he wanted to. Since then, Gilbride had grudgingly come around and shown respect for Sage. Gilbride was a top-notch nano-surgeon with a lot of experience, a good med person to have out in the field with a unit.

"Anders is doing really well," Gilbride said. "He should be up and around in another week or ten days, once the cloned skin settles in."

"That's good to hear, sir. You people do good work here."

"Thank you, Top. I wanted to talk to you about Private Jahup." Gilbride waved to the boy in the bed.

Sage's interest sharpened. "Is something wrong, sir?"

"No, nothing like that. I've got him sedated, as you requested. The ribs have already knitted, so he's ready to get back to work if that's what you want."

After a brief consideration, Sage shook his head. "That's not what I want. Yet."

"I thought as much, given the attack last night and his relationships with the girls. I want to know how long you want me to keep him here."

"How long can you give me?"

"I can turn him into Rip Van Winkle."

Sage frowned, not knowing what Gilbride meant.

Gilbride waved a hand in dismissal. "Old Terran literary reference. I can give you a couple days if you want, no problem. Frankly, Jahup can use the downtime. That young man came in here nearly exhausted. Sleep will be a good thing."

"It shouldn't be more than a few more hours. I've got to set some things up without him being in the way."

"Just let me know." Gilbride hesitated for a moment. "I've got to ask, Top. Are we going to start seeing more wounded in here anytime soon?"

"I'm going to try to prevent that, sir. But I think we're all going to have to be prepared for things to get worse before they get better."

SIXTEEN

Colonel Halladay's Office
Fort York
2051 Hours Zulu Time

Sage entered the colonel's office after the corporal outside announced him.

Halladay returned Sage's salute and told him to have a seat.

Sage took a chair in front of the colonel's immaculate desk. The holo behind Halladay took up nearly the whole wall and showed the river that wound through the jungle where the Phrenorian base lay. Onscreen, there was no mysterious structure.

Halladay turned to face the holo. "This is the sat view of the area where you say the Phrenorian installation is."

"It's there," Sage said.

"No foul, Top. I believe you. As you can see, there is no sign of the structure."

"Satellites can be fooled, sir. That's why we send in scouts to verify intel. We didn't pick up any sign of the

Phrenorian base before Jahup and I went in there either. There are a half dozen different camo possibilities that would hide that installation from the air and space. If you want a true look at that site, you're going to have to send in specialized drones."

"Which would alert the Phrenorians that we're onto them." Halladay cursed under his breath.

Sage didn't say anything. That was the downside of the drones.

"If I were in charge of a hidden base that had just gotten discovered," Halladay said, "I would evacuate everything I had in that place and go on an immediate offensive. That sound right to you?"

"There's no other way to play it, sir. If you keep your units there, you're a sitting duck. You can't deploy them and just expect them to disappear. Going on the offensive would be the only way to handle it."

"And I'd stock that fortification with anti-aircraft weps to repel an air-based attack, as well as minefields to keep a ground attack at bay. You confirmed the existence of a minefield?"

"Yes sir. The minefield runs a half klick deep, packed tightly enough to make sure you can't get a unit or crawlers into the area without taking damage. Try that and you'll lose soldiers and vehicles. Jahup and I negotiated the minefield easily enough, but it was just two of us and we went slow. The systems are redundant. By the time you try to remove the mines, the drone patrols will have targeted you as a threat."

"We need more information about that installation." Halladay sat forward in his seat. "Since getting someone inside that base seems impossible, there's only one way to get the information we need."

"We find someone who's been inside and take that

person," Sage agreed. He'd already been thinking about that himself.

"Exactly, and Zhoh has been inside."

"That doesn't mean he's seen everything there, sir. Like I said, I didn't get the impression he was a guest."

"He'll have seen more than we have."

"Even so, Zhoh will be hard to get to."

"There's friction between Zhoh and General Rangha that we might be able to exploit." Halladay consulted his PAD and put it down next to the holo projector. An image of Zhoh formed above the projector. "I've got a buddy in a Sensitive Operations Group who's studying Phrenorian language cryptography, and who has managed to hack into some of the Phrenorian comms. I had to pull in a couple of deep favors to get this intel, so this is just between us."

"Yes sir."

"Have you ever heard the Phrenorian term *kalque*?"

Sage thought for a moment and shook his head. He'd concentrated on learning how to fight the Sting-Tails, their abilities and their unit tactics. He was sure whatever *kalque* was, it didn't have anything to do with fighting.

"It's the closest verbal approximation of the Phrenorian word we can make," Halladay said. "What *kalque* basically means is a being without a future. A living dead being. The Phrenorian culture is based on a caste system, from the primes on down to the *kalques,* and those divisions are made based on family lines, history, performance, and exoskeleton color. There are a lot of shades of differences in between, and even SOG doesn't know all of them. The Phrenorians are, according to my source, a deeply stratified community. Normally *kalque* are identified at birth, separated and streamlined straight into positions of no power. Colonel Zhoh GhiCemid was declared *kalque* months ago, busted in rank and benefits, and dumped onto Makaum to serve General Rangha."

"How did that happen?"

"We're not sure. Xenosociologists believe that the only time the Phrenorian Empire would render a being of Zhoh's stature *kalque* was if a genetic deficiency showed up, one that before had gone unnoticed. Their marriages and unions focus on improving the bloodstock."

"The way the old royalty did in ancient Terra."

"Exactly."

"That led to a lot of inbreeding. Physical deformity. Mental problems and full-blown insanity."

"The Phrenorians evidently dealt with that as well, which is one of the reasons they are so driven to keep the gene pool strong. Some of the Xenohistorians who have studied captured Phrenorian documents say that the Sting-Tails had their share of insane leaders in the past, and once a pandemic wiped out nearly eight percent of their populace in the Iaerad System a few hundred years ago because the genes were too similar. It made them all susceptible to the sickness. After that, the Phrenorian primes instituted a review for any union that was proposed and insisted that the gene pool remained varied."

"Zhoh found a female who tweaked his *chelicerae*, decided to get hitched, and got declared genetically deficient?"

"Something like that, Top. There's nothing definite about this information." Halladay tapped the PAD and an image of another Phrenorian appeared. "You didn't see this Sting-Tail this morning at that base, did you?"

Sage studied the Phrenorian. Sometimes it was hard to tell the Sting-Tails apart because they looked so similar and only subtle shifts in color, striation, and patterns marked them as unique. On the battlefield, with weapons blazing, differentiating the warriors was almost impossible. Sage had killed all that had confronted him.

This one seemed slightly smaller than Zhoh, less threatening. There were no scars. He looked pristine, like a showpiece.

"I don't think so, sir. There were a few of the Phrenorians out there, and it was dark. With the color of their exoskeletons, they blend into the dark pretty well."

"Understood. This is General Rangha, the Phrenorian in charge of the 'trade' agreement here on Makaum."

The name meant nothing to Sage. "Do we know anything about him?"

"Rangha is as close to true royalty as the Phrenorians get, I'm told," Halladay replied. "He is *yaloreng*, which translates into something like 'valued.'"

"'Valued?'"

"He had an ancestor who was recognized as a Phrenorian champion in some war, and he has the proper coloration. The *yaloreng* bloodlines are those the Phrenorians want to see continue. They keep careful track of those and make sure the descendants are placed in positions of power. The Phrenorians treasure their heroes."

"What kind of history do the SOG people have on him?"

"Not much. Rangha is a figurehead, for the most part. The Phrenorians figured Makaum for an easy win at some future point. The only reason Rangha's out here is to amass more glory for the Phrenorian Empire by being in charge when that victory rolls around. And to get more accolades for himself. Since he's *yaloreng*, the Sting-Tails want to inflate him, give their people someone to look up to."

"Sounds like he's already sitting pretty."

"He is, but Rangha has developed some interests outside of acceptable Phrenorian limits. He's likes wealth, and he's been involved in some of the black-market activity taking place onplanet, investing through fences and managing to allow shipments to be made. Rangha has pulled a small crew of like-minded Phrenorians together. It would be death for the other Sting-Tails to be found out, but I'm betting General Rangha's involvement would be overlooked or covered up."

"How did you find this out?"

"Mr. Huang."

Sage knew Huang. In addition to making noodles at his shop, Huang was a first-class independent spy who sold spicy meals and secrets. The old man was a veteran of wars out in the frontiers. In his youth, he had been a soldier, but whatever name he'd gone by had been deleted from files. Now he was Huang, the noodle maker.

"Yes. As you know, Mr. Huang has other uses," Halladay said. "He tipped me off to General Rangha's little sideline a few weeks ago, but I didn't know how to use that information until now."

"What did you do?"

"I arranged to have Mr. Huang turn the information over to Wosesa Staumar."

Sage couldn't place the name. "I don't know who that is."

"No reason you should, Top. Staumar is a civilian mover and a shaker in the Makaum trade interests, and he's also pro-Phrenorian. On top of that, he's deep into the black market onplanet."

"What makes you think Staumar will inform on Rangha?"

"Getting Rangha out of the black market will leave a void. Nature, and greed, abhors a vacuum. Staumar will happily move into that void to add to his own profit margin. He's also been trying to curry favor with Zhoh."

"Why?"

"Because when push comes to shove on this planet, you can bet Zhoh will be leading the Phrenorian warriors, not Rangha. Staumar knows that. He wants to side with a winner."

"So you're betting what? Once Zhoh finds out about the black market deals Rangha's been doing that he will inform the Phrenorian Empire?"

"I don't know, Top. That's what we'll be waiting to see. At the very least it should create some confusion and give us some breathing room while Zhoh tries to figure out what to do with that information. If we get really lucky, we might be able to find out who is among Rangha's inner hierarchy and grab one of those warriors for information about what's in that complex. Before Zhoh steps up as the new Phrenorian military leader."

"That's risky. Doing this could accelerate whatever the plans are for that base."

"We have to hope that accelerating those plans leaves some weaknesses too. If we wait till they hit their time-table, we're too far behind what's going on to do much about it."

Sage silently agreed, then he had another thought. "What does General Whitcomb say about this course of action?"

"The general doesn't know." Halladay grimaced. "If I told him we *think* the Phrenorians have a base out there, the general might jump the gun and send out a drone swarm to check it out. Or he'll kick the intel upstairs to Terran Alliance Command and let them deal with it. Which means we'll be sitting here till they figure out what they're going to do. We'll be vulnerable. I don't like either of those ideas, so until we find out exactly what the Phrenorians' plans for that installation are and can pass that information on, we're going to keep this between ourselves."

"Command will hang us both when they find out."

"Let them try. By that time I figure we'll be up to our ears in Phrenorian warriors and they'll all have more pressing concerns. I know we will." Halladay blanked the PAD and Rangha's image faded. "In the meantime, you and I have to meet with Quass Leghef to figure out our next move regarding the people who attacked our fort."

SEVENTEEN

Red Light District
Makaum Sprawl
5819 Akej (Phrenorian Prime)

Zhoh didn't like skulking. He was a Phrenorian warrior and skulking didn't suit him. He was born to walk onto a battlefield and take up arms against all opponents who had the courage to face him. Then he would destroy all who dared face him. That had always been the way of things after he had forged his *patimong*.

Tonight, though, required a more deft touch. He was capable of that as well, but he didn't like it.

Cloaked in loose-fitting clothes under the shadows cast by the moonlit night, Zhoh knew he could pass without being immediately recognized as Phrenorian. Many offworlders wore such cloaks against the incessant barrage of night insects. The wearing of the disguise chafed him and he pulled irritably at the garments with his lesser hands, keeping his primaries folded next to his body and his weapons.

Hiding himself seemed cowardly, but he knew the value of an ambush. He settled on thinking of this as a surprise attack and felt only slightly vindicated. He preferred a foe he could call out onto a battlefield, but the person he searched for tonight was not so inclined.

Mato Orayva and five other Phrenorian warriors Zhoh knew from previous campaigns, spyrl members he felt he could trust who would stand at his side, walked along the meandering plascrete road between offworlder houses.

Of them, Zhoh trusted Mato most. They had grown up together, and became warriors at the same time, after their fourth *lannig*. Mato was the son of Zhoh's mother's sister, and that bond was tighter than most on Phrenoria. Mato was a good warrior in his own right, but many officers would have been threatened by his skills, thinking that he would soon surpass them. Zhoh had no such concerns. Mato had long ago tied his fortune to that of Zhoh's, so Mato was as much interested in returning Zhoh to a position of power as Zhoh was.

Senses alert, Zhoh scanned the neighborhood around him with distaste.

Most of the Makaum people still lived in the houses they grew out of the trees and brush, but many others who had chosen to liaise with the offworlders lived in prefab buildings dropped there by corps who wanted front men to represent them with the populace. This newer part of the sprawl was constantly changing as it was added to, and it was showy with wealth and possessions.

Zhoh's own home, until it and his lands had been taken from him in his disgrace, had been small and clean, made of stone and carboweave and set next to the Eron-urn Ocean, the most ancient of the Phrenorian seas. Those lands and his home had been a place of honor, earned by the blood he had shed in the name of the Empire, by the victories of his progenitors. Skulls of conquered opponents from dozens of worlds had lined the walk leading to his door.

Angrily, Zhoh put the thoughts of that house and the dreams he'd fostered there from his mind. Sxia and her twisted genes had ended all of that for him. But some of those things might be able to be won back. He would lay his foundation for that here on Makaum, and the first head he would take would be that of General Rangha.

The being Zhoh wanted to see tonight was a Hoblei trader named Sazuma. The Hoblei were materialistic beings whose sole drive was to accumulate as much wealth as they could. Their worlds were divided up into great trading houses that sent emissaries out to buy and sell goods and companies, and they were good at it because they had so many connections. Those connections were also used to fund and supply wars, because they could transport people and weapons and credits into and out of places no one else could.

Zhoh was of mixed feelings about the information Mato had brought him. Mato was more gifted in espionage than Zhoh was, and Zhoh readily acknowledged that. As soon as Mato had landed onplanet, he'd started building up a network of informers.

Wossea Staumar, the informant for tonight's mission, was one of the Makaum trade counsel representatives. The man reminded Zhoh of a *krayari,* always snuffling around underfoot for choice bits of detritus left by others that he could use to his advantage. He was fat and focused, a being whose desire for things and power could never be quenched. But he was also not a being who would come as a warrior would: boldly and sure of himself.

No, Staumar was a *gasyg*, a sly blade, a poisoned

weapon an assassin would pull in the middle of the night to strike at a warrior from behind. Or, better yet, while the warrior was sleeping or wounded. Killing an enemy or a rival without risk was a *gasyg's* greatest desire. Normally, Zhoh did not suffer a *gasyg* to live around him, but occasionally they had their uses. Those who wielded them had to remember that, like a blood-covered *patimong,* the blade could twist with the greatest of ease at the wrong moment and cost dearly.

As Zhoh crossed the plascrete road, he wondered if Staumar's story about General Rangha's improprieties was true. Or perhaps this was only bait in a trap. Rangha himself was not so clever, but the general had advisors, warriors placed with him by the primes to ensure his success. One of Zhoh's lesser hands caressed the hilt of his *patimong* while another slid around the butt of his Kimer pistol.

Small Phrenorian drones flitted over the houses, the alleys, and the road. Their vids fed into Zhoh's HUD and he tracked the overlay constantly. Several pedestrians walked the road as well. Most of them wandered in small groups from the bars and sex clubs in the red light district, and only a few traveled alone. No lights lit the road along the housing area because they drew masses of insects that clogged the air-conditioning units.

With the sharp night vision that came with being a Phrenorian, Zhoh negotiated the road without mishap and easily read the address for the Hoblei trader. Sazuma lived on the fifth floor of the Calthea Building. All of the buildings in this block were named after Terran flowers, and the area was one of the more affluent. A nano-wafer exterior covered the plascrete walls, turning the structure into a glamorous mountain of artificial ice. According to

Staumar, the Hoblei female kept six live-in guards and rented the whole floor and roof.

The door was locked and required an access key. The building also had a top-of-the-line exterior security system and two Turbellan guards in the evening on the door.

Turbellan sec men used chems to alter their growth, turning them into muscle-bound monsters. They wore armor and carried Garond needler machine guns.

As Zhoh put a foot on the steps, one of the guards challenged him. The guard's face was broad and long. Chrome showed where added armor had been implanted in his flesh.

"I do not recognize you."

"I am a guest," Zhoh replied as he kept moving.

The guard shifted the needler up into firing position just as Mato shot him in the throat with a concealed coil-gun that short-circuited the Turbellan's brain functions. One of the other warriors did the same to the other guard.

Mato turned and put up a no-peek barrier that bent the moonslight away from the entrance. Passersby might notice some movement in the area but they wouldn't be able to tell what it was in the darkness. The no-peek didn't work except in lightless areas, and even then it couldn't fool thermographic or infrared vision.

Four of the warriors grabbed the dead guards and carried them around to the alley. The waste container creaked open and the thud of the bodies being thrown in sounded a moment later.

"The security is a Bannyad system," Mato said with a hint of admiration as he knelt to examine the lock. "There's a monk sect living on that planet that does nothing but dream up intricate puzzles for their locks."

"This system is hard to break into?" Zhoh hadn't considered that getting inside the building would be a problem. Mato was good with locks and sec systems.

"It is exceedingly hard to break through one of these."

"But you've had experience with them before."

A spicy fragrance wafted from Mato that indicated his satisfaction with himself. "Of course. Give me a moment." He pulled a small device from inside his cloak and attached it to a lock that was bigger than one of Zhoh's primary hands.

Lights flashed on the lock and Mato used his lesser hands to manipulate the device he used. Zhoh didn't know what the symbols on the lock's viewscreen meant, but he assumed Mato did because there was no hesitation in his efforts.

After dispersing the warriors accompanying them so they wouldn't stand out so much, Zhoh divided his attention between the device Mato attached to the door and the overlays provided by the sec drones zipping over the area. Five minutes passed and Zhoh knew they were in danger of drawing attention from the passing pedestrians. They could not stand there so long.

"Mato . . ."

"A moment more, *triarr*," Mato responded. *Triarr* meant "family of my family," and it was used only by close family members. It was almost a sentimental thing, something that Zhoh didn't allow from anyone but Mato. "I almost have it."

True to his word, the lock *snicked* open in one of Mato's lesser hands. As he put the lock manipulator away, he drew a Lyduc gauss pistol set to stun.

Inside the building's foyer, Zhoh stationed two of the five warriors outside the door. The sec drones would provide early warning, but the warriors would make certain the way remained clear.

Zhoh glanced at the cams watching over the foyer, which was clean and held wall holos advertising products and corps from several galaxies. The trade sector that had come down on Makaum concentrated on selling everything it could.

"We are being recorded," Zhoh said.

"It's not a problem." Mato crossed the foyer to the bank of three elevators and pressed a button. "I have a program that will eviscerate all of the security vids from five minutes before we arrived till after we leave."

Even though he knew Mato was capable of doing exactly what he said, Zhoh didn't like having to trust complex solutions. He would have rather dealt with things personally, the way he was going to deal with the Hoblei trader colluding with Rangha.

The elevator arrived with a melodic chime and the doors separated. Mato stepped inside and turned his attention to the chrome access panel by the control box. Tools filled his many lesser hands and the access panel popped off into his hands. He took out wire cutters and a solder torch and began patching in a small PAD.

"Hold the elevator for just a moment," Mato said.

Zhoh shoved a foot in front of the door and blocked it from closing.

"You have company," one of the warriors outside the building warned.

Zhoh checked his faceshield overlay and saw a squat Wedoid turning toward the building. "Let him pass."

"Yes, Captain."

"Mato . . ."

"I see him. There are other elevators."

The Wedoid strode through the doorway, paused only a moment to finish a conversation on his wristcomm, then headed for the elevator where Zhoh and his group stood. "Hold that elevator."

Zhoh didn't like Wedoids. They took up a lot of space and they smelled bad. Despite their large mass, they moved deceptively quickly. Their native planet's gravity was twice that of Makaum's, so they moved even more easily here.

The being's head massed two of Zhoh's and looked like it had been plunked down tight onto his shoulders so there was no neck. His body was a meter and a half across and only a little more than that in height. He wore business clothing, something in subtle shades of turquoise, but none of that disguised the massive muscles beneath a soft layer of fat.

The Wedoid looked at the wires and at the PAD in Mato's hands. "Is something wrong with the elevator?"

"You chose the wrong one tonight," Mato replied.

Too late, the Wedoid realized the trouble he was in. He tried to flee the elevator, but Zhoh wrapped a primary under his massive chin and dragged him back.

Partially breaking free, the Wedoid whipped around and reached in his pocket. He had nearly pulled out a Birkeland mini-coilgun, which was named for the weapon's size, not for the particle charge it produced. The pistol was meant for close defense and could take out a raging *kehund*, a noxious predator that could smash small boats on Phrenoria.

The hum of the pistol's arming phase rang inside the elevator. Zhoh seized the Wedoid's wrist before he could pull the weapon free of his pocket, trapped it there. Following through on the attack, Zhoh whipped his tail around to pierce his opponent's eye. The curved tip of his stinger missed the Wedoid's eye, but it buried in the soft

flesh at the side of his nose. Zhoh knew the nasal channel led to the brain as well, so he evacuated venom and
yanked his tail free.

The Wedoid's constitution allowed him to continue to
grapple for a time and he bore Zhoh back against the wall.
The three warriors had hold of the being by then.

"Leave him," Zhoh commanded.

When the warriors released the Wedoid and stepped
back, Zhoh thrust his right primary up against the being's arm that held him pinned to the elevator wall. The
Wedoid's grip on Zhoh's neck was not immediately life
threatening. He breathed through spiracles on his meso-
soma, not his head like a human or Wedoid.

Provided the being did not rip Zhoh's head off.

Zhoh hit the Wedoid's arm twice more, and on the last
blow he heard the being's elbow crack. By that time, the
Wedoid was losing strength as the venom shut down his
brain. Zhoh kicked his opponent's leg out from under him
and yanked, toppling the being over. The Wedoid gasped
for breath, then seized up and lay still. His eyes glazed.

Mato pressed the controls on his PAD and the elevator
doors closed. The elevator started up smoothly.

Composing himself, Zhoh adjusted his cloak and
smelled his own spicy pheromones at the success of his
battle. That scent elicited echoing spoors from his warriors and Mato, stepping them all toward bloodlust.

"I have control of the elevator," Mato said. "Our next
stop will be the fifth floor. I have also installed the software package that will erase all of the recordings of our
time here."

"Good." Zhoh drew his Kimer and turned to his warriors. "Kill the guards, but leave the Hoblei female to me."

"Yes, Captain." The warriors drew their weapons as
well.

"Do you have the layout of the fifth floor, Mato?"

"I'm uploading it now to our HUDs."

A moment later, the fifth floor blueprints overlaid Zhoh's faceshield. The elevator came up in the center of the building.

EIGHTEEN

Quass Leghef's home sat in a tiny glen near the center of what was becoming known as the "old" Makaum sprawl. With the onslaught of prefab buildings, the Terran Army fort, the various corps setting up shop, the (ta)Klar embassy, the Phrenorian embassy, and the growing assortment of offworlder shops showing up to snag profits and deals, the conservative member of the community had quickly imposed a separation of new and old.

The sprawl had grown 200 percent, and the offworlders now outnumbered the Makaum people two to one. "New" Makaum was a boom city of flashing lights, street vendors, and deals that attracted that section of the native populace who thought offworlders were bringing a new way of life.

Eventually, Sage knew, the boom would bust. If the Phrenorian War encroached on the planet, those corps and execs would pack up and Gate to their next providence. If the patents on new pharma products got too dicey, or the price of labor rose too much so that getting natural resources offplanet wasn't as profitable, they were just as gone.

Sage had seen it happen before. Planets that had been fat with credits got busted back to poverty almost overnight. They were left without technology to get into space because they hadn't had it before the arrival of the corps, and there had been no need of it as long as the offworlders were there.

Those economies went on for a time, but eventually they floundered. Then the tech went away because no one left behind could fix all the new toys. Crawlers that lacked power cells, comm devices that could no longer receive broadcast media, and energy infrastructures gave out because parts for hydroelectric engines and windmill generators couldn't be machined and were too costly to buy.

A way of life went away and the city additions built by the corps lasted only a little while, as long as renters could pay for them, and eventually became slums reclaimed by whatever environment surrounded them.

If the corps had been there too long, if they had made life too easy for the native people, too many of the old ways of living were forgotten. A generation or two were lost before they could pull out of a downward spiral. And sometimes that didn't happen.

"You with me, Top?"

Realizing that Halladay had been speaking to him, Sage replied, "Here, Colonel. Just didn't expect the Quass's house to be so small." They both wore hardsuits under spidersilk coveralls that were more like serapes and were designed to keep bugs and lizards away. The oil worked into the cloth smelled a lot like the salve Jahup had used to keep them insect-free in the jungle. They carried their rifles slung and their helmets at their hips, but wore ear-wigs to keep in touch with the eight-person sec team that surrounded them fifty meters on all sides.

"You haven't met Quass Leghef?"

"No sir."

Halladay smiled faintly. "I have. She's quite the lady, and I mean that with all due respect. She's got a lot of bark on her and doesn't take much off of anyone. That's why I'm glad she's on our side."

"Yes sir."

Sage walked beside Halladay as they entered the waist-high gate to the Quass's house. The road that led to her house was covered in *lordina,* a thick, resilient moss that handled heavy foot traffic and kept the ground fairly solid during the rainy seasons. The fence was waist-high as well, created by brambles a third of a meter thick that grew in perfectly straight lines. Spindly branches with tiny leaves wove in and out of the branches to create a solid barrier.

Flowering shrubs and trees filled the interior of the yard. The scent of dozens of sweet nectars assaulted Sage's nose and made the air almost too thick to breathe. Ripe fruit, like the *corok* melons he recognized by the small porch, hung ready for the picking.

Wide flagstones made of river rock created a forty-meter pathway that led to the two-story house under a sweeping arbor of tall trees. Four of the moons shone down through the branches. Some of the trees had been used to create the house, becoming the walls on all sides. Interlaced branches filled with moss created the peaked roof.

Sage had wondered how the houses stayed dry and Jahup had tried to explain it to him. Mostly it had to do with the absorbency of the moss and natural funnels grown from a type of hollow grass the Makaum called *fimus*. Building a house was an art, Jahup had said, and not every Makaum person could do it well. There were *stroitath* among the Makaum, people who could sense where roofs might leak, and who could influence *fimus* to grow there and control those areas. The excess water was carried away in the hollow grass and kept in rain barrels or ran into gardens.

As Sage looked at the home, he realized his mother would have loved to see something like Quass Leghef's house, but he couldn't help noticing how indefensible the structure was. A powersuit would tear through it like paper.

The house was a sanctuary, set off from the violence that surrounded it. New Makaum was a blot of light pollution in one corner of the sky, and only a few thrusters showed shuttles carrying cargo to the stars or landing with a new shipment of goods.

Sage hated the fact that he was bringing the war to Quass Leghef's door. But she had invited them there.

Halladay looked at a bell mounted by the door, hesitated, then lifted his hand to knock on the plain wood door, but it opened before his knuckles could make contact.

"Good eve, Colonel Halladay and Master Sergeant Sage. Won't you please come in? The Quass awaits you in the meeting room." The speaker was as thin as a reed and withered. He had sad, small eyes set into a bony face. Scars had grayed with time and folded into wrinkles, but a trained eye could still see them. Sage knew the man must have been a warrior at one time. His hands were scarred too. He wore simple clothing and pulled his white hair back with a black beetle shell.

"Thank you, Pekoz. Is the Quass well?" Halladay asked.

"The Quass is always well, Colonel." Pekoz smiled, but the effort didn't quite reach his eyes. "Please come this way."

Sage followed Halladay and the old man through the house. The rooms were small but neat, and held mostly chairs where people could sit and talk. The walls were polished wood and held a layer of what smelled like beeswax. Branches created the roof overhead, all of them lying in a geometric pattern that supported the bright green moss that grew thick and heavy among them.

The Quass sat in front of a comm in one of the back rooms lit by a jar containing a chemical. The windows were covered by thick drapes so the outside insects wouldn't be attracted.

Leghef was small and commanding even sitting in the chair at a desk that grew out of a wall. She wore plain spidersilk robes and not one of the ceremonial suits she usually had on in public. Some kind of soft slippers covered her feet. Her black-and-gray hair hung down to her shoulders.

The walls around the room were heavy with books and bookshelves. One of the books lay open and Sage could see the neat lines of script that covered the pages. An inkwell and a slim wooden stylus sat beside it.

"Thank you, Pekoz," the Quass said. "Please bring our guests some tea. And I would like a fresh cup myself."

"Of course, mistress. Do you have a preference?"

"Surprise me. I have made far too many decisions this day, and I have one more yet to make." The Quass turned from the comm.

Onscreen, a media piece about the Phrenorian War was airing. The drone view of the urban battle between the Phrenorians and the Terran Army whipped by at a dizzying speed. Toppled buildings lay everywhere. Powersuits fired cannons and machine guns as well as particle-beam and laser weps, according to however their battle array was set up. Ground troops sprinted between the masses of plascrete, searching for fighting positions. Jumpcopters sailed by overhead, spewing death and dropping more troops in AKTIVsuits and powersuits.

The holo blanked for a moment, leaving the screen blank, and Sage realized the media drone had taken a direct hit. A moment later, another view of the battle filled the holo with violence as a Terran powersuit took a direct hit from a sabot round that first peeled the armor open, then pureed the soldier inside, leaving traces of the person outside the armor.

The Quass waved her hand over the comm and the screen blanked again. "We've never had a war on Makaum," she said softly. "Not once. Our ship fled from a war back in our home system, whatever that was. Over the years the names have become jumbled or misinterpreted. You tend to lose the past when you are forced to deal with a hostile present."

"You don't lose all of it," Sage said before he knew he was going to speak. Halladay looked at him from the corner of his eye. Sage stopped himself. "Forgive me. I spoke out of turn."

"Actually, you didn't, Sergeant Sage," Leghef said. "My husband was an honest man. Always spoke his mind. So did my son. And—well—you know Jahup. As soon as he thinks something, he generally speaks what's on his mind."

"Yes, ma'am."

"Continue with what you were saying." The Quass watched him with avid interest.

"There's not much else to say, ma'am. I just don't think you lose everything. Maybe you've forgotten what planet you came from, but the values you have here, the way you take care of one another, has to have been learned somewhere."

"I don't know about that. The ease with which my people have picked up vices and criminal activity leads me to believe that we may have buried those things while we concentrated on survival."

Sage didn't say anything.

"My husband always said that we were lucky to have such a small world to ourselves, and to be so dependent on one another. I was Quass during those times, having taken over from my grandmother when she died. I was young. I wanted to change the world. That's the folly of youth. Always wanting to change things when everything is all well and good. He and I used to have some long arguments about that. Now I imagine him sitting here in this room saying, 'See, you have to be careful what you wish for.'" The Quass quieted for a moment. "And I would have to tell him that he was right."

Pekoz returned to the room carrying a clay teapot and cups on a tray. He set the tray down, then poured tea into each of the cups. "Would you like honey or berry juice?" he asked.

The Quass took honey, but Halladay and Sage both declined.

Sage sipped the tea and found it hot and strong.

"I'm not avoiding why you came here, Colonel," Leghef said. "I'm just gathering my thoughts." She waved at the comm. "This is the only piece of technology I have allowed into my house, and I hate it."

Halladay looked uncomfortable. "I'm sorry you feel that way, Quass Leghef, but it is a necessary evil if you're going to communicate quickly with the fort. Plus, there is an added benefit that your medical people can be quickly called."

"Oh, the medical people could be quickly called before so many people had these," the Quass said. "Every house—every house *we* make—has a bell out front. As this one does. Perhaps you saw it when you came in."

"Yes, Quass," Halladay said.

"If we had a medical emergency, someone in the house simply rang the bell. Then the neighbor along the road would ring the bell, till a line of ringing bells led our physicians to the house that needed them. The same thing occurred when we had an occasional fire, which was a seldom thing before your arrival."

Sage felt a twinge of guilt over the fire that had started when the DawnStar assassins had tried to kill Kiwanuka and him. He hadn't been able to control that, and a lot of damage had been done.

"Most of my people enjoy these things," Leghef said. "They play games on them. They see entertainment they never dreamed of. Hardly anyone goes to the town square to listen to the musicians these days. Things have changed." She paused and looked at them. "But you're not here to talk about how things have changed, or what my thoughts on that are. You're here to talk about arresting people you think attacked your fort, and possibly adding fuel to the fire of civil unrest among my people."

And just like that, Sage knew they were in the middle of it with a hostile audience.

NINETEEN

Fifth Floor
Calthea Building
Makaum Sprawl
5943 Akej (Phrenorian Prime)

When the elevator came to a stop, Mato held the doors
closed for a moment and worked on his PAD. A
moment later, he had a view of the foyer outside the
elevator.

The foyer was small but ornate, covered in cycling
holos that advertised goods and services.

"Do you have access to vid of the other rooms on this
floor?" Zhoh asked.

"No. Those run on an internal security system. I've cut
off all outgoing feeds, so no one outside these rooms can
be contacted, but it will take longer to acquire the floor's
private system. And I can't do that from here."

"Can you find out which room the Hoblei female is in?"
Zhoh asked.

"No. She's had the floor rented for months." Mato

checked his weapon. "There have been remodelers in, so I can't even guarantee that the blueprints I have shown you of this floor are the same."

That was frustrating. Before stepping into a battle zone, Zhoh at least liked to have some idea of what was waiting for him. But he was adaptable, capable of evolving. That was the core statement of *lannig*.

Zhoh held the Kimer pistol at the ready. "Open the doors."

The elevator doors slid open with a liquid hiss and the cooler atmosphere of the fifth floor blew into the compartment. The holo ads kept cycling, showing tech products, bio mods, and resorts on other worlds.

Zhoh ordered one of the warriors to stay with the elevator while another covered the stairwell in the southeast corner. He, Mato, and the third warrior would search out the premises.

Once the elevator opened, Zhoh stepped out into the foyer, then into a large room filled with comfortable furniture for many different beings. There was even a large aquarium set up for (ta)Klar that occupied a central area in the room. One of the white-furred blue aliens floated inside the tall aquarium and held a specially adapted comm unit in its hands.

The (ta)Klar glanced up as Zhoh entered the room, then froze as prey always froze in the hope that a predator would pass by if it didn't move. The (ta)Klar didn't have time to swim to the protective suit that sat on the aquarium floor, and living outside the water habitat would only extend life for minutes.

Feeling contemptuous of the being, Zhoh fired the Kimer instantly, not wanting to give the (ta)Klar the chance to warn anyone else at the other end of the comm link. The particle charge hummed shrilly as it released, then shattered the thick transplas holding the water. The beam caught the (ta)Klar in the chest and ripped the being open. The comm sank to the bottom of the aquarium as purple blood spread through the water remaining in the tank below the waterline where the hole was.

A wave of spilled water cascaded over Zhoh's feet as it rushed across the floor.

Knowing guards would attend the invasion immediately, Mato and the other warrior crouched and took cover beside large pieces of furniture.

A Dra'cerian guard peered around one of the three doorways leading out of the room. Dra'ceria was known for its hired muscle and turned out some of the best flesh-and-blood killing machines ever bred. They were lean and covered in tan- and brown-splotched fur that lay smooth and shiny. Mostly, they reminded Zhoh of Terran cats he'd seen on ships with the soundless way they could move and the quickness they possessed. Their faces were pushed in, with useless noses, but they had sharp eyes and peaked ears and a hunter's instincts.

This one had scars on his face that showed below the protective red goggles that linked him to his weapon. He held a machine pistol in both hands as he swiveled around the corner to take in the room. He locked on Zhoh and fired immediately.

Zhoh stepped to the side and fired the Kimer, blasting a hole in the wall beside the Dra'cerian's head. Solid projectiles bounced off Zhoh's exoskeleton. He knew at once that the bullets were underpowered, designed to stop an intruder in a home, but not to penetrate the walls. Plascrete from the shattered wall showered the Dra'cerian and he shook his head and roared a savage challenge.

Before the guard could set up again, Mato's coilgun delivered an electric charge that burned his face off and

fried his brain. The stench of charred flesh filled the floor
as the Dra'cerian's loose body toppled to the floor.

"What about the emergency notification systems,
Mato?" Zhoh asked as he went forward.

"They're off-line as well. No one can send for help from
this building."

Mato and the other Phrenorian warrior dropped two
more Dra'cerians who edged out of the two other doors
leading from the reception room.

Three down. Zhoh kept count, then moved that total
up to four when the warrior guarding the elevator let him
know another guard had gone down beneath his weapon.

As Zhoh walked through the rooms filled with exotic
goods from hundreds of worlds set on shelves and display cases, he cursed the extravagance. So many races
were weak, trying to hold on to things they didn't need,
wandering through life with no reason for being except
accumulation.

One of the things he'd respected about the Makaum
when he'd first arrived onplanet was that they had lived
simple lives with modest pursuits. In those days, the
Makaum had continued to gather in the town square to
trade and feast and sing. Now many of them were as bad
as the Terrans and the Hoblei and all of the others. They
filled the bars and pleasure places chasing fantasies and
momentary luxuries. Zhoh had no mercy for them now,
but they were a resource he wanted to preserve. Slave
labor was invaluable.

"Five are down," Mato said.

Zhoh tracked his warriors through the overlay and saw
that Mato was two rooms away. One Hoblei female lived
here alone with all her treasures to impress others.

He stepped into another room, this one whose walls
were covered in brocaded fabric and skins from large

creatures that he could not identify. He smelled the faint
trace of blood that hadn't been able to be removed from
the skins. Vases filled with flowers and plants and spices
sat around the room on small tables.

The Hoblei female lay on her side on a large couch in
front of a fireplace on one wall. She was mammalian,
with four breasts instead of two because Hoblei had mul-
tiple births, which explained why they spread through
space like a virus. A golden coat of fine hair covered her
curvaceous body and lay sculpted around her face.

Hoblei females were legendary lovers, and fetched high
prices as slaves for races who wanted that kind of conquest. This one wore red clothing that barely covered her
genitals. She held a glass of greenish liquid in one hand.
As Zhoh watched, a small *ingokel* surfaced in the glass
for a moment, then swam back down to join two of its fel-
lows, kicking with its tiny arms and legs.

The creature was smaller than the Hoblei female's
smallest talon and as black as space. The *ingokel* were
native to Ratorenth but had spread to a number of planets that wanted them for the narcotic pleasure they gave
when devoured whole. Some said that the *ingokel* were
intelligent because they had limited tool application,
and that eating them went against several protection-of-
species acts. Trading in them was illegal on most planets.

"I suppose you're to blame for why my comm system
has gone down?" the female asked in a low, unperturbed
voice. She spoke the trade language, which Zhoh understood. She waved her free hand at the large holo screen
covering the wall opposite the fireplace. A PAD lay on the
couch beside her.

The holo screen had frozen in mid-refreshing, showing
stocks on one side and comm channels with six people in
a two by three block on the other side.

Zhoh didn't answer her as he swept back his cloak. "You are Sazuma." She looked like the image Mato had shown him, but many of these beings all looked the same.

"You interrupted an important trade talk," Sazuma told him. "I've been negotiating this particular deal for the last three months and I had it to the point of culmination. I was set to make a fortune. A small fortune, but a fortune nonetheless."

Despite the fact that he was in her home, that nearly all of her guards were dead, and that he held a weapon on her, Zhoh couldn't smell the fear stink on her. It was possible that she was too intoxicated to feel afraid, but he thought maybe it was because the Hoblei as a species believed there was no problem they couldn't deal their way out of.

"I came to talk to you," Zhoh said.

The Hoblei female smiled and the effort looked far too predatory. "If you went to all this trouble to see me, there must be something I have that must be worth a lot to you. I don't mind making a profit, but I confess I have no idea what you have come here seeking."

"The most valuable thing in all the worlds," Zhoh answered.

Sazuma's eyes opened in mock surprise. "And what might that be?"

"Information."

Sazuma shook her head. "You'll have to find someone else for that. I trade only in goods. Information is much too dangerous because you can sell it to one person, then another person you don't know can track you down and kill you for that. I'm not interested." She drank from the glass, caught one of the *ingokel* in her tiny, sharp teeth and bit down. The small creature ruptured with a tiny shriek and a bright blossom of pale pink blood stained the

Hoblei female's teeth and lips. She swallowed, then licked the residue away with a narrow black tongue.

"You have the information I seek," Zhoh told her, "and you will give it to me."

A red haze fogged through the trader's eyes as the narcotic from the *ingokel* fired through her brain. She seemed more removed from things, but she remained cognizant. "You've stated what you want, but what do I get out of this transaction?"

"A faster death."

That caught her attention and some of the euphoria she was feeling cleared away. "I see no bargain here."

"Have you ever seen someone take days to die?"

Sazuma's pointed ears dropped and curled in submissively. "If you are going to kill me, I will not tell you what you wish to know."

"You will. Once you are broken, you will tell everything you know."

The Hoblei female drew up into a tight ball on the couch, no longer feigning disinterest. Zhoh smelled the fear in her then, and it was as thick and cloying as a thing dead for days.

Mato called over the comm. "We have searched the rest of the rooms. The remaining guard isn't here. We're coming to you."

"You are doing business with a Phrenorian general by the name of Rangha," Zhoh said.

Sazuma hesitated, then she nodded weakly. "I am. He came to me months ago. It's not often I conduct trade with a Phrenorian. Usually your kind remains so virtuous that doing any kind of illegal business is impossible."

Zhoh took some pride in that, but also felt excited as he wondered who else the Hoblei female had done business with. "What have you been doing with Rangha?"

Before she could reply, the sixth Dra'cerian slid down from his hiding spot in the chimney. Hanging upside down, framed in the fireplace, the bodyguard aimed and fired two shots. Both rounds hit Zhoh in the chest and caused him to stumble backward, but he pointed the Kimer and fired.

The particle beam blasted the Dra'cerian's head into blood and bone splinters and ruined flesh. Twitching in death spasms, the guard dropped from the chimney and landed in a loose-limbed heap in the fireplace.

Sazuma leaped from the couch and tried to run, but Zhoh caught her by the scruff of her neck with his primary and lifted her from the ground. The drink spilled from her hand and the *ingokel* that survived hopped madly on the thick carpet.

Zhoh held her in his primary so that her feet dangled centimeters from the floor. He brought his tail up and stopped the sharp point ten centimeters from her face.

"We are going to talk, and you are going to tell me all that I want to know about General Rangha. If I believe you, I will grant you a simple, painless death."

"Why can't you let me go?" she pleaded.

"As you said, information is a dangerous thing." Zhoh thrust his face into hers and shoved his *chelicerae* into her features, then released enough poison to cause her sharp-etched pain, but not enough to render her unconscious. "Now start talking. The agony only increases from this point on."

TWENTY

"Let me assure you that we're not here to make things worse for your people, Quass Leghef," Colonel Halladay said. "We're trying to bring some balance in these troubled times."

Halladay's words sounded weak even to Sage, but he didn't know any other way to state their reasons for being there. Fort York had been built on Makaum with the intention of helping the local populace. Also to potentially keep the Phrenorians at bay. But they were there to help.

"Perhaps you'd like to point out where I have erred in my summation," the Quass countered.

Halladay reddened a little. Despite all the maneuvering he was used to in the Army, this one little woman was throwing his game off. Sage was impressed, and equally grateful he wasn't the one under fire.

"Before we get to that," the Quass said, "perhaps it

might be better if we got to know each other a little more. After all, you are in my home as my guests. I would be remiss were I not to extend some courtesy."

"Yes, Quass," Halladay said, looking like he'd just been granted a stay of execution. "That sounds like a good idea."

Except that they didn't have time for playing games, Sage thought. They needed to be moving now. The people who attacked the fort could be disappearing as they spoke. Besides that, he didn't trust the old woman to lighten up. More like she had a whole minefield planned for the colonel.

"Where were you born?" Leghef asked.

The question caught Halladay by surprise. "I was born in London, Quass, but my father was an officer in the Terran Army. I grew up in a lot of places. Mostly military bases on different worlds."

"So change has always been a part of your life."

"Yes. We moved every two or three years. My mother got used to it and looked forward to decorating our new home each time we moved."

"Then you might not know what it means to put down roots." The Quass switched her attention to Sage. "What about you, Sergeant?"

"I grew up in a village, ma'am. A little place called Sombra de la Montána. The name is Spanish, a Terran language."

Interest glimmered in Leghef's eyes. "What was growing up in Sombra de la Montána like, if I may ask?" The Spanish words came out twisted but she made it through them okay.

"Life was simple there. The people hunted for food in the jungle. Game and fruits and nuts. Other things. They gardened. They built their own homes near a stream that provided fresh water."

"No technology?"

"No, ma'am. It wasn't needed and it was too expensive. Some of the people had a few things, but life was hard there. Everybody had to work to get by."

"You two came from the same world, but you lived such different lives."

Halladay let Sage answer since the Quass was focusing on him.

"Yes, ma'am, I guess so. Despite everything you might see on holo ads on the comm, Terra is not one huge world filled with technology. There are still places where people have to do a lot of manual labor just to survive."

"What did you do there in that village?"

Sage grinned a little, thinking he could deflect the question, become uninteresting. "I was a kid, ma'am. I hunted, I fished, I tried to get out of chores every time I could. But when it came time something needed to be done, I was there. My mother made sure of it."

"You must have a very good mother."

"I did, ma'am."

The Quass sat a little straighter and took a breath. "I'm sorry. I didn't intend to bring up painful memories." Her discomfort and embarrassment were small things, but they were there.

"No, ma'am. The memories are good ones. What happened in the end wasn't so good. The Colombians, people who lived south of Sombra de la Montána, were at war with Mexico, people who lived north of my village. For a long time, the war stayed away from the mountain because the country was hard and it wasn't easy to travel, which is why not many other people lived there. But one day the Colombians invaded our village and killed most of my mother's people before they could escape."

"Forgive me for asking, but is that how you lost your mother? In that attack?"

"No, ma'am. My father and I lost her to sickness a few years later. My father was a soldier. He and his group got us safely off the mountain and to the United States."

"Your father was not from the village?"

"No, ma'am. He was a soldier from the United States. He'd been assigned as part of a deep insertion team in the area. A guerilla. Someone who operates behind enemy lines."

"He met your mother there."

"Yes, ma'am. He stayed on throughout the war when he could have walked away or rotated out."

"It sounds like he loved your mother very much."

"Yes, ma'am, and that made the Colombian War even more personal to him."

"So you and the colonel both have a legacy you follow."

"I suppose that's right, ma'am."

"Your father is not an officer?"

"No, ma'am. He was a sergeant. A good soldier."

" 'Was'?"

"He died in battle against the Phrenorians only a short time after I enlisted in the Terran Army. He chose to be a soldier all his life." Sage could still see the death notification in his mind. It was permanently recorded there, as were the doctor's words about his mother's passing.

"I'm sorry for that loss as well." Leghef regarded him in quiet speculation. "You have experienced all of this, being caught in the middle of opposing forces, and losing family because of it, and now you're here to advise me to allow you to arrest some of my people, knowing the hard feelings and distrust such an action will set into motion."

"Ma'am," Sage said, wishing the Quass had never

gotten him to talking, wishing he could have remained invisible, "I think the colonel can make a better case for what we're proposing."

"You came here together, so I'm assuming you both agree on a course of action."

"Yes, ma'am, we do." Sage wasn't going to leave Halladay swinging in the wind. "Those people who attacked the fort have to be made an object lesson of so that we can continue to push for peace."

"Then I want to hear your proposal from you. Explain to me why I should allow you to arrest the people you think are responsible for the attack on your fort."

"I don't just *think* those people attacked the fort," Sage said. "Noojin identified them."

Concern flickered in the Quass's eyes. "Is she all right?" Accusation turned her words into jagged shards that bit.

"She's fine, ma'am."

"Then why didn't she come with you?"

"She feels like she betrayed her people. She's not ready to deal with that guilt yet, and I don't think she was ready to face you. I think she would have liked to speak to you before she answered my questions."

"Yes, I think she would have wanted to do that. She's young. This whole experience has been a hardship for her."

Sage didn't say anything. The Quass was also accountable for the situation Noojin had been left in, and everyone in that room knew that.

"I only have your word that Noojin has been treated well."

Sage looked at Halladay, but the colonel shook his head, leaving the discussion in Sage's hands. Feeling a little uncomfortable, Sage continued. "I can let you talk to her over the comm, ma'am. Noojin is with Sergeant

Kiwanuka. I can call the sergeant and get a connection for you."

"Is this sergeant holding Noojin prisoner?" The Quass's voice tightened and her gaze became steely.

"No, ma'am. Noojin is with Sergeant Kiwanuka for her own protection."

"From your soldiers?"

"No, ma'am. There are civilians working at the fort. We thought it was possible that some of the people behind the attack might want to keep Noojin from talking. It isn't hard to think maybe someone might have wanted to harm her."

The Quass shook her head in dismay. "This is what we have come to? That my people will now kill each other?"

"To be honest, ma'am, yes." Sage held his gaze steady on the old woman. "That's why Colonel Halladay has had soldiers placed around you all day. In case someone tried to hurt your granddaughter."

"Telilu?" The Quass glanced at Pekoz.

"Telilu is fine, Quass," Pekoz stated. "I checked on her as I was making tea. She's sleeping."

Looking a little relieved, but angry at the same time, Leghef returned her attention to Sage. "I have seen no soldiers."

"No, ma'am, you weren't supposed to. They're dressed like civilians but they're armed to the teeth. We've rotated them in and out so the same faces aren't out there all the time."

"You think the men who attacked your fort will try to attack my family?"

"The attack this morning changed things, ma'am. I know you stopped the violence this morning, but the people who did this, they'll get more and more brave the longer they get away with this. Other people will see that those attackers are unpunished and may decide they're unhappy enough to strike out at the fort too. Or at a soldier who's in the sprawl on duty or on leave."

"You could keep them at the fort."

Sage nodded. "We could, but then we wouldn't be doing the job we've been sent here to do. So far no one has been killed, but once that happens, all bets are off." He paused for a moment. "You can feel the tension ratcheting up in this sprawl. I can feel it. Since I've been on Makaum, your people have been torn about whether or not they want off-worlders here."

"Many of us would like to return to the life we knew before you offworlders found us."

"Ma'am, all due respect, but that's not a decision anyone gets to make anymore. If the Terran Army pulled out tomorrow, you people will be left to the mercy of the corps and the Phrenorians, and it won't take the Sting-Tails long to send the corps packing, then the Sting-Tails would own you."

Leghef returned his gaze full measure. "Why should I think Terrans are any better than the Phrenorians?"

Sage decided to be blunt because Quass Leghef seemed to favor that. "This conversation we're having right now, ma'am? This wouldn't be taking place if that attack had been against the Phrenorians. They would have already tracked down those people responsible for the attack, or some people they claimed were guilty of the attack, and put their heads on pikes out in front of their embassy."

Quietly, the Quass put her teacup and saucer to the side. "You have the names of the people you suspect?"

"Noojin named three men she recognized. There were more."

"*Corok* melons grow on the same vine."

"Yes, ma'am. I'm guessing if we find the three, we'll find the others soon enough."

"Tell me this: How did you get Noojin to give you those names? She can be quite stubborn."

"I just told her the truth, ma'am."

"What truth?"

"That Jahup would find out the names from her, and he would go after those men on his own. I've seen that in him."

The Quass took a long breath and let it out. "Jahup has much of his grandfather in him. As his grandmother, I knew that would be the case. And I wanted him to be protected. I wanted you to find those men without my permission if you felt it needed to be done to save Jahup from his pride. But I cannot always be a grandmother. I also must be Quass. So I wanted to hear your argument in this matter." She turned to the comm and waved a hand over it.

Immediately, several rectangles showing faces of a couple dozen Makaum men and women formed in the holo above the comm. All of people at the other end of the link listened attentively as Leghef faced them.

The Quass took a brief count. "We still represent a majority of the Quass and you have heard the facts these men have stated representing their interest in this matter. Those of you who agree that the Terran Army should have the authority to make arrests in the matter of the attack on the fort please vote now."

Sage glanced at Halladay, who shook his head, letting Sage know he hadn't known they were being recorded either. Evidently Quass Leghef was more knowledgeable about technology than she let on.

TWENTY-ONE

The Home of Quass Leghef
"Old" Makaum
2209 Hours Zulu Time

In his rectangle on the holo projection, a burly Makaum man with a shaved head and full beard looked displeased. He frowned and the scars on his face deepened. Sage recognized the warrior's scars. This man had fought for his life on several occasions. He spoke with grim authority. "Leghef, it is my opinion that we should be the one to enforce the laws."

"The attack took place on the fort, Quass Tholak," Leghef said. "As we have agreed under treaty, this places the onus of justice on the Terran Army."

Tholak slapped the table in front of him. "When are we going to start taking our lives back from the offworlders? We cannot let them continue to take everything from us. If we allow them to arrest our people . . ."

"We already allow them to arrest our people," Leghef cut in. "Whenever Makaum people are guilty of trading in drugs or weapons, or anything else that we have declared illegal, the Army takes them into custody."

"And they give those people to us," Tholak said. "That is why we now have a containment building for our people that we have never had before."

"Those people are counseled and returned to their families, Quass Tholak. Even repeat offenders are given to us."

"Except for those who are killed," Tholak replied.

Sage knew that less than a dozen Makaum people had been killed during arrests. The soldiers had been careful of the local population. More Makaum had died at the hands of offworlder criminals and other Makaum than under the guns of soldiers.

"Those people made their own choices," Leghef declared. "They were lost to us before they died."

Several others were lost who left on ships, signing on as crew or with criminal organizations. Makaum had a dwindling native population. Most of those departing were young people, and Sage knew the Makaum feared losing the future to the vices and to the freedom of space.

"What is going to happen to those who are accused of attacking the fort?" Tholak demanded. "Will they be returned to us as well?"

Leghef looked at Halladay.

"Our intent is to lock them up in the Army stockade for a time," Halladay said. "To make our point. The actual time and punishment of those men will be left up to you people. But this attack was personal. Our response needs to be the same."

"We cannot agree on this, Leghef," Tholak stated, shaking his head vehemently. "I will not condone an offworlder action in this matter. If we give them this, we are giving them all our liberties. I would sooner die." His screen blanked immediately.

A few more screens blanked out as well, leaving noticeable gaps in the original pattern.

Leghef gazed at the holo. "We still have a majority, so the vote can go forward. How many are in favor of allowing the Terran Army to go after those who attacked them?"

Answers came quickly, with only two voting no.

"Well," Leghef said, "we appear to be deadlocked, Quass Kekish. You are the only one who has yet to speak. How do you vote?"

A young man on the lower left side of the holo shot Leghef a calculated smile. He was perhaps in his midtwenties, surely the youngest member of those assembled. His black hair was neatly groomed and came to a point over his forehead, shadowing his dark eyes. His mouth was narrow and he had thin lips. His clothing was an offworlder style, sleek and expensive.

Sage tried to place the name and couldn't, but it sounded familiar.

Kekish put his hands together in front of him, obviously very much filled with his own self-worth. "As you know, Quass Leghef, since my father abdicated his place in this assembly and nominated me to take his seat, you and I have not often agreed on many things."

"No, Quass Kekish, and I didn't often agree with your father before you either."

The young man chuckled. "I am moved to vote 'no' regarding this matter, simply because you and I agree on so little. But I also know that when these arrests take place, our people are going to want to know who allowed them to happen. Perhaps the Quass assembly will have voted for it, but it is *your* name our people will remember as being the person who championed the offworlders in this matter."

Leghef said nothing, merely waited in quiet dignity.

"So I will give you your deciding vote," Kekish went on, "and I hope that it will be enough to poison your roots."

"Thank you for your consideration, Quass Kekish," Leghef said in a tone that was still pleasant. "Thank you all, and I will give you information regarding this matter as I receive it." She waved her hand over the comm and the holo blanked. She leaned back in her chair. "I do detest that yipping little *ageew* and his self-important airs." She let out a breath. "But he is of his vine as well. His father is Roddarsay, one of the wealthiest men in Makaum."

That was a name that Sage remembered. Roddarsay was one of the first Makaum to start dealing with the corps and had secured a fortune for himself by licensing specialized healing plants he'd hybridized. According to the intel Sage had read, the man had already been wealthy before the deals with the corps.

"I know who he is," Halladay said. "I've had some dealings with him."

"Then you know how difficult Roddarsay can be."

"I do."

"There are days I think Roddarsay put Kekish on the Quass solely to torment me. Then I see how much Kekish offends others and I know he's not my burden alone to bear." Leghef sat up straighter. "The last I heard from my grandson, he was with you, Sergeant, so where is Jahup now?"

"Back at the fort, ma'am," Sage answered. "I had the doctor give him something to help him sleep till we figured out what we were going to do about this. Frankly, I didn't want him involved in this until we'd decided on a course of action. Having him run loose could have complicated matters."

"I agree. As you have stated, he would have gotten the

names from Noojin and the present situation would have grown worse."

"He needed the rest anyway."

"You look like you could use some rest yourself, Sergeant."

"Soon, ma'am. Soon as I can. Once this is taken care of."

"There is one thing that I ask."

"If I can, ma'am."

"Jahup has been assigned to you in his expertise as a scout. Take him with you when you arrest these men. That way people will know that he is there because the Quass has allowed these arrests to take place. And it will satisfy his need to punish those who tried to hurt his sister and Noojin."

Sage looked at Halladay.

Halladay nodded.

"Yes, ma'am."

"Can you look out for him while you're doing this?"

"I look out for all of my people, ma'am."

"This thing is best done quickly. I will deal with the repercussions from the people as best as I can, but now that the other members of the Quass know what's going to happen, news will spread."

"Thank you, ma'am." Sage stood.

The Quass stood as well and searched him with her eyes. She looked tired, but compassion sounded in her voice. "I have heard the sadness in your voice when you talked of your lost village and lost parents, Sergeant. These are terrible losses to bear. But I would like to offer you this, if I may."

She reached to one of the bookshelves and took down a bracelet made of purple and white wood that swirled in a complex pattern, weaving and separating. A silver medallion on the bracelet's front held a single bright orange seed that had been carefully worked into the wood so that it was level with the rest of the surface.

"Ma'am, I can't accept a gift."

"It's not a gift. It is a symbol of my authority and you will take it. Many people in Makaum will recognize this piece and pay more attention to you because they will know where you got it." Leghef took Sage's big hand and slid the bracelet over it, not stopping till the bracelet bottomed out against the AKTIVsuit's sleeve on his wrist. Her hands were unexpectedly strong and callous.

Sage was surprised the ornament fit because he had big hands and thick wrists. The bracelet stood out against his dark skin.

"That was my husband's," Leghef said. "It's called a *draorm*, which translates in your language, I believe, into 'seed of my seed.' Each *draorm* is unique, and none may be copied. They are made from different woods, from the heart of a mighty tree, and then carved in a single piece. Every Makaum parent makes one for sons or daughters on our Counting Day, when a child is declared an adult and chooses his or her vocation to serve our people. My husband's father gave this to him."

"Ma'am, I really can't take something this personal—" Sage started to slip the bracelet off.

"No." Leghef laid her hand on Sage's wrist, halting his efforts. "Vergit, my husband, would want you to have this. He would have seen the sadness in you too, and he would have seen the strength you carry with you. This wasn't made to gather dust on a shelf, Sergeant. It was made to adorn the wrist of a man who helped us stay safe and strong and true to ourselves. I did not allow this to be buried with my husband because I could not let all of him go. I'd thought I was wrong to do that. I'd thought I was being selfish. But now I see that there was a reason for me to hold it back."

"Ma'am—"

Tears glimmered in her eyes as she patted his hand and he relaxed, knowing he couldn't refuse the gift.

"Among our people, the *draorm* is believed to bring good luck, and to be a constant reminder that we are all seeds. When we landed on this planet all those generations ago, we had to move to elude predators, to find lands that we could tame, to find a place where we might anchor ourselves and flourish in spite of all that stood against us. We did. Each child is a seed as well, a part nature has promised us to spread and change and become more than we are. You too are a seed, blown from your Sombra de la Montána to our world. So take the luck the *draorm* gives you."

"Yes, ma'am. Thank you."

Quass Leghef released Sage's hand and he stepped back. Pekoz appeared and guided them back to the door. Sage respected the woman's determination to take care of her people, but he couldn't help wondering if she'd feel so certain of the future if she knew about the Phrenorian base.

Outside the home, he and Halladay pulled their helmets on, opened their comms, and set about organizing the raid they had planned.

TWENTY-TWO

We have a problem," Kiwanuka announced over Sage's comm.

Sage didn't break stride as he entered the med center. Ahead of him, Jahup was sitting on the edge of his bed and looking a little groggy. "We're about to do an op. We don't have time for problems."

"Noojin is insisting on going along on the raid."

"No. Bad idea."

"We're going to have to tranq her to get her to stay here. Or else have a sec team sit on her while we're gone."

"Either one of those is fine to me. Choose one."

"I think she needs to go, Sage," Kiwanuka said.

"I don't."

Kiwanuka's voice sharpened a little. "You're leading this op, Top, so you hold rank here, but I am acting in an advisory capacity."

"Wait one." Sage stopped beside Jahup as Gilbride ran a med unit over him. "How are you feeling?"

"Woozy. My head feels thick." Jahup narrowed his eyes and raised his voice accusingly. "The doctor told me you were the one who decided to keep me asleep till now."

"He was," Gilbride said as he slipped the bioscanner into a thigh pouch on his medsuit.

"I did," Sage admitted. "There was nothing you could do till now."

"I could have been talking to Noojin and finding out who those people were that nearly killed her."

"That's already done."

Jahup stared at Sage in disbelief. "She *told* you?"

"Yes. I need you suited up in the next five minutes if you're going."

"I'm not going anywhere until I talk to Noojin."

"That would be fine with me, except your grandmother wants you there when we arrest the people who attacked the fort. And she wasn't asking as your grandmother. She was giving orders as the Quass."

"My grandmother?"

"Soldier, you're a day late and a credit short. You need to pick up the pace if you're coming with me." Sage turned to Gilbride. "I need the fog out of his head."

Gilbride nodded. "I thought you were going to say that." He reached into his thigh pocket and took out a compressed air delivery hypo, dialed in a med and measurement, then pressed the device to Jahup's naked arm.

"Ouch! *Rhaiz*! Warn me before you do that."

"Trust me," Gilbride said as he put the device back in his pocket, "it's a lot better if you *don't* know it's coming." He took out a small flash and shined it into the boy's eyes. "He's perking up now. He'll be good to go by the time you get him suited. The armor will adjust him from there."

"Follow me," Sage told Jahup.

"I'm naked! Where are my clothes?"

"Getting cleaned," Gilbride said. He looked at Sage and offered his hand. "Good luck out there, Top."

Sage nodded.

"I'm not walking through the fort naked," Jahup protested.

Sage motioned to a passing female medtech. "I need to borrow your smock."

The medtech slipped out of her smock. Sage took it, said thank you, and handed it to Jahup, who grabbed it.

The scout shrugged into the garment and had to hurry to catch up with Sage. "We're going after the people who attacked Telilu and Noojin?"

"Yes."

"Who is it?"

Sage handed Jahup his PAD and kept walking. His faceshield showed the preparations being made by the small, handpicked team he had selected.

"I know these people." Jahup sounded confused and disbelieving at the same time.

"Then identifying them will be easier," Sage said. He went back to Kiwanuka on the comm, looking at her face on the overlay as he made his way down the corridor toward the rendezvous point. Now that things were in motion, it wouldn't take long for word to spread around the fort. The soldiers would know, and so would the civilian workers. "Make your case."

"Noojin has earned the right to go with us on this," Kiwanuka said. "She was nearly killed by these people. She's had to deal with snitching out her people. And she had you bullying her into giving up those names."

Sage felt a little irritation at the last accusation. "I didn't bully her. I gave her a choice."

"You put her in a position of emotional distress."

"She was already there," Sage argued. "I just pointed it out."

"You boxed her in and gave her no choice to do anything except what you wanted her to do. That wasn't fair."

Sage took a breath and reminded himself that everyone needed to be calm before an op like this. "Sergeant Kiwanuka, we're not here to be fair. We're here to be soldiers."

"So is Noojin. She's been training just like the rest of the Makaum reserve you set up. She wants to participate in tonight's op."

"She's too involved." Sage had worked with Noojin. She wasn't as driven as Jahup, but she showed some natural ability in the hardsuit. The HUD interface was more difficult for her, but the physical capacity was there.

"I would make that same argument about Jahup."

And you would probably be right. Sage looked at the boy walking at his side. Jahup walked with purpose now that the stim had cleared his mind of the leftover sleep meds.

"Jahup is going along at the insistence of Quass Leghef," Sage said.

"To take the edge off of his feelings. Sure, I get that. But if anyone needs some get-back here, it's Noojin. You made her feel helpless. And she probably saved the lives of those soldiers this morning."

And that was another truth. Kiwanuka wasn't pulling any punches. Sage respected that about the woman. He would have done the same thing. He'd known the two of them might bond while Kiwanuka was watching over Noojin.

The girl wasn't from a world where litigators handled things. She was from Makaum, where people took care of their own needs. She did need to come if she wanted to. Sometimes he outsmarted himself.

"How is she in an AKTIVsuit?" Sage asked. "I haven't seen her latest drills."

"The reports are on your PAD," Kiwanuka replied. "She's good."

"She'll be your responsibility, Sergeant."

"That's fine with me. She's spent more time in the jungle fighting for her life than most of the soldiers we have here. I don't doubt that if things go sideways she'll stick. She managed to warn those soldiers this morning, and get herself and Jahup's little sister to safety before we killed her."

"You've made your case."

"I just wanted to make certain we were clear."

"Crystal," Sage said. "Get her suited up and meet us out front. If you're late, we're leaving without you."

"We're already suited up and waiting for you, Top."

Of course you are.

Fort York
2352 Hours Zulu Time

Eight soldiers, including Kiwanuka and Noojin, stood out in front of the motor pool when Sage arrived with Jahup. Noojin's hardsuit was the smallest among them. She stood to one side with her arms crossed, her Roley hanging over one shoulder and a Birkeland shoved into the hip holster. Sage couldn't see through the faceshield, but he could recognize by her body language that she was angry.

Beside Sage, Jahup was gesturing forcefully with one hand. Knowing what was going on, Sage overrode the private comm link between the two Makaum reserves.

"—should have told me," Jahup was saying at the same time Noojin was saying, "—same way you could have told me where you went with your *lobufa* when you left the fort."

Sage couldn't remember exactly, but he thought *lobufa* was a crush or a new love.

"I told you," Jahup argued, "I was under orders to—"

"I was being held in an 'interview' room," Noojin responded.

"Enough," Sage ordered. "This stops now or you're both staying here. Do you read me?"

"Yes, Top," Jahup said.

"Yes," Noojin answered.

Neither reply was heartfelt, but Sage wasn't going to put up with distractions. "Those people this morning meant business. You're wearing hardsuits tonight. Everyone is going to think you're one of us, and they aren't going to hesitate about shooting you if that's where this goes."

Sage climbed into the passenger seat of one of the crawlers. The vehicle had six wheels and comfortably sat six passengers with full gear on. It had armor all the way around, bulletproof and beamproof windows, and a pop-up mini-turret particle-charge cannon. They were designed for fast-strike situations.

Jahup and Noojin stopped beside Sage's crawler for just a moment. Jahup plastered a stick-on replica of the Makaum flag onto Noojin's back. The red flag featured an *ypheynte*, an insect built along the lines of a Terran dragonfly, over a green disk that represented Makaum and the Quass. The *ypheynte's* segmented wings glistened like jewels.

Sage had never figured out why the *ypheynte* was so important to the Makaum people.

Noojin turned around to put one of the flags on Jahup's back.

"Those are going to make you stick out," Sage said.

"You need us to be identified," Jahup said. "Otherwise the people we meet tonight will think it's just the Army taking the ambushers down. You don't want them to think that."

"Many of our people want peace," Noojin added. "They need to know that peace can still exist." She pointed to symbols in the upper right corner of the flag. "That is Jahup's name, and it lists him as a hunter. They will know us."

Kiwanuka cut in on a private comm channel. "They're right, Top. With them accompanying us and easily identifiable, the innocents may get out of the way faster."

Jahup joined Sage in the seat that had been left in that crawler while Noojin joined Kiwanuka.

Sage figured they were all right about the situation and identification, but he couldn't help knowing that unique look might come back around to bite them. There was a reason soldiers all dressed the same, and it wasn't just so they could identify each other. It was also so they looked the same to opposition.

"Colonel Halladay," Sage called over the comm.

"Here, Top." Halladay sounded a little anxious, and part of that was because he'd guaranteed General Whitcomb there would be no fallout. Sage had gathered from Halladay's attitude after talking to the general that Whitcomb wasn't a big supporter of the operation. Still, the Quass had "requested" intervention, and that had gone through channels as well.

"We are go," Sage said.

"Then roll. Blue Jay Twelve and Blue Jay Fourteen are with you."

At the other end of the fort, two fully armed jumpcopters lit up their drives and ascended into the dark sky, standing out only briefly against the largest moon before rising into the clouds.

"Roger that, Top," a woman's voice said. The comm link confirmed her as one of the jumpcopter pilots. "This is Blue Jay Twelve, and we'll be standing by."

"We appreciate the support, Blue Jay Twelve." Sage pointed toward the gates and the crawler pilot sped into motion. Now that they were moving, some of the tension that Sage felt started to drain away.

TWENTY-THREE

Tanasam's House of Luck!
Makaum Sprawl
6019 Akej (Phrenorian Prime)

In addition to the large casino that had set up shop on Makaum, smaller clubs had been established as well. These were designed for the criminals because they had money to spend. Some of the proprietors of the big casinos owned dives too, in an effort to get all the creds they could.

Some of those dives were merely fronts for other businesses.

Zhoh walked in the shadows that lay across the narrow, rutted dirt road. The roads in Old Makaum neighborhoods were covered with moss, though many of the downtown areas had plascrete or were now worn down to hard-packed earth.

This road had been put in by offworlders too cheap to provide either a covering or improvement. Every time the rains came, more of the road washed away. Even now sewage drained down open ditches to great ponds that had been dug into low spots in the surrounding terrain. Not even Makaum's voracious jungle tried to reclaim the area.

The passersby wandered in twos or threes and wore cast-off clothing and ragged bits of cloth. Most of them were offworlders who had gotten trapped, either by a vice or by bad luck, on the planet, or they were beings who operated much as the *krayari* did, picking up enough bits and pieces of garbage to keep them going. Occasionally they would attack a being smaller or weaker or alone and take what they wanted. Some of them begged for food and credits and medicine. Both genders sold themselves to get whatever fix they needed.

A few of them were Makaum.

Zhoh stared at the low-tech sign that hung in front of Tanasam's House of Luck! The identification was an icon of a blue robot from *Ytasi*, a holo game that consisted of combat between two robotic armies. Players and onlookers wagered on the turn-by-turn play of the game.

Vines and shrubs scaled the casino's earthen walls. Construction cost of the structure had been minimal. Whoever had built it had simply cut chunks of earth with a vibro-shovel, stood them up, and chem-sealed the surface with a thin layer of plascrete to make it more durable. Most of the buildings along the road were the same, but some of them were merely large tents made of a variety of materials.

A being wrapped in rags reached from one of the narrow alleys and grabbed Mato's ankle. It was so shrouded in cloth and so disease-ridden that Zhoh could not determine the gender. The stench was so bad that even that made determination impossible.

It pleaded in a raspy voice and looked up at him with its one good eye.

Mato stopped, looked around, and reached down for a broken branch almost two meters in length and at least five centimeters thick. With an economy of movement, he rammed the branch through the being's head, putting it out of its misery. It only squeaked a little, shivered, and was still.

Still using the branch, Mato shoved the body deeper into the alley, withdrew the makeshift weapon, and tossed it into the darkness as well. He cursed as he cleaned his exoskeleton with a handful of dirt.

"Someone should go through here and eradicate these worthless beings," Mato snarled. "They suck up resources and do nothing to give back to anyone. They don't even make worthwhile slaves. You can't teach them anything."

As they continued forward, two other beings dressed in rags quickly drew back into the shadows away from Mato.

"They can be taught," Zhoh commented. "With just one lesson, you have taught them to fear you."

"That is something that should not have to be taught. I am Phrenorian." Mato slid a hand over his Kimer pistol. "I have to wonder, *triarr*, if the Hoblei woman has tried to send us to our doom by giving us the name of this place."

"You are concerned?"

"Of pestilence and plague, yes. These beings can be carrying any number of things."

"Disease is not a problem for us. We are too different from these."

"I hope so. Still, the sooner we are gone from this place, the happier I will be."

"It won't be long." Zhoh stopped under the casino's sign and peered at the casino.

The carbo-alloy door hung from simple hinges and opened easily. The sonics inside that were there to keep the local wildlife out were turned on so high that Zhoh felt uncomfortable entering the building. His insides shook and shivered as he continued through the door, and a pair of small lizards raced across the floor. Zhoh had barely enough room to stand under the low ceiling.

Small flocks of insects hovered around the chem-candles that hung on the wall and from the split logs that supported the roof that had been made the same way as the walls. The plascrete fixative that caked the walls, ceiling, and floor glistened in places and looked dull in others. Many branches and shrubs had torn through the walls and had been hacked off by sharp instruments. Other growth had small leaves that showed they'd come through recently.

Tables scattered around the room were covered with card games, dice games, and holo projectors. Stacks of chips stood on a few of the tables and bright blue and red robots battled each other in games of *Ytasi*. The crowd noise brayed loudly inside the room. Human, humanoid, and other beings celebrated or wailed over the way the cards fell or the dice rolled or the combat sequences in *Ytasi* worked out.

The stink that lay over the casino was oppressive, filled with the thick odor of human and humanoid sweat, smoke from various plant and chem products that provided hallucinogens, and alcohol.

Zhoh was certain he had been in worse places on other planets, but he could not remember at the moment where that might have been. The players and guests of the establishment took him in, as well as Mato and the three warriors who accompanied them. Two other warriors stood outside the casino to assure a way out when the time came.

Scanning the room, Zhoh spotted the being he was looking for at one of the *Ytasi* tables. A large group had gathered there, and that was where most of the cheers and curses flew from.

Erque Ettor sat against the back wall of the building in the corner. He was from one of the Vorough clans, gypsies who hauled cargo from planet to planet. Some of them worked Makaum, hauling oxygen and water to miners working the asteroid belt out near Lodestone.

Ettor was a tall, skinny being with pale white skin and arms and legs that looked too long and too frail. His clothing colors reflected those of his clan, bright and colorful and in layers. Voroughans were known as gluttons and loved to eat. Since they lived in space and generally didn't spend any time in anything more than .3 gravity, none of them could afford to put on weight because their muscles and bones wouldn't support them on a planet with a standard gravity. Makaum was .8 gravity, so being onplanet had to be painful for the being.

Of course, Ettor was dirtside to make a profit, and part of those profits was funneling into General Rangha's accounts.

Zhoh crossed the room and beings stepped back from him, giving him room. As he neared the table, the final battle started. Robot warriors sped across the holo battlefield and went to pieces when hit by missiles, sniper fire, and land mines.

Ettor's opponent was a scruffy human with long hair and a beard. He wore an old Rodine Corp jacket and the patches indicated he worked on shuttle engines. He was missing a thumb and two fingers on his left hand, and the left side of his face was a mass of burn scarring that pulled at the corner of his mouth.

When the last of the blue robots flew into pieces, the human cursed loudly and kicked the table.

"Don't be a sore loser, Bill," Ettor said while laughing

at the other being's expense. "You can work off your debt by fixing my shuttle engines."

The human got up from the table and walked to the bar. "Stand me a beer, Erque. You've got all my credits."

Ettor called for the bartender's attention and confirmed the order. He locked his pale silver eyes on Zhoh. "Do you fancy a game?"

"I do." Zhoh sat in the chair on the other side of the holo table. Those beings closest to him backed away, but that might have been because of Mato's presence as well. The other three Phrenorian warriors spread out around the room.

"It will cost you a hundred credits to play me."

The stakes were more than the last player had had showing on the table. Zhoh took a credstick from his Kimer pistol holster and slotted it in the table.

Ettor waved a hand through the holo field and the robot warrior pieces lit up on the screen. "Did you bring your own cheering section, *doqua*?" The term was Voroughan clanspeak and loosely translated to "friend."

"I did."

"You're the challenger, so I get to pick the armament." Ettor made his selection quickly and a stockpile of bows and arrows, swords, and spears showed up on the holo. There was enough of each weapon to arm each warrior. "You pick the terrain."

Zhoh swept a primary through the holo and went through the menu of available terrains. Mountainous country, swampland, and deserts awaited selection. Zhoh selected an urban area with tall, closely packed buildings.

The computer designated the engagement area, limiting it to a few blocks.

Ettor grinned. "Not many people would pick an urban area with archaic weapons like these."

"I'm fine with blades and bows," Zhoh replied as Ettor's

small army disappeared from the screen. He quickly assembled his own army and placed them in the buildings and on the street.

"I didn't know the Phrenorian military ever fought with bows." Ettor took a sip from the bottle that sat at his left elbow.

"I have trained to fight with every weapon I have ever encountered." Zhoh waited, and in his 360-degree vision, two of the beings standing behind him made small signs to Ettor, who gave no indication that he had seen them, though Zhoh knew the being had.

"This should be interesting then." Ettor waved a hand through the holo again and part of the battlefield stood revealed. The first turn went to him. Three of his robots armed with bows shot one of Zhoh's captains, which automatically caused a penalty for Zhoh's team.

"I've done most of my fighting in urban areas," Zhoh said. "I've never lost."

Ettor smiled. "Maybe your luck will change." Another battery of robot archers took out another of Zhoh's captains.

"The game could have been a true challenge," Zhoh said. "I like to play. But I don't like a cheater."

Ettor frowned. "I'd watch what you say, *doqua*. I'm not just a player in this bar. I own this place."

Zhoh moved his primary toward the screen, as if he were going to make an adjustment to his pieces, but his lesser hand stole down to free the Kimer from its holster. Aiming on the fly, he shot the two beings standing behind Ettor because both of them doubtlessly had weapons to protect their boss.

Before those bodies could slide down to the floor, Mato and the two other warriors had opened fire as well. Mato blasted both of the beings who had signaled Ettor.

Zhoh stood and shot the being to his left as he drew his *patimong*. The blade sliced the air, then whipped through the segmented thorax of the Gaedghan standing beside the table to the right just as she freed her particle beamer. She fell in pieces.

Ettor got out of his seat, but Zhoh pinned him to the wall between his dead guards by holding the *patimong* to his throat. When he looked around, Zhoh saw that everyone else in the casino was dead.

"What do you want?" Ettor asked. "I don't even know you."

"You've been doing business with a Hoblei female named Sazuma," Zhoh said.

"Yes."

"I want you to tell me about the cargo you recently secured for her. A shipment of weapons." According to what Sazuma had said, Rangha had put a lot of his credits into a weapons shipment, intending to turn a profit on them by selling them to pro-Phrenorian Makaum people who wanted to arm themselves.

Since the weapons had been black-market stock robbed from the Pagor System by looters before it fell to the Phrenorians, they had been purchased cheaply enough through the Hoblei female. On Makaum, the weapons would sell for four and five times as much as he had given for them. The Hoblei female had taken a cut of the action and never had to invest a single credit.

Ettor, with his connections among his clansfolk, had arranged the transportation of the weapons to Makaum.

The Voroughan didn't look happy as he considered his options.

Zhoh thrust the *patimong* into Ettor's body, purposefully missing vital organs. Ettor stumbled and would have gone down when his weak muscles betrayed him. Zhoh grabbed the being with his free primary and pressed him back against the bloodstained wall. He left the *patimong* in his side.

"Okay," Ettor gasped. "Okay. I brought the weapons down, but I don't have them."

"Where are they?"

"In the old market square. In a unit in Cheapdock. Sazuma arranged for the weapons to be sold to a Makaum man named Roddarsay."

"Tell me how to find the unit," Zhoh ordered.

Once Ettor had given up the location of the weapons cache, Zhoh quickly drew the *patimong* from the Voroughan and slammed it back though the being's heart. Ettor gave a last cry of pain just before life left him.

Zhoh paused long enough to clean his sword on the dead being's colorful clothing, then gazed around the casino. He approached the bar and fired a particle-beam blast into the rows of bottles behind the wooden counter. The alcohol spread quickly as he walked toward the door. Stopping at the entrance, he nodded to Mato, who took out a laser weapon and fired into the pooling alcohol.

Soft blue and yellow flames manifested with a *whumpf* and ran back toward the bar, pushing heat back over Zhoh.

"Now that you have this information," Mato said, "what do you plan to do with it?"

"I'm going to find evidence of Rangha's profiteering and I'm going to prove him unfit to lead this command," Zhoh said. "Then we're going to take this planet."

TWENTY-FOUR

No matter how well planned, an op never ran smoothly after encountering the enemy. Sage reminded himself of that as the crawlers sped through the dark streets of "New" Makaum. He focused on the plan and on the options they had, and hoped for a good result. He had calculated for everything he and Kiwanuka could think of, given what they knew about the site, and he had a good team assembled. Still, once events were in action, things didn't always go the way they were supposed to.

The magnetic drives of the vehicles were silent, but the mil-spec crawlers drew attention from the few people out braving the insects that leeched blood or feasted on flesh. The offworlders scattered first, knowing that anyone in the red light zone was fair game for the peacekeepers. The Makaum natives carousing a walk on the wild side were a second slower, but picked up the pace.

According to Noojin's intel, and that was corroborated by Jahup, the three men she had recognized from the ambush all frequented the same offworlder bars. Before the arrival of the corps, the Makaum populace usually gathered at people's homes or around the well house in the town square. But the corps had dropped in plascrete rectangles with integrated plumbing, heat, air, and electricity generated by solar power and provided those services in exchange for the right to mine and for rights to biological products grown onplanet. The bars were just a sideline for the corps to recoup a few credits, provide entertainment for the imported labor, and spy on the local populace.

Several of the bars had garish color schemes, patterns and images, infused by nano-wiring that ran through the plascrete. Zorg's Weeping Onion was a Lemylian bar that specialized in high-octane drinks because it took a lot of alcohol to incapacitate a Lemylian. The intel packet indicated that the Lemylians had set up moonshine stills outside the sprawl to supplement their liquor stores.

Lemyli was a poor world, harsh and unpredictable due to solar flares and high winds. The people had never achieved a technology that launched them into space, but their planet was rich in iron ore that was needed for the construction of space stations and starships, and it had been located on a major Gate path that had been laid in to take advantage of neighboring systems.

For years, the cheap labor pool onplanet had been a major draw as well, but several of the Lemylians had chosen to become steelworkers in space as well as cargo handlers on corp docks on other worlds when the mining boom waned. Several areas on Lemyli were now biohazards and the Terran Alliance hadn't been able to make the corps provide restitution in any form. Industry there had slowed and only corp outliers dug for the dregs of profits left there.

Zorg's Weeping Onion featured silhouettes of exotic dancers shimmering across the front wall of the building. There were at least a dozen different species in the mix, limned in emerald green, red, violet, and gold. Music blared from an exterior aud system, but it warred with the music of other bars along the same road.

Sage had the crawlers park along the next road a block over from the bar. People who had been standing under the awnings in front of the buildings started walking away. Part of the Terran Army's service contract with the Makaum people included policing the red light district. The Makaum had never needed personnel to handle the rough trade, and they weren't equipped to combat the weapons the offworlders carried in, or the hostilities that broke out when sex, drink, or drugs were involved.

One of the most frequently violated rules in the red light district concerned the carrying of weapons. Sec men and mercs carried all the time and were licensed to do so, but most of the offworld clientele in the area did too, illegally. The Makaum that ventured here these days tended to arm themselves.

Sage pulled up a history of the times the Terran Army had been involved in businesses along the nearby roads. This was a high-incident neighborhood, filled with violence and the occasional murder. Over the past three months, four Terran Army soldiers had sustained serious injuries during peacekeeping calls.

"Dangerous place," Sage commented to Kiwanuka over a private comm.

"It is."

"You've been inside the Onion before." Sage had

picked that detail out of the reports that flashed across his faceshield.

"Twice," Kiwanuka said. "Last time was a little over a week before you arrived."

"The blueprints we have are solid?"

"They were the last time I was here."

Sage flicked through the scans he'd pulled up. Zorg's Weeping Onion had three exits, the double doors in the front and two doors in the back that led out to an alley. He assigned four of his team to the alley and they peeled off from the group, double-timing through the neon-lit shadows.

"There's also the hidden crawlspace behind the bar," Kiwanuka said. "That wasn't discovered until my second call out here. The bartender disappeared and I knew I hadn't lost him in the confusion. It took me a while to find the door in the floor."

"A bug-out tunnel?"

"Yes. Like you noticed, the bar deals with the blue-collar crowd. Some of the regulars come for a beer and to watch a fight, but they sell weapons under the table to the right clientele."

Sage knew the type of bar. He'd been in his first back in Juarez while in boot in Texas. His father had already spaced to fight the Phrenorian War and there hadn't been anyone to go home to. The weekend pass had turned into a whirlwind of violence and narrow escapes. "Where does the tunnel go?"

"Building to the east. It's a brothel owned by the same people who own the bar."

"We're not here for the bartender. Just make sure no one we're looking for goes down the rabbit hole."

"Copy that. As soon as we're inside, Noojin and I will cover the bar."

"You're sure she's going to be okay?" Sage was still undecided as to what he thought would happen when Noojin saw the men she had identified.

"She's solid, Top." Kiwanuka used her sergeant's voice, the one with the tone that ended all questioning.

Sage hoped Noojin was ready and calm, then he put that thought out of his head and focused on the op as he closed on the bar's double doors. Taking a room was all about concentration and reacting quickly, getting ahead of whatever play was made by the men they were there to apprehend.

A Lemylian male stood sec at the door. Like all of his kind, he was mostly shoulders and chest, and the rest of his body tapered down to legs ridged with muscle. His features were narrow and pointed, his jaws wider than his forehead, and his eyes shone like crystal-blue gems. He wore a reinforced combat helmet and lightweight armor and had a Rakan tranq pistol holstered on his hip. A shokton hung by a sling from his left wrist. Sage was sure the sec man carried a knife. Lemylians set a lot of store by knives.

"Terran Army business," Sage said. "You buying in or stepping off?"

"Stepping off," the Lemylian said in a deep voice. His right hand slid up to button at the waistline of his armored jacket. He started to walk away, but Sage caught the Lemylian's hand and stopped him from touching the button.

"We'll announce ourselves," Sage said. He pulsed a degaussing charge through his glove that rendered the electronics in the alert button inert.

"Sure." The Lemylian nodded and moved away when Sage released him. "I get paid to take out drunks, not stand up to the Army."

Sage pushed through the doors and stepped into the bar.

The place covered a lot of square footage and was much bigger inside than the exterior advertised. Whirling, kaleidoscopic music from spinning broadcasting drones hammered Sage's hearing till the helmet filtered them out. Lights swept the smoke-drenched walls in neon rainbow hues. Dancers collided out on the dance floor, some of them weaving drunkenly while others battered each other in hyperkinetic oscillations, driven wild by drug-fueled abandon.

Lemylians partied hard, and there wasn't much in the way of alcohol or stims that could harm them. Overdosing wasn't a problem, with their enhanced constitutions, but they could get a full-on crazy going.

As he moved through the crowd, which parted reluctantly before him, Sage pulled Noojin's vid feed into his HUD and overlaid to his right. Managing two feeds in close proximity was difficult for him and started a headache at the back of his skull.

Your stress levels have risen. Do you wish a stim to be administered? the suit's near-AI asked.

"No." Sage kept circling.

The bar occupied the wall to the left that abutted the brothel next door. The Lemylian bartender noticed the Terran Army and Sage's suit picked up the recording equipment that suddenly flared to life at either corner of the room on that wall.

"You've picked that up?" Kiwanuka asked Sage over their private comm.

"Yes." Sage magnified the vid equipment. "The hardware looks bigger than it needs to be."

"They're packed with smoke and aud foolies. When they trigger, it sounds like ship-to-ship action in space. Loud and scary, and visibility goes to near zero when the smoke pours out. It gives the bartender time to grab the currency, the digital bank box, and scamper."

"Let the others know."

The plascrete floor felt uneven beneath Sage's boots. His helmet cycled constantly, adapting to the rampant light show that slammed into his faceshield again and again. Dealing with twice the filtering because the same thing was going on with Noojin's helmet, Sage ignored the assault as well as he could and kept moving. He hated looking for targets in a civilian populace. Things went sideways too quickly and the wrong people got hurt too often.

I have found one of the subjects of your search, the near-AI informed Sage. The face-recog software matched a Makaum man in the corner to the three images Noojin had picked out from citizen records maintained in the fort's database. All civilian workers and vendors had to have Terran Army identification to come on base.

The targeting software outlined Vekaby in red and estimated the distance as thirteen meters to where he sat at a table between the two back doors. Stunning Vekaby at that distance would have been no problem if not for all the dancers in the way.

Vekaby looked like he was in his late twenties. Shaggy black hair trailed down to his shoulders, looking out of place with the neatly trimmed beard that covered his rugged face. He wore a blue plasfab jacket and red plasfab pants that doubled as armor and provided cooling as well. He drank from a green bottle.

The information the fort had on the Vekaby was sparse, only containing what Noojin had given them earlier. The man had visited the fort once on a tour pass, which was the only reason he was in the system. He had been the leader of another hunting group, but lately he'd been guiding drug traffickers out into the jungle.

The other two subjects are verified as well, the hardsuit's near-AI informed Sage.

Mosbur had burn scarring that marred the left side of his face and ear. According to what Noojin had said, Mosbur and Vekaby had been rivals in different hunting bands before the corps ships had hit dirtside. Like Vekaby, Mosbur wore offworlder clothing and armor.

Delshy was an older man, heavier and more muscle-bound than the other two. His hair was gray and hacked off to an even length. Noojin had said Delshy was selfish and an outlier from most of the Makaum people. Maybe there hadn't been much in the way of crime until the off-worlders made planetfall, but there had been a few people who didn't play nicely with others and insisted on walking a different path.

"There they are!" Noojin called over the comm. She started to reach for her weapon.

Kiwanuka stepped smoothly in front of the girl and blocked her from view, managing to throw an arm around her and keep her arms in without being noticed by the ambushers. Noojin calmed immediately and Sage suspected Kiwanuka was conversing with her over private comm.

Sage clicked over to a private channel with Jahup. "You follow my lead. Understand?"

"Yes sir." Jahup's voice was tightly controlled but he moved smoothly. The young man's hardsuit told Sage his blood pressure was up, but he was keeping himself calm.

"We need them alive," Sage said, "and able to answer questions. The colonel and I want to know where the weapons came from, and we want to know if the ambush this morning was an isolated event or part of an organized movement."

Vekaby and his cronies watched Sage and grew restless in their chairs, shifting and trying not to make eye contact. Vekaby coughed into his hand as Sage headed in their direction.

Sage came to a stop in front of Vekaby and the others. "Vekaby, I need to speak to you."

Before Vekaby could speak, Delshy erupted from his seat and shoved a Lemylian male dancing beside Sage. The Lemylian only staggered a little, probably more from drinking than from Delshy's push, but he came around angrily and drove a hard left fist into Sage's head, taking him for the person who jostled him.

"*Ril'eru!*" the Lemylian shouted. The bright blue eyes narrowed in pools of inflamed red. "*Orkim lorser!*"

Despite the armor's strength and gyro-aided balance, Sage stumbled sideways, striking another Lemylian and getting hit again instantly by that man. Lemylians were about as strong individually as any race Sage had ever encountered. The armor had taken some damage.

With the Lemylians primed by drugs and alcohol and whatever brain stim software they favored, they had no problem throwing themselves into battle. On their planet, they'd had to fight the environment, Terra-plus gravity, huge predators, and each other.

Vekaby and his companions headed out the back door, plunging into the neon fluttering through the night outside.

"Corporal Rasheed," Sage called over his comm. The first Lemylian grinned broadly as he hurled more curse words in his language and threw another big punch. Sage caught his opponent's fist in one hand and managed to stop the blow centimeters from his faceshield.

"Yes, Sergeant," Rasheed responded.

"Five men just left this building headed your way. All are armed and presumed hostile." Sage dodged the Lemylian's blow with his other hand and still hung on to the one he had. The Lemylian jerked Sage off balance but Sage recovered.

"There are more than five, Top."

Checking his HUD, Sage saw that a torrent of people was leaving the bar.

The Lemylian behind Sage tried to hit him. He side-stepped the Lemylian's blow by sliding, and shoved his gloved hand to his opponent's throat. He pulsed an electric charge through his glove and watched the Lemylian jerk and stutter-step backward, then fall to his knees gasping for air through his partially paralyzed throat.

"Find them, Corporal. Don't let them—"

A deafening explosion roared from outside, and the door Vekaby and his men had gone through blew into the bar in plasteel shards that struck Sage and the Lemylian he still held.

TWENTY-FIVE

Zorg's Weeping Onion
Red Light District
New Makaum
0039 Hours Zulu Time

Knocked off balance by the concussive wave and the debris, Sage tried to recover and got hammered again by the Lemylian he had hold of. The Lemylian didn't seem to register the explosion. Sage was his total focus. The blow to his chest knocked Sage back and he lost his grip on his opponent.

"Rasheed!"

There was no answer.

Armor has taken 13 percent damage, the near-AI stated.

Advancing with his fists in front of him, the Lemylian grinned and shouted more invective in his language. Around them, several bar patrons lay stunned and bleeding. No one appeared dead, but they hadn't caught the brunt of the blast. Most of that had occurred outside in the alley.

Setting himself in an L-shaped stance with his left foot

behind him, Sage blocked the Lemylian's left-handed blow with his right forearm, then swiveled his hips as he swung his left hand into his opponent's face. The blow rocked the Lemylian's head back, but he set himself to return the attack. Blood trickled from a split lip and he pulled his chin farther down on his barrel chest.

Small-arms fire chattered out in the alley and muzzle flashes tore holes through the darkness and the neon.

"Blue Jay Twelve," Sage called over his comm. "Can you see my team outside the bar?" He focused on the Lemylian, concentrating on removing one obstacle at a time. He'd forgotten how dangerous Lemylians were in close quarters.

"Top, this is Blue Jay Twelve," the jumpcopter team leader called. "Your team at the back of the building is down. Looks like they were hit with a high-explosive round. Maybe an Arayo Defender munition."

"Copy that, Blue Jay Twelve." Stepping forward, Sage shifted his lead foot, blocked the Lemylian's right hand with his left forearm, and swung his right foot in a round-house kick that caught his opponent in the face. While the Lemylian tried to recover, Sage placed his right hand on his opponent's face and pulsed an electrical charge.

Overcome, the Lemylian staggered back with his hands covering his face and fell onto a table, shattering it and dropping heavily to the ground.

Sage turned toward the door and pulsed electrical blasts into the next Lemylian that tried to engage him and caught a third Lemylian in the throat before he could block the blow. Both went down.

"Rasheed." Sage strode out into the alley as his software sorted out his people inside the confusion raging inside the bar. All the Terran Army soldiers inside the bar were still on their feet, heading for the back of the

Weeping Onion while the bar's clientele headed for the front door because they'd recognized it as the path of least resistance. The explosion had sealed the deal.

Jahup took up a position behind Sage. Overhead, both jumpcopters continued to circle the area. Sage patched into the overhead feeds and saw himself looking around the downed bar patrons in the alley. The dizzying spin provided by the jumpcopter views almost proved disconcerting, but Sage dealt with them.

"Here, Top," Rasheed croaked. He and his fellow soldier lay sprawled on the ground, only now trying to get to their feet. Their armor glowed phosphorus white and made them stand out in the night and the neon. "Caught us by surprise. Wasn't expecting something so powerful."

Sage figured the explosives Vekaby and his people had used were Arayo Defender rounds. The Defender was used in close proximity to blast opponents back and disorient them, throw their tech off-line for a short time, and mark their armor for suppressive fire and snipers.

Kiwanuka and Noojin, followed by the remaining two soldiers, joined Sage in the alley.

"These guys are carrying serious hardware," Kiwanuka said as she observed the other two white phosphorus soldiers stirring on the other side of the door. "Somebody's bankrolling them. There's no way they got that kind of tech on their own."

Sage silently agreed, and that was going to be one of the first questions he asked the ambushers when he caught them. He scanned the alley as bar guests ran toward either end. "Which way did Vekaby and the others go?"

"Don't know, Top," Rasheed answered. The other recovering soldier answered similarly. "They were in front of us, then we got hosed."

"I've got your targets, Top," the jumpcopter leader announced. "Two of them caught trace blowback from the phosphorus and are lit up. I'm assuming the group is staying together. Sending coordinates now and we'll keep them in sight."

"Copy that." Sage waited till the signal relay popped up on his street map overlay, then turned and ran past Rasheed and his men while assigning the two soldiers who had followed Noojin and him inside to remain with Rasheed and his team till they recovered.

Sage pounded down the alley, pouring on the speed available to him through the hardsuit. The AKTIVsuit's power drained faster when the bumped-up strength and speed and electrical shocks were used, but the levels remained satisfactory.

Several people, most of them offworlders but with a few Makaum mixed in, had come out to the street to find out what all the noise was. As they took in the Terran Army hardsuits running toward them, they dodged back inside the nearest building or alley. Several of them reached for weapons, then relaxed when Sage and the others passed them by.

The op had already exceeded the parameters Sage had hoped for, but if Quass Leghef could manage it, he planned on stepping up the police action in the red light district. More weapons than they'd believed possible were hitting the streets. The Terran Army had to make more of an appearance.

Sage spotted the phosphorus-stained figures 53.67 meters ahead and locked on to them. He drew the coilgun as he ran and made sure it was set to stun. He wanted the men alive so he could talk to them about the attack and about the weapons.

An old man driving a cargo cart pulled by a *dafeerorg* unintentionally blocked the street when he tried to turn around. Seeing the Terran Army soldiers bearing down on him, he struggled to turn the big lizard around. Already frightened by the loud explosion and the action going on around him, the *dafeerorg* fought the reins, shaking his head and bawling in deep-voiced terror.

Without breaking stride as he closed in on the cart, Sage leaped the *dafeerorg*, which stood 1.5 meters tall at the shoulder. Covered in light gray scales, the lizard stumbled in the harness as it tried to avoid Sage.

Effortlessly, Sage landed four meters on the other side of the cart, gaining quickly on the fleeing men. Vekaby spun and brought up the big-barreled Arayo Defender and fired a gel round at Sage. Already twisting, anticipating the trajectory of the round, Sage dodged to the left, dropping down far enough to put his fingers on the ground to keep his balance.

The Defender munition zipped past his shoulder, missing him by millimeters. Five meters behind him, the gel HE round slammed into the corner of a massage parlor. The blast shredded the building's corner, reducing it to a cloud of flying plascrete shards. A section of the roof collapsed onto people gawking beneath it.

Sage lifted the Birkeland and fired at Vekaby, but one of the other Makaum men with him stumbled into the stun charge and went down like he'd been poleaxed.

"Jahup," Sage called over the comm. "Secure that man."

"He's down," Jahup argued. "He's not going anywhere."

Vekaby and the other four men split up. Two of them went to the left and two of them ran to the right. All of them disappeared in the tangle of people in the alleys.

"He's alive and we have him," Sage said. "I don't want him to disappear."

Jahup cursed, but he dropped out of the chase and took the unconscious man into custody.

The jumpcopters split up as well, staying out ahead of the chase so they could provide support in case other people tried to stop the soldiers.

"Sergeant," Sage called as he slowed and took the corner, following Vekaby and his companion. A knot of people blocked the way. Sage ran toward the wall on his right, leaped, triggered the boot sole claws, and hit the wall with both feet. For a moment his velocity held gravity at bay and he managed three long strides across the wall with the claws digging purchase. As gravity pulled at him again, he leaped from the wall and landed in an open area past the crowd bottlenecking the alley. He stumbled for a second, then retracted the boot claws.

"We have the others," Kiwanuka replied. She and Noojin were stride for stride together as they veered off in pursuit of the other two men.

Twenty meters ahead of him, Sage saw Vekaby turn to the right, following the twisting path of the alley.

Red Light District
New Makaum
0041 Hours Zulu Time

Your blood pressure, respiration, and heart rate are elevated outside of recommended parameters, the near-AI said. *Do you require adjustment?*

"No," Noojin replied. "Leave me alone."

Her anger flared at the AKTIVsuit. Even after all the training she'd endured to learn to operate the hardsuit, just trying to keep up with Jahup's new interest, she still resented the combat gear. She didn't like not being able to feel the air around her, to hear sounds in their natural environment rather than the electronically enhanced versions of them the hardsuit provided, and she missed the smells of everything around her that told her so much. The Terran soldiers didn't realize how much they gave up by being in the armor.

Then again, when the hardsuit's mechanical "muscles" were engaged as they were now, she was faster and stronger than she'd ever be on her own. Taking meat from the jungle wasn't just about strength and speed, though. A hunter had to be clever, had to know the terrain, and had to be patient.

Noojin watched Mosbur running ahead of her. He was easy to spot because he was one of the men who had gotten marked by the phosphorus blowback. When the man glanced over his shoulder and saw that she was within twenty meters of him, panic widened his eyes. She enjoyed that more than she knew she should, but she couldn't help remembering how Mosbur had tried to kill her and would have killed Telilu as well if he'd gotten the chance.

Mosbur split off from the other man and they went in different directions in the same alley. Turning, Mosbur fired a particle-beam weapon that threw up a cloud of dirt and rock and grass in front of Noojin. She ran through it and leaped the crater that had opened up in the ground.

"I've got Mosbur," Noojin said as she and Kiwanuka closed on the intersection.

"Be careful," Kiwanuka told her.

Unable to turn right as sharply as she'd thought she could in the soft dirt of the alley, Noojin bent her knees and lowered her center of gravity, shoving her left foot out to broaden her base. Her feet skidded through the dirt, leaving tears centimeters deep. Then, when the majority of her momentum had been exhausted, she started forward again.

Above, the jumpcopter trailed after Kiwanuka.

Mosbur continued running, but the AKTIVsuit's amplified hearing picked up the ragged breaths he was sucking in. Sometimes the hunting band had to run down creatures as well, but usually they ran in teams, some resting while others gave chase as long as their prey was boxed in.

The alley wasn't a proper box. Realizing he was going to be overtaken, Mosbur darted left into a bar, shoving through three Makaum people coming out.

Noojin switched over to thermographic vision and tracked the hot spots on Mosbur as he ran through the building. More patrons choked the doorway, making a human barrier.

Checking the other side of the large plate-glass window that took up a three-meter by two-meter area on the wall a short distance from the door, Noojin saw that no one was there. She drew the Birkeland from her hip holster and leaped through the window.

Noojin crashed through the transplas. Shards flew in all directions and people still inside the bar dropped to the floor. She landed on the plascrete surface and slid for just an instant before locking down.

Panicked, knowing he'd exhausted whatever lead he'd had, Mosbur seized a young Makaum woman who had been trying to escape unnoticed with a young man. Her companion protested and reached for Mosbur. Mosbur slammed his weapon's barrel into the young man's temple and he slumped to the floor, unconscious.

Mosbur pulled the woman in front of him as a shield and pressed the barrel of the particle beam weapon against her neck. "Stay back, Terran! Stay back or I'll kill her!"

"I'm not a Terran." Noojin cleared her faceshield so that her features could be seen.

Several of the people in the bar were Makaum and recognized her.

Mosbur grinned, but his breathing was still ragged. "Noojin. So you're responsible for the Terrans hunting us." He raised his voice. "Do you see? The Terran Army is here to make us their slaves. They're already luring away the young people among us, turning them against those of us who wish to remain true to our people."

Anger surged inside Noojin and she switched the Birkeland from stun to lethal.

"Noojin," Jahup said over the comm. "We agreed that we would bring these men in alive."

"He's a killer," Noojin argued. "He doesn't deserve to live any more than a *khrelav* who's learned to hunt at the fringes of the sprawl." Killing the occasional flying lizard that turned to hunting people was dangerous because they were big enough and powerful enough to take down a jumpcopter.

"If you shoot him, he may kill the woman."

"I'm not going to let him go." Noojin addressed Mosbur: "Lay down your weapon and you won't be harmed."

"So the Terrans can lock me up?" Mosbur shook his head. "Maybe you're going to turn traitor to your people, Noojin, but I'm not."

"I'm here acting on the authority of the Quass. You and Vekaby and other men were responsible for the attack on the fort this morning. You have jeopardized the treaty we have with the Terrans."

"They're just as bad as the others." Mosbur backed slowly toward the door, pulling his hostage with him. People behind him cleared out of the way. He shoved a table over, clearing it from his path. "All the offworlders want our resources. They're all *poldyn*, determined to leech our blood until we're just skin and bones." He reached for the door. "Now put your weapon down or I'll kill her."

"Is she an enemy to you, Mosbur? Does she side with the Terrans?"

Mosbur pressed his weapon into his captive's neck more forcefully. "Do it!"

Noojin stretched her left arm out and started bending to lower her weapon to the floor. She deployed the grappling hook set in the housing of her left forearm. The grapple came online silently and established a reticle on her faceshield. The hook penetrated in slim line formation, then flared out when it reached its target.

When Noojin released her pistol, Mosbur took his weapon from his hostage's neck and swung it toward Noojin. Aiming at Mosbur's right calf where it was exposed outside the woman's leg, Noojin fired. The grapple was designed to penetrate plasteel and plascrete. It drove through flesh and blood with ease, tearing through Mosbur's calf and breaking his shinbone.

Squalling in pain, Mosbur stumbled to his right, away from the woman, and looked at the bloody wound that had exploded out of his leg. He managed to remain standing and tried to pull his weapon up.

Noojin gripped the thin buckyball strand attached to the grappling hook and yanked. Mosbur screamed in agony as his wounded leg flew up and he fell back. He left a bloody streak as he skidded across the floor like a hooked *jasulild,* but he was the smallest of those Noojin had ever taken.

Moving swiftly, Noojin plucked the beam weapon from Mosbur's hand and laid it aside. She roughly rolled the man over onto his stomach, then she reached into a thigh compartment for a binding strap to secure his wrists behind his back.

Mosbur continued groaning in pain.

Taking her knife from her sheath, Noojin sliced through

the buckyball strand and secured the hook back in her forearm compartment where she would rearm it later. She removed a slap patch and compression bandage from the medical kit in her chest armor and put the patch on Mosbur's neck, rendering him unconscious at once. Then she put the compression bandage on his leg to stop the bleeding.

She didn't feel sorry for Mosbur. With the way the man had menaced the young woman—with the way he had threatened Telilu—he deserved death. Noojin wouldn't have hesitated to kill him.

Using the suit's enhanced strength, she stood and threw Mosbur over her shoulder. She still felt conflicted about aiding the Terran Army against her people, but after what Mosbur had done—this morning and now—her actions felt more certain.

TWENTY-SIX

Red Light District
New Makaum
0043 Hours Zulu Time

As Sage turned the corner of the alley, he threw himself backward to avoid a direct hit from the Arayo Defender, but the gel charge struck the building above him as he crouched and tried to bring the Birkeland to bear. The explosion dropped a large chunk of the building onto him, burying him in a glowing pile of plascrete.

Sage pulled his arms free and levered himself up, shoving through the debris, which fell away all around him. Static filled his systems for a moment, throwing the feeds into a vortex of confused images across his faceshield. He searched through the confused haze of information filling his faceshield and tried to make sense of it as he scanned the alley.

Vekaby and his companion had disappeared.

"Sage?" The voice belonged to Blue Jay 12, hovering somewhere overhead. The jumpcopter pilot said something else, but he lost her words in the jamming effects of the munitions charge.

"I'm here." Sage scanned the alley ahead of him, seeing that it opened out into a small street forty meters away. He was certain Vekaby and his partner hadn't returned past him. They would have been brought down by the wreckage if they'd tried to retreat. "I've lost my targets."

"They're in the street ahead of you."

Sage lurched forward through the rubble. He hadn't heard from Halladay since the explosion in the Weeping Onion and guessed that the colonel had had his hands full dealing with public relations—or the general. Sage ran, opening his faceshield and using his eyes as the hardsuit's systems and musculature came back online. Unfiltered dust and pollen filled his nose, causing him to sneeze and choke as his lungs tightened.

Faceshield and programs are back online, the near-AI whispered into his ear.

Dropping the faceshield back into place, Sage checked on Kiwanuka and Noojin's status, seeing that they had each taken down their targets. Jahup stood over the man he'd been assigned to.

At the alley mouth, feeling the strength and speed back in the hardsuit once more, Sage followed the jumpcopter's laser designation and spotted Vekaby and the other ambusher hijacking a crawler. Vekaby held the large-caliber pistol on the driver, then hauled the man out of the vehicle.

Sage ran toward the crawler and saw Vekaby's head swing around as the man spotted him. Vekaby fired another gel charge but missed by a meter as it sailed past Sage. The resulting explosion struck a neon sign and tore it to shreds, raining debris over the street but not doing much more damage. A plume of writhing orange flames and gray-black smoke clawed toward the night sky.

Vekaby engaged the crawler's magnetic drive and sped forward. The passenger tried to shoot Sage with the Arayo Defender and spread a line of carnage along the street on both sides as he cycled the magazine dry.

Fifteen meters from the crawler and closing, Sage saw the passenger reloading the Defender, then aiming at him through the rear window. Vekaby yelled at the man, no doubt expressing what would happen if the gel charge hit the window and triggered detonation. The man reached down for another weapon, coming up with a solid projectile machine pistol. The near-AI identified it as a new German-made firearm.

Five meters away and accelerating, Sage holstered the Birkeland, threw himself forward, and landed on the crawler's top hard enough to dent the surface. Momentum exceeding that of the vehicle, Sage started skidding forward and slammed his left hand down as he pulsed a magnetic charge through the glove. Vekaby took evasive action and tried to shake him off.

Sage allowed his body to swing around, anchored by the magnetized glove. He slid over the crawler's windshield till his legs trailed across the front of the vehicle. Sage pulled himself to his knees, pulled his left glove to the side, and spotted the passenger wheeling around with the large-capacity machine pistol in both hands. The man fired, stitching a line of holes through the transplas windshield. The bullets ricocheted off Sage's armor with bruising force.

Driving his hand forward through the windshield, Sage fisted the passenger's shirt and jerked to the left, bouncing his head off the side window. Fractures ran through the transplas and the man dropped the machine pistol as his eyes rolled up into his head. The seat belt held him in place.

Anxiously, Vekaby swerved and reached for the Arayo Defender between the seats. He'd just managed to fist the weapon only a split second before Sage grabbed it and tore it from his hand.

"Stop the crawler," Sage commanded.

Instead of obeying, Vekaby accelerated and whipped the crawler sideways. The sharp right turn, especially with the combined weight of Sage and his armor making the vehicle top-heavy, caused the crawler to flip onto its side and slide across the plascrete.

Before Sage could demagnetize his glove and kick free of the crawler, the vehicle overturned again, rolling onto its top and pinning Sage beneath it. A momentary flicker of panic filled him, but he kept himself calm as the suit held and he could breathe.

Warning, the near-AI said. *Sustaining this much weight can cause armor to—*

Ignoring the hardsuit, Sage continued getting battered on the rough street. He managed to get his right arm into position to provide purchase and shoved as hard as he could. Slowly, the crawler overturned onto its side and freed Sage.

"Are you all right, Top?" Blue Jay 12 asked.

"Yeah. I'm good." Still sliding out of control, Sage got his balance and got to his feet while skipping like a stone behind the rolling vehicle. Ahead of him, the crawler hit a closed electronics store and demolished the front wall. Arriving only a second later, Sage raced around to the front of the car, which sat upside down.

Battered and bruised, cut in several places—but none of it life threatening—Vekaby struggled to get out of his safety harness. When he saw Sage standing in front of him through the shattered windshield, Vekaby slumped back into his seat in surrender.

"Are you and your people all right?" Colonel Halladay asked.

"Yes sir," Sage answered over their private comm channel. He stood on top of a three-story plascrete building where one of the jumpcopters had touched down to take on the prisoners. He and his team had taken them into custody, bound them, and carried them up the stairs that led to the rooftop. People in the streets and in the surrounding buildings stared up to see what was going on.

Sage was uncomfortably aware that the jumpcopter made an attractive target for anyone who wanted to try for it. In anticipation of that, Sage had stationed his team around the rooftop. Armed drones deployed by the jumpcopter circled the area, feeding vid of the crowd standing down in the streets. Most of them were just gawkers, but there was a large gathering of anti-Terran protestors as well. They cursed and made offensive gestures at the soldiers.

"This didn't turn out to be the quiet arrest we were hoping for," Halladay said.

"No sir. Things went sideways pretty quickly. Vekaby and his people were outfitted with high-tech armament that we hadn't expected, and they didn't want to be taken into custody."

On board the jumpcopter, the crew secured the five prisoners in the cargo area.

"Where are they getting the weapons?" Halladay asked.

"Vekaby's not saying, but two of the other men say they got them from a supplier in Cheapdock." Sage turned and gazed to the north, where the Offworlders' Bazaar lay.

The location was only minutes away. He didn't mention that to Halladay because the colonel would know that.

"Who's selling the hardware?"

"The two men who told me where the weapons came from don't know. They went with Vekaby to pick them up, but they weren't party to the negotiations."

"Where did Vekaby get the credits to buy the munitions?"

"That's another unknown, sir."

Halladay cursed. "I want to know if the attack yesterday morning is an isolated event or just a preview of what we can expect."

"Yes sir. My team and I are ready to pursue that line of the investigation."

"I know, Top, but I don't have to tell you how General Whitcomb is taking this police action."

Through the HUD's feed with the other jumpcopter cycling the area, Sage saw the line of destruction that trailed out of the Weeping Onion and flared out into two trails, one of them leading to the building where he stood.

"No sir, you don't." Sage had already formed a good idea of what Whitcomb was all about. The general wanted to end his career with a quiet posting.

"It's a nightmare for the diplomatic corps, and believe me, they've already been contacting me to let me know they're not happy."

"Yes sir."

"Luckily, Quass Leghef has gone to bat for us and is taking some of the pressure off. She wants to know where the weapons are coming from too, and she's made sure the general knows that."

Sage's hope rose a little. He didn't like the idea of not following up on the weapons trail, and there was no time like investigating while the trail was still hot. A few days, or even a few hours for that matter, and the trail to whoever sold those weapons to Vekaby and his people would vanish.

"General Whitcomb knows we have a limited window of time to act, so he's cleared your team for this follow-up, but he wants to speak to both of us at oh eight hundred in the morning."

"Yes sir."

"You and your people are up for this?"

"Yes sir. I wouldn't have it any other way."

"Then get moving, Top. Good luck."

As the jumpcopter cleared the rooftop and headed back to the fort with the prisoners, Sage gathered his team.

Offworlders' Bazaar
Makaum Sprawl
0132 Hours Zulu Time

Sage left the crawlers a block from the Offworlders' Bazaar with a driver in each vehicle to provide support in case they needed an exit strategy. The air support—both jumpcopters, now that delivery of the prisoners had been accomplished—was left in the area too, so they wouldn't alert the Cheapdock personnel. Then, dressed in cloaks that blunted the straight edges of their armor, the remaining six soldiers followed Noojin and Jahup into the area while maintaining comm silence.

Noojin and Jahup were used to working together as scouts and hunters, and they had been to the Offworlders' Bazaar on several occasions, so Sage had them lead the troops in. Corporal Culpepper walked slack, covering the soldiers with a heavy plasma blaster that was barely hidden under the cloak.

At the northern end of the bazaar, a three-story building stood above a loose ring of one- and two-story buildings that all faced the dirt-packed courtyard. Sporadic lights lit the rooms and sec lanterns hung over the entrance to the main building, keeping the darkness at bay.

Keeping ten meters apart, Noojin and Jahup stayed to the right and kept to the shadows as much as they could. Other people walked through the marketplace, but they kept to themselves and all conversations were low rumbles. A few of the shops were open, nearly all of them catering to vices: flesh and drugs and alcohol.

The offworlder businesses looked grafted onto the old Makaum buildings. The neon and sec shields and vids stuck out like cancerous growths against the smooth symmetry of the buildings grown from trees and built from cut stone. The bazaar had been built to be a permanent fixture for the Makaum people.

Sage remained amazed at the changes the corps had wrought in the amount of time they'd arrived before Fort York had been established. He'd seen vid of Makaum as it had been when it was discovered. The sprawl had been primitive by comparison to what it now was, and several areas still remained so.

But the sins of the universe had come knocking. In one generation, the planet would be so changed that the new generation would have little in common with the last. Technology transformed things that fast, mostly because it homogenized all the cultures in an area into one entity. It didn't build bonds as much as it dropped everything into the lowest common denominator.

They skirted the area and kept moving.

Outside Cheapdock
North of Makaum Sprawl
0145 Hours Zulu Time

Cheapdock lay to the northeast of the bazaar three klicks distant. Small shuttles from cargo ships and space stations landed there when they couldn't get a berth at the main ports. Cheapdock was an oval that was 2.3 klicks in diameter across its widest point east to west and 1.9 klicks north to south. The stardock was open-ended from east to west and had hangars and cargo areas on the north and south sides that were several buildings deep.

It was the old port, quickly built and used by the corps when Makaum had been discovered, then quickly abandoned when the profits started to roll in and the new starport was built. The Terran Army fort planners had considered the site for the post, but they were too far away from the sprawl to be as effective as the Terran Alliance wanted them to be. On top of that, Cheapdock was separated from the sprawl by a slow-moving river, seventy-three meters across and eighteen meters deep, which provided a natural choke point for a land-based attack.

The corps had built a retractable bridge across the river, which was controlled by bashhounds on the Cheapdock side. Green Dragon Corp still managed the bridge, provided upkeep, and charged for access, but the execs also ran a lot of the black market as well.

Sage and his people stayed off the main road and stuck to the north side of the slope so they could peer down on the terrain. They made their way through the jungle and only had to dispatch a few predators before they reached the Tekyl River.

Crouched along the bank, Sage studied the river. The

retractable bridge was 217.4 meters downriver. The jungle had been cleared out at either end and bashhounds stood guard in small forts on either bank as well. Drones sailed along the surface of the water and swept the waterway.

"Security's pretty tight," Kiwanuka commented. She knelt down only a short distance from Sage.

"On the surface, yeah," Sage agreed, "but I'm not picking up anything in the river."

"*Jasulild* live in this river," Jahup said. "I know we can walk across the river bottom in the hardsuits, but if we chance upon a *jasulild* while we're down there, things could go badly. This is the spawning season and they're even more aggressive now than they normally are."

"The hardsuits have sonar capabilities," Sage countered, "and the *jasulild* aren't going to pick up a scent trace from us."

"*Jasulild* hunt based on movement." Noojin sounded pessimistic. "Not scent."

"We're crossing. The answers we need are over there." Sage pulled his cloak off, put it into his equipment pack, then closed the watertight seals on the Roley and shoved the Smith and Wesson .500 Magnum into an expandable waterproof thigh pouch. "Jahup, let's go."

Jahup nodded, stored his cloak in his pack, and remained crouched down under overhanging branches as he eased into the river. In seconds he was submerged. No trace marred the river to show his passing.

Sage started forward, but Noojin intercepted him.

"Wait," she ordered. "I need to be over there with Jahup." Without waiting for a reply, she stepped into the water and disappeared as well.

Sage let thirty seconds tick off the chronometer on his faceshield and started down into the river. His boots sank several centimeters into the mud and grew heavy with accumulated mass. The hardsuit's skeletal system quickly adjusted for the weight of the mud and the restriction of the water.

Right before his helmet sank beneath the river, Sage heard the whisper of the seals closing and saw the air supply indicator form in a soft glowing blue line, marking the time he could be submerged. Provided he didn't over-exert himself underwater, the hardsuit could filter oxygen from the river water to extend the oxygen in the reservoir.

Darkness and sediment restricted visibility in the river. Night vision was only slightly better, and thermographic vision was problematic. Sage used echolocation, bouncing sound waves off his immediate surroundings. The sonar provided a reliable image of the riverbed and surrounding water, but didn't reveal the soft areas covered by a thin layer of mud. Sage sank three times, once up to his hip, and had to extricate himself with care so he didn't sink deeper.

Echolocation revealed another hardsuit behind him when he reached the midpoint of the river. A discreet ping identified Kiwanuka.

Ten meters from the opposite bank, on the slow rise toward the surface, the echolocation beeped a warning and revealed a huge mass coming toward him from sixty meters away and closing rapidly.

At first, Sage thought someone had a small submersible in the water. The object was seven meters long and three meters in diameter. Then its tail flicked in a movement that was too organic for a marine vehicle.

"Kiwanuka," Sage called out in warning over a short-range comm frequency.

"I see it." Kiwanuka hunkered down till she was lying in the mud.

Sage did the same thing. He gazed up at the surface

of the river as the current swept silt and debris over him. If neither of them had a profile and there was no scent, whatever the creature was should pass them by without noticing them.

Instead, the creature came at him, closing swiftly. The echolocation revealed the *jasulild* in limited terms. Sage knew the creatures were usually covered in blue and purple scales and looked like Terran cuttlefish, only uglier and with teeth like a piranha.

The *jasulild* swam over to Sage, held its position with its fins, and scraped at the hardsuit with its teeth in an effort to pluck him from the muddy river bottom. The sound echoed inside the armor because there was no way to filter that noise.

Swimming backward a short distance, the *jasulild* approached Sage again and once more tried to dig him out of the mud. Reaching up with his left hand to touch the *jasulild's* massive underjaw, Sage blasted the creature with a short burst of electricity that flared for only a second.

The *jasulild* shivered and only moved weakly afterward. The gills still worked, so Sage knew he hadn't killed the thing, but it was stunned. He pulled himself up from the mud with difficulty and continued toward the opposite bank.

He came out under low hanging branches and remained within the shadows. After confirming Noojin's and Jahup's positions farther up the bank at the ridgeline, Sage knelt and watched as Kiwanuka surfaced and came out as well while he readied his weapons.

After Culpepper and Pingasa and the other two soldiers crossed and there were no more incidents, Sage gave the order to continue to Cheapdock. The answers to the weapon supplies lay ahead of them.

TWENTY-SEVEN

S how me your pass." The Green Dragon bashhound was blunt and direct. All four limbs were cyber replacements and whatever was left of his original flesh and blood had been enhanced by steroids. His armor was olive green, almost black in the night. A yellow Chinese dragon reared proudly on his chest plate. He carried a double-barreled plasma blaster on a sling at his side. He had not put in an appearance till after the retractable bridge had clanked back across the river.

Mato sat behind the controls of the Phrenorian aircar and extended his PAD to the bashhound. The five warriors that accompanied Zhoh and Mato sat in the two backseats of the vehicle.

In the passenger seat, Zhoh remained calm and assumed a look of disinterest, but his eight eyes took in everything around them. Three other bashhounds worked the outpost and they were connected to a team inside the Cheapdock sec offices. If anything happened on the bridge, automated defense systems would pop up and reinforcements would be on the way in seconds.

The gate just ahead of the aircar was a pair of massive tungsten rectangles four meters tall by eight meters wide.

The bashhound flicked on the PAD and scanned it into his own reader. The information contained on the PAD Mato had given him contained well-entrenched lies. There was a Captain Achsul Oretas, who served on General Rangha's personal staff and who had sometimes been a go-between for the general and Erque Ettor, the Voroughan black marketer, but he had not given permission for anyone to visit the storage bay tonight.

So far, news of Ettor's death had not reached the Phrenorian embassy. Mato had flagged the being's name so they would know if anyone picked up that news in the media, or if the name was searched for through Phrenorian channels.

Zhoh was certain the general would be searching for word of Ettor before long. The visit to the storage bay in Cheapdock would guarantee that.

"Your pass is accepted, Captain Oretas," the bashhound said, returning the PAD, "and your presence has been logged."

Mato took the PAD and stored it between the seats.

The bashhound passed over a small beacon. "Clip this to your outerwear and keep it on your person at all times. Keep your group with you. If your group separates, anyone not with you will be arrested or killed. If you lose the beacon or stray from the areas you have been cleared for, you will be arrested or killed. Do you understand this?"

The security was much more strict than Zhoh had expected, but it was nothing he had not eluded before. Not only that, but he intended to comply with the rules. All he needed was proof of General Rangha's extracurricular activities.

"I understand." Mato clipped the two-centimeter-square blue beacon badge to his armor. A small ruby light winked as the security system pinged the badge.

"Do you require any assistance?" The bashhound didn't sound interested.

"I know the way," Mato said. Ettor had given them the location of the storage bay where he had arranged for Rangha's weapons to be kept secure.

The bashhound stepped back and the massive gates to the starport swung open soundlessly.

Mato engaged the magnetic drive and the aircar lifted a half meter from the ground. He eased forward. As soon as they had cleared the area, the gates swung closed behind them.

The plascrete road that led to the starport had been re-finished lately, but not replaced. Another layer had been positioned over the top of the one already in place, but it had been so thinly done that the cracks and imperfections that had scored the previous one remained as ir-regularities. The aircar passed smoothly over the road, but a large cargo crawler in the other lane bumped and rocked as it approached. The aircar's windshield tinted automatically as the crawler's high beams flickered across the surface.

Warbur traders clung to the crawler's sides. Their wide skulls, large mouths, blue fur, and arms that were longer than their legs identified them easily. They wore savage tribal markings that scarred their broad faces and had only flaring slits for nostrils. All of them carried assault rifles and bandoliers of extra charge magazines.

Mato swore as the trade crawler rumbled past. The

bitter, salty stench of the Warburs hit Zhoh like a physical blow. He held his breath until they were gone.

"Those creatures are filthy," Mato declared.

"They're also dangerous," Zhoh reminded him as he studied the rows of storage units ahead. The Warburs didn't wear their scars as decoration. They had a reputation for being low-end transport for cargo, but they fought to defend their business. "They probably got trade rights for air or water and are supplying the mining colonies out in the asteroid belt."

Once Makaum was secure, Zhoh intended to take over Lodestone and the surrounding asteroids. The large planetoid drew in a lot of wayward meteors rich in ores that could be used to build Phrenorian ships. Getting control of that would be a good thing. Zhoh had already been planning on depriving the miners of their limited spacecraft and opening negotiations with them. If they objected to working for the Phrenorians for air, water, and food, Zhoh would cut those things off as he had before in similar situations. In days, everyone in those rocks would be dead. Removing the bodies could be easily done as the miners were replaced from the slave population left on Makaum.

Knowing the Warbur were out there changed the dynamics of the situation in the asteroids. The Warbur worked for credits. They could be bought off, but if they couldn't be, cutting off their source of income would send them on their way.

Either way would serve.

6189 Akej (Phrenorian Prime)

Mato drove through the rows of storage bays. The one Ettor had given them the number to was located in the back north row and halfway down. Drones maintained security but the jungle encroached on the units more than Zhoh would have permitted had he been in charge.

Someone had been through the area recently in an effort to clear away the jungle. Ash, charred roots and branches, and soot shadows on the broken plascrete offered mute testimony that the Green Dragon Corp had tried to fight back the jungle. Only a few meters away, huge burn pits showed where more trees and brush had been shoved in and burned.

The smoky residue choked Zhoh as he climbed from the settled aircar. He was conscious of eyes on him as he approached the storage bay. The line of units stood twenty meters tall and was at least forty meters deep, judging from what he had seen during their approach. Ettor had stated that several weapons of varying origins were inside.

Drones cycled on rounds overhead while armed Green Dragon bashhounds occupied rooftops with sniper rifles.

The dull metal lock face was programmed in Brootan, the language of one of the dead worlds the Empire had left in its wake as it conquered its enemies. That in itself pointed to a Phrenorian renting the storage bay because the symbols were used only in the Empire these days, and then only for mathematical research regarding plasma engines. The Brootans had excelled in math and music.

Mato joined Zhoh at the door and set a bag of tech gear on the plascrete at their feet. Mato knelt, opened the bag, and withdrew a small, sophisticated unit that fit neatly into his lesser hand. He checked it briefly, powering it up so that an amber light glowed strongly, then extinguished.

"This will tell us if any surprises were left in the lock mechanism." Mato removed the lock cover and attached four leads to the circuitry within.

"You will find any potential traps with this?" Zhoh didn't like snooper tech like the device Mato used. He preferred a battlefield, a plasma rifle, and his *patimong* for close fighting. He would win back his honor and his place among the Empire with those. But he appreciated Mato's knowledge.

"If I do not find them, *triarr*, you will be the first to know."

Zhoh smelled the sweet pheromones from Mato that told him the warrior was pleased with himself. Zhoh was not amused. He did not want to die tarnished in the eyes of his family.

Mato punched in the code Ettor had given them with one of his lesser hands.

Although he did not wish to experience any anxiety, Zhoh felt himself grow tense as Mato entered the last symbol.

The locking mechanism cycled, clicked hollowly, and ratcheted as it opened. The recessed handle popped out. Carefully, Mato took the handle in one of his lesser hands and pulled. The three-meter door opened, grinding in the grooved tracks in front of the bay. Ash and bits of bark popped and snapped as the door cut through them.

"Wait." Mato knelt again, put the first device away, and took another from the bag.

The new device was cube-shaped and threw out a light spectrum that Zhoh could scarcely see. Mato eased into the room with the device extended before him and a maze of lights the size of Zhoh's *chelicerae* created an interwoven pattern throughout the bay.

"This is a trap." Mato's scent changed dramatically. The pleasant pheromones disappeared, replaced at once by the dry, bitter stink of concern.

"What kind of trap?" Zhoh asked.

"What would you put in a place you did not want anyone to find out about?" Mato countered.

"A plasma charge. Something that would get rid of everything I did not want seen."

Mato moved the cube around and took care not to break any of the light beams. He picked up his bag and slowly walked to the left. After a moment spent examining the wall, he took out a device that activated with a hum, and a section of the wall slid away to reveal another keypad.

Mato looked at Zhoh. "Ettor only gave us one code."

"Perhaps it was for both keypads."

"Should I enter it?"

"Can you bypass it as you did the other?"

"This one is more complicated. It will take longer."

"Bypass it. As much pain as Ettor was in, I do not see how he could keep from telling me everything, but it is possible." If Zhoh had been about to die and had knowledge that would ensure his killer would die with him, he would have made sure that happened.

Mato took the first device out again and set to work. Almost as soon as he started, a red light flashed on the keypad and a digital viewscreen opened up.

Cursing, Mato stared at the keypad. "It's counting down."

TWENTY-EIGHT

T he security fence is no problem, Top," Corporal Pingasa said as he surveyed the seven-meter-tall plascrete
barrier only centimeters away. Even in armor, he was a
small, compact man with a soft voice. He held his hand out
and a blue light field stood revealed only a few centimeters
above the surface of the sec wall. "I can bypass a section
of this wall easily enough." He pointed to two small boxes
at the top of the wall that were twenty meters apart.

According to Halladay, Pingasa was the best sec tech at
the fort and usually worked on the drones and automated
systems. He'd grown up in a village outside Llongwe,
Malawi, where his father had worked as a cybernetics
professor at the University of Malawi. Pingasa's mother
had designed security programs. He'd had no problem
getting them past the first layer of security outside the
starport.

"Sounds good." Sage had used foolies on similar sec architecture himself. As he stood waiting, feeling the pressure of time passing by, he also felt fatigue creeping over him. He'd been up, more or less, for sixty-nine hours straight except for the quick nap in the med center. He was running on empty, but he didn't want the stim the suit's near-AI regularly recommended because the payback for that would drop him like a rock in a few hours and he didn't know where the present op was going to lead. "So what's the problem?"

Pingasa reached into his chest pouch and removed four drones about the length and thickness of his forefinger. As he held them in his palm, the drones opened and spread small rotors that doubled their size. The rotors spun over the skeletal body that was left and they deployed with an almost silent hiss. A pair flitted toward each of the small sec boxes and the other two stayed together.

Two of the drones landed on the boxes while the second pair met in midair and started spinning a single gossamer strand between them. They worked slowly and Sage chafed at the delay, feeling exposed even in the underbrush. As the strand elongated, the two drones flew in opposite directions.

"The problem is that this network is also wired into drones and into the bashhounds walking perimeter." Pingasa moved his hands in front of him, twitching and gesturing, controlling the drones. "It's a three-deep system: stationary, mobile drone, and mobile flesh-and-blood. We have to take a drone and one of the guards walking this perimeter as well."

Sage pulled up Pingasa's faceshield vid and saw the intricate visual representation of the work being done. All of the corporal's work manipulated the drones, pulling them together.

"The drone and the guard have to be taken at the same time, and they can't get any farther than twenty meters apart when we shut them down." Pingasa continued working and his hands flashed more quickly. "They'll be wired to each other. If one signal goes down, the other is alerted, and if they're separated, the general alert goes out and we'll be eyeball deep in bashhounds. Green Dragon doesn't mess around when it comes to sec."

"Understood." Sage dropped out of Pingasa's feed, overwhelmed by the layers and layers of images the corporal was sifting through. "How do we get by that?"

"I've got a foolie for the drone. Someone will have to take out the guard. Without killing him. If his vitals crash, then the alarm is triggered. I can't work around that." Pingasa dropped his hands.

On the wall, all four drones had joined up. The gossamer strand stood taut between them only a few centimeters above the barrier. They scuttled over the sec boxes and cut through the cover with small lasers.

Pingasa held his hand out again. The section of wall in front of them remained dark, but the sections on either side still glowed with blue energy. The strand also glowed blue.

"Okay, now we can climb the wall, but you and I will go first, Top."

"How are you planning on taking out the bashhound without crashing his vitals?" Kiwanuka asked.

"With a Pacifier," Sage replied. The paralytic drug rounds were used to knock down civilians during an urban firefight and keep them out of harm's way so soldiers could do their jobs. They were often used in cases when opponents used human shields. The paralytic turned the hostages into limp, dead weight, allowing a sniper to shoot the hostage taker.

"A Pacifier round isn't going to penetrate armor," Kiwanuka said.

"It won't have to," Sage said.

Before Kiwanuka could ask him what he meant, Noojin spoke up. "The guard walking this perimeter is smoking *drequeurn*. I have smelled it both times he has been by."

"That's right," Sage said, impressed by the girl's alertness. *Drequeurn* was a mildly narcotic local plant that was one of the first trade goods the corps had insisted on.

Noojin turned her head to look at Sage but her faceshield showed only darkness. "You have opened your faceshield to know that."

"I did. The first thing you learn about an AKTIVsuit is that it can't completely replace a soldier's senses or translate a battleground."

Noojin glanced at Jahup and crossed her arms. Her body language suggested that he had said something over private comm that she didn't particularly care for.

Sage chose not to intrude on that conversation. He opened the Roley's action and started to insert a paralytic round.

"Not to demean your skills, Top, but I'm a sniper." Kiwanuka readied her rifle.

"Agreed. Go." Sage pocketed the Pacifier round. He was getting tired. He should have suggested Kiwanuka make the shot. He was running a team, and some of these soldiers had more skills than he did.

Slinging her rifle over her shoulder, Kiwanuka surveyed the bypassed barrier and stepped to a section where the verdant growth hung low over the wall. In another few days, the tree branches would have to be cut back so they wouldn't foul the security. Sage made a stirrup of his gloved hands and she stepped into them. As he lifted her up the wall, she popped short claws from the palms of her

gloves and the toes of her boots, then climbed slowly to
the top of the plascrete barrier.

Sage opened his faceshield slightly and the redolent,
sickly sweet odor of the *drequeurn* drifted into his helmet.
The bashhound was circling again. His circuit was fifteen
minutes long. If they missed him this time, they'd have to
wait another fifteen minutes, and every minute they stood
there was risky.

After Sage gave Pingasa a hand up, the man climbed
to the top of the barrier as well. He reached into his chest
pouch and took out another drone, then sent it off, staying
clear of the bypass strand. As he waited, he removed another device, this one as large as a deck of playing cards,
from his chest pouch as well.

Kiwanuka reached the top of the wall and locked on
with her left hand, the cyber limb easily managing her
weight. Slowly, she eased her sniper rifle into position
atop her arm only a centimeter under the strand. She held
her position, moving only slightly to follow her target.

Tense, making himself breathe naturally, emptying his
lungs and drawing air back in to keep his oxygen levels
up, Sage accessed Kiwanuka's and Pingasa's vid feeds.
He didn't allow himself to think of all the things that
could go wrong in the next few seconds. They had their
exit strategy in place.

The starport was a thousand meters distant through
jungle that was already nearly a meter high, growing in the
gray ashes of the latest burns. Three hundred and seventy
yards to the southeast, a pair of powersuits trekked through
the jungle, burning down a taller section of the growth.

A shuttle flared through the sky as it descended and the
crackling thunder of the solid fuel engines washed over
the area. On the tarmac, two shuttles were busy unload-

ing and taking on cargo. In addition to their black-market dealings, Cheapdock also did legal business with small corps and individual companies and haulers.

Automated units as large as crawlers beeped and flashed as they resurfaced the tarmac over gray ash where plant growth had been burned. Maintaining the starport against the encroaching jungle was a full-time job.

Thirty meters away from the wall, the flat, black circular drone hovered two meters above the jungle growth and moved ten meters behind the bashhound smoking the *drequeurn* stick. The bashhound's faceshield was raised just above his top lip, providing just enough room to smoke. The coal flickered bright blue for an instant, then dark purple haze spewed from between his lips.

Kiwanuka's sniper rifle reticule centered on the sliver of the bashhound's face revealed through the raised faceshield. Her voice was calm and steady when she spoke. "Ready when you are, Corporal."

"It will be just a moment." Pingasa flicked his fingers and the code vids filled his faceshield again.

Sage withdrew from the tech's view and concentrated on Kiwanuka's. She kept the reticule steady as the bashhound came toward them. Eight meters away, Pingasa's drone flitted slowly, mimicking the insects that flew around it.

"If you don't get the drone there soon," Kiwanuka warned softly, "I'm going to lose the angle on this shot."

Sage made himself relax and remember that Kiwanuka was a better marksman than he was.

Pingasa's drone flitted and slid sideways as it closed on the guard. The sec drone continued on. Pingasa whispered, sounding hypnotized. "Three seconds, Sergeant. Three . . . two . . . *one.*"

The small drone swooped just as Kiwanuka's finger tightened on the trigger and pulled through to fire her weapon. The Pacifier round struck the bashhound at the corner of his mouth and left a yellow dye splotch the size of a demicredit to mark the hit.

At the same time, Pingasa's drone mounted the sec drone. Sage couldn't see anything that was taking place there, but the sec guard toppled over and went limp.

"I have the drone," Pingasa said. Careful of the strand bypassing the sec barrier, he threw a leg over the wall and dropped to the ground on the other side, crouching to show only a low profile. He raced toward the fallen bashhound. Only a few meters away, the sec drone continued on its path.

Kiwanuka also dropped to the ground and took up a support position with her rifle in a kneeling pose. She wrapped the sling around her forearm and waited. Her biometrics never shifted off of normal.

Jahup approached the wall and popped his claws.

"Wait," Sage ordered. "If Pingasa finishes the foolie, then we go. Until then, we stay here to cover any retreat we may have to make."

Jahup lowered his arms and backed away from the wall. "All right."

From his tone, Sage knew Jahup wasn't happy with the command. Jahup and Noojin were inexperienced at working as soldiers, but they knew the jungle and they knew how to survive. Maybe they didn't understand tactics in a military unit, but they had a better chance on an op like this than some of the green soldiers back at the fort.

And the few experienced people in the ranks needed to remain there in case another attack took place this morning.

Reaching the fallen bashhound, Pingasa dropped to his knees and scanned the man with the device he held. Sage tracked the sec drone and pinned a distance reference on it and the bashhound. They were now four meters apart and the twenty-meter invisible tether between them was steadily running out.

Sage made himself wait. Pingasa would be aware of the distance himself. Reminding the corporal of that wouldn't help.

Moving smoothly, as if he had all the time in the world, Pingasa took out another small drone and ran it under the device he held. The sec drone was at sixteen meters. Just before the sec drone hit nineteen meters, Pingasa flicked his hand and tossed the small drone forward to follow the Green Dragon unit.

The distance separating the sec drone from the downed guard hit twenty meters, then twenty-one. Nothing happened.

Sage released a tense breath.

"The second drone is cycling the guard's biometrics." Pingasa stood and took small computer chips from his chest pouch that were no bigger than shirt buttons. "It's programmed to follow the sec drone, which is blind to us now, so their sec system is going to show this area as secure."

"Good enough, Corporal." Sage went to the base of the barrier and motioned to Jahup and Noojin. "Let's go." He cupped his hands together to make a stirrup.

Noojin stepped into Sage's hands and he eased her up the wall, then he did the same for Jahup.

While the two Makaum worked their way up the wall using claws, Sage turned his attention to Corporal Dundee and Private Selzler. "You two are here to cover our retreat." He pointed to the barrier. "Mine that wall so we can drop it in a hurry if we need to. Set up some anti-personnel claymores from here to the river. If anybody comes after us, I want to stop them or slow them down."

"You got it, Top." Dundee was an experienced munitions man and he'd picked Selzler after he'd seen her work in training. He and Selzler broke out their equipment and set to work.

Sage cupped his hands for Culpepper.

"Not me, Top. You're next." Culpepper shouldered his heavy plasma rifle and cupped his hands. "When I cover your six, it stays covered as long as I'm drawing breath."

"Copy that." Sage stepped into the other man's hands and maintained his balance as Culpepper lifted him over his head. Sage popped his claws, leaned into the plascrete, and climbed. He reached the top, checked Kiwanuka's vid to make certain the way was clear, navigated the bypass strand, and dropped to the ground, sinking into a crouch immediately and freeing the Roley.

A moment later, Culpepper dropped into position behind him.

Pingasa handed one of the button chips to Jahup, then offered one to Sage.

"What is it?" Sage asked.

A smile sounded in Pingasa's voice. "A little something extra. These button chips are coded with Green Dragon sec information. Their sec system will read them and assume we're starport guests."

"I haven't heard of anything like this." Sage affixed the button to his shoulder the same way Jahup, Kiwanuka, and Noojin had done.

"I was not always a Terran Army soldier. I helped my mother with a lot of the design work she did on sec systems. She tells me I am a most apt pupil."

"Glad to hear it." Sage opened his pack and took out the cloak to disguise his armor again. "Now let's go find that weapons cache." He started toward the starport buildings and pulled up the map of the storage units. The one they were looking for was on the north end.

TWENTY-NINE

Zhoh watched the countdown taking place on the locking mechanism and remained calm. There was time. There had to be time. He couldn't get this close to achieving his goal of exposing General Rangha's unacceptable greed and watch that chance slip away.

"Enter the code again," he told Mato.

Without pause, Mato did as he was told. He was a warrior and he would obey. All of the other warriors stood with Zhoh. They were spyrl. Nothing would break that. They would only retreat when Zhoh gave the command.

When Mato finished, the countdown continued.

Cursing Rangha's treachery even in this, Zhoh prepared to give the command to save his warriors. Then another idea struck him. Rangha was not that clever. He had secrets, but they would be simple secrets. He was not a tactician. Rangha was a pampered pet of the Empire.

"Enter the code backwards, Mato." Zhoh couldn't back down from the challenge. He wouldn't walk away and have nothing to show for his efforts.

Mato didn't question the command, didn't mention that they were almost out of time, and his lesser hand was steady as he tapped the code sequence into the keypad.

With only four ticks left on the counter, the symbols stopped, winked, and faded from sight.

Ettor had told the truth, but he had withheld a fraction of it. Zhoh's estimation of the being rose, but only slightly.

Along the storage bay, the light beams winked out.

"Allow me to check for further surprises." Mato scooped up his bag and walked through the storage bay.

Impatiently, Zhoh watched and waited as minutes passed. Presently, Mato returned and slung his bag over his shoulder.

"Everything is clear," Mato said.

Zhoh stationed two of his warriors at the entrance and walked deeper into the storage bay. He surveyed the weapons stacked on shelves and racks around him. Rangha had amassed a variety of ordnance.

"Captain." Yuen, one of the more seasoned warriors among them, lifted a Vesokan plasma launcher.

The weapon was thick and heavy and took at least four appendages to wield. The Vesokan possessed transmutable bodies contained within shells and could manifest as many limbs as they needed.

Despite their lack of definite shape, they had a propensity to mimic those around them. Some of them had psi abilities that allowed them access to the memories of those they consumed. Offworlders who made planetfall at Vesoka didn't live to regret that landing. As a result, the Vesokans learned quickly and took to the stars and to war.

The Phrenorian Empire had battled the Vesokans to a standstill, then drew lines that separated them from the other galaxies and the Gates. If the Vesokans reproduced more quickly, they might have stood a chance against the Empire. The Terran Alliance had quarantined the Vesokan system even before the Phrenorians had to beat them back.

"Yes, Lieutenant?"

"This weapon came from Tianyse."

That caught Zhoh's attention. Tianyse was one of the outer worlds of the Empire and had suffered tremendously when the war with the Vesokans started. Ten years ago, nearly every Phrenorian on that planet had been killed before the Empire even knew the Vesokans were a threat. Zhoh had been part of the offensive that had beaten the invaders back at great cost, but the glory had been worth it.

"How do you know?" Zhoh asked.

"This is a seventh gen iteration of the weapon, sir." Yuen was a heavy weapons expert. "The only place we saw these was Tianyse."

Zhoh didn't ask if Yuen was certain of that. The warrior knew his weapons.

"General Rangha was also on Tianyse," Yuen said.

"Not during the fighting," Zhoh said. He'd interfaced with every combat general on Tianyse. Several of the successful campaigns had been ones he had designed.

"No. General Rangha was there afterward. During cleanup."

Basking in the glory the Empire gave him as a blooded hero. Zhoh barely restrained a curse.

"I was assigned to the cleanup effort," Yuen continued. "We catalogued weapons like these. As I said, that was the only planet where we encountered them." He replaced the plasma cannon on a rack with at least twenty others. "These other weapons, they're all from campaigns we've fought in, sir."

Evidently Rangha had been building his inventory over the years, so his treachery had been going on far longer than Zhoh would have imagined.

"Make a list of the weapons, Lieutenant," Zhoh ordered. "We'll match them up against other campaigns the general was involved in."

"Yes sir."

"And take vid."

"Yes sir."

Zhoh was torn between emotions as he walked through the aisles of weapons. He was angry that Rangha had gotten away with so much, and he was enthusiastic about finding so much corruption the general was responsible for. The presence of the storage bay filled with weapons was leverage, but he wasn't certain if it was enough. Bloodline heroes were fiercely protected by the Empire. None of them had ever been toppled.

That thought gave Zhoh pause, but he pushed past it. Simply accepting the lot he had been regulated to on Makaum was intolerable. He would have his victory and his life as a warrior returned to him, or he would die trying.

He was more warrior, more of a champion, than Rangha would ever be.

"Captain," Mato called from the back of the storage bay. "I have something you should see."

Zhoh walked back to where Mato stood in front of a climate-controlling unit. He'd attached a PAD to the unit.

"What?"

"I have discovered who has access to this storage bay."

"Through a climate controller?"

Mato's pheromones gushed and in a cloud of sweetness. "Climate controllers are programmed through the starport mainframes, *triarr.* I overlaid an *orrach* virus I've designed into the system."

An *orrach* was a small, vicious aquatic predator on Phrenoria that laid its eggs within the eggs of other creatures. The embryos matured quickly in their egg-within-an-egg, ate the other unborn creature, and hatched with poison lethal enough to bring down a full-grown *ighttas,* one of the thirty-meter-long bottom feeders that scavenged the Phrenorian oceans. They were more deadly as young than they were as adults.

"The virus looks like code that the Green Dragon Corp uses," Mato went on, "but it gathers in the mainframes and gives me access."

"What do you have?"

"As we knew from Ettor, Rangha's personal *jolaf,* Captain Achsul Oretas, has been visiting the storage bay, but there is also a Terran woman who has come here as well."

"Who?" Zhoh peered at Mato's PAD.

"Her name is Ellen Hodgkins."

"Who is she?"

"I'll have to do more research on her, but what I see here is that she's registered with the *Hooded Vorol.*" Mato flipped through the PAD. "That's a small, transitory starship that doubles as a space station. A traveling casino that offers sex and drugs."

"A smuggler." Zhoh understood at once. Such ships set up in orbit to make a profit sometimes for weeks or months, fleeced everyone they could, then headed for brighter waters.

"Yes."

"What would Rangha want with a Terran?"

"He could use her as a go-between to sell to Terrans

and other races onplanet." Mato checked through a few more screens. "Hodgkins has a history of criminal behavior and was previously an employee of DawnStar Corp."

"How long ago?"

"She was released from DawnStar weeks ago by Velesko Kos."

Zhoh considered that. "Kos was operating DawnStar's illegal drug factories. Was Hodgkins affiliated with Kos before arriving at Makaum?"

Mato flicked through screens of data. "Yes. She worked with Kos in the Awver system as a strikebreaker. Apparently there are still bounties on Kos and Hodgkins and several of their collaborators in that system."

"Rangha mentioned Kos when I talked with him this morning." Zhoh's angered deepened as he remembered the conversation he'd had with the general at the hidden base, and he wondered if any of the weapons that were supposed to be there were now here in this storage bay. "He all but accused me of favoring the Terran sergeant, Sage, by standing with him against Kos."

"Perhaps the agreement with Hodgkins was begun with Kos."

"It's possible. I want to speak to that female."

"Getting access to the *Hooded Vorol* will be difficult. We can't force our way aboard, and they do not favor Phrenorians with any kindness."

"There must be a way to get to her."

"Captain," one of the warriors called from the front of the storage bay. "A sec team is headed our way."

Zhoh looked at Mato.

"It wasn't anything I did here." Mato unplugged his PAD. "I would have known if I'd tripped any alarms."

"Get outside. We've got all the information we need for

the moment." Zhoh strode to the front of the bay. "Lock this place down."

The Green Dragon sec team arrived at the storage bay as the door closed. The officer in charge was young and crisp, new to authority and proud of his position. He looked at Zhoh and his warriors.

"I am Lieutenant Fu and I am in charge of security. Who is Captain Achsul Oretas?" the young lieutenant asked.

Zhoh squashed the impulse to split the man with his *patimong*.

"I am," Mato said, following the plans they'd made before they'd entered the starport. "Is there a problem?"

"Your identification seems flawed."

"There must be some mistake."

"There is no mistake."

"I have access to the storage bay," Mato argued. "Only myself and Ms. Hodgkins have the codes."

Fu hesitated for a moment. "Please come to my office. We can get affairs straightened away there."

Zhoh rubbed the fingers of his left lesser hand, letting Mato know that following the lieutenant's suggestion would be fine for the moment.

"Of course, Lieutenant." Mato gestured with one of his primaries, getting close enough to Fu to make the young man step back just a little. "After you."

Zhoh followed Mato and the other warriors trailed after them. The Green Dragon sec men surrounded the group but did not act threatening. Zhoh felt no fear, trusting that his warriors could easily dispatch the sec men if the need arose. Until then, he would see if Mato's skills could smooth over the temporary setback. It would be better if the Hodgkins female had no warning they had knowledge of the weapons.

THIRTY

Sage held his position in the shadows beside the last row of storage bays. Out on the starport, one of the loaded shuttles launched, speeding down the runway for a short distance before leaping adroitly into the night sky and sailing over the trees. Only a little farther on, it arced sharply upward, kicked in the thrusters, and headed for the starry space. The thunder of the engines rolled over the starport.

"In place, Top," Kiwanuka called. She'd climbed to the top of the building and lay on the roof to provide cover fire if necessary.

Sage checked her vid and swept the aisle between the rows of storage bays. No one was in the narrow alley between.

"Pingasa," Sage said, "you're with me. The rest of you grab cover and wait."

Pingasa joined Sage and they stepped out of the shadows. The cloaks covered the armor for the most part, and evidently Pingasa's button chips were doing their job because no alarms sounded.

Sage scanned the storage bay numbers, looking for the one where Vekaby's companions had said they'd taken delivery of the weapons.

"Bannyad locks," Pingasa said.

"That doesn't mean anything to me," Sage told him.

"Expensive locks. Hard to break."

"Is that going to be a problem?"

"No, but I'm going to make it look easy and I want you to know it's not and that you should be impressed. Very impressed." Pingasa knelt in front of the unit and dug into his chest pouch.

Sage stood guard with his hand on his Roley underneath the cloak. The spidersilk material shifted slightly as a gentle wind gusted. Sage breathed the thick air through the slight crack he'd left open in his faceshield. The humidity had risen and it smelled like rain. It was getting on toward one of Makaum's rainy seasons.

Lightning flickered across the sky, and rolling thunder followed shortly after. Sage's faceshield told him that the temperature was starting to drop, which could mean storms, but he already knew that because he felt the cooler air cycling inside his helmet.

An alarm suddenly screamed.

Pingasa stood and grabbed his bag. "That wasn't me, I swear. I barely touched that thing."

Grabbing the corporal's arm, Sage pulled the man into motion back toward the jungle. "Move!"

6198 Akej (Phrenorian Prime)

Zhoh stood under guard in the sec office as the lieutenant watched the computer clerk sift through the starport's files. Cheapdock did a lot of business, and there was a massive amount of files. Some of them, probably like the storage bay where the weapons were kept, were not accessible to every Green Dragon officer.

The sec office was large, filled with sec screens that watched over the starport. A big map at one end of the room showed the locations of the sec guards and accompanying drones. Zhoh's warriors stood in a group under the watchful eyes of the guards.

The lieutenant was growing impatient with his lackey's inability to sort out the problem with the identification Mato had presented at the gate.

The being at the computer station shook his head. "There is a problem, Lieutenant Fu, but I cannot isolate it."

"Perhaps there is not a problem," Mato said. "Perhaps the problem lies in your software." He acted calm, but he put a note of rising irritation in his voice. "I cannot be held here for long. I have responsibilities. If I am not back to my unit soon, I will be missed."

"That is not my problem," Lieutenant Fu said, raising his voice as well. "The security of this spaceport is my responsibility."

So far, Zhoh held himself in check. They had not been relieved of their weapons, merely detained.

The security alarm shrilled to life out on the starport.

Lieutenant Fu watched as one of the screens at the front of the room shifted over to another location. In the shadows in front of the storage bay where Rangha kept his illicit goods, two cloaked shadows pulled back and ran.

Lights tore away the night, chasing the two fleeing figures and Zhoh noticed the armored boots of the Terran Army.

Energized by the security breach, Lieutenant Fu glared at Mato. "Those men tried to break into your unit! When

I brought you in here, I put that unit on immediate lock-down! Why are those people out there?"

"I don't know," Mato replied.

Cursing, Fu turned to his guards. "Lock these people down! I am going to find out what is going on!"

Zhoh knew that was not going to happen. He unfolded immediately, drew his *patimong*, and cleaved the lieutenant from crown to jaw with one blow. Blood and brain matter flecked the screens and the computer officer.

Even as Zhoh unlimbered his Kimer pistol, his warriors exploded into action. Particle beams, lasers, and solid rounds filled the air. The Green Dragon sec men fell in pieces.

Mato crushed one guard's face and skull with his primary and shot another with his particle beam weapon, vaporizing a large hole through his chest.

Zhoh only had time to kill one more guard, who managed to wound Lieutenant Yuen in one of his lesser arms, before the fight was over.

The alarm continued to shrill and the comm on the computer called for attention. One of the warriors had shot the computer operator in the back. His clothing and his flesh smoldered and set off a smaller smoke alarm.

"Which way?" Mato asked.

"To the storage bay," Zhoh replied.

Doubtless, Mato knew that many sec guards would be closing in on that area, but he asked no questions, simply led the way out of the security office.

0306 Hours Zulu Time

Sage knew they couldn't outrun the sec lights even with the assists from the hardsuits. His mind raced, trying to figure out their best exfil route.

"Top, I'm sending air support and ground support your way," Halladay said. "Blue Jay Twelve and Fourteen are two minutes away."

"That would be a waste of time, sir, and a diplomatic nightmare. We don't have any authority here. This starport is Green Dragon territory."

"They're running drugs and guns out of that place," Halladay said.

"Can you prove that? Or are renters simply abusing their storage privileges?" Sage followed Pingasa around the corner of the nearest building as two Green Dragon sec guards opened fire.

Bullets chewed holes in the plascrete wall and a laser burned a meter-wide swath from the corner, leaving slag running down to the ground.

Watching Kiwanuka's overlay on his faceshield, Sage saw both sec guards go down to her armor-piercing rounds. Chunks of armor blew out from their chests, showing where the bullets had gone. Sage knew that the Green Dragon Industrial Trade was a purely criminal corp, so he didn't sweat the body count. Those men wouldn't have hesitated to kill his people.

He hated the fact that he hadn't been able to uncover the secrets in the storage bay. There probably wouldn't be another chance.

"Top!" Culpepper called. "We've got incoming!"

Glancing back at the corporal's position, Sage spotted three powersuits headed their way in long, loping strides, cutting off their retreat.

"Time to come down, Kiwanuka," Sage said. "We've got to find a new exit strategy. Corporal Culpepper, close it up. Noojin, Jahup, in with the group."

The three joined Sage just as Kiwanuka dropped to the ground a meter away. The lead powersuit fired a short-range missile that struck the rooftop where Kiwanuka had been. Plascrete shattered and a ten-meter section of the wall toppled free to land on the ground nearby.

"Move!" Sage shouted, and led the way back down the aisle between the rows of storage bays.

Figures swept around a building fifty meters in front of Sage and ran toward him and his team. He pulled the Roley up and prepared to fire, then got slammed to the ground as another short-range missile hammered the ground behind them.

A crater opened up and threw a landslide of plascrete rubble and dirt at them, covering the whole area in a haze. Knocked from his feet, Sage skidded for several meters and watched as the approaching group got blown from their feet in a near miss as well.

Rolling to a prone position, Sage pulled the Roley to his shoulder and took aim at the man in front of him. Before he squeezed the trigger, he recognized Captain Zhoh GhiCemid seventeen meters away.

"Wait!" Zhoh had his rifle pointed at Sage's head.

"Hold your fire," Sage told his people.

"Those are Phrenorians," Culpepper argued.

"We're not fighting Phrenorians on Makaum," Sage said. *Yet.* His aim never wavered. He opened his faceshield. "You know who I am."

"I do," Zhoh replied. "When I saw Terran Army armor, I expected it to be no other being."

The powersuits came nearer. Kiwanuka turned around and fired at one of them, putting armor-piercing rounds through the pilot's head and shoulders. The powersuit lost coordination and fell, taking down the one following closely behind it. The third one sidestepped his companions and laid down a barrage of fire that filled the air with bullets and explosives.

Choked by the roiling dust, Sage coughed and closed his faceshield again, letting the hardsuit filter out the impurities.

Two of Zhoh's warriors opened fire on the powersuit. Hammered by bullets, the pilot retreated. He paused only long enough to help the other survivor to his feet.

"I suggest we work together," Zhoh said. "Our chances of getting out of this will be better."

Behind him, three of his warriors laid down suppressive fire to hold the Green Dragon bashhounds at the other end of the aisle at bay. But holding a position wasn't going to work for any of them and Sage knew it.

"Agreed. We work together to get out of this," Sage answered over the team comm so his people would know what was going on.

Culpepper opened a private channel. "You've got to be kidding, Top! You can't trust Sting-Tails!"

"How well do you think we're going to do fighting them *and* the Green Dragons?" Sage spotted a nearby aisle that headed to the jungle to the north, behind the last row of storage bays.

Culpepper cursed.

"We go north." Sage pointed at the aisle so there would be no mistake. "We head into the jungle and try to fight our way back to the river."

Zhoh clambered to his feet as well and saluted Sage with his sword. "Fight well, Sergeant."

"You too," Sage responded. He waved to Noojin and Jahup. "See if you can find us a way out of here."

The two Makaum recruits dashed ahead. At least two rounds slapped into Jahup, partially turning him around, but he didn't appear injured as he sped up to catch Noojin.

Sage and Zhoh followed the two and Kiwanuka hung back so she could cover the Phrenorian captain. As they emerged at the other end of the aisle thirty meters behind Noojin and Jahup, Sage took up a position at the aisle, knowing the bashhounds would overtake them and trap them out in the open. He readied his weapons.

"What are you doing?" Kiwanuka asked.

"Buying time," Sage replied. "If they catch us out in the open without fallback positions, they'll cut us to pieces."

"I'll stay."

"No, Sergeant, you won't. I'm depending on your sniping ability to give me time to reach you. Now go."

Kiwanuka went and the rest of the soldiers followed her. Culpepper protested almost inaudibly, but he knew Sage was right. As he passed, he slipped Sage two claymores.

Sage shoved the claymores into the ground just inside the aisle and activated them. He shortened the Roley's stock so he could maneuver it more easily in close quarters. Then he waited and hoped he could buy his people—and himself—enough time to get out of the death trap they'd stepped into. He watched the end of the aisle as shadows from the approaching bashhounds filled it.

6217 Akej (Phrenorian Prime)

"What is the sergeant doing?" Zhoh watched the human as he ran back toward the storage bays, surprised at how Sage stopped at the end of the aisle they had just come through.

"A foolish thing," Mato replied. "He's going to get himself killed."

Zhoh stopped, remembering how the sergeant had stood up alone to Velesko Kos and his guards in the nightclub in Makaum, calling Kos a murderer to his face. That had been impressive, worthy of a warrior, worthy of glory.

"Come on, *triarr.*"

Zhoh took a fresh grip on his *patimong* and turned back to join Sage. "Go, Mato. That is an order. Get the warriors set up so they may defend the sergeant's retreat and mine when the time comes. Work with the Terrans."

"You're going to get yourself killed." Mato's pheromones smelled like metal, indicating his apprehension.

Excitement filled Zhoh as he thought of the coming battle. It would be glorious. He should have considered the tactic of slowing down their pursuit himself. His respect for the sergeant grew. "I have no intentions of dying today. Go."

THIRTY-ONE

Sage watched the Green Dragon sec guards fill the aisle, confident that their quarry was still running for the jungle. Behind him, Zhoh GhiCemid rushed back toward him, and for a moment the thought crossed his mind that the Phrenorian captain was going to attack him.

Then Zhoh ran to the opposite side of the aisle and took up a position holding his sword and pistol. His lesser hands filled with grenades.

"This is a daring move, Sergeant," Zhoh said.

"We can't fight a running battle on all fronts," Sage replied grimly.

"So we hold them here as long as we can, then fall back?"

"Yeah. I've got anti-personnel munitions set up here."

"So we will soften them up and then go on the offensive?"

The mention of *we* surprised Sage only for an instant. Zhoh was, after all, experienced in combat. He would appreciate the effort. "If we let them get out of there and surround us, we're dead," Sage said.

"Agreed. We kill these opponents until we can kill no more or until our people are in position."

"Yes. Good luck, Captain."

"We do not need luck," Zhoh said. "In this, we are in our element." His synthetic voice included a hint of pride and anticipation.

Sage waited till the bashhounds were halfway down the eight-meter-length aisle. "Take cover, Captain."

Zhoh ducked back around the corner of the aisle, his back pressed into the plascrete wall.

Sliding back into cover as well, Sage set off the first claymore. The explosion unleashed a maelstrom of depleted uranium pellets that hammered the bashhounds' armor and broke their approach. The four security lights shining down into the aisle winked out in quick succession and pieces of transplas fell. The feed from Kiwanuka's hardsuit showed she had taken out the sec lights and was setting her sights on the guards racing across the rooftops.

She shot one of the guards through the head and the man spun out of control as his momentum carried him over the edge. His corpse dropped onto the mass of confused bashhounds in the aisle.

Sage popped the two ParaSights from his armor and interfaced their vid links, allowing him to see the combat area from above as well. He set off the second claymore, this one packed with plasma, and hellfire pummeled the bashhounds that had pushed through their dead to resume the fight. The heat slagged their armor and the men inside died screaming.

Zhoh pitched grenades among the survivors and more plasma erupted in smaller pockets.

The advancing line stalled and broke. The bashhounds at the back began to retreat. Another sec guard on top of the storage bay to the left dropped over the side, wounded and flailing like a bird trying to take wing. Zhoh shot the man in the head before he hit the ground, quieting the screams.

Sage set off the remaining two claymores and added to the chaos and death toll. A mound of bodies choked the aisle.

"Sage," Kiwanuka called.

"On our way." Sage waved to Zhoh. "Time to go." He turned and headed toward his team, locating them on the HUD. They had taken cover amid knee-high brush behind a natural depression that only provided slight cover, but slight cover was better than no cover. Zhoh jogged effortlessly at Sage's side five meters away. Adrenaline pounded at Sage, dumping into his system. He accepted a tranq to level him out, to keep him focused. Too many things were going on around him and maintaining the links to the ParaSights was demanding. The tranq flooded through him, slowing things down and allowing him to be more attentive.

He would never have believed he would ever fight alongside a Phrenorian.

Three crawlers carrying Green Dragon bashhounds roared out of an aisle between storage bays five hundred meters to the east. They flared out into a one-two formation and streaked for Sage and Zhoh.

Knowing they would never make the holding position with the others, Sage stopped and brought his Roley to his shoulder, cycling a gel-grenade into the launcher mounted under the assault rifle. He centered on the lead crawler, put the reticule over the driver's head behind the windscreen, and pulled the trigger.

The gel-grenade sailed true, but the crawler climbed on a small rise and the explosive struck the vehicle's undercarriage. The resulting blast lifted the crawler on its left side and took out the wheels. The crawler returned to the ground but the wrecked wheel assemblies dug into the ground and flipped the vehicle. Swapping ends and turning over, the crawler rolled to a stop and landed on its side.

The crawler behind the lead vehicle swerved to miss the wreck. One of the bashhounds in the back stood on the rear deck behind a squat, ugly weapon that Sage couldn't immediately identify.

"Move!" Zhoh ordered. "Quickly!"

Evidently the Phrenorian captain recognized the weapon because he dove to the side. A heartbeat after Zhoh leaped away, Sage jumped as well, staying low.

A small sun erupted from the mouth of the weapon, struck the ground where Sage and Zhoh had been standing, and left a crater twelve meters wide.

Sage couldn't believe the portable cannon could deliver such destruction. Dirt rained down over his armor and dust clouded the area, wiping away his own field of vision. He brought up the views provided by the ParaSights and got himself situated.

"Top," Kiwanuka called over the comm.

"Still here." Sage pushed himself to his feet as the first crawler closed on him. Small arms fire burned through the air around him and bullets ricocheted from his armor. He leveled the Roley and shot the driver through the head with a depleted uranium round, then dodged to the side.

Unable to get completely away, or perhaps the driver yanked the wheel at the last minute in an attempt to save his own life, Sage got hit by the front of the crawler and flew eight meters before crashing into the ground. His senses reeled, but the near-AI automatically compensated, hitting him with another stimpak that blocked the pain and cleared his mind.

The bashhound holding the cannon fired another round as a bullet struck the side of his head. The HUD tracked the trajectory of the round back to Kiwanuka and Sage saw the group there was under attack as well. The cannon round struck the ground in front of the out-of-control crawler, creating a crater that the vehicle dropped into.

Through the ParaSights' view, Sage saw Zhoh standing his ground and firing particle beam blasts into the last crawler's windshield. Holes appeared in the transplas, and one of the blasts killed the bashhound in the passenger seat, but the driver remained hunkered down behind the wheel.

Stepping aside calmly, Zhoh avoided the crawler by centimeters, then flicked his tail out with blinding speed. Sage only just managed to see the tail pierce the thinner armor under the driver's chin. The venom acted immediately, causing the man to scream in agony and reach for his face.

Zhoh and Sage stood for a moment in the roiling dust cloud. The survivors of the second vehicle climbed from the crater. Sage pulled a lethal tangler grenade from his ammo rack and threw it at the men. When it struck the ground, buckyball strands erupted from the grenade, threaded around the bashhounds, then collapsed, pulling through the armor and bodies. The sec guards hit the ground in pieces.

On the run, Zhoh picked up the squat mobile cannon that had landed only a few meters away. The Phrenorian swept the weapon up in his arms and aimed it at the crawler whose driver he'd slain. Demonstrating more than a familiarity with the weapon, Zhoh opened fire and sent a miniature sun streaking for the crawler as the bash-hounds struggled to crawl from it.

The plasma charge hammered the crawler and turned it into a glowing pile of radiation and heat. The concussive wave blew Sage off his feet and knocked him back several meters.

You are losing consciousness, Sergeant, the near-AI said. *Taking steps now to alleviate stressors. You have no debilitating injuries.*

Sage tried to speak, tried to take a breath, then felt the new stimpak soaring through his system, reconnecting all the synapses in an Arctic rush. A headache dawned in the back of his skull and his jaw muscles quivered for a moment. Getting to his feet, he ignored the headache as his jaw unclenched. He still gripped the Roley and he brought it up into the ready position.

Zhoh lay a few meters away. The Phrenorian had been closer to the blast.

"Captain," Sage said when he approached the Phrenorian. Zhoh lay silent and still. Sage wasn't even sure if the captain was still alive. "Do you require—"

The sword came up in a blur and the segmented tail tip hurtled toward Sage's faceshield.

6259 Akej (Phrenorian Prime)

Rising up through the blackness that engulfed him, Zhoh felt like he was returning from *lannig.* Then he felt an iron hand gripping his primary arm and his tail tip slamming against something.

Vision returned to him and he saw the Terran sergeant

leaning down over him. Memory returned to Zhoh in a flash, ripping away the paralysis that gripped his mind and senses. He had attacked Sage while unconscious, but he couldn't apologize, not even with the truce behind them. He gazed at Sage's faceshield, trying to see the being's features and perhaps guess at what he was thinking.

Knowing the tension between them had to be broken, Zhoh drew a leg between him and Sage and shoved the human from him. From the way the sergeant's body shifted, Zhoh knew Sage had contemplated an attack, but he allowed himself to be disengaged. He held the assault rifle at the ready, but did not point it at Zhoh. However, it would only take a moment to bring it to bear.

Conscious of continued firing going on around him, Zhoh rolled backward and rose to his feet. He held the Vesokan portable plasma cannon in his lesser hands.

Bowing slightly, Zhoh spread his primary arms in a peaceful gesture. "I was not in my right mind."

"Copy that," Sage replied, pulling the Roley aside. "I had my bell rung too. Whatever that thing is, it packs a punch."

"It is very powerful for a single warrior to carry."

A small aerial vehicle rose out on the tarmac and sailed at them with cannon blazing. The rounds ripped into the surrounding terrain. Four powersuits approached at a run from nearby aisles through the storage buildings.

"We've got to get gone," Sage said.

Zhoh's mind churned, thinking of the storage bay and of Ellen Hodgkins and of General Rangha. He wasn't sure what had brought the sergeant and his team to the storage bay, but there had been far too much interest shown in the contents of that place. Despite his desire to prove General Rangha as unfit to command the action on Makaum, Zhoh couldn't let the general's complicity in the weapons black market be discovered.

So there was only one thing to be done.

Swinging the Vesokan plasma cannon toward the storage bay, Zhoh fired three times as quickly as he could. The miniature suns burned through the fortified plascrete walls and set off some of the munitions within.

The storage bay became a raging inferno as the ammo contained therein cooked off in quicker and quicker detonations. Some of the debris hit the aerial vehicle and knocked it off course. Before the pilot could recover, the aircraft struck the ground only forty meters from Zhoh and Sage and blew up, showering them in metallic and ceramic fragments.

The explosions continued to spread, throwing fire in all directions. The approaching powersuits held back as chunks of the buildings blew over them.

"Now we go," Zhoh told Sage.

Together, they ran toward the Terran soldiers and Phrenorian warriors. And as they ran, an idea of how Zhoh could use the Terran sergeant to get to Ellen Hodgkins occurred to him. He knew he would have to be sly, but it could be done.

0311 Hours Zulu Time

With the starport now in flames and still more explosions rocking the area, Sage and his group ran toward the river. The Green Dragon sec teams would cover the two entrances, thinking them the weakest and most logical points for invaders to escape by. And they would cover the aircraft because those would be a temptation for someone needing a quick getaway.

They covered the 1,452 meters to the wall in a short time while running flat out and only met minimal resistance, but the Green Dragons had vectored in on their escape path and knew which way they were headed. Crawlers, powersuits, and aircraft led the chase ahead of the foot soldiers.

"Corporal Dundee," Sage called over the comm.

"Here, Top, and I see you're bringing a crowd with you."

"That I am. I hope you're ready for them."

"Party favors are all assembled. Just give me the word."

"Drop the wall." Sage noted that they were 106.7 meters from the barrier, and should have been well out of the blast radius.

Bright orange flames showed through fracture lines that suddenly appeared in the wall. The cracks grew larger and the fire grew brighter. Then the wall fell into a jumble of fragments and the plasma charges died out. There was hardly any sound.

Dundee was an artist with explosives.

Noojin and Jahup led the way through the jungle, skirting flora and fauna that Sage knew he would have never seen. *Strof*, bloodsucking vines with limited intelligence, trembled restlessly from tree branches. Jahup blasted an *oskelo*, a flying snake, while on the run. There were more they narrowly avoided, but Sage didn't have time to identify them.

Detonations lit up the night with fire and thunder behind them. Through the ParaSights' views, Sage saw that the first line of Green Dragon sec had reached the hole in the barrier. The claymores knocked the lead powersuit down, but it recovered quickly.

"Figured on ground troops coming through first," Dundee admitted, "but I got something for the powersuits coming up next."

The powersuit muscled through the opening in the barrier and started down the gradual slope leading to the river. Three steps out, a munition exploded and unleashed a buckyball tangler that wrapped around the powersuit's legs and cut through them above the knees. Unable to stand, the powersuit went down.

The pilot of the second powersuit evidently thought the way would be clear and hurried past. A second tangler erupted from a tree and wrapped around the unit's chest. Man and machine were sliced in half.

That gave the rest of the sec team pause, but they fired their weapons from where they gathered. Craters erupted around Sage and his team as they hunkered down with Zhoh and his warriors.

The river was only 22.3 meters away, but fording the water would be impossible.

"Sergeant Sage, this is Blue Jay Twelve. Blue Jay Fourteen and myself are going to clear the way for you."

Sage looked up into the sky amid the lightning and the thunder that suddenly cut loose again. He magnified his view and spotted the two jumpcopters streaking toward them from Makaum.

"Copy that, Blue Jay Twelve. Any time you're ready." Sage relayed the information to Zhoh and his warriors.

Ten seconds later, air-to-ground missiles hammered the broken barrier.

"Go!" Sage urged.

The soldiers walked along the ground and the Phrenorians took to the water like they were born to it.

As Sage came back up on the other side, he spotted three sec crawlers on the retractable bridge. One of the jumpcopters swooped down and unleashed another flurry of missiles. The bridge blew into pieces and scattered across the river.

One of the aerial vehicles from the starport locked on to one of the jumpcopters and strafed cannon rounds in-

terspersed with green tracers. The jumpcopter pilot tilted
the nose down to avoid the barrage and to let the aircraft
pass. Then the jumpcopter wheeled around and fired its
cannons, catching the Green Dragon aircraft squarely.

Doomed, out of control, the sec aircraft crashed into
open jungle. Flames jetted up from the trees, catching in
some of the canopy and spreading briefly before settling
into a steady burn.

On the riverbank, the Terran soldiers and the Phrenorian warriors unconsciously separated into groups, each
to their own.

Sage studied his people and was glad they were all
alive. Some of the Phrenorian warriors looked worse for
the wear.

"Well," Zhoh said as they headed back toward the Offworlders' Bazaar, "it appears our brief détente on this
world has accomplished some good. The Green Dragon
slionunt have been set back here, and the damage surely
runs into millions of credits."

Sage decided the Phrenorian captain sounded happy,
and realized that he'd never heard that particular emotion
from them before. "I'll settle for that, Captain."

"We work well together, Sergeant. It is a shame that we
find ourselves on different sides in this war."

"You can always surrender, sir," Sage suggested.

One of the Phrenorian warriors started toward Sage,
but Zhoh held up a primary and waved the Sting-Tail back
into position.

"Perhaps there is a way we can continue our association
for a bit longer."

"I appreciate the help back there, sir, but I don't see that
happening." Sage watched the Phrenorian captain and remembered how Zhoh had been shamed on his own world
and assigned to Makaum. They were both blooded fight-

ers, both deserving of duty out on the front line where the war was hottest. Yet they were both stuck here.

"You were at Cheapdock for a reason, Sergeant. As was I. We ran afoul of the Green Dragons during our investigation of the same storage bay you were so interested in." Zhoh shrugged a little. "Perhaps you would allow me to buy you and your soldiers a drink and we could talk about that."

Sage flipped over to the comm channel he shared with Colonel Halladay. "What do you think, sir?"

"I think that you and I are buried so far in drek once General Whitford has us in his office regarding a 'semi-authorized' probe into Green Dragon business that went this badly we won't see sunlight for a month."

"The information Vekaby's men gave us led to that storage bay, sir," Sage reminded. "We were working on the ambush, shutting down illegal weapons, and I can guarantee from the way that storage bay exploded, weapons were kept there."

"I agree, but the general isn't going to like the fact that we've rocked his boat, and I don't think the locals are going to be happy with us either."

Sage studied the burning starport in the HUD. "That's probably true, sir."

"Do you think you can trust Zhoh?"

"No. He's after something. I just don't know what it is."

"I'm thinking we should try to find out."

"Yes sir."

"If you take him up on the offer of a drink, do you think you can keep yourself and your people alive?"

"That will definitely be on the agenda, sir."

"Then get it done, Top. If we're invited to go down the rabbit hole, we've got to follow it out."

"Yes sir."

"Be careful, Top."

"Copy that, sir." Sage swiveled his helmet back to the Phrenorian captain who waited patiently.

"Well, Sergeant?" Zhoh asked.

"If we're still talking after the first round, Captain, the second round is on me."

THIRTY-TWO

The bar was on the east side of New Makaum, distant from Zorg's Weeping Onion, but news of the Terran Army police action that had taken place in the bar and spilled over onto the street was on holo on the display at the back of the bar. The establishment was called Venom of the Ightskel and was operated by an independent company that was associated with Huang the noodle maker. Sage thought he remembered the men were cousins or something, but they didn't favor each other. Huang's family tended to be large and varied, and Sage suspected that kinship wasn't always by blood.

Only minutes before Sage and the others had reached the bar, the sky opened up and unleashed a monsoon. They'd ended up walking through mud the last kilometer and a half, and now part of that was tracked into the bar. Two of the servers worked to clean the floor with scoops and mops.

Sage had apologized for the mess, but Cai, the owner, shrugged and asked them what they wanted to drink. Judging from the prices he charged, he was making up for the janitorial inconvenience.

By the time Sage looked for a table amid what appeared to be a fusion of South Sea Isles décor and seventeenth-century Terran pirate Jolly Rogers flags and antique compasses, cutlasses, and sailcloth, the scattered clientele had deserted the bar, braving the rain and the wind.

Sage pointed to a table in the back corner. "Does that table suit, Captain?"

"It does."

Sage led the way, but even in his armor he felt vulnerable with his back exposed to the Phrenorian. The whole meeting felt wrong, but he wanted to know what was so important about the storage bay that Zhoh felt compelled to talk to him about it.

The soldiers and the warriors scattered around other tables, but they didn't fraternize. Sage thought that the mere fact they weren't shooting at each other was about the best they could expect even under the circumstances. A lot of blood had been spilled on both sides during the war. All of the individuals in the bar, except for Noojin and Jahup, were veterans and had lost fellow soldiers and warriors.

The chairs hadn't been made to a Phrenorian's scale, but Zhoh made do. The captain reached into a pouch on his thorax armor and took out a small flat black device in one of his lesser hands. The instrument was devoid of controls except for a small button.

"This is a white noise generator," Zhoh said. "I thought it best that we speak in private. This place is known to associate with Huang the noodle maker, and he can be a *foseby* if left unfettered." The Phrenorian term most closely translated into "busybody" in Terran.

"Yes sir."

"At this range, once I activate it, your soldiers will not be able to hear us, and you won't have any access to your comm."

"Copy that, Top. We're not going anywhere." Kiwanuka sat closest to Sage, only two tables away. She drank with her left hand and her right was beneath the table. Sage had no doubt that she was holding a weapon. If he had been her, he would have been holding one.

"All right," Sage agreed.

Zhoh pressed the button on the device and placed it on the table between them.

Sergeant, all comm access outside this unit has been severed, the near-AI said. *Suggest—*

"Cancel that," Sage interrupted. "Suspend comm links until I tell you to reconnect."

Affirmative.

Sage removed his helmet and set it on the floor beside him. Switching from the 360-degree view to only what he could see in front of him and peripherally was disturbing. He felt limited in a dangerous situation. He ignored the feeling and picked up his glass. "What are we drinking to, Captain?"

"A successful joint venture." Zhoh lifted his glass in one of his lesser hands.

"Past or present, sir?"

"This one to the past, and the next—if you are willing to proceed with what I am about to suggest—to the present."

"All right." Sage tossed back the sake, felt it burn his throat, then explode in his stomach, reminding him of how long it had been since he'd sat down to have a real meal. Drinking on an empty stomach wasn't a good idea.

Zhoh finished his drink and set his glass back down. "According to the holo in back of the bar, you had an encounter with the beings who attacked your fort yesterday morning."

"It's not my fort," Sage corrected.

"As you say." Zhoh dismissed that with a wave. "Since you have arrived here, you have had a great impact on Terran Army operations, so I associate you with the new measures I have seen."

"After the ambush that killed Sergeant Terracina the first day I got here, we had no choice but to go on the offensive. Things changed."

"Of course. You did find the beings responsible for the attack on the fort?"

"We did."

"And that led you to the storage bay in Cheapdock."

Sage thought about the question for a moment, turning around all the possibilities.

"You are not giving away any true secrets, Sergeant. Simple logic dictates that the beings were responsible for your appearance at the storage bay."

"Because there were weapons there?"

"Yes."

Sage leaned forward a little. "I didn't see what was inside that storage bay, Captain Zhoh, so how did you know what was in there?"

6259 Akej (Phrenorian Prime)

Too late, Zhoh found that he'd been trapped by Sage. The sergeant was more quick-witted than he had any right to be. Zhoh stared into the human's two eyes and had to tamp down his anger. For a moment he considered killing the sergeant. Sage was going to be dangerous in the future. He'd proven that time and time again.

In fact, Sage was dangerous now. Even if Zhoh succeeded in manipulating the sergeant, knowledge of his work with the human would reach the Empire. If they were successful in their coming endeavor, that would prove to be only an inconvenience.

"We watch what is going on," Zhoh said. "We were tracking the weapons as well."

"You weren't tracking them along the same lines I was, Captain." Sage's voice remained flat.

"No, I wasn't." Zhoh thought quickly and came up with what he believed was a simple enough lie with enough truth to hook the sergeant. "Yesterday, three of my warriors were killed out in the jungle. I began an investigation. From what was discovered, it appeared the murderers who killed my warriors were Makaum."

"Not the same men I went after."

"No. This was another group." Zhoh knew the sergeant would believe that. The attack on the fort wasn't a singular event. Maybe others hadn't happened yet, but they would as long as those weapons remained unsecured.

"Did you find out who they were?"

"We tracked them from the scene."

"Who were they?"

"Those beings no longer need names, Sergeant. Phrenorians are not known for their mercy."

Sage paused for a moment, then nodded. "Fair enough. So these men told you about the storage bay?"

"No. They told me about a Voroughan black-market dealer."

"Erque Ettor?"

Zhoh considered the question. Ettor had no connection to General Rangha. Sazuma would not have given Ettor Rangha's name. She would have kept her business private. He could give the sergeant information about Ettor.

"Erque Ettor will no longer have need of his name either," Zhoh said. "He gave me the location of the storage bay and the passcode to get in. We went to Cheapdock with falsified identification and opened the storage bay. It was filled with weapons."

"I could tell that from the way it blew up, and that explains how you knew shooting that building would set off the munitions."

"Yes."

Sage's gaze consumed Zhoh again. "But it doesn't explain why the Green Dragons allow a group of Phrenorians onto their starport."

Zhoh suddenly realized that lying to a Terran was much harder than he'd expected. "I went there under the guise of a customer."

Lieutenant Fu and his men were dead, even if the Green Dragon Corp decided to share information with the Terran Army. The lie could not be unwoven.

Zhoh decided to plunge ahead and lay down the bait he was hoping to use before the sergeant could pick at his story any further. "I claimed I was meeting with the person who owned the storage bay. Her name is Ellen Hodgkins. I believe you are familiar with her from your involvement with Velesko Kos."

Sage's expression remained unreadable to Zhoh, but there was a slight shift in his body language. He leaned back in his chair a little. "I'm familiar with Ellen Hodgkins. She was part of Velesko Kos's drug cartel."

"I know where she is," Zhoh stated.

A moment passed as Sage considered that. Zhoh let the sergeant think about the information as long as he wished.

"I'm surprised you haven't gone after her, sir."

"I plan on going after her, but in order to do that, I need your help."

"My help?"

"I can't go where she is."

Sage was silent for a moment, thinking. Zhoh watched the sergeant and knew that when the day they were true adversaries came, Sage would make a dangerous opponent. Killing the sergeant here and now would be a wise move, but he couldn't do that. Not yet. He needed Sage for now, and there was a matter of honor between them. He might have saved Sage's life in the club against Velesko, but the probability was greater that Sage and his soldiers had saved not only Zhoh, but his warriors as well. The debt was not yet balanced.

"She's not on Makaum," Sage said.

"She is not."

"But she's within your reach, otherwise we wouldn't be having this discussion. So that means she's on one of the space stations."

"Yes." Zhoh didn't feel threatened giving away so much information. Chances were good that Sage would be able to find the female on his own, but it would take time, and he would know that might not be time he had to give. News of the attack on Cheapdock would spread, and it wouldn't take long for people to figure out what had happened there.

"You'll tell me where she is," Sage said, "but only if you get what you want."

"Yes."

"Then what do you want, Captain?"

0426 Hours Zulu Time

"Zhoh's not telling you everything," Kiwanuka said over a private comm link as she walked beside Sage along the road leading from the Venom of the Ightskel.

"Of course he's not." Sage's stomach growled but he knew it would be a while before he had a decent meal. He pulled a protein-sub bar from his pack, opened it, and bit into it. "We're not telling him everything either."

The road was mostly deserted at this time of the morning, but there were a few stragglers limping or lurching home. Insects and flying lizards continued pelting Sage's faceshield. His eyes burned from going so long without sleep.

"I'll bet he knows more about the black-market weapons business than we do," Kiwanuka said.

"That's a sucker bet. He knows why we're here, but we don't know why the Phrenorians are interested."

"You're not buying his story about three Phrenorian warriors getting killed out in the jungle?"

"Not for a minute. If that had happened, they would have put the heads of *someone* out on poles in front of the Phrenorian embassy."

"Exactly. So explain to me why you're letting him accompany us—"

"*Us?*"

"Somebody's got to watch your back, Top. That's me. Noojin and Jahup haven't spent any time in space, even on a space station, so taking them out of their element wouldn't be smart. Pingasa is a tech jockey and he was out of his element tonight except when it came to breaking and entering. I'm better than anyone else you've got here."

"There's Culpepper."

"Culpepper alone with Phrenorians for backup? No. Not gonna happen. He'd drive himself insane trying to look in two directions at once, not knowing who to trust."

"You don't trust the Phrenorians."

"No, but I won't let it get in the way of taking care of business and you know that."

"I do."

"So I'm in?"

"Definitely."

"Then why didn't you tell me?"

"Something this risky, Sergeant? I only want to take volunteers." Sage shifted gears. "I want Ellen Hodgkins and whoever bankrolled the attack on the fort off the board. We're drawing a line tonight, and nobody's going to think twice about what we stand for." He paused. "In the meantime, we hold Zhoh close to us, try to figure out what he's really doing here."

Sage flagged down the two crawlers he'd sent for while an aircar floated down to settle in front of Zhoh and his warriors.

"Still following the rabbit hole, Top?" Halladay asked over the comm.

"Yes sir, and we're going offplanet to do it." Sage quickly explained the situation as they boarded the crawler. Halladay wasn't happy, but he didn't call off the op.

THIRTY-THREE

On every planet Sage had ever served on, there was a "North Star Spaceport." He'd heard that the actual owners were an interplanetary criminal syndicate that used the small spaceports to launder credits, or maybe to ship their own black-market goods. Or maybe there was a small corp somewhere that had licensed the name throughout the known star systems, spread the gossip themselves, and charged licensing fees to the people who wanted to set up shop under the North Star name.

Sage wasn't sure what the true story was, and he didn't really care. He and Kiwanuka left the other soldiers at the spaceport. Culpepper didn't care for the idea, but he was a soldier who followed orders.

Faceshield lifted, Culpepper scowled at the Phrenorian warriors milling around the aircar. "I'll be here till you get back, Top."

"I know you will, Corporal. I'm counting on it." Sage walked toward the spaceport office, a small plascrete block that had the name painted across it.

The spaceport was only large enough for four shuttles at any one time. There were no storage areas. Refueling and repairs were done in space in rented mechanics' bays on space stations. Profits were taken through quick turnover traffic, dealing with regular deliveries as well as taking in overflow from other corps' ports.

One of the shuttles sat out on the field. It was a no-frills scarred box with a rounded nose, stubby wings, and three large thrusting engines. There wouldn't be anything comfortable about the ride.

The small man in the office window had white hair and bowed shoulders, and age had written a story in the wrinkles on his face. He was a man who had been countless places and seen countless things, but now he stared out at Sage with bewilderment.

"Sergeant Sage?" the clerk asked.

Sage responded that he was. He had called North Star because he hadn't wanted to use a Terran Army shuttle and risk tipping off Ellen Hodgkins.

"You requested four seats on the shuttle?"

"Yes."

The clerk motioned toward Kiwanuka and Zhoh and the Phrenorian warrior that accompanied them. "For the four of you?"

"Yes. Round trip."

"For all of you?"

"Yes."

For a moment longer, the clerk stared. His bewilderment became disbelief, then he firmed his jaw, processed Sage's credstick, and handed them the tickets. The little man continued staring after them as they went to the shuttle.

Near Space
6259 Akej (Phrenorian Prime)

Zhoh endured the launch, felt the giant primary of gravity pressing him back into the foam seat, and concentrated on the mission he had set for himself. Breathing was difficult, but he worked at it and kept himself calm.

Being in space was no problem, but leaving a gravity well or returning to one came close to unnerving him—though he would never admit that to anyone. Give him his *pati-mong* and a place to stand and he would battle any being, but he dreaded the excess gravity because it always felt like his exoskeleton would give way under the increased forces. He had never seen that happen to anyone, though there were those who claimed to have seen such a thing, and he did not think it could happen under normal conditions.

But he only had to remember Sage and the female sergeant lying in other foam seats to know that these conditions were not normal.

"When we find Ellen Hodgkins," Mato said over the comm link from the foam seat beside him, "we cannot control what she will tell the sergeant."

Zhoh didn't know how Mato could think to speak at the moment, or how he found the breath.

"What if she tells the sergeant about General Rangha's involvement in the weapons dealings?"

Zhoh already knew the answer to that. "Then we kill them all, Mato. At that point, we will have no choice." He felt angrier that he had to find these loose ends and deal with them so carefully. This was Rangha's mess, and it should have put his head on a pole. But Zhoh's honor would not allow him to let the Empire be embarrassed in such a manner. A Phrenorian warrior was a fighter. Not a thief or profiteer. What a warrior did when he took up his weapons was to further the interests of the Empire, not himself.

For a moment, Zhoh caught himself on the horns of that dilemma. There might be some who would say his actions now were to further his own interests, not the Empire's. His future and that of the Empire were aligned. He would not think—could not think—any other way. Whether the Empire admitted it or not, it needed him to clean up Rangha's dishonor, and it needed him to take Makaum.

Finally the shuttle broke free of the planet. Zhoh breathed deeply while his body was suddenly weightless. Then the shuttle pilot kicked in the nose jets and started the spacecraft spinning fast enough to provide 0.3 g. The weightlessness went away and Zhoh felt comfortable.

The *Hooded Vorol*
Orbiting Makaum
0746 Hours Zulu Time

"I can't allow you to carry arms aboard this ship." The tall, thin Cheelchan female looked imposing in her black *smaup*-hide coverall. Her own dark skin looked leathery and jaundiced. Her eyes were slits and sat too far apart on either side of her head to be considered attractive by Terran standards, but it echoed the fine bone structure of her body.

Cheelcha was a small backwater world that came naturally to crime, especially smuggling. It was a stopgap planet, a place between Gates where ships would meet and trade in illicit goods that were outlawed at the end of one Gate or the other.

The people had lived in clans and fought each other for the resources, till the offworlders had discovered them.

Then they had banded together, more or less, in the sprawls and had stolen from those who came among them. Once they had ships, they spread to the stars, usually in the same line of work.

Sage gave her a flat stare. "You will step out of my way and allow me to do my job."

"You have no right—" the Cheelchan said.

"I have every right," Sage roared in his drill instructor's voice. The Cheelchan ensign drew back from him. "The Terran Army signed on to protect Makaum."

"This isn't Makaum." Her voice took on a strident tone.

"You're in orbit around Makaum and you do business onplanet," Sage replied. "As such, that makes you part and party to Terran Army peacekeeping efforts, including the right for Terran Army personnel to board and search your ship at any time."

That was why Zhoh had needed Sage, to pull rank on the ship while they looked for Ellen Hodgkins.

"Check your manifests, ensign," Sage continued, "or pull the ship's captain away from breakfast and break the news to him. Either way, I'm going to do my job." He strode through the hatch to the small security area and the young Cheelchan stepped back from him.

She tapped her comm badge and connected to the captain. Sage didn't stay to hear the conversation. He'd done enough raids to know how that would go. He stopped in front of the ship's computer, tapped the keyboard, and scowled at it as the device immediately locked down.

"Wishing you'd brought Pingasa now, Top?" Kiwanuka asked over the comm.

"Do you know anything about breaking into these things?"

"If it doesn't involve a sledge or explosive materials, no."

Sage turned to the Cheelchan female. "Open these records."

She stood up to her full height and quivered a little. "I have sworn to protect the rights of our guests."

"If I search through this computer and match it against warrants on this planet and others, I may end up taking all of your clients into custody." Sage knew that was probably true.

"Tell me who you are looking for," the ensign said.

"That's not happening."

The Phrenorian warrior with Zhoh stepped forward. "Perhaps I can be of assistance, Sergeant." He held up a PAD configured for Phrenorian use.

Sage looked at Zhoh.

"Mato is good with electronics systems," the Phrenorian captain stated. "He got us through traps set in the storage bay."

Sage remembered how impressed Pingasa had sounded when looking at the locking mechanism on the storage bay in Cheapdock. If Mato had gotten through problems there, then the warrior had to be good with tech.

However, allowing the Phrenorian to access the data first was risky. Sage didn't trust Zhoh to share everything.

Time was also a concern. Ellen Hodgkins, if she was still on the *Hooded Vorol,* could hear about what had happened at Cheapdock at any time, realize that the storage bay had been at the center of that, and elect to jump ship. The only thing Sage was banking on was that she wasn't an early riser and that no one had tipped her off.

Sage stepped back from the computer to allow Mato access. "Get it done."

Mato moved into the space, opened the computer with a small screwdriver he handled like a surgeon, then attached clips from his PAD to the circuitry within. In seconds, he had access to the computer network and appeared to be scouring screen after screen of information.

"I have the information." Mato took his leads back and deposited his PAD into his chest pouch. "I can take us to our destination."

Sage let the Phrenorian take the lead and followed him.

Out in the wide metal-and-ceramic hall, Sage glanced up at the cams located along the hallway. "I know you didn't mention our destination back in the sec office, but they're going to track us. They may warn everyone on whatever floor we stop at."

"They will not be tracking us," Mato said with calm authority. "I have blinded their vid and aud sec systems, and I have created a passcode that will allow us access to most compartments on the ship." He stopped in front of the ship's elevator and used a lesser hand to punch a keypad.

The doors slid open with a *whoosh*.

"You did all that in the little time you spent on their computer network?" Sage asked.

"Some things you prepare for ahead of time, Sergeant." Mato stepped into the elevator and held the door till everyone entered, then he pressed the D Deck button.

Sage was impressed, and he made a mental note to talk to Pingasa when they returned. Computer security at the fort needed to be hardened—immediately.

The elevator dropped toward D Deck.

D Deck
The *Hooded Vorol*
0751 Zulu Hours

When the elevator doors opened, Sage blocked the way with his arm and looked at Mato. "I want to know where we're going."

Mato turned to Zhoh. "Captain?"

"Tell him," Zhoh said.

"Of course, sir." Mato turned back to Sage. "Our destination is Unit Forty-seven. She was registered as Deborah Jones. An innocuous name. Other Joneses are listed as being on the ship. It seems to be a popular name."

Sage chose not to explain why Jones or Nguyen or Ivanov might be so popular and focused on the mission. "You're sure it's her?"

"The *Hooded Vorol* keeps a vid log of its guests. I matched her photo. She has changed her hair length and color, and the color of her eyes, but it is her."

"I'll take the lead," Sage said, pulling his Birkeland and setting it to stun.

"Of course, Sergeant," Zhoh said.

Sage stepped into the hall and kept going. The first units were numbered 61 and 62, but the living quarters were tiny, claustrophobic areas for most people who weren't used to them, so Unit 47 wasn't so far away.

Only a few guests were in the hallway. One glance at the black, battle-scarred Terran Army AKTIVsuits—or maybe it was the Phrenorians, Sage conceded—sent them scurrying.

Just before Sage reached the door to Unit 47, two men stepped out of the unit across the hall. They wore armor and carried weapons, so Sage knew the no-weapons rule wasn't enforced on the ship. The men looked seasoned, carrying scars and the air of men used to combat.

One of the men—a short, swarthy older man with an obvious cyber eye and the smooth way of moving that advertised he had wired reflexes—triggered the face-recog programming in Sage's near-AI. *Attention, Sergeant, the man before you has been identified as Xander Singh, a known associate of Velesko Kos from time spent in the employment of Domanska Mining Corp in the Awver system. He is a wanted fugitive in three different—*

The door to Unit 47 opened and Ellen Hodgkins left the room in a hurry. Evidently the ensign had managed to send out an alert somehow from the sec office.

THIRTY-FOUR

D Deck
The *Hooded Vorol*
0753 Zulu Hours

Hodgkins had cropped her hair as Mato had said, cutting it to jaw length, and it was now electric blue with silver streaks. She wore black-lensed eye protectors, so he couldn't be sure about the eye color, but her profile was a match to the facial-recog that had been dug up when they'd investigated Velesko Kos. The skintight sky-blue bodysuit flaunted her curves, making her stand out yet be instantly dismissed as window dressing for some corp exec. She carried a small matte-black case in one hand.

Singh stepped forward, putting himself between Sage and Hodgkins. He spoke over his shoulder to the woman. "You need to go." He drew a vibro knife from the sheath at his hip. The blade was as long as Sage's forearm and the weapon hummed in readiness.

"Ellen Hodgkins." Sage drew the shokton he'd equipped himself with for use on the ship. Fighting in space was problematic. Beam weapons and depleted uranium rounds ricocheted off the bulkheads when they didn't punch holes in a hull. "By the authority of the Terran Army, you're under arrest for conspiracy regarding the attack on Fort York and for weapons trafficking."

Hodgkins ran for the stairwell doorway at the other end of the hall. The second man trailed after her, drawing a sonic mace capable of delivering hydrostatic damage to anything that held fluid. The sonic blast could do significant damage even through a hardsuit.

"Get out of the way," Sage told Singh.

The man shook his head. "That's not going to happen."

Sage feinted with the shokton, then he delivered a backhand blow with the weapon aimed at Singh's head. Singh stepped back to avoid that, and when he did, Sage tossed a non-lethal tangler grenade at the man's feet.

Moving smoothly and quickly, Singh swept the grenade behind him with the vibro blade and ducked away from the released plaswire coils that exploded out of it. The strands looped uselessly in the empty expanse between Singh and the other bodyguard.

Still in motion, Singh went on the attack. The vibro blade blurred in front of him. If not for the musculature of the hardsuit, Sage knew he'd never have been able to keep up with his opponent. Again and again, the blade bit into the armor on Sage's forearms as he blocked thrusts and slashes. The cuts ran deep, drawing sparks from wiring and sometimes blood from Sage's flesh beneath the armor. The nano-circuitry repairing the hardsuit scrambled to rewire all the systems to keep Sage's hands online and operational.

Warning, Sergeant. Suit integrity in forearms and hands are at 57 percent. Continuing to battle in this manner will result in eventual failure of—

In the past, Sage had been up against opponents wielding knives and swords, and he'd fought them on the battlefield and in rough bars, in the hardsuit and unassisted. Singh was one of the best he'd ever encountered, but the man had dropped into a rhythm. Perhaps fights didn't normally last this long for him, or the rhythm had come from sparring with the same partners too long, but Sage spotted the cadence and anticipated Singh's next strike before he made it.

When Singh struck, Sage closed his hand around the man's knife hand and squeezed, feeling the bones in the hand shatter even though they were reinforced. To his credit, Singh ignored the pain and dropped the vibro knife into his other hand. He stabbed at Sage's stomach and managed to get at least six centimeters of blade through the armor on Sage's right side.

Administering pain blocker. Administering coagulant. Do you require—

Before Singh could drive the vibro blade any deeper, Sage backhanded the man on the side of his face, breaking his jaw and slamming his head into the wall. Singh's eyes glazed and rolled up into his head. Sage allowed the man to sink to the floor when his legs gave out beneath him.

"On your left, Sergeant." Zhoh brushed by Sage in the narrow hallway, quickly followed by Mato.

Ignoring the fading pain in his stomach as the meds kicked in, Sage wrapped a hand around the vibro blade and pulled it out. Nausea swam through his mind and it knew it was more from shock combined with lack of sleep over the last three days than any damage he'd suffered. This wasn't the first time he'd been stabbed.

Blood pooled inside the armor, but it was already responding to the coagulants and nanobots in his system.

"Clear my head," Sage said as he steadied himself.

Administering stimpak. Recommending med center and sleep. You are nearing exhaustion.

"Sage." Kiwanuka stood beside him.

"I'm fine," Sage told her, and started toward the other end of the hallway, where Zhoh had engaged the other bodyguard.

The Phrenorian captain stood his ground and blocked the sonic mace again and again with his sword. The stims hit Sage's system and his vision narrowed to dark tunnels. For a minute he didn't think his legs were going to hold him. He'd pushed himself too far, too hard, and for too long. If it hadn't been for the hardsuit and the microgravity in the ship, he didn't think he would have managed to remain standing. Stab wounds tended to have that reaction more than bullet or beam wounds. There was something visceral about getting pierced by a knife.

Beyond Zhoh, Mato, and the bodyguard, Ellen Hodgkins opened the stairwell and went through.

6313 Akej (Phrenorian Prime)

The female was getting away.

The realization of that infuriated Zhoh. He resented the bodyguard standing in front of him, preventing him from reaching his prey. At another time, he might have respected his opponent's knowledge of arms and the bravery with which he fought, but that time was not now.

Zhoh thrust at the bodyguard again and once more found the sonic mace intercepting his blow before it could be delivered. The initial block shivered along Zhoh's arm, but the immediate sonic discharge that followed threatened to tear his arm from his body. Zhoh didn't dare expose a limb to the destruction the sonic mace would carry. A humanoid's skeleton would fracture under the onslaught, but under the chitin, his body would be destroyed. *Lannig* would not remedy that.

The stairwell door closed and erased sight of Ellen Hodgkins.

Cursing, Zhoh lashed out again. This time the bodyguard was not quick enough to block the keen blade completely and it sliced along his brow over his right eye. Enduring the sonic blast again, aching from the injuries he'd suffered, Zhoh moved to the bodyguard's right and took advantage of the temporary blindness caused by blood weeping into his eye.

Zhoh thrust again, but the *patimong* only delivered a glancing blow. The blade cut into the bodyguard's armor, but didn't reach the flesh beneath. Knowing he had an opening, the bodyguard whipped the sonic mace toward Zhoh's head. Zhoh managed to get his other primary up to block the bodyguard's blow, avoiding the weapon and striking his opponent's wrist.

Twisting slightly, Zhoh whipped his tail forward and sank the tip into the bodyguard's jugular, putting his strength and weight into the strike. Envenomed, already dying and losing motor control, the bodyguard stumbled back and grabbed at his throat as his air passages closed down.

Mercilessly, Zhoh shoved the soon-to-be corpse to the hallway floor and continued on. Mato followed him, and the sergeant was once more moving, with the female sergeant at his side.

Zhoh's thoughts raced as he opened the stairwell door and went through. He could not allow Ellen Hodgkins to tell what she knew about Rangha's criminal activities, and he didn't want to fight Sage and the other soldier here.

If he and Mato killed them on the *Hooded Vorol*, Zhoh was certain the ship's crew would never let them leave the vessel alive.

Defeat seemed determined to snatch victory from his grasp. Pausing in the stairwell, Zhoh smelled the woman's scent and knew that she had gone up rather than down. He rushed up the steps that were built for humans more than they were constructed for Phrenorians.

He opened a comm to Mato. "You have seen the ship's blueprints?"

"Yes."

"The woman is going up. What is up there?"

"Three decks up, there is a shuttle holding area. If she can get one of those vessels, she can leave this ship."

Zhoh redoubled his efforts, launching himself up several steps at once, taking advantage of the microgravity.

G Deck
The *Hooded Vorol*
6371 Akej (Phrenorian Prime)

Stepping out of the stairwell on G Deck, Zhoh gazed around the wide-open desk. Bulkheads set the 5,000-meter-long space off from the rest of the *Hooded Vorol* on three sides. The fourth side held three door bays that allowed shuttles to leave the ship.

The shuttles were small, space-use only, and not meant to make planetfall. Several shapes and sizes occupied the rows before Zhoh, ranging from single-pilot slingers to small cargo carriers.

"Hey." The speaker was one of five Cheelchan sec guards emerging from around a boxy cargo shuttle much like the one that had brought Zhoh and the others to the

Hooded Vorol, only this one was on a much smaller scale and looked more frail. "Put your weapons down and stand against the bulkhead." His battle armor gleamed and he held a pistol in his hands before him.

The other sec guards looked like copies of the first and only maintained a ragged sense of combat, not spread out the way they should have been.

Mato, Sage, and Sergeant Kiwanuka joined Zhoh in the shuttle area.

"I'm Terran Army," Sage declared, flashing his ID on a holo in front of his hardsuit. "We're here on a peacekeeping matter. These people are with me. Now back down and let us get our jobs done."

"We have orders to detain you," the sec leader said. "Now get up against the wall."

A handful of beings stepped out from the other side of the shuttle space, saw what was taking place, and quickly retreated.

"Captain," Sage said quietly over the comm link, "I'm not going to let these men stop me."

"Agreed," Zhoh replied. "Mato and I will go to the right—"

"Sergeant Kiwanuka and I will go to the left. If you have to hurt them, hurt them. But do not kill them unless you're forced to."

"Understood, Sergeant." Zhoh readily agreed to forestall an argument, but he would do whatever he needed to in order to achieve his goal. If these beings had to die, then that was the way it would be. "Go!"

Zhoh hurled himself to the right and Mato was right behind him. Sage and the female sergeant split off to the left. Immediately, the Cheelchan sec guards fired their assault weapons. Zhoh expected the rounds to ricochet from the bulkhead the stairwell door was located on, but they shattered against the surface instead. Dye marked the impact areas around small projectiles that studded the wall. Almost instantly, the projectiles sizzled with energy.

Mercy weapons. Zhoh wanted to scoff at their opponents' weakness. Such weapons would never be allowed in the hands of a Phrenorian. He slid behind the bulk of a nearby shuttle and smelled the air, getting a sense of the direction the female had taken.

Listening to the flurry of armored boots striking the metal deck, Zhoh knew the sec guards had split up in an effort to apprehend Mato and him as well as the Terran soldiers. Zhoh ran to the back of the shuttle and ended up between it and the bulkhead.

The wall was part of a machinist's bay. Magnetic strips held heavy torque wrenches and other tools Zhoh could not identify. Except as potential weapons.

Seizing a fire extinguisher from the wall, Zhoh tossed the red container to Mato, who caught it easily and grasped the intention. He armed the extinguisher and pointed the nozzle at the corner of the shuttle as the sec guards approached.

Zhoh picked up two wrenches as long as his primary arm, kept one, and tossed the other to Mato, who caught the tool in his lesser hands. Together, they awaited the sec guards.

When the Cheelchans rounded the shuttle, bunched too closely together to be effective instead of spread out as Zhoh would have trained his warriors, Mato emptied the fire extinguisher in a single, long blast as he dove to the deck.

Purple foam struck the sec guards and covered them, bonding instantly the way it was supposed to in order to smother a flame. The fire retardant could be lethal to an unprotected being.

The foam blinded the guards and turned the deck slippery beneath their boots. Zhoh stepped in with his wrench before they could recover and swung at the first Cheelchan's head and nearly took off his helmet when the blow landed. Unconscious or nearly so, the guard dropped.

From his position on the deck, Mato lay beneath the stream of mercy rounds that sprayed a full meter above him. He swung his wrench and knocked down the nearest sec guard, then, when the guard hit the deck, he hammered the Cheelchan again. The sec guard's helmet bounced against the deck and he lay still.

By that time, Zhoh had thrust his wrench into the remaining sec guard's helmet and drove him backward so suddenly that his feet shot out from under him. Before the Cheelchan could fall to the deck, Zhoh swung again, slamming the heavy wrench against the sec guard's helmet.

The guard quivered and lay still.

Zhoh kept hold of the wrench and followed Ellen Hodgkins's scent.

Three rows down, the female was climbing into a small shuttle, ducking beneath the uplifted hatch. Zhoh ran to her and reached her before she knew he was there. He gripped her foot and yanked her from the spacecraft, throwing her down to the deck. He stood there, towering over her.

She'd lost her goggles and gazed up at him with cold, cruel eyes. Her hands were outspread. She no longer carried the black case.

Zhoh motioned to the shuttle. "See if you can find the case she had."

Mato scrambled up into the shuttle cockpit as autofire sounded from the other side of the shuttle. Sage and the female sergeant must have engaged the remaining sec guards.

"What do you want?" Hodgkins demanded.

Zhoh squatted down beside her and held the wrench upright beside him. He swung his tail forward, making his captive tilt her head back to keep the venomous tip from breaking the skin at her throat.

"To see you dead for your treachery," Zhoh answered.

"Who are you?"

"I am Captain Zhoh GhiCemid, a true warrior of the Phrenorian Empire."

Recognition flared in her dark eyes. "Rangha told me about you. You're *kalque*, and not fit to be part of the Phrenorian Empire. They sent you out here to bury you."

Zhoh barely restrained the rage that filled him. His grip on the wrench tightened and all he could think about doing was crushing the female's skull with it. He raked her with the tip of his tail enough to leave a scratch that must have burned from the venom. The poison wouldn't kill her, but she would be in pain until she got meds.

"I am going to bring Rangha down," Zhoh promised. "His association with you is going to cost him everything."

"His association wasn't with me," Hodgkins said. "It was with Velesko Kos. I just picked up the pieces after Kos got himself killed." She rubbed at her jaw, careful not to touch the scratch, which already looked inflamed. "Are you planning on cutting yourself into the deal?"

"No."

The noise of assault weapons being fired died away on the other side of the shuttle bay and Zhoh knew he was running out of time.

Mato shoved his head out of the shuttle cockpit. "I have found the case. It contained a computer that has records of the transactions she has done with General Rangha and others."

"Can you delete mention of the general?"

"Yes."

"Then do it."

"That will leave gaps in the information. It would be easier to simply destroy it."

"That would be even more suspicious than the gaps," Zhoh said. "I don't want the Terrans to have any information about Phrenorian involvement with this woman."

The female laughed sharply. "So that's what this is about? A cover-up?" She scratched her neck and reached to the back of her collar.

Zhoh stood and hefted the wrench.

Sage and the female sergeant rounded a shuttle a hundred meters away and approached at a run.

"This is going to be interesting," Hodgkins said. "You're working with the Terran Army and they're going to arrest me. How are you going to keep me from talking to them?"

"You will be dead before they get here," Zhoh promised, knowing he was giving her no choice.

Hodgkins reached into the back of her collar and brought out a small handgun. Zhoh had no chance to identify the weapon before she fired, and he was already swinging the wrench.

The bullet slammed into Zhoh's chest, hitting him high and hard, penetrating the chitin and knocking him back just as the heavy wrench split Hodgkins's head open and scattered blood over the deck. The small pistol dropped from the female's quivering hand.

Letting go of the wrench, Zhoh calmly reached into his medpack and drew out two bandages. The bullet had cored through his chest and exited his back, leaving a much larger wound on its departure. A whistling hiss of air sounded behind him where the round ripped through the bulkhead and atmosphere was leaking out the hole.

A Klaxon shrieked and red lights started spinning around on the ceiling.

"Captain!" Mato called from the shuttle.

"I am fine," Zhoh replied, even though he felt weak and his insides still trembled from the shock of the bullet passing through his body. It had not killed him. He would grow strong once more. "There should be a patch kit aboard the shuttle. Give Hodgkins's computer to Sergeant Sage and see to the hole in the bulkhead. Things are going to be confusing for a time, and it would be best if we could eliminate one of the most critical threats while the rest gets sorted."

"Of course, Captain." Mato handed the computer off to Sage, who appeared to be distracted, either from the wound, which had bled down his armor, or by communicating with the ship's captain and arranging the situation as best as he could before more sec teams arrived.

Zhoh thought Sage's disengagement from the dead woman was probably a combination of both. The bullet wound in Zhoh's chest throbbed painfully, but he ignored that, thinking of his coming meeting with General Rangha and how that would go.

But the female sergeant was engaged in the here and now. She stood before Zhoh in a challenging manner that he would not normally have allowed. However, temporary accommodations had to be made.

"Did you have to kill her?" the female sergeant demanded.

"I did not wish to be shot again, Sergeant. Her aim might have improved." Zhoh knew there was no argument to that.

"You should have searched her for weapons."

"I was about to do that."

"Why did she try to shoot you with you standing right there?"

Zhoh focused on the dead female, knowing he had pushed her to the limit. "I think, Sergeant, she was distressed. We all live in desperate times these days."

Frustration showed in the female sergeant's body language. She hesitated a moment, as if she might speak further, then she walked away to help Mato with repairing the bulkhead.

THIRTY-FIVE

Compartment 683-TAOPHQ (Terran Army Offplanet
Headquarters)
Space Station DSC-24L19
Loki 19 (Makaum)
LEO 332.7 kilometers
1128 Zulu Hours

Sage hadn't dreamed of Sombra de la Montána so
deeply in years. That place and the years spent there
were things he took out occasionally in the quiet times
in a bar or during PT, places and instances when he could
be alone with his thoughts because he didn't want to share
that part of his life with anyone.

He wasn't sure why the village was so much in his mind
now. It wasn't just his parents. He kept memories of his
mother and father close to him at all times. Usually he
thought of them, but they had lives in the village and in
Texas.

Since he'd gotten free of the *Hooded Vorol*, he'd been

commanded to ship over to the DawnStar space station, where General Whitcomb kept his offices, to be debriefed. Colonel Halladay had met him there, and had brought a physician to tend to Sage's wound and the stimpak shakes that had settled in.

Halladay hadn't spoken much, just listened while Sage related what had happened aboard the *Hooded Vorol*, and had taken possession of Ellen Hodgkins's computer. He'd sent it by military courier to Pingasa at the fort with instructions to get all the information off of the device that he could.

After that, they had gone to the general's outer office and taken seats to await the general's pleasure, which seemed like it might be some time in coming because there was a steady flow of diplomats and lawyers from various corps. All in all, the general had a circus on his hands and Sage didn't feel guilty in the slightest. They'd been chasing things since yesterday morning and still hadn't gotten out in front of them.

Even with the thought of having his stripes yanked, possibly being discharged from the Army, and almost certainly being returned to his old training position, Sage slept in an uncomfortable chair outside the general's office. He knew he'd done what he could today, and tomorrow would have to wait. If he got sent back to training, he'd start fighting all over again.

Or maybe he would hire on with a private security firm trying to save assets from the Phrenorians. One way or another, he could get back in the war. He wanted to stay with the Terran Army, though. That had been the only other family he'd ever had.

Maybe that was why he dreamed of Sombra de la Montána. He'd lost that family then, and he guessed he was about to lose this one. Most of the dreams were of that day the Colombians attacked and killed so many of the people he had known and grown up with.

He was kneeling with his mother, trying to stop all the blood pouring out of Manolo Paredes, the old man who took children fishing with him from time to time, when a soft hand gripped his forearm and shook it gently.

Sage blinked his eyes open and found Quass Leghef standing in front of him. The woman looked tired, but she was dressed in full regalia, a spidersilk dress festooned with jeweled insect wings and polished bits of wood. For a moment Sage thought the Quass's hands were covered in blood as his mother's had been in the dream, but she was wearing long maroon cuffs to accentuate the dress.

"Master Sergeant Sage, I apologize for waking you," the Quass said.

Sage started to get to his feet, but Leghef held him down. "No, ma'am, it's not a problem." He glanced over at Halladay, who was awake now as well. Sage distinctly remembered the colonel snoring.

"I'm glad you're all right," Leghef said.

"Thank you, ma'am."

"I also hear that you captured the men who attacked the fort."

"Yes, ma'am."

"Apparently that trail led you to other successes."

"Yes, ma'am."

"I understand that you can't talk to me about it, but I believe I have most of the story."

Sage didn't know what to say to that.

Behind the Quass, also looking resplendent, Pekoz stood patiently.

"I assume you're waiting to talk with General Whitcomb," the Quass said.

"Yes, ma'am." Sage didn't think there was going to be a lot of talking going on once he and Halladay were in the office with the general.

"Let's see if we can hurry things along." Leghef tapped the purple-and-white *draorm* that encircled Sage's left wrist, smiled as though pleased, and took him by the arm to get him to stand. "Colonel, if you'll join us."

Looking a little uncertain, Halladay got to his feet. "Yes, ma'am, but the general likes to do things his way and in his own time."

"I'm sure we won't take up much of the general's time," Leghef assured him, and she guided Sage to the general's door.

The blond female corporal Sage had met the first time he'd gotten an earful of General Whitcomb sat at the desk. She looked over at Sage in disbelief, who shrugged slightly, then put on a sterner look as she addressed Leghef. "Ma'am, you can't just—"

"It's all right," the Quass said. "I know the way."

The corporal started to say something else, but Pekoz interrupted. "Young lady, this is the Quass Leghef. I believe it will be fine for her to see the general. He's expecting her."

Defeated, the corporal raised her eyebrows at Sage and silently mouthed, *Wow*.

In spite of his current situation, Sage winked at the corporal, and then he followed Leghef into the general's office.

General Howard Whitcomb sat comfortably at his desk. He looked older today than he had the last time Sage had been there. Short gray bristles covered his round head and the gray beard growth showed he'd been up for a while. He sucked in on his right cheek as he listened to the man before him, and the effort made the old scar there pucker

more deeply. He looked small against the vid port of open
space behind him. Other space stations and starships
floated in orbit below the green planet that claimed a large
chunk of the view.

Sage and Halladay stood straight and saluted, their
covers put under their elbows.

"General, sir," Halladay said in a firm voice, "Colonel Halladay and Master Sergeant Sage reporting as requested."

Whitcomb stared at them, and a red flush darkened his
face. "You two were supposed to wait outside till I sent
for you."

"I asked the colonel and the sergeant to join me,"
Leghef said. "They're wasting their time sitting outside
when they have so much to do." She looked at the man
sitting in one of the two chairs in front of the general.

Seated comfortably, wearing an expensive suit, the man
looked to Sage like he was part of the diplomatic corps.
He had that perpetual young, energetic look about him,
like a polished stone in someone's collection.

"Quass Leghef, it's so good to see you," the diplomat
said. "I'm sorry it has to be under these circumstances."

"Thank you, Guariento, but you can go now," Leghef
said.

Guariento blinked his eyes and looked shocked. The
youthful look aged about ten years and he didn't look so
peppy. "Excuse me?"

"I'm going to need that chair and two more," Leghef
said, "so go fetch them from outside and go on about your
next appointment."

"Quass, have I done something—"

Leghef sat herself in the other chair in front of the general's desk. "Not yet you haven't. I still need those chairs."

Guariento looked at Whitcomb but got no help there.

He stood, nodded, and buttoned his jacket. "Of course, Quass." He left the room.

"Quass," Whitcomb said hoarsely, "with all due respect, I have a calendar full of appointments. Surely you realize—"

"Would you like to compare calendars, General?" Leghef asked with an edge of contempt. "You're running a fort from up here, and I'm down there running a world that is trying to fall to pieces. I've got meetings scheduled with you, with the Phrenorians, with the (ta)Klar, and with several of the corps, in addition to my own people. If you don't wish to talk, I'm certain I could shorten my list."

"Madam, I would like to meet with you, but I'd like to suggest another—better—time." Whitcomb almost sounded polite.

Leghef gestured to Sage and Halladay. "Return their salute, General, so they can join us."

"I don't see why they need to be party to whatever discussion we're about to have."

"Your inability to see such a thing is partly why we're having this discussion," Leghef said.

Reluctantly, Whitcomb saluted and leaned back in his chair, preparing to recover his battleground.

Guariento returned with two chairs. Pekoz helped him with the door, then took one of the chairs for himself. Halladay, closer to the diplomat, took the other chair, crossed the room, and sat his chair beside the Quass, leaving the chair on the other side for Sage.

The diplomat stood looking lost.

"Thank you, Guariento," Leghef said. "That will be all."

Guariento left, and he looked relieved to be doing so.

"Quass Leghef," Whitcomb said, obviously deciding to

fire the first salvo, "forcing your way in here is egregious."

"You're right. I should have made you force your way into my house, but I'm particular about who I invite there."

Sage made himself keep a straight face, and he couldn't believe how adamant the woman was.

"As to the order of business," Leghef went on, "I want these two men to return to my planet with me. Nothing else will be acceptable. They both have things to do to continue providing protection for my people, and I disparage of the way you've seen fit to take them away from us."

"Madam, Quass or not—"

"I am Quass for certain, General, and make no mistake about that. I have the majority of the Quass behind me and I am here representing their wants. And they want these men returned. They—*I*—want soldiers who are on the planet with us, who are facing the same dangers we are."

Whitcomb's face purpled. "You cannot come into my office and tell me how to run my army."

"No, but according to our treaty agreement with the Terran Alliance, I do have the power to say whether you have a fort on Makaum." Leghef let that hang for a moment. "So do you want to listen to my *suggestions*, General? Or would you rather pack up your fort and go?"

Whitcomb glared at Leghef. "Do you know how long you people would last against the Phrenorians? The minute the Terran Army pulls out, they'll take you people."

"They will," Leghef agreed. "And with the way the Phrenorian War is headed this way, Makaum is going to be an important world to have for resources to fight that war. Do you want to tell the Terran Alliance that you cost them this world? Because that's exactly what I'll tell them."

For a moment, Sage thought Whitcomb was going to continue the fight, that he was going to test Leghef's resolve, then the general's shoulders bowed slightly and Sage knew it was over.

"I have received a bill for reparations to the damage that was done to your city," Whitcomb said. "I needn't tell you that we're not going to pay that. Since you expressly desired Colonel Halladay and Master Sergeant Sage to pursue the people who ambushed *my* fort."

"You weren't going to get it done," Leghef said. "As for payment, don't bother. The Phrenorians have already been in touch and are offering to pay the cost for repairs. I think all of us are glad to hear that Green Dragon corp has decided to pull out of Cheapdock, and probably off of Makaum." She stood. "So do whatever you see fit, General." She turned to Halladay and Sage. "Let's go. Tonight there is a party, and both of you are going to be my guests."

Halladay and Sage stood, saluted Whitcomb, who delivered an unenthusiastic response, and performed an about-face before following the Quass out of the office.

As they waited for the elevator to take them down to the shuttle to return to Makaum, Sage looked at Leghef. "Thank you, Quass."

She smiled at him and touched the *draorm* again. "I could do no less, Master Sergeant, and I am happy to have helped."

THIRTY-SIX

Freshly showered, dressed in gym shorts, Sage sat at his desk in his private quarters and stared at the sat recon of the river where the Phrenorian base lay hidden. It lay out there like a bomb waiting to explode. He and Halladay hadn't quite gotten a handle on how to proceed with that threat at the moment.

The holo projection of the footage scrolled by in 8x speed, time and time again. The river remained undisturbed and continued to flow unimpeded through the jungle. Watching the projection over and over again was frustrating, but seemed to make him more awake than drowsy.

He'd tried to sleep, knowing he needed it, especially since the Makaum were going to turn out for the party tonight and the Terran Army was providing security. He and Halladay had spent time trying to talk Quass Leghef out of the festivities, but she had been adamant. With the way the Makaum people were split over the role off-worlders were having in their lives and would continue to have in their lives, the Quass insisted on the holiday to remind them of the things they had in common and the crises they'd already weathered.

The Festival of the Beginning was celebrated every year and marked the day the survivors had climbed from the wreckage of the starship that had crashed on Makaum. It was a day to remember those who had gone on before, and think of those who would come after.

A knock echoed through his door.

Sage blanked the computer holo and leaned back in his chair. "Come in."

Kiwanuka entered the room carrying a couple of meal bags. Like Sage, she wore sweat pants, but she also had an olive drab ARMY tee shirt that made her dark skin look even darker. "You haven't eaten, have you?"

"There was a protein-sub in there somewhere," Sage replied with a smile. "But it's long gone and barely remembered."

"I saw you coming out of the showers a little while ago." Kiwanuka put one of the bags in front of Sage and pulled up the other chair in the room to his desk.

Sage cleared gear from that side of the desk and put it on the floor to make room for her. "I should bring you a meal one of these days."

"You'd have to bring enough for three, Top." Kiwanuka reached into her bag and took out a carton of what smelled like lasagna.

Sage reached into his own bag to explore the contents, found a similar carton, and took it out. When he opened it, he discovered it was lasagna. "Three?" He looked at Kiwanuka.

"I have a roommate. Sergeant Bianca Dobell." Kiwanuka took out plastic flatware and passed it around.

"She works in the motor pool."

From what Sage remembered of the sergeant, she was an old-school hardliner. Diligent and tough.

Kiwanuka shook her head sadly. "And she snores like an out of alignment magno-drive."

Sage smiled. "No fun to be you."

"Not all of us get to be First Shirt and have our own quarters." Kiwanuka opened up a carton of salad and added dressing, then she opened up a stay-hot containing small yeast loaves. "You've got the wine."

"Special occasion?" Sage reached into his bag again and found two wine bulbs. Both were marked with Terran brands.

"Since we're not going to be drinking at the party tonight, I thought we could celebrate now." Kiwanuka picked up the bulb of deep red liquid. "There's not enough in one of these to last till the party. When does it start?"

"At dark. About twenty fifteen."

"When all the bugs are out. Yum."

"As I understand it, the bugs are a big part of the show."

"I'm glad I'll be in armor."

"Yeah. Me too." Sage got out his carton of salad, dressed it, and dug in.

"I assume the secret project you've been working on with Halladay has to do with the Phrenorian base Jahup found."

"Yeah. It's out there."

"What is it?"

Sage shook his head. "Don't know yet."

"Tell me when you find out?"

"As soon as you're cleared. This is strictly need-to-know."

They ate in silence. When they finished the meal, Sage felt better, more whole. He helped Kiwanuka clear away the remains of the meal. "Thank you," he told her.

"Have you slept yet?" she asked.

"Some while I was waiting in the general's office."

"I was told Quass Leghef read the general the riot act."

Sage was surprised.

"I heard that from the colonel," Kiwanuka said.

"Doesn't seem like something the colonel would tell people."

"He had to explain why you were still allowed in the fort after everything we did last night and this morning. He didn't tell us everything, but I know how the Quass can be, and I read between the lines of what the colonel told us."

Sage smiled.

"So?" Kiwanuka looked at him intently.

"So what?"

"So was that woman fabulous or what?"

Sage's smile widened. "She was. Entirely fabulous."

"Good." Kiwanuka stood and pulled Sage to his feet and pushed him toward his bed. "It's sixteen eighteen now. That gives us four hours of sleep before the party tonight."

"Us?" Sage looked at her.

Kiwanuka pursed her lips. "Look, you're not sleeping and I haven't gotten very much sleep since this morning—or yesterday morning, actually—so I thought maybe we'd try sleeping together."

"Together?" Sage knew he must be tired if he couldn't do anything but repeat what she was saying.

"Bunk buddies, soldier. Nothing else."

Sage nodded. "And if we can't sleep?"

"Then we get up and make sure our gear is right. Again."

"All right." Sage let her pull him onto the bed and lay on his side. She spooned in next to him and closed her eyes. Cautiously, he threw an arm around her and held her. When he didn't get an objection, he thought everything was fine. He felt her breath soft and warm on his forearm, felt her heart beating, closed his eyes, and felt more at peace than he had since he'd hit dirt on Makaum.

He was asleep before he felt her breathe again.

Piyosa's Spring
West of Makaum Sprawl
0753 Zulu Hours

Even though she gave no indication, Jahup knew the exact moment Noojin knew he was there. He sensed her awareness of him through that bond that they sometimes shared. When they were younger, they could almost touch each other's minds, could know instantly how the other was feeling.

Now that he thought back on it, he wasn't sure when knowing each other had become so difficult.

She sat on the edge of the small spring, her bare toes in the mud and the water, letting the tiny *blutinny* nibble at her toes. Actually, when they were small, she had insisted the small fish were kissing her toes. Jahup had never been able to think of it like that. He'd always thought it was too silly for boys to think of the sensation in that way. The *blutinny* simply ate whatever stuck to a person's bare feet or licked the salt from their skin. Besides that, the fish got to know a lot of their world through their mouths.

The spring sat isolated from the sprawl, off the beaten

track, and most hunters didn't go there anymore because the place was so small. Jungle surrounded the spring, which bubbled up in waves that never ended. Before the offworlders came, children had come here to explore the pool and to play.

Now, with so many evil people in the jungle doing bad things, the children weren't allowed out of the sight of parents or other adults.

"Are you just going to stand there and stare?" Noojin demanded.

She wasn't wearing her hardsuit like Jahup was. When he'd returned to his grandmother's home instead of the barracks because he'd wanted time to think, Jahup had cleaned his gear the way he'd been trained. He'd even invited Noojin to join him, but she had politely refused.

Now she wore her hunting gear instead of her armor and she didn't sound polite at all.

Jahup popped his faceshield up. "I didn't know if coming over to you was safe."

"The *blutinny* won't hurt you."

It wasn't the *blutinny* that worried Jahup. Noojin got like this sometimes. Jahup didn't understand why exactly, but Grandmother had always insisted that those times would pass, and they did.

Jahup crossed over to the spring and knelt down beside her. With the armor on, he was heavy enough to sink into the bank, which made her scowl at him.

"Why did you come here?" Noojin asked.

"Because this is where you are."

"Did you need something from me?" Her voice sounded sharper and she sounded angrier.

Jahup didn't know what he'd done wrong, but he'd obviously done something to offend her. "No, I just wanted to make sure you were all right."

"I'm fine."

"Because we nearly got killed and I couldn't help thinking how close I'd come to losing you." Jahup said that before he really knew he was going to.

Silently, she picked up a twig and drew in the water. Jahup couldn't tell what she was drawing. The waves broke her efforts apart before she even finished them. The *blutinny* thought it was a game and followed the end of the twig as it darted around.

"We nearly died because you insisted on being part of the Terran Army," Noojin said at last. "We are not them. They are not us."

Jahup chose not to argue with her because he knew they wouldn't see things the same way. He didn't know why Noojin couldn't understand that they had to help the Terran Army fight to get their lives back.

"No matter what you think, Jahup, the Army is not helping us get back to who we were." Noojin sounded calmer, almost sad. "Nothing will ever be the same again."

"Is it okay if I just sit here?" For a moment, Jahup thought maybe she hadn't heard him.

"It's fine."

He looked at her because she didn't sound right and saw that tears dropped from her cheeks into the spring. The *blutinny* swarmed the tears where they fell in the water.

Jahup knew better than to mention the tears. Noojin didn't cry often, and she *never* wanted it mentioned. She went straight from crying to being fighting mad.

He sat there beside her, almost touching, and never felt farther away from her.

THIRTY-SEVEN

Lareta's Rapture
New Makaum
7078 Akej (Phrenorian Prime)

He's up there," the voluptuous *A'shtasser* female told Zhoh as she entered the room he'd rented in the bordello.

She was humanoid, but she had green skin, blue hair, and a prehensile tail that she was in the habit of flicking when she presented herself to anyone with money. The thin wisps of spidersilk she wore barely covered her nakedness.

She'd told Zhoh her name was Ineena, but he didn't care. The only thing he was interested in was the fact that she knew Captain Achsul Oretas, who visited Lareta's Rapture regularly when he was in the sprawl.

Ineena slid onto the round bed in the center of the room and played with the chains and other devices that dangled from the mirrored ceiling. Images of people and creatures having sex played on a holo overlay at the foot of the bed.

"Is he alone?" Zhoh asked.

The female shrugged. "He's with a friend."

"A friend like you?"

"I'm better." She smiled provocatively at him and her tail twisted languorously around her forearm. "That's lucky for you."

Zhoh went to the door and closed it, then turned around to the woman. The room smelled of sex and drugs and alcohol and disease. It almost choked Zhoh in its intensity and he couldn't think of many worse places to be.

The female mistook the closing of the door for his increased sexual interest. Phrenorians couldn't have sex with humanoids, but the humanoids' secretions were pleasantly intoxicating.

Zhoh did not know that himself. It was just something he'd been told by others. He would never lie with a beast.

"Come to me and I'll make you glad that you did." The female crooked her finger at him and grinned salaciously. At least, that's what Zhoh thought she did. He wasn't certain of all humanoid emotions. He pulled a silenced pistol that fired depleted uranium rounds and put a hole between her disbelieving eyes. Blood flew through the holo images of sex partners as her body toppled onto the bed to stare sightlessly up at her own reflection.

Flipping his cloak over the pistol he held in his primary, Zhoh opened the door, walked outside, and punched in the lock code on the keypad. The door would not open again until the time he'd paid for had passed.

He walked along the hallway and did not look at the bar below. When he reached the room where Achsul lay with a human female, he used the cyber lockpick Mato had given him on the keypad, watched the symbols cycle. They stilled and the lock opened with an almost silent click.

Pushing the door open, Zhoh followed it inside the room, which was exactly like the one he had just left. A human female lay on top of Achsul. She was laughing, like she was enjoying her experience.

At least she would die happy. Zhoh shot her through the back of the head as he approached the bed. The corpse collapsed on top of Achsul.

The captain tried to push the dead female from him, but he was drunk on her nectar and he couldn't quite manage it.

Zhoh placed a primary on the corpse's back and pressed down, keeping Achsul trapped on the bed. Zhoh shoved the silenced pistol into Achsul's face, tearing off two of his *chelicerae* as he did.

"Silence," Zhoh ordered. "One sound other than when I tell you to speak and I will kill you. Lift your left primary if you understand my directions."

On the other side of the bed, Achsul's primary rose a short distance.

"Other than you, is there anyone else in General Rangha's command who knows about the weapons he has been hording from past campaigns? Speak softly when you answer."

Achsul's mouth opened and closed a moment and he drank his own blood from where the *chelicerae* had been sliced off. "No. I have been with him the whole time. I hid what he was doing. He swore me to secrecy. It was not me, Zhoh, I was only following orders. I had to serve General—"

Zhoh put two uranium rounds through Achsul's face, killing him immediately.

"Not anymore," he said. He saw himself out.

There was only one more loose end to take care of.

The Canopy
New Makaum
1628 Zulu Hours

On the shaded rooftop bar of a two-story building not far from the Offworlders' Bazaar, Sytver Morlortai drank imported beer from Hon'qua and looked at the holo images he had taken of the market square of what was now referred to as Old Makaum. A casual passerby might have thought him a tourist reviewing images he'd captured while on a stroll through the sprawl.

The bar was called the Canopy and was one of the least inspired names Morlortai had ever heard. Most of the shade came from large trees that grew up through the center of the building and extended six meters above Morlortai. Someone had worked at keeping the trees pruned, but they hadn't worked hard at it.

The place suited Morlortai because the clientele tended to be self-absorbed offworlders who were distracted with deals they were doing over comm or who drank while they were crunching numbers.

From where he sat, Morlortai could see some of the destruction left by the Terran Army action done earlier that day. Construction crawlers labored to carry the damage away and the verdant growth that had been harmed was already reestablishing itself.

"Did you pick your spot yet?" Turit asked over the comm.

"Already done," Morlortai replied. "All I'm waiting for now is the party to begin." He reached for the sweating beer bulb and took a sip, finding that it was not as cold as it had been, which was a shame because Hon'qua beer was meant to be drunk cold. "All we're waiting for is the contact that brought us to this *enthche*."

After spending almost two days onplanet, Morlortai was convinced the world was a cesspool just waiting for someone to pull the drain. He was going to do his part to help that when he killed Wosesa Staumar. Ny'age, one of his merc family, had trailed the Makaum man all day yesterday to build as much of an idea of the man's routine as she could.

According to her, Staumar was a parasitic growth who profited from his own people's misery. He had sold out Makaum to the big corps and was cashing in on the bio market in a big way. Since getting wined and dined by the likes of DawnStar, Green Dragon, Silver Spin, and Tri-Cargo, Staumar had totally adopted a life of immorality and wickedness. But he currently lived on the Phrenorian's tab, soliciting his friends and neighbors to believe the Sting-Tails would be the best partner for the future of their world.

Killing Staumar would be a pleasure. Morlortai lived on the fringes of lawful society, and maybe he did murder for hire, but he had a code and he didn't kill innocents. Ny'age had discovered that Staumar had killed two prostitutes at the pleasure palaces, one woman and one boy. The Phrenorians had disposed of the bodies.

Remembering that left a strong distaste in Morlortai's mouth. He finished his beer and waved down a server for another, relishing the thought that it would at least be cold for a while.

After the drink was delivered to his table, Turit hailed Morlortai on the comm. "Your contact has arrived."

Morlortai's senses quickened and he was instantly more alert. "You're sure."

Turit made a choking sound, which was as close as the translator could come to emulating an Angenen's laughter. "He's the only Phrenorian in the bar."

And that was the real surprise on the job that had brought Morlortai to Makaum. The price he would get paid for killing Staumar was only a drop in the bucket compared to what had been offered for the other contract.

"I would like to join you," a deep synthesized voice announced.

Morlortai turned and gazed up at the blue and purple Phrenorian standing beside his table. The colors told him at once that he was dealing with a higher-up in the Empire. In his career as an assassin, Morlortai had never worked for the Empire. Life these days was interesting.

With an air of largesse, Morlortai waved toward the chair on the other side of the table. He kept both hands in view on the table despite the way the Sting-Tail was armed. After years of experience with Turit, Morlortai trusted that the Angenen would put a bullet through the Phrenorian's brainbox before he could finish drawing a weapon.

They exchanged the passwords the fixer who had arranged the meeting had prepared for them so they could identify each other.

"Would you like something to drink?" Morlortai asked.

"No. I won't be here long. I came only to give you the name of the target you're here for."

"And half of the agreed-upon amount."

"Of course." The Phrenorian extended a credstick and Morlortai pocketed it immediately.

"You know if the credits are not all there, I will come looking for Blaold Oldawe."

The Phrenorian hissed angrily. "Have a care. Throwing names around like that can get you killed."

Morlortai shrugged. "I can promise, General Rangha, if I am betrayed, you will never live to see if I make good on my agreement to kill the target."

If the Phrenorian was rattled by all that Morlortai knew, he showed no signs of it.

General Rangha produced a small datacube. "All the information you need is there. Do not fail in this."

"I never fail," Morlortai said.

The general left the table without another word. Morlortai didn't worry because he knew Turit would keep the Phrenorian in his sights until he was out of the area.

"So who is the target?" Turit asked.

"Curious?" Morlortai loved tweaking the Angenen's natural curiosity.

"Yes."

Morlortai laid the datacube on his computer and brought up the holo. A single file was contained on the cube.

"Captain Zhoh GhiCemid. Apparently Blaold Oldawe intends to get rid of his ex-son-in-law."

"It's a waste of credits. It would be better to see if Zhoh dies here."

Morlortai shut down his computer and pocketed it, finished his beer and got up to leave. "It's a payday. A big one. I haven't met many who have hated someone as much as Blaold Oldawe does."

THIRTY-EIGHT

The insects turned out to be a big part of the Festival of the Beginning.

The Makaum people gathered in the town square near the partially rebuilt well house, which had been nearly destroyed by Velesko Kos's kill team weeks ago. They lit the area by torches and lanterns instead of off-worlder lamps and lights. Sweet-smelling gray smoke drifted up from the flames.

Standing there looking at the shattered pieces of the *ypheynte*, an insect that instantly reminded him of a Terran dragonfly, Sage felt guilty for his part in the near destruction of the historic monument.

Most of the *ypheynte's* body had been rebuilt and it stood on six arched legs over the cistern below, which reflected the lights. Vines grew over a structure made from bent trees specially shaped to create the *ypheynte's* wings. At night, the vines, called *irdenroth*, glowed a soft blue when all five of the moons were visible, as they were now. The moons clustered above the sprawl, looking big and bright, and blossomed in pink, gold, green, yellow, and orange pastels. The night was lit almost well enough that the torches and lanterns weren't needed.

"What do you think, Top?" Clad in her hardsuit, Kiwanuka stood beside Sage and gazed at the moons-filled sky.

"I didn't think the moons would all show up at once," Sage replied.

"It only happens every seven years. This is the first time offworlders have seen it. Have you ever seen anything so beautiful?"

"No." Sage felt a little uncomfortable around Kiwanuka. They'd slept together, and that was all that had happened, but he had really slept, trusting her. It was the first time in a long time that he'd let someone get that close to him. He suspected it was a first in a long time for her as well.

Later, when they'd woken up, they'd separated as though nothing had happened. Sage wasn't sure what he was supposed to think about that, and he didn't want any distractions with everything that was going on between all the players on Makaum at the moment. The claws were out now, and things were only going to get bloodier.

The Makaum people sat around the well house on spidersilk blankets and shared snacks they'd brought from home. They sang songs, with only a little accompaniment on instruments, and their voices lifted to fill the area.

At first there were no insects and none of the small flying lizards that usually filled the nights in Makaum. Sage guessed that maybe the smoke kept them away. Then the winged creatures came and landed on the well house and the cistern and filled the trees that made up the nearby houses.

As if in response to the songs the Makaum people sang,

the insects lit up in waves of color and began crooning and buzzing, joining in at times.

"Isn't this lovely?"

Hearing the soft voice beside him, Sage glanced down at Quass Leghef. He'd gotten so consumed by the show going on around him that he hadn't seen her walk up to him. He resolved to be more attentive. He was here as security.

"It is," Sage said, meaning it.

"Every day of our lives on Makaum, we live with the knowledge that this world is filled with predators that want only to kill us. Insects and lizards and spiders and aquatic creatures. And that's not even mentioning the lethal plant life." Leghef took in a deep breath of the smoke-scented air and let it out. "But this one night, just after the sun sets and all five moons are in the sky, Makaum changes and provides a temporary sanctuary. I think that's a fascinating thing."

"Yes, ma'am, it is."

"Our ancestors noticed that the predators don't feed on these nights. None of them stalk prey. Once we discovered that, we made this a night that we did not kill either. Meals are made early, and they're shared out here."

"When I was small," Sage said, "our village used to have holidays and feasts like this. Everyone worked to provide something for the meals, and no one went away hungry those days."

"You'll have to come by and visit me again, Master Sergeant. I'd like to hear more about your village and your life there, and what you think of our lives here."

"Yes, ma'am. As I get time."

"For tonight, though, would you be kind enough to walk me to the well house? I've got to offer a rebuttal to Wosesa Staumar tonight. He's going to be lobbying for the Phrenorians and I want to make sure I get a chance to let everyone know what a fool he is."

"It would be my pleasure, ma'am."

Leghef took Sage by the arm and he carefully guided her through the thronging crowd to the well house. Kiwanuka followed him, acting as his wingman for the security assignment. Once they arrived at the well house, he stood by Leghef's side. Pekoz stood a short distance away.

"I'm fine here, Sergeant. Thank you, but isn't there somewhere else you should be?" she asked.

"No, ma'am. For right now, my job is to take care of you."

"I assure you, I can take care of myself."

"Yes, ma'am, but I was thinking maybe you could help me."

She smiled at him, then turned her attention to a heavy-set Makaum man walking toward them. "Ah, here comes my sparring partner."

The Terran Army had a thick file on Staumar. When the military had first hit the dirt on Makaum, he had been one of the chief go-to people onplanet. Then, as the corps, then the Phrenorian lobbying credits grew higher than the Terran Alliance was willing to pay, he'd gone over to the Sting-Tails.

Sage felt an instant dislike for the man. Staumar was an opportunist, ready to seize whatever deal best worked for him. He'd gotten fat since the arrival of the corps. His face was round and he wore the latest fashion in suits. He smelled of offworld products, not the herbal scents that Leghef and other Makaum people favored.

"Quass Leghef," Staumar said as he walked up to join her, "you're looking well tonight."

"It's because I'm here to bathe in the spirit of fellowship," Leghef replied, "and in remembrance that our people have survived on Makaum against all odds because we learned to care for each other."

Staumar smiled, but there was no warmth in his dark

eyes. "We no longer have to survive on this planet, Quass. We can drift through space, the way the seeds of an *ardenang* ride breezes. There are whole worlds out there waiting for us to take root on them."

"I choose to keep myself rooted here. And you should find another comparison. Despite its proclivity for drifting to wide-open places, no offworlder has successfully managed to grow *ardenang* anywhere else, and they want to because no one has ever found another spice like it in all the worlds. Many things are unique on Makaum, and I believe that her people are among them."

"I swear," Kiwanuka said over a private comm to Sage, "the more I'm around this woman, the more I like her. I wish I'd been there in Whitcomb's office. You have got to tell me about that. You owe me. I brought you lunch today."

"Maybe," Sage replied. "In the meantime, look sharp. We don't know if we took out all of the weapons any other anti-Terran protestors might have access to."

"Copy that."

Sage scanned the surrounding houses and buildings. Behind the rows of Makaum people, there were rows of offworlders, all drawn like the insects and flying lizards by the music and the lights. Between them, a line of Terran Army soldiers was there to maintain order.

As beautiful as the night and the festival was, Sage couldn't wait for the event to be over.

2037 Zulu Hours

"You're not wearing your suit." Jahup felt betrayed as he stepped up behind Noojin.

She sat on a blanket and wore one of the gowns his grandmother had helped her make this year. Since Noojin had no parents, Leghef had helped her spin the spidersilk and sew the clothing she needed. They had invited Jahup to help when he started complaining about the sewing getting in the way of hunting. He'd found other things to do, but he'd also noticed how beautiful Noojin looked in the gowns, though he wouldn't tell her that because that would make him uncomfortable. And it would probably make her feel the same way.

"No," she responded in that warning voice, "I'm not wearing armor. This is only the second Festival that has occurred since I've been alive. You're locked away inside that hardsuit and you're cut off from the experience tonight that will not happen again for another seven years. Or *ever*."

Jahup didn't want to fall into that argument again, about whether the Terran Army would be able to help them. So he stood nearby and watched Noojin talk and laugh with a couple of the girls she knew.

Telilu came out of the crowd wearing one of the dresses Grandmother had made and a crown of light orange night blossoms wound through her hair. She stopped and gazed at Jahup hesitantly.

"Jahup?"

Grinning, Jahup popped his faceshield up and looked down at his little sister. "Hello, Twig."

"Don't call me that."

"All right."

"Why are you wearing that?"

"So I can take care of you."

Fear rounded her eyes and the sight of it made Jahup instantly feel guilty.

"Is something going to happen?" Telilu asked quietly.

Noojin got to her feet and walked back to take Telilu by the hand. "Nothing is going to happen. He's a boy.

Sometimes boys say dumb things. Come up here with me. It'nyi brought some fresh *corok* melon and honey-roasted *tiarkal* nuts she'll share with us."

Jahup cursed himself for being a fool. He hadn't even considered that what he'd said to Telilu might scare her.

Noojin glared at him again, burning the feeling into his bones. She sat and placed Telilu in her lap, then talked softly to the girl and placed food in her hands.

Sighing, Jahup continued on his rounds as Wosesa Staumar called for attention.

2.6 kilometers West of Makaum
2052 Zulu Hours

Listening to Staumar ramble on over the drone relay that flew between the well house and the hide in the trees over two kilometers from the market square, Sytver Morlortai decided the man was a born politician. Staumar liked the sound of his own voice, and that had been immediately apparent.

For the last fourteen minutes, the man had blathered on, recounting stories and jokes about past festivals. He showed no sign of slowing down, but Morlortai didn't have a timetable for how long the man was going to speak.

Nestled into the canopy of the tree, the mercenary had a clear line of sight through the scope of the Yqueu sniper rifle. The weapon fired a 50mm round, heavy enough to do impressive damage. The distance would allow him to get off a second shot, if it was needed, before the sound of the first shot rolled over the festival goers.

It was also a round and rifle model favored by many of the Terran Army snipers.

A wind speed and direction indicator hung from a nearby branch and showed digital displays.

"Do you plan on camping in that tree overnight?" Turit asked over the comm.

Morlortai laughed. "No. I'm just checking to see if I can bag both targets tonight at one time. Since Staumar is proselytizing for the Phrenorians, I figure there is a good chance Captain Zhoh GhiCemid will be there as well."

"Don't get greedy."

"It's just good business sense, my friend. Think about it. When I drop Staumar, the (ta)Klar pay us. If I tell them I dropped a Phrenorian captain too, in order to heighten the impression the targets were taken out by Terran gunners, I think I'll be able to talk them into a bonus situation."

"Then get it done. Onineo is making dinner tonight at the ship and I don't want it to get cold before we get back."

Morlortai searched the fringe crowd and spotted General Rangha in the group of Phrenorians. The general had not yet noticed the tracker Ny'age had planted on him after their meeting earlier. Morlortai had been hoping to take both targets at the same time from the beginning.

He followed Rangha through the scope and saw another Phrenorian join him.

"The general has just made contact with your second target," Turit announced.

"I told you I felt lucky." Morlortai focused on Zhoh. Although he wasn't an expert on Phrenorians, he was pretty sure the two Sting-Tails were arguing. They stood by themselves a short distance away from the other warriors.

Even though his heart rate hadn't changed, Morlortai knew he was excited when the cool thrill of death washed over him. Since he'd left Fenipal, all he'd wanted to do was be able to decide his own fate. Now he decided the fates of others.

He put the rifle's reticule on Staumar's chin and started taking up trigger slack till the rifle fired and smacked into his shoulder. He slid the scope over and readied his second shot.

Market Square
Old Makaum
7516 Akej (Phrenorian Prime)

Zhoh kept his hands, all of them, from his weapons because he sorely wanted to take one of them and kill General Rangha. He'd been surprised Rangha had turned out for the Makaum festival, even though Staumar was there to plead the Phrenorian case to his people.

Then again, as a chosen hero of the Empire, politics was a skill Rangha would have learned as one of their pampered bloodline warriors. If the Empire primes only knew what they were holding so close, they would kill him.

"You went up to the *Hooded Vorol* with the Terran sergeant," Rangha said. This was the first he had talked of the action aboard the ship.

Zhoh had known the confrontation was coming, but he hadn't thought Rangha would presume to have it here. This choice didn't make sense.

"You consort with our enemy," Rangha continued, "and you expect me to believe you have the interests of the Empire at heart?"

The accusation stung. Zhoh's wound still pained him and he had not slept since yesterday. There had been too many things for him to do once he returned to his base. He shouldn't even have been here, and wouldn't have been if he'd had a choice. The argument between the Makaum people, the foolishness of them even thinking they had a choice in their future, was a waste of his time.

Only Rangha had insisted Zhoh be here as a show of support.

"What were you doing, Captain?" Rangha demanded.

No longer wanting to take the abuse from Rangha, Zhoh took the white noise generator from his chest pouch and activated it, shutting down his and the general's comms, leaving only the two of them talking.

"I went with Sage this morning because you left a trail to that storage bay containing all the weapons you've been stealing from past campaigns," Zhoh said in a tightly controlled voice. He couldn't stop the words. They poured out of him. "Your partner, the human female Ellen Hodgkins, had a computer that named you as the seller of those weapons. She had a copy of every transaction you have made on this planet."

Rangha drew back from Zhoh's wrath and his pheromones stank of fear and rage, but the fear was stronger. "You're lying!"

"I still have copies of those records."

"What are you going to do with them?"

"I'm going to send them to the Empire."

Regaining his composure, Rangha stood taller. "Do that and I will tell the Empire you falsified those records, that you were the one doing business with the Hodgkins female. We'll see if they take my word or that of a *kalque*."

Zhoh knew then that Rangha was speaking the truth. Given a choice of whom to believe, the Empire would side with their general and bloodline hero because it was in their interests to do so. The best that Zhoh could hope for in that instance was a quick, painless death.

And he knew they wouldn't give him that. Despair

swept over him as he tried to figure out how he was going
to fix his mistake.

At that moment at the well house in front of the Makaum
people, Staumar's head exploded into bloody chunks.

Zhoh moved, automatically seeking shelter, and he felt
the wind of a large-caliber bullet sizzle by, missing him
by only millimeters.

Rangha felt it too, and he gazed at Zhoh with fury in his
eyes. "You should have been dead! He should have killed
you! Try to hide! He'll find you!"

Zhoh ran back toward Rangha, taking the general down
to the ground as a few Makaum people in the crowd unlimbered concealed weapons and started fighting.

Lying on top of Rangha, knowing the general's personal
bodyguards were even now racing to his aid, Zhoh pulled
his Kimer pistol, used his body to block the view of what
he was doing, and slid the weapon under Rangha's thorax
armor and fired three times.

Rangha jerked with the impacts, then he lay still.

Pushing himself up, Zhoh yelled at the approaching
bodyguards. "Form a circle and get a medkit. The general
has been shot."

2058 Zulu Hours

When Staumar's head blew up—and Sage couldn't think
of any other way to describe what had happened—he'd
reacted immediately and wrapped his arms around Quass
Leghef, protecting her with his body. The woman didn't
know what had happened to her debate opponent. All she
had seen was Staumar had been injured.

"He's hurt," she cried. "He needs help."

"He's dead, ma'am," Sage said as he picked the woman

up and started for the nearest house. He and Kiwanuka had chosen it for their fallback point in case something happened. "You can't help him. Now let me take care of you."

Sage stumbled around other people, not wanting to hurt anyone, as the cracks of two large-caliber rounds echoed over the distance. "Kiwanuka."

"Yes, Top?"

"There's a sniper out there. Find him and put him down."

"Copy that. Already on it."

Sage ran, dodging people and occasionally jumping over them, making the straightest course he could to the safe house. They had reinforced the walls just that afternoon with carboplate that would offer defensive measures against bullets and beam weapons.

Small arms fire broke out from three or four areas on the Makaum section, and more fired from the rows of offworlders. Several rounds peppered Sage's back as he ran. The Terran soldiers were slow out of the gate, but they responded swiftly once they got into motion.

"Use mercy rounds!" Sage ordered as he entered the house. He started to set the Quass down, then noticed she was as limp as a rag doll. As he held her back so he could see better, he saw all the blood that had stained the front of the woman's dress.

He put a gloved hand to her throat and verified that her vital signs were all over the place. He opened up a comm channel. "I need a medic—*now!*"

Two medics raced through the doorway and huddled over Quass Leghef, breaking out equipment and meds from their carryalls.

"Take care of her," Sage ordered.

"Copy that, Top," one of the medics said. They worked smoothly and efficiently.

Sage pulled his Roley into position and stepped back into the town hall. Everything was in a pandemonium. Terran Army soldiers, citizens, and Phrenorians all fired at each other. Dead and wounded lay strewn across the ground, some screaming in pain.

Sage felt echoes of Sombra de la Montána hammering through his mind. He went forward to get control of his men and help where he could, but he knew he was already too late.

EPILOGUE

Sage sat on a chair outside the triage center with his helmet on the ground beside him. He replayed what had happened in the market square over and over in his mind. He'd already seen recorded events on the HUD screen of his suit.

So far, there were 37 confirmed deaths and 183 injuries. Those injuries were of the Makaum people who had come to Fort York to be seen by doctors. Others hadn't come, and the numbers were going to climb.

Fatigue overwhelmed Sage. He'd helped control the outbreak of violence, helped sort the quick from the dead, but that hadn't been helping. Not really.

Captain Gilbride found him a few minutes later. The doctor wore bloody scrubs and looked worn to the bone. "Top."

"Yes sir." Sage started to get to his feet and saluted, following the training when nothing else made sense. He kept seeing Quass Leghef limp in his arms.

"They just told me you were here."

"We finally got everything out there sorted, sir."

"You came here to check on the Quass?"

"Colonel Halladay told me to get out of the market. He thinks maybe I could be a target too. I came here because I couldn't think of anywhere else to go." Sage didn't want to ask about the Quass because he was afraid he knew the answer.

"She's alive, Top." Gilbride shook his head. "I did what I could for her, but her still being with us—well, that's more because of how stubborn she is, not how good I am."

Sage nodded.

"We'll have to wait and see how it goes from here."

"Yes sir."

"If you feel up to it, maybe you could join Jahup. He's in the room with her. She's in a coma now, so we'll have to wait to see how she does."

"Yes sir. Thank you."

Gilbride told him what unit the Quass was in, clapped him on the shoulder, and went back to surgery.

JAHUP LEANED ON the bed and held on to his grandmother's hand. The Quass looked small and still in the sterile sheets, nothing like the energetic woman she had been only a few hours ago.

Feeling awkward, Sage stood in the doorway.

"Come in, Top," Jahup said without turning around.

"You're alone?" Sage crossed the room and stood beside the boy.

"Yeah."

Sage had checked the list of KIA. Noojin hadn't been among them.

"Noojin has Telilu," Jahup said. "She doesn't need to be up here and see Grandmother the way she is now. Pekoz is still in surgery."

Guilt stung Sage. He'd forgotten about the old man. By the time he'd remembered and checked on him, he'd been told Pekoz had been medevaced on a jumpcopter.

Tears rolled down Jahup's cheeks, cutting through the dirt smeared there. The *draorm* on Sage's wrist caught his attention. "Grandmother gave you that?"

"She did. I tried to tell her I couldn't take it, but she wouldn't listen. She said it belonged to your grandfather."

Jahup smiled a little. "You can't give something like that back." He looked at Sage. "Did she tell you what it meant?"

"She said fathers make them for sons and that it had belonged to your grandfather."

"She didn't tell you anything else?"

"There was a lot going on."

"A *draorm* signifies family, Top." Jahup's voice broke a little at the end but he held it together.

Sage waited and the machines beeped in the silence while he tried to figure out how he felt about that, and why the Quass had given him the *draorm*. He didn't have any answers and thinking that hard right now just made his head swim.

Looking back at his grandmother, Jahup asked, "What do we do now? Everything's so messed up."

"We fight for your world, Jahup, because that's what she expects us to do. We rest, we look at what we know and what we need to know, and we figure out what we need to do. The colonel's already working on that, and tomorrow, we get started."

Jahup nodded. "Do you have somewhere else to be?"

"Not right now. I figured I'd stay here with you for a while. If that's all right."

"Yes. Thank you."

ZHOH LAY IN the nutrient-rich waters of his homeworld in his private tank. Warriors were posted on his door, but that was for his protection. No one suspected that General Rangha hadn't died at the hands of an assassin. Once the violence had broken out, events had become tangled.

Now he lay back and rested, letting his chest wounds heal. The wounds hadn't been enough to trigger a full *lannig*, but he knew he would be stronger in the morning, and then he would make his case to become the commander of the forces on Makaum. He would lobby for his advancement based on his past performance, and—if he had to—there were primes he could contact to help him. They would not want to lose a bloodline hero, and the facts Zhoh had collected would strip Rangha and his legacy away from them.

First he would deal with that battle, then he would go to the base that Rangha had set up out in the jungle and take a proper inventory of what was there. Zhoh had already started plans for how he would deal with things, and going head-to-head with the Terran Army was on that list.

In order to do that, he was going to have to limit contact to Makaum. Too many freighters came and went on the planet. It would be too easy to resupply the army. Zhoh intended to trap them, isolate them, and eradicate them.

He also needed to find out about the assassin Rangha had intimated was out there. That could not be allowed to stand.

For now, though, Zhoh closed his eyes and healed as dreams of conquest slid through his mind.

IAN DOUGLAS's
STAR CARRIER
SERIES

EARTH STRIKE
BOOK ONE
978-0-06-184025-8

To the Sh'daar, the driving technologies of transcendent change are anathema and must be obliterated from the universe—along with those who would employ them. As their great warships destroy everything in their path en route to the Sol system, the human Confederation government falls into dangerous disarray.

CENTER OF GRAVITY
BOOK TWO
978-0-06-184026-5

On the far side of human known space, the Marines are under siege, battling the relentless servant races of the Sh'daar aggressor. Admiral Alexander Koenig knows the element of surprise is their only hope as he takes the war for humankind's survival directly to the enemy.

SINGULARITY
BOOK THREE
978-0-06-184027-2

In the wake of the near destruction of the solar system, the political powers on Earth seek a separate peace with an inscrutable alien life form that no one has ever seen. But Admiral Alexander Koenig has gone rogue, launching his fabled battlegroup beyond the boundaries of Human Space against all orders.

DEEP SPACE
BOOK FOUR
978-0-06-218380-4

After twenty years of peace, a Confederation research vessel has been ambushed, and destroyers are descending on a human colony. It seems the Sh'daar have betrayed their treaty, and all nations must stand united—or face certain death.

ID2 0515

IAN DOUGLAS'S
MONUMENTAL SAGA
OF INTERGALACTIC WAR
THE INHERITANCE TRILOGY

STAR STRIKE: BOOK ONE
978-0-06-123858-1

Planet by planet, galaxy by galaxy, the inhabited universe has fallen to the alien Xul. Now only one obstacle stands between them and total domination: the warriors of a resilient human race the world-devourers nearly annihilated centuries ago.

GALACTIC CORPS: BOOK TWO
978-0-06-123862-8

In the year 2886, intelligence has located the gargantuan hidden homeworld of humankind's dedicated foe, the brutal Xul. The time has come for the courageous men and women of the 1st Marine Interstellar Expeditionary Force to strike the killing blow.

SEMPER HUMAN: BOOK THREE
978-0-06-116090-5

True terror looms at the edges of known reality. Humankind's eternal enemy, the Xul, approach wielding a weapon monstrous beyond imagining. If the Star Marines fail to eliminate their relentless xenophobic foe once and for all, the Great Annihilator will obliterate every last trace of human existence.

IDI 0515